The RED Chrysanthemum

Linda Beutler

Oysterville, WA

Acknowledgments

Beyond the timeless genius of Jane Austen, whose vibrant words bring thirsty readers back to her well of inspiration time after time, I wish to thank two of her acolytes, Abigail Reynolds and Mary Street. The first Jane Austen what-if I ever read was *What Would Mr. Darcy Do?* by Abigail Reynolds, and so learned that answers Jane Austen never supplied could be imagined by modern writers in a compelling way. In Mary Street's *The Confession of Fitzwilliam Darcy,* the world was taught how to think like Darcy. That Reynolds, Street, and myself found "ample sources of delight, each in our own way" in the brilliant and unequaled performances of Jennifer Ehle and Colin Firth in the 1995 BBC television adaptation of *Pride and Prejudice,* propelled to life by Andrew Davies' exquisitely crafted screenplay, seems obvious but cannot be overstated.

My heartfelt gratitude is extended to everyone at Meryton Press, especially Gail Warner, my generous editor. When I found myself through the looking-glass with a nearly completed manuscript in my computer, they did not seem in the least surprised or hesitant to lead me forward.

Chapter 1

Fitzwilliam Darcy rode up High Street in the village of Lambton, approaching the town's best inn as if pulled by a magnetic force. His intent was to contrive a private conversation with a young lady staying there, Miss Elizabeth Bennet, even though he would be entertaining her and the relatives with whom she was travelling, her Aunt and Uncle Gardiner, that evening at his estate. How Elizabeth would respond to his chosen topic was unforeseeable, but he hoped for the best. In fact, he felt more hopeful about everything than he had for several months.

Edward and Madeleine Gardiner turned away from a shop window and noticed Darcy proceeding toward them. They were beginning their day of visits with a leisurely stroll to St. Swithin's, the church at the top of High Street. Mr Darcy saw them and doffed his hat but did not dismount. "Mr Gardiner! Mrs Gardiner! Good morning! Where does your visiting take you today?"

Mrs Gardiner curtsied as her husband removed his stylish beaver with a friendly bow. The lady answered, "You see us bound for St. Swithin's Church, Mr Darcy. It was where my family belonged when I was a girl, and I have fond memories of it."

"A charming chapel. I have attended two or three weddings there. I hope Lambton is living up to your memories, madam?"

"Indeed it is, sir, as are the people. I have been able to renew several of my old acquaintance."

"I hope the absence of Miss Elizabeth from your visit to the church does not mean she is unwell?"

"Oh no, sir, not at all. Lizzy is never unwell," replied Mr Gardiner. "She has just received a letter from her sister Jane by this morning's post and begged to have a few moments to herself to read it. We shall call back for her in an hour."

"Will she, or yourselves, be offended if I interrupt her?" Darcy asked. His face looked surprisingly hopeful.

Mr Gardiner, as the male relation and therefore guardian of his niece on their tour of Derbyshire, responded, "I do not see what harm could come of a public conversation in the guest sitting room, as long as all the doors are open." He spoke with a twinkle in his eye that Darcy recognized in his niece.

To Darcy's amazement, Mr Gardiner was the brother of Elizabeth's mother, the altogether ignorant, shrill, and nervous Mrs Francis Bennet. Other than general colouring and the same chin, he never would have guessed such an amiable, sensible and lively man—and to his credit a fine fisherman, Darcy had learned—could be the brother of such a one as Mrs Bennet. That he was the uncle of Elizabeth Bennet, however, made abundant sense.

"Nor can I imagine my niece taking offence. It was in that room that we left her."

Darcy suppressed a smirk. He could all too easily imagine Miss Elizabeth Bennet taking offence. "Thank you, sir." Darcy reseated his hat. "If I do not see you again before our conversation is finished, I look forward to seeing you tonight. I shall send a carriage, so you need not book transport with the inn."

"You are very kind, sir, but it must be said that we travel by our own carriage." Mr Gardiner bowed again. He did not mention his business was carriage making.

Darcy blushed a little. *Still supposing your own vast superiority, eh Darcy?* "Ah, of course. Excuse my presumption, please. Until this evening then…"

When Darcy turned his horse down High Street, Mr and Mrs Gardiner exchanged a significant look. They believed Fitzwilliam Darcy to be in love with their niece, and every encounter with the man seemed to add evidence to their supposition. Darcy wore his heart on his sleeve, though appeared unaware of doing so. How their niece felt about him in return, they could not yet say, and she did not seem inclined to speak of what was obvious to them.

Gaining sight of the inn, Darcy scanned the second story windows. In one, he spied Elizabeth's back with her dark coil of lustrous hair pinned carefully upon her head. His heart increased its pace.

Inside the inn, he asked after Miss Bennet, and the affable and efficient maid, who always wore an obliging smile, led him to the guests' sitting room where two days before he had introduced his sister, Georgiana, to Elizabeth. The introduction had been a great success on Georgiana's side, as had Elizabeth's return visit to Georgiana yesterday. Now his sister was forming the habit of quoting to him, in private moments, clever things Miss Bennet had said. Darcy was delighted.

Because it was a chamber available for use by any guest of the inn, the servant merely tapped on the open door to attract Elizabeth's attention then stepped in and announced, "Mr Darcy to see you, ma'am." Darcy strode past the maid to see Elizabeth look up with surprise and a fleeting smile.

"Thank you, Hannah," said Elizabeth. The servant withdrew, leaving the sitting room door open.

Upon entering the room, Darcy noted Elizabeth's posture and the manner in which her legs were curled beneath her upon the window seat as she read her letter. Her bonnet and gloves were on a nearby table and her spencer was untied. Clearly, she had intended to walk out with her aunt and uncle when the post arrived.

As Darcy bowed, Elizabeth scrambled to her feet, her skirts briefly riding up before slipping down to the toes of her boots. Darcy did not miss a flash of pink stockings just over the tops of her worn but clean walking boots, causing blood to roar in his ears. *Such well-turned ankles! Certainly the result of her being a great walker...* He straightened and tried to gather his wits enough to remember what he had come to say. He glanced around the room; they were alone.

"Mr Darcy! I had not expected to see you until this evening. My aunt and uncle have gone out—"

"Indeed, I met them, and they explained you had remained behind with a newly arrived letter from your sister. I hope you will not resent my interruption, but it is about your sister that I would speak to you."

"You could scarcely have chosen a topic, Mr Darcy, with which I would more eagerly agree to converse," Elizabeth replied, although she could not help colouring slightly when she remembered the last time they had spoken of Jane.

Darcy removed his hat and gloves, placing them on the table next to Elizabeth's. He paused—the sight of his hat and gloves next to hers arrested his breath—before drawing up a straight chair to face Elizabeth as she settled herself upon the window seat.

Is she glad to see me? Did I catch the ghost of a smile when I was announced, or was she already smiling at something in her letter? Elizabeth settled her hands in her lap and looked down at them. With a start, she noticed the open ties of her spencer. Even though she knew full well Darcy had seen her in this walking gown without a wrap on several occasions, she suddenly perceived the open spencer as somehow provocative. She stood up precipitously and turned her back to him. It would be more improper to remove the garment in his presence, so she retied the three bows across her bosom. "I pray you, sir, excuse my appearance." When she turned back to him, her cheeks were a becoming shade of pink.

Darcy stood when she did, and they were now almost toe-to-toe. He managed to refrain from saying, *"You are lovely,"* and said instead, "Of course! I have caught you at your leisure."

They sat down again. There was an awkward pause before Darcy continued. "As I said, I would speak to you about your sister…er, Miss Jane Bennet."

Elizabeth smiled at his hesitation and chuckled. "Yes, one must be specific when mentioning sisters to me; I have far too many."

He returned her smile. "Let me begin by saying how gratified I was when you accepted a visit from Bingley on Wednesday. I would not have blamed you had you spurned the opportunity." He searched her eyes for some clue to her emotions as he spoke but she had fixed her gaze at a point over his shoulder at the mention of Charles Bingley. "I fear, to my shame and through my fault, he may not be a popular man in Hertfordshire." Darcy looked down.

Elizabeth searched his face when he finished speaking. His eyes were on his hands, which sat in loose fists upon his knees, and his cheeks had joined hers in being now a little rosy. *I shall not shy away from this,* Elizabeth decided. "*I* have no complaint against Mr Bingley that would be served by such an incivility as you suggest. How proceeds his tender regard for your sister?"

10

Darcy looked up, his confusion evident. *"My* sister?"

"Why, yes. Jane wrote to me from London, when I first arrived in Kent in March, with the information that Caroline Bingley had *finally* called at Gracechurch Street and expressed the expectation of an announcement of a betrothal between Mr Bingley and your sister."

Ah, that *is how Caroline dissuaded Jane.* Darcy gave his head a slight shake of disapprobation. *So Caroline was that cruel.* "Let me assure you, Miss Elizabeth, the expectation is entirely on Miss Bingley's side and hers alone. Georgiana and Bingley are only as companionable as friends of the opposite sex, much separated in age, might be. After last summer…" Here Darcy paused to give Elizabeth a meaningful look. He referred to the foiled elopement of his sister with the wastrel George Wickham, of which he had informed Elizabeth in April. "…I am afraid Georgiana's confidence in all things has suffered a blow from which she has yet to fully recover. And Bingley's affections remain quite firmly lodged elsewhere. *That* is the point I wish to convey to you, Miss Bennet. *That* is what I have come to tell you."

Darcy watched as several distinct emotions crossed Elizabeth's countenance. Finally, her mouth settled into a thin line of temper, her tempting lips compressed. She was not most pleased by what he had hoped was good news.

"I have long suspected Miss Bingley of greater spitefulness than Jane ever would dare accuse her. Jane is too good. May I take it from your response you were not aware, sir, that your sister's imaginary attentions to your friend, and his for her, were offered as the fictitious reason for Mr Bingley's defection from my sister?"

"Most assuredly not. Once again, I own I am annoyed by the presumption of Miss Bingley. She *will* continue to assume everyone's motives are as mean as her own."

"Since the very night we met, Miss Bingley's motives have *always* been abundantly clear to *me,*" Elizabeth spat. "At least in *her* case my first impressions were entirely correct. I expect the worst of her and am *never* disappointed." Elizabeth paused, sensing an imminent loss of control and willed herself to be calm. She could not, however, keep from adding, "If Mr Bingley's regard for someone other than your sister is as constant as you say, I wonder that he has not returned to that lady's neighbourhood."

Their eyes locked. Darcy could see the anger Elizabeth was attempting to subdue. He drew in a deep breath, returning her implacable gaze with what he hoped was equanimity. Elizabeth perceived an unexpected vulnerability in Darcy not previously displayed.

"That he has not done so has been entirely my doing. I thought I knew Bingley's character, but after conversing with him these past two evenings since your reunion, I realize I have greatly misjudged him. You see, Miss Bennet, before his acquaintance with your sister, Bingley was given to a series of idle flirtations characterized as 'being in love,' but which came to nothing. I thought his particular attentions to your sister were simply more of the same until I began to seriously observe him at the Netherfield ball." Darcy sighed and then continued, "But you know all this. I have written it to you. That I also misjudged and slighted your sister's affections when I had no real knowledge of her character has become intolerable to me, especially now that *your* presence has revealed Bingley still admires her to the exclusion of all others."

Elizabeth's countenance did not change, but she nodded acknowledgment of the letter Darcy had written following his unsuccessful proposal of marriage.

"I understand why Bingley has hidden his continued and unabated regard for your sister. He assumes I will discourage him, and even with you here, he will not speak her name to me. It pains me that my previous ridiculous attitude has created this wedge in our friendship. When I overheard Georgiana ask Bingley to describe your sisters, he would only speak of Jane. He made it plain he is as devoted to her as he ever was."

Elizabeth thought of her meeting with Bingley two days previously and his particularly accurate remembrance of the date of the ball where he had danced almost entirely with Jane. She had expected him to ask after Jane particularly. *But of course, he would not. Mr Darcy was there.*

"And yet he does not pursue her." Elizabeth, exercising taut self-control, returned to the material point.

"What hope has he? He is well aware of the appearance of his actions. He has no expectation of success." Darcy felt moved to defend his friend.

Elizabeth all but snorted her disdain. "So he does not credit Jane with the constancy of affection so apparent within himself? Were *your* tales so believable, Mr Darcy? Or is he afraid of the scorn of Meryton society should a man of pleasing and generous manners return to a house he has legally taken and renew his addresses to the most beautiful and charming lady of the county? Since when have gentlemen become so missish?" She looked away from Darcy. This was a terrible muddle, started by Darcy's preposterous interference and abetted by Bingley's sister, but now continued by Bingley's caution and deference to his friend. *What more dare I say?*

A minute passed and then another. Darcy rose and started pacing. *I must not lose sight of my reason for coming here. I knew I might bestir her anger at me, but I will not have her angry with Bingley. I must make this attempt.*

"Miss Bennet, I now know, beyond any doubt, my friend is still in love with your sister. If you can assure me her regard for him is likewise steadfast and she bears him no ill will, I believe I have it in my power to right a very great wrong."

That the happiness of her sister might be restored made Elizabeth's heart soar, but she responded in a steady voice. "Indeed, sir, when last Jane and I spoke of Mr Bingley, her regard for him was not in the least diminished. If I may quote her, she said, 'He is still the most amiable man of my acquaintance, and so he shall remain.' You see, Mr Darcy, despite her attachment to him, Jane now has no expectation of ever marrying for love. Her heart is quite fixed, but you know my family's circumstances. Since she is the most beautiful of us all, she is resigned to marry where opportunity presents itself in order to secure all of us from eventual poverty."

Darcy halted his pacing. Elizabeth stood to face him, and he regarded her with new eyes. He found it remarkable Elizabeth did not consider herself quite as beautiful as her sister. *Perhaps she is being modest, but she sounds utterly sincere. Perhaps she has heard it from her mother for so long that she has come to believe it herself. She is confident enough of her wits but thinks little of her other charms.* It further occurred to him that, never once in their acquaintance, not when they danced at Netherfield—when she was by far the most entrancing woman in the room—and not even during his ill-starred proposal of marriage, had he told her he thought her bewitchingly handsome. Now she stood before him, speaking with the fierce gravitas of a she-wolf defending her den. There was a majesty to her even as she spoke of the want of her family's connections and the entailment, which might leave a family of women to destitution. He longed for her—to comfort her, to make everything in her life easy, to release her from all worry, to gain some of her passion for himself.

Darcy's throat tightened. "She still loves him?" His temples were throbbing. *As I still love you.*

"Most assuredly," she replied, nodding for emphasis.

He wanted to embrace her, to calm her in his arms, but instead said, "Let us be seated, Miss Bennet. I would continue this conversation if we can regain our composure."

Elizabeth lifted her chin at the implication she had neared the sharp edge of civil discourse, but she knew he was right.

They sat. "I fear, in restoring your sister to Bingley, I must reveal to him information that will damage our friendship, perhaps irretrievably, but it cannot be helped. I have no right to request your assistance, but I may have need of it."

"It will be a pleasure, Mr Darcy, to aid you in this particular cause however I can. What do you ask of me?"

"For this evening, you could merely assure Bingley he would receive no disapprobation *from any quarter* were he to return to Netherfield. He regards your opinions very highly, and your kind reception heartened him. Then, after you and the Gardiners take your leave, I will explain my nonsensical, indeed abhorrent, behaviour to him." He paused. "I may need to reveal my proposal to you in April to illustrate and prove the absurdity of my actions. May I have your permission?"

"You have not already told him?" Elizabeth was surprised.

"No, I have only spoken of it to my cousin Colonel Fitzwilliam. After all, *that* poor fellow had to endure what must have seemed an excessively long carriage ride to London with me. If it is any consolation, he offered me no sympathy and judged my proposal one of the most inept he had ever heard. Even Georgiana does not know."

"Of my own acquaintance and family, I have told only Jane. I told her you had revealed the truth of Wickham's character, but I withheld your part in separating Bingley from her. I would not be a party to any increase of Jane's heartache. Please understand by this, sir, I was not seeking to protect *you* in any way."

Darcy could not meet her fine eyes. He looked down and turned partly away. He had reminded her of her first and deadliest allegation against him when she refused him in April and his feeble attempt to defend his indefensible actions. *If Elizabeth has started to improve her opinion of me during these last three days, I have surely undone all my good work.* "Miss Bennet, I do not deserve anyone's protection, least of all yours." He turned back to her and the supplication in his eyes was very near to melting her heart. "You owe me nothing. I am in your debt for making those reproofs that were so necessary but that no one else had dared. The several flaws in my character to which you alerted me, I have... I am *attempting* to correct. You accused me of arrogance, and never was an accusation more deserved. 'Your selfish disdain for the feelings of others...' you said. You were right and just."

Elizabeth was mortified to hear her pitiless words repeated and astonished he remembered them. She looked away and could not form a reply.

"Have I your permission, Miss Bennet?" His question came in a whisper.

She nodded emphatically. Finally, she managed a smile, being naturally unable to sustain ill humour. "That episode reflects poorly on us both, Mr Darcy," she replied, attempting to coax a smile.

When he met her sparkling eyes, the corners of his mouth turned up, and his dimples deepened. He looked more like his portrait. "You have a charming smile, sir. You should employ it more often."

He was relieved she was teasing him. Or was he mistaken? Was there a sincere compliment hidden in her chuckle?

"Thank you, Miss Bennet, for your advice. And thank you for any service you may give to increase Bingley's confidence in the affections of your sister."

"If we are together successful, how soon do you think he might return to Netherfield?"

"With Bingley, it is difficult to say." They both smiled. "He is to stay here three weeks, then he and his sisters travel north to Scarborough to attend a family christening, and there they are to stay for some weeks. We had not spoken of meeting to share the autumn pheasant shooting."

Elizabeth looked down; then her eyes returned to Darcy with a wry smile. "If only Jane were here instead of me and I were home tending my little cousins. But she is not afflicted with my sense of adventure."

Before Darcy could check himself, he blurted, "But *I* am glad you are here..." He coloured and looked away. Standing abruptly, he said, "I forget myself; I have guests at home. Please accept my thanks, Miss Bennet, for your time and for agreeing to assist me." He picked up his hat and gloves.

Elizabeth stood and walked to the door with him. "It is I who should thank you, Mr Darcy. You must know how grateful I am for anything that leads to Jane's happiness. I feel certain when Mr Bingley understands the whole of it, all will be forgiven." She laid her graceful hand on his forearm. "Less naturally amiable tempers than his have found ways to forgive you." She paused, her eyes flitting to his then away. "And if I have seemed insolent or ungrateful to you this morning, please accept *my* apologies." Her eyes, usually so ready for mirth, were earnest when she took a last look at him. *Oh dear, I may be falling in love with him… I seem to be sinking, yet floating at the same time.*

Darcy lifted her hand and kissed it quickly. "You have said nothing to regret; indeed, you are too generous, Miss Elizabeth. Until this evening." He released her hand and left the room. Once again, the blood roared in his ears as the scent of lavender tingled his nose.

Does he still love me? Elizabeth asked herself as she settled back on the window seat. She heard the hostler bring up a horse and saw Darcy mount his steed to return to Pemberley.

Darcy looked over his shoulder at the window where he had seen Elizabeth when he arrived. Now, she had returned to that seat and was watching him. He doffed his hat to her, half turning his horse. She smiled at him in return. It was a full happy smile, such as he had seen her bestow upon Jane and her father, but this smile was meant for him alone. His face warmed, and he turned away. *I have pleased her!* He was quite certain.

Elizabeth picked up her letter from Jane, which she had nearly finished when Darcy was announced. It was full of tales of the Gardiner children and trivial gossip from Meryton. The letter had been addressed ill and was sent before any of Elizabeth's travel memoirs would have arrived at Longbourn. She could not now attend her reading, her mind too full of other thoughts. *His regard for Bingley does him credit. If my presence has brought Bingley's suppressed feelings to the fore, then I am pleased to have visited Pemberley after all.*

Elizabeth mused upon that great manor, a handsome house that suited its handsome owner. The words of the housekeeper in praise of her master sounded in her ears. Once Mrs Reynolds was made aware Elizabeth had met Mr Darcy, were they shown more of the house than they otherwise would have seen? Would she have been so particularly taken to the striking portrait of him?

Elizabeth felt her heart pounding as she relived the moment of encountering a dishevelled Darcy approaching his home and his disarming confusion upon discovering her. Her chest had tightened in a way she never felt before.

And she had the same tightening when he reappeared a quarter of an hour later, properly dressed to walk with her party. Indeed, upon reflection, such a clutching within her was now an accompaniment to Darcy's every appearance. *I am falling in love with him. How do I stop this now it has begun? It can lead to nothing. It will not do...*

Arabian Jasmine
"Amiability"

Chapter 2

Fitzwilliam Darcy felt a strange lightness as his horse returned to Pemberley. He was fortunate to have chosen a mount that knew the paths, for the man himself was pleasingly distracted. *She said 'less naturally amiable tempers than Bingley's have found ways to forgive.' I hope she was referring to herself. And her smile... I should have run back inside and taken her into my arms when I saw it.* He sighed. *This will be a long, tedious afternoon.*

After avoiding Miss Bingley for the afternoon with the excuse of work to be done in his study, Darcy pestered his valet with more than his usual fastidiousness as he dressed for the evening. His man was giving his lapels a third brushing when there was a tap at the dressing room door, which could only be Georgiana. "Come!" Darcy said curtly.

Georgiana entered, wearing an unadorned muslin gown of pale pink and a single strand of small coral beads at her neck. After the disastrous episode with Wickham, Darcy surmised Georgiana had again affected the styles of girlhood to make herself less noticeable to men. But even before last summer, he was glad that, despite her London education, Georgiana did not respond to the changing modes of fashion with over much interest. Even before Wickham's schemes, she preferred simple styles as became her youth, height, and pale colouring. He had seen, more than once, the disparaging humour in Elizabeth's eyes when observing the latest styles on Caroline

18

Bingley and her sister, Louisa Hurst, covered in every manner of decoration in the most garish colours. He felt at times that it was all Elizabeth could do to swallow her laughter. Indeed, he had to admit he often felt so himself.

"Do I look well?" Georgiana asked, giving a little twirl. "Will I please my new friend, do you think?"

"You always look charming." Darcy smiled at her, pleased that she seemed in lively spirits. Was Elizabeth already having such a good effect upon his sister?

"Yes, I know."

Darcy reached to tweak her nose for such impertinence, but she spun out of his reach, giggling.

"But tonight I wish to *be* charming, Brother, and it is so difficult with Bingley's sisters jumping on my every syllable as if I were as wise as Aristotle. It is embarrassing."

"Is it not a wonder they are related to Bingley? I marvel at it constantly." Both brother and sister were pleased to see the other in such good humour. Georgiana readily marked the improvement in her brother from the sudden appearance of Miss Elizabeth Bennet and her friendly aunt and uncle. Miss Elizabeth was the only lady her brother had ever mentioned in letters, quoting their animated debates during her brother's stay at Bingley's Hertfordshire estate last autumn. He had not mentioned her again until letters arrived from him whilst he was in Kent for Easter, the second of which seemed to be preparing her to meet Miss Elizabeth. He had implied Georgiana would have occasion to get to know the lady much more intimately. And then…nothing.

Now, it was clear Darcy was quite in love with her. "Miss Bennet puts one at ease where Miss Bingley puts one on guard as our dear cousin the colonel might say. It is little wonder Miss Bingley speaks so shabbily of Miss Bennet, Brother, for how can Miss Bingley possibly compete?" Georgiana eyed her brother carefully as she said this and was not at all surprised when his countenance turned dumbfounded. She watched, vastly entertained by the effect of her words as he gathered himself.

Darcy adopted what Georgiana referred to as his grumpy-brother face and feigned impatience. "I think you should leave me to finish dressing before I decide your impudent mood is not fit for polite society."

Georgiana trotted to him dutifully and kissed his cheek. "Oh, your secret is safe with me."

He did not need to ask what secret she meant.

When she reached the door, Darcy stopped her. "Georgie…" She turned back and smiled. "I'm relieved you like her." He quickly looked down to hide the colour advancing to his cheeks.

Georgiana whispered fondly, "You love her! How could I not like her?"

As his sister slipped from the room, Darcy turned to his valet, who had pursed his lips in a valiant attempt not to grin. The servant had a tuft of lavender stems in his hand from which he expertly snapped the flowering ends and tucked them into his master's buttonhole. "That will be all, Garrick, thank you." Darcy nodded. He wondered whether Elizabeth would notice he had chosen lavender—for her.

WHEN DARCY REACHED THE ENTRY hall, Georgiana was already waiting while Bingley could be seen descending the stairway from the guests' wing of the house, fussing with his shirt cuffs. It was a clear, bright evening, and the three met under the front portico to await the carriage.

"You are joining us in greeting the guests, Bingley? Did I tell you I called on Miss Elizabeth this morning?" Darcy attempted to sound nonchalant.

Both Georgiana and Bingley turned to look at him in surprise.

"Did you indeed? Your morning ride took you to Lambton, did it, and not into the wilds of your estate as usual?"

Darcy ignored the question. "She had just received a letter from her sister Jane, who is having a happy time with the Gardiner children at Longbourn whilst their parents are travelling with Elizabeth."

Bingley looked at Darcy with more astonishment than he could conceal. Sounds of a carriage approaching abruptly ended the conversation.

The guests were welcomed, and Darcy deferred to Bingley to escort Elizabeth into the house while he and Georgiana accompanied the Gardiners.

"Miss Elizabeth, you look remarkably well this evening," Bingley observed, smiling.

"I thank you, Mr Bingley." She leaned in and whispered, "You see me in fine spirits because I am wearing a new gown." Elizabeth knew she could speak of a frivolous topic without Bingley thinking her a frivolous lady. Servants approached to take away the outerwear of the ladies and Mr Gardiner's hat and gloves.

Once her pelisse was removed, Bingley took Elizabeth's hand and turned her elegantly. "Georgiana, Darcy," Bingley said, calling their attention to Elizabeth. "Miss Bennet is debuting a new gown this evening."

Elizabeth laughed and blushed. "I did not tell you for you to make an announcement of it, sir!"

The Gardiners smiled at the younger people admiring their niece. Mrs Gardiner had made a present of the creamy-yellow silk, suitable for a fine evening event, at the start of their journey to Derbyshire. It had been decided this would be the perfect opportunity for its first airing.

Georgiana cleared her throat, her earlier whimsy now subdued by her usual public shyness. Elizabeth turned to her with kind eyes and stepped a little closer. "The colour favours you, Miss Bennet," Georgiana spoke haltingly.

"Thank you, Miss Darcy." Elizabeth nodded and smiled.

Georgiana glanced nervously at her brother. "Miss Bennet, I would like it very much if you would call me Georgiana."

Elizabeth's eyes sparkled into the younger girl's earnest gaze. "And so I shall. Please call me Elizabeth, or Lizzy if it suits you."

The conversation was in murmurs, causing Darcy to strain his ears to hear every word. His heart filled with pride at his sister's overture of friendship, and when Elizabeth turned away from Georgiana, he met her eyes with a smile, making his dimples deepen. Mr Gardiner squeezed his wife's hand, a gesture she returned.

The three couples climbed the main staircase to the second floor and approached the drawing room. Their conversation lagged in time to overhear Caroline Bingley crowing, "Which do you think it will be, Louisa? Shall Eliza Bennet wear that horrid pink print or is it time, again, for us to see the pale green muslin?"

"My sixpence is on the pale green, Caroline," Mrs Hurst tittered. Both sisters erupted in shrill derisive laughter.

Elizabeth stopped, suddenly breathless. She turned red from the neckline of her gown to her hairline and felt her feet were stuck to the floor. Bingley looked away, redder even than Elizabeth, partly because his colouring was prone to blushing but mainly due to the rude behaviour of his sisters.

Darcy immediately stepped to Elizabeth's side, holding out his arm for support and meeting her alarmed gaze. "You are always the most handsome lady in the room, no matter what you wear. I have seen you with petticoats six inches deep in mud, and yet you were not diminished in the least. Please take my arm." His voice was low and intense, his eyes imploring.

Mr and Mrs Gardiner exchanged another significant look.

Elizabeth raised her eyes to his and lifted her chin. She was too mortified to smile but took a deep breath and laid her hand upon his arm. His kind words enveloped her. *That is the most gentlemanly thing he has ever said to me in the whole of our acquaintance.*

Darcy and Elizabeth advanced into the drawing room, straight-backed and full of regal hauteur, followed by the Gardiners—pale with anger—and then Georgiana on Bingley's arm, both vividly pink.

Darcy settled Elizabeth on a settee at the opposite end of the large room from Bingley's sisters and sat next to her. "Bingley is correct, Miss Bennet. You are looking remarkably *handsome* this evening." His voice was slightly louder than it needed to be. He held her eyes, willing Elizabeth to smile at him.

She smiled and nodded. "Thank you, sir." Her smile then faded with her courage.

No one of the party acknowledged Bingley's sisters.

Bingley sat Georgiana in the armchair to Elizabeth's right and then advanced on his sisters. They were seated together on a settee and he stopped behind them, put a hand on the shoulder of each and squeezed. "You have surpassed yourselves," he hissed. "*And* you were heard as I am sure you meant to be." Both sisters grimaced at the pressure on their shoulders, which was unrelenting.

As the Gardiners sat together on the settee opposite Georgiana, Mr Gardiner slipped several coins into his hand from his pocket and sorted out two sixpence coins. He leaned forward to his niece and whispered mischievously, "Would you like to settle their debts for them, Lizzy? It appears they both lost."

Elizabeth glanced at Darcy and Georgiana, and her smile this time was spontaneous. "Indeed, Uncle, thank you."

Under normal circumstances, Mrs Gardiner would have discouraged her husband from forming such a conspiracy of revenge with her niece, but she was livid at the insult, which she fully believed was meant to be heard, and looked forward to a comeuppance.

Elizabeth stood, and the gentlemen did, likewise. She walked calmly to the other end of the room and stood before her tormentors. Only upon her arrival, did Bingley release his vise-like grasp of their shoulders.

"Good evening, Miss Bingley, Mrs Hurst." Elizabeth curtsied and then held out her hand, revealing the two sixpence. Bending slightly, she continued as if speaking to naughty children, "I understand *both* you ladies have lost a wager this evening? I would not have you without pocket money for cards on *my* account." She carefully deposited a coin into the hand of each sister. They were too nonplussed to refuse.

"There, you can settle your debts between you." Elizabeth beamed at them, turned, and returned with stately bearing to her seat next to Darcy, who smiled warmly when her eyes met his. Georgiana, in an attempt to retain her dignity, put the back of her hand over her mouth and turned away from the other end of the room to chuckle. Bingley followed Elizabeth down the room after giving his sisters a final glare, sitting in the chair next to Georgiana.

The sisters sat in appalled silence. Elizabeth had resettled herself when Marcus Hurst entered the room. "Ah, Mr Gardiner," he began, "do you suppose we shall be fed the trout we caught yesterday?"

"I certainly hope so, sir!" was the amiable reply.

Hurst was introduced to Mrs Gardiner just as servants entered with a variety of beverages. Everyone advanced for refreshments to the round table in the centre of the room except Bingley's sisters.

"We are awaiting one more person," Darcy said to Elizabeth in a low voice as he handed her a cup of wine punch. "I have invited the vicar of Kympton. He was appointed three years ago, Miss Bennet, and I thought you would be interested in meeting him. I think you will enjoy making a study of him and how he compares with others who could have taken that position."

Elizabeth nodded, an eyebrow raised knowingly. It was the living that might have gone to George Wickham had he been a better man.

In just moments, the vicar was announced and introduced. Shortly thereafter, the butler entered to announce supper would be served, and footmen opened the doors into the dining room.

Darcy took Elizabeth's arm and seated her to his right. The Gardiners followed, and Darcy indicated they should sit on his left. Bingley escorted Georgiana to the hostess's end and then, by pre-arrangement with Darcy, sat to Elizabeth's right. The Hursts came in together, and Georgiana asked them to sit on her right. The vicar, a Mr Egerton, stood dumbly for a moment before offering his arm to Miss Bingley, who wordlessly accepted it and found herself seated between the vicar and her brother and across from Louisa. She felt she was being spontaneously punished for her rude remark, it not being in her nature to apprehend that Darcy and his sister must have arranged the seating plan earlier when they finalized the menu with the butler and cook.

As the first course was served, Elizabeth turned to Bingley. "I have had a letter from my sister Jane today, Mr Bingley," she said, smiling brightly. "Imagine her surprise when I respond that I have had the pleasure of your company. She will be so pleased to be remembered to you and to know you and I have rekindled our friendship."

Darcy was pleased at what he was hearing, even as he saw Bingley's blush and wary glance. He turned his attention to Mrs Gardiner. "I understand Miss Bennet is tending your young children, Mrs Gardiner?"

While Bingley longed to listen to *that* conversation, he responded to Elizabeth in a low voice. "I think there are *some* who might not wish her to be remembered to me."

Elizabeth held her smile steady. "Perhaps, but I believe they sit nearer the middle of the table, sir, and *not* at the head of it."

Bingley now looked completely surprised. "Indeed?"

"Yes! Mr Darcy was saying this morning that he hopes to visit Hertford-shire again for the sport after you have been to Scarborough. I know Jane would be pleased to have you both return to the neighbourhood."

"You are full of wondrous information, Miss Elizabeth." Bingley looked self-satisfied, as if trying to suppress a grin.

Elizabeth nodded, accepting the compliment. "I am glad you find me so."

Bingley and Elizabeth then addressed themselves to their food, listening to Mr and Mrs Gardiner discuss the high regard their children had for their cousin Jane. The opposite end of the table was nearly silent, with the exception of Mr Hurst asking after the courses yet to come, to which Georgiana quietly responded.

The soup arrived, a simple consommé flavoured with herbs. As Darcy ate, he absently touched the lavender flowers at his lapel and smelled his fingers, a faint smile evident by his dimples. Elizabeth watched him and wondered whether he had ever noticed her scent was lavender and if the association was the reason he wore those particular flowers. She mustered her courage. "Mr Darcy, I see you are wearing lavender tonight. Are you fond of the scent?"

Only then was he aware that he had absently touched the flowers to release their fragrance. Mrs Gardiner glanced at him then to her niece. She nudged her husband's knee under the table; he understood he should attend and followed his wife's eyes to their object.

Darcy looked into Elizabeth's dark eyes and felt himself quite lost in their bright quizzical expression. "I am, Miss Bennet. It first became attractive to me last autumn. Now I find I am fonder of it than ever…certainly more fond of it than I was in, say, April."

Elizabeth's eyes widened, and she felt her cheeks grow warm. She inhaled and almost forgot to exhale. *Is he telling me he still loves me?* She caught the corner of her lower lip between her teeth to keep from smiling and tried to appear as if she was considering her reply.

Mrs Gardiner glanced at her husband, who had nudged her knee in return, and his eyes were questioning. She shrugged, not knowing what to make of Darcy's odd references to the times of year when he enjoyed the scent of lavender. It was evident from Elizabeth's response that she knew exactly what Darcy meant.

Darcy watched Elizabeth as she bit her lip; she intoxicated him. As she breathed deeply, her creamy bosom rose and fell beneath the garnet cross on a thin gold chain that she never was without. He wanted to believe she took his meaning, although he was aware he had been wrong, very wrong, in such beliefs in the past. But now her teeth released her lip, which he had every inclination to kiss, and she smiled at him. It was the sort of smile any *other* man, even a simpleton, would recognize as the smile of a lady in love.

"Are you aware, Mr Darcy, that lavender is considered one of the soothing herbs?" Elizabeth asked.

"Is it indeed? I own I find it more stimulating than soothing."

Elizabeth's blush deepened.

Bingley watched the exchange, and although not an unusually perceptive man, he knew what he was seeing. He had sensed in Meryton that Darcy had formed a reluctant and guarded admiration for Elizabeth Bennet, as she was the only local lady with whom Darcy had danced at the Netherfield ball. At the time, Bingley did not think Elizabeth cared for Darcy in the slightest, although she did seem challenged by him and was moved to retort whenever Darcy made one of his pretentious statements. Bingley found their conversations fraught with a certain hostility from whence he could not identify the source, but for Elizabeth's part, he assumed it had sprung from Darcy's ill-tempered remarks at the Meryton assembly. At that time, he had the discomforting sense Elizabeth had overheard Darcy—the truth of which was later confirmed by Jane—and Bingley could not blame Elizabeth for being insulted. However, from the current turn of her countenance, one could surmise she undoubtedly had buried her grudge.

Bingley stopped eating and stared at Darcy, having reached a much fuller realization. He now saw that in the days after the ball—when Darcy left Hertfordshire as if chased by demons—Darcy was trying to convince Bingley of Jane Bennet's indifference because Darcy felt himself in danger from her sister. *If I had continued to pursue Jane, Darcy would have seen much more of Lizzy. All that cant about their lack of family connections and Jane not caring was just so much twaddle, excuses to keep from falling in love with Elizabeth. But now he has! He assumed I was merely infatuated again, but he now sees I still love Jane, and he loves Elizabeth. That must be why he is no longer concerned about Jane being spoken of so freely.* Bingley determined to speak with Darcy directly after the evening's guests departed.

The fish course arrived, composed of the boned fillets of the trout caught the day before in a light almond sauce. Elizabeth thought it heavenly.

"Have you made much study of the uses and meanings of herbs, Miss Bennet?" Darcy asked, once all his guests had been served.

"Yes, I have. I find I quite enjoy it. I have taught myself to make a tea my mother finds most soothing, which she takes in the evening. And I make scented oils and eau de cologne for myself and all my sisters."

"So, you make your own scent?"

Elizabeth looked down, her lashes appearing to rest on blushing cheeks. *Oh, now Lizzy, you reveal much too much. And he already knows the answer. Do not ask me the next question, sir; please do not ask me...* She willed Darcy not to inquire what scent she had chosen for herself. He knew perfectly well, and she did not wish to speak it aloud. She saw her aunt and uncle taking a great interest in the conversation, and she had very little left to hide from them. *If only I could stop blushing at everything he says. Why am I being so silly?*

"Yes, I do," she murmured.

Darcy was pleased; he had teased her successfully and knew he needn't push the point further. He lowered his voice in mock conspiracy. "You know, I believe my sister would be quite delighted to have a scent of her own. Her seventeenth birthday is approaching, and what a marvellous gift it would be! How long does it take?"

Elizabeth looked up, and her eyes warmed into his, thanking him silently for taking another path without an obvious change of subject. "Not so very long. The dried ingredients are combined and bottled and then must sit to gather strength. When is her birthday?"

"It is mid-month, August, and you are to be in Lambton for another week. Could I persuade you to make use of our stillroom? I am sure we could arrange that Georgiana not know you were here."

Darcy and Elizabeth looked at Mrs Gardiner hopefully, aware she was listening to their discourse. "One does not like to impose upon a new acquaintance, Mr Darcy, but perhaps, if you were to invite my husband to go fishing again, Lizzy could come with him unannounced?"

Darcy leaned to Mrs Gardiner. "Consider it done! Tomorrow? The day after? We have nothing fixed for the next few days, and on quiet mornings, Georgiana practices at her harp or pianoforte for hours at a time."

Mr Gardiner pricked up his ears. "Either would suit me!"

Mrs Gardiner reminded her niece and husband they were to spend the early half of the following day with her former schoolmistress. "...so it must be the day after tomorrow. Oh! But that is Sunday! How one loses track of the days when one travels."

Darcy paused, considering. "When will you be free tomorrow? After what time?" He addressed the whispered question to Mrs Gardiner.

"The engagement is in Lambton, a brief walk from the inn, and my husband and niece need not stay for the whole of it. May they arrive late morning? Would eleven o'clock suit?"

Darcy smiled and looked from Elizabeth to her uncle. Mr Gardiner spoke up, "I must confess, Mr Darcy, I have been hoping for such an opportunity. You see, sir, I indulged in a treat for myself. I bought a new rod from a local craftsman this afternoon. A Mr Tilney?"

"Oh, ho!" Darcy chuckled in appreciation. "Hurst! Listen to this! Bingley, are you attending? Mr Gardiner has been to Tilney's and has made a purchase."

"Lucky man!" Hurst leaned around his wife to grin at Mr Gardiner. "He does not always have rods on offer. Most are bespoke." He raised his wine glass to Mr Gardiner's good fortune.

"I was indeed lucky. Someone had ordered the rod and then found it did not fit. The customer did not like the heft. I tried it in the shop, flung it about a bit with some line and found it admirable." Mr Gardiner smiled, his eyes merry.

"You are most forbearing, Mrs Gardiner, to allow so much fishing whilst on holiday," Louisa Hurst remarked.

"It makes him far more bearable once we are at home if I show forbearance now," replied Mrs Gardiner with the good humour of a knowing wife.

"So it is a settled thing, Mr Gardiner; you will join us for more fishing tomorrow?" Darcy asked in a louder voice to ensure Georgiana would hear.

"Indeed, sir."

At that moment, Georgiana, who had been concentrating on her fish, noticed the vicar had not eaten so much as a bite. "Reverend Egerton, you do not like fish?"

Just then, there happened to be a lull in the conversation and all heard his response. "Indeed, Miss Darcy, I never take it. Fish are God's wild creatures and I find their means of death so violent that I cannot tolerate it. I only take flesh when I know it to be domestic and killed quickly."

Elizabeth raised her napkin to her mouth to hide her response, and Darcy could not meet her mirthful eyes, though he longed to, knowing they would both laugh.

"Killjoy," Mr Hurst was heard to mutter.

"Let me assure you then, sir, the duck we are about to be served is from the Pemberley domestic flock. They were killed with all due dispatch," Darcy informed the vicar.

Georgiana glanced up at her brother, aware his tone was light, even—dare she say it?—a little amused.

"Thank you, Mr Darcy, for informing me," replied the vicar seriously. He then looked down, embarrassed to think his patron had heard his unguarded remark.

The table was quiet until the fish course was cleared away. Some guests left portions on their plate but Darcy was pleased to see Elizabeth had eaten all of hers. "You like fish, Miss Bennet?"

"I am particularly fond of trout when I know my uncle has provided it." She smiled across the table to her relative.

During the poultry course, Miss Bingley had sufficiently recovered from her earlier mortification and censure to ask, "Mrs Gardiner, I understand you spent some portion of your youth in Lambton?" At that lady's nod, she continued, "Did your family enjoy the patronage of the Pemberley estate?"

Mrs Gardiner eyed Miss Bingley calmly but warily. "My father's business was patronized most frequently by the next estate over, Broadvale, and the Wentworth family—an estate smaller than Pemberley but populated by a larger family. My father was a wheelwright and trained apprentices. When he had the opportunity to buy a business in London, we moved to the city, and there I met Mr Gardiner."

"Our grandfather was a carriage-maker, Mrs Gardiner!" Bingley cried, delighted. "He invented a cunning axle, so I am told, and therein lies the Bingley fortune."

Caroline's eyes widened before lowering, annoyed with her brother for announcing the family history so forthrightly. Louisa caught her sister's eye and shrugged, hoping Caroline would throw off her pique and make some attempt to be entertaining. It was perfectly clear to both Elizabeth and Louisa that Caroline was attempting to remind Darcy of the low connections of the Bennet family but only succeeded in giving her brother the opportunity of honestly delineating that the Bingley connections were neither significant nor historic.

The roast veal added no revelations or uneasiness to the evening. Georgiana was relieved no other wild game was served to disquiet the vicar and spoke primarily to him. Bingley and Elizabeth talked of the beauties of Pemberley, which Darcy was pleased to overhear, and Bingley asked what she had seen on her tour before arriving at Lambton. The Gardiners' comments added to the conversation by enhancing details supplied by their niece.

The topic of travel continued into the dessert course of fruit and the local Stilton, when Darcy asked Mrs Gardiner, "So you have already been further north, well into the Peaks?"

"Indeed, we have. I could not wait to see them again and share them with my niece. Lizzy is a good traveller and delights in wild country. You should have seen her, Mr Darcy, scrambling over the tors as if born to it. You would not know she was raised in such mild country as Hertfordshire."

Elizabeth half-smiled at her aunt but with a scolding shake of her head. "Now she will start telling tales of me, Mr Darcy. I implore you not to believe half of what she says, although I fear all of it will be true."

Darcy smiled at Elizabeth then turned to Mrs Gardiner. "Tales about Miss

Elizabeth Bennet? I do hope they have the potential for her embarrassment."

Mrs Gardiner chuckled. "It is I who should be embarrassed for being so silly. Lizzy is exceptionally sure-footed, but she did climb very high, and I took a fright. I had a sudden vision of having to confess to her father that she was injured in a fall! I made her come right down. I do hope you were able to enjoy something of the view, my love, before I took a panic?" Mrs Gardiner addressed the last to her niece.

"Indeed, I did, Aunt. As I climbed, I paused from time to time to ascertain how much further I could see. And, of course, with this fine weather, it was spectacular." Her eyes bright with the recent memory, she turned to Darcy. "If I may say, sir, you live in breath-taking country."

Darcy was momentarily tongue-tied. The image of Elizabeth cresting the Peaks like winged victory, the wind whipping her skirts, her escaping curls caught in the breeze, looking on his home county with excitement in her eyes; yes, he could imagine it all very thoroughly. He blinked. Was the present reality any less thrilling? That she was sitting at dinner with him at Pemberley, the woman he loved, and looking so exquisite in her pale yellow gown? She had smiled at him, he thought, with something like friendship, or at least easiness. He heard her praise his home and Pemberley woods to Bingley. And she would be back the very next day.

It was all too easy to let hope run away with him, and Darcy tried to settle his thoughts. He cleared his throat and gathered himself. "Yes, Miss Elizabeth, you may say it as much as you like! But do I infer correctly that you have made other journeys with your aunt and uncle?"

"Only one, and not so long as this, but three summers ago, we ventured west to Stonehenge. The three of us discovered we travel rather well together," Elizabeth replied, looking fondly at the Gardiners. "That journey was their gift to me when I came out at age 18."

"Ha! Most young ladies flock to London for their coming out, but Elizabeth Bennet left it! You are always unique!" Darcy chuckled. "But I thought you were not yet one and twenty?"

"I have had a birthday since we met in April, sir." Elizabeth looked down, not liking to refer to their last meeting in Hunsford. She found herself wanting only to speak of that which would increase his good opinion of her.

There was a silence during which Caroline Bingley rolled her eyes to her sister in deep resentment.

Finally, Darcy restarted the conversation. "And what did you think of Stonehenge, Miss Elizabeth?"

"Most evocative! Spiritual, yet somehow dangerous… We can only guess what the Druids did there, but it is clearly a place of profound meaning and a marvel of stonework."

"We have a henge in Derbyshire called Arbor Low," Darcy said, turning to the Gardiners. "It is not so well preserved or dramatic as Stonehenge, but I would be delighted to form a party to visit it. I have not been since I was a boy of fifteen or so, and I do not know that Georgiana has ever seen it."

"We would not wish to trouble you, Mr Darcy," replied Mrs Gardiner. She added, glancing down the table, "Your guests may not wish to make the journey. I do not remember seeing it when I lived here, although I have heard of it. We three might go on our own without inconveniencing you."

Darcy knew this response to be a civil formality and brushed it away. "Nonsense, Mrs Gardiner! It is just outside Bakewell. Georgiana?" he spoke up to attract his sister's attention and she looked at him. "Would you like to make the trip to Arbor Low? We will take the Gardiners and Miss Elizabeth, and any of you who wish to join us." Here he looked at Bingley. "It will take half a day if we include a picnic."

Mr Gardiner spoke up, "We would be delighted, sir, if we are not taking you from your guests."

"I certainly intend to join you," exclaimed Bingley. "I shall like it very much."

The next Wednesday was fixed upon, and the ladies withdrew to the music room to await coffee and the gentlemen. The vicar took his leave.

Once alone together, the ladies found their mutual society to be tense in the extreme. Georgiana and Elizabeth sat at the pianoforte selecting music to play. Caroline and Louisa stood to the side, feeling the dreadful slight of not being asked their opinion or invited to perform. Mrs Gardiner chose a seat with the intention of requesting Mr Bingley sit next to her. She was interested in him on Jane's behalf.

Fortunately, the men did not tarry over their port. Darcy, in his desire to spend every possible moment in Elizabeth's company, propelled them out of the dining room. They brought their drinks to the music room and settled in to listen. Darcy secured the chair with the best view of the pianoforte. Louisa and Caroline sat by themselves, facing Darcy and away from the instruments and performers.

Elizabeth played the pianoforte and sang two songs, ones she already knew well. When she looked up from her fingering, Darcy's eyes were beaming at her, and she smiled a little as she sang.

Elizabeth is here in my home, singing like a linnet as if for me alone. It could only be bettered if we were, in truth, alone. He applauded heartily when she finished.

Georgiana suggested another song, but Elizabeth demurred, saying she had heard it sung but did not want to make her first attempt at playing it a public one. Georgiana said in a low voice, "Elizabeth, I do not sing in company, but if you will be my voice, I shall accompany you as I have practiced this piece several times. My brother loves to hear you sing; he has told me so."

Elizabeth nodded, blushing, and her eyes involuntarily went to Darcy, where she became momentarily engrossed in the affection in his dark eyes. *Where do I stand in his esteem?* she wondered. *How I wish I knew.* She smiled at him, which deepened his fond expression, and turned her attention to the next song.

While Elizabeth was singing, Darcy was oblivious to everything and everyone else in the room. He allowed his fancies to run away with him, imagining long winter evenings with just his sister and Elizabeth for company, his two favourite ladies playing duets until he would take Elizabeth's hand and lead her to their bedroom. Detecting the beginnings of arousal, he closed his eyes and attempted to master his breathing.

"Her singing is not as horrible as that, is it Mr Darcy?" The hiss-like whisper of Caroline Bingley's voice jarred in his ear. She had walked behind the chair where Darcy sat. The enticement he was feeling vanished.

"Miss Bingley, you once again reveal a distinct inability to accurately read my thoughts," Darcy murmured. "I wonder that you still make the attempt." He glanced up at her with extreme irritation then away. "I can offer no suggestion of improvement to Miss Elizabeth Bennet's voice. There is no lady I would rather hear." He stood abruptly and walked to the end of the pianoforte.

Mr Gardiner attended the exchange, and although he could not hear what was said, the sneering insolence of Caroline Bingley and Darcy's resulting disturbance of mind were evident. He turned to catch his wife's eye and discovered her to be in serious conversation with Bingley, that gentleman looking very interested in what Mrs Gardiner was saying. They were so occupied in discussion that they neglected to applaud at the end of Elizabeth's song, nor did they stand and approach the serving table when, as the music ceased, a footman delivered the coffee service.

Darcy noticed the tête-à-tête and was filled with a sense of foreboding when he saw Bingley, his countenance ever a map of his feelings, glare openly at his sister Caroline, all the while leaning in to catch Mrs Gardiner's every word. Elizabeth and Georgiana moved to the serving table, and they were met with kind words of appreciation from Darcy and Mr Gardiner. Hurst approached on wobbly legs, picked up the port decanter and carried it back to the corner where he had been dosing.

"Your singing is every bit as lovely as I remember, Miss Elizabeth," said Darcy, pulling his attention away from Bingley's unprecedented grave expression. Bingley was still eyeing his younger sister with exasperation.

"You are too kind, Mr Darcy, but your sister assures me you never lie and are never wrong, so I must assume you mean what you say." Her eyes were alive with their usual teasing sparkle. "It would be difficult for anyone's voice not to sound its best when accompanied on such a fine instrument, played by someone who performs as well as Georgiana."

Georgiana and Elizabeth began to compliment Darcy on the quality of the pianoforte, which had only just arrived, an early birthday gift from brother to sister. Caroline Bingley silently poured herself coffee, hearing with irksome annoyance that Elizabeth and Georgiana addressed each other by their first names, a civility Miss Darcy had never extended to *her*. Her deeply rooted dislike of all things Bennet was ready to erupt, and she did not notice her brother's fixation upon her as his talk with Mrs Gardiner continued.

Georgiana did not care for coffee and returned to her instrument, selecting music to continue playing.

Darcy and Elizabeth were alone at the serving table, and both were now inescapably aware of the intensity of Bingley's eyes upon his sisters. Darcy's perplexity was difficult to mask, and Elizabeth tried not at all.

"What can they be speaking of, do you suppose?" Elizabeth asked as she watched her aunt's face, so earnest in whatever she was saying to Bingley.

"Miss Elizabeth, did your sister mention in her letters to you from London whether your aunt was present when Miss Bingley paid her call?"

Both Mrs Gardiner and Bingley were now looking at Georgiana, and Bingley was shaking his head.

Elizabeth's eyes grew wide with concern, answering Darcy's question in the affirmative by the very nature of her expression. It was at that moment Bingley jumped to his feet and approached Darcy like thunder. His actions were so incautious that Georgiana stopped playing.

"I say, Darcy? May I have the immediate use of your study for a few moments? I would speak with my sisters—both of them." He turned and fixed them with a look of such glowering resentment as they had not seen since they teased him as a boy. But the anger of a man thwarted in love was much more intense than any fleeting childhood indignation.

Darcy spoke in a low voice. "Perhaps this should wait until morning when our dinner guests have gone?"

Bingley responded hotly, "This involves everyone here, it seems, but it starts with my sisters."

"No, Bingley, I think you will find it starts with me." Darcy spoke as if bestowing his own death sentence.

Bingley turned a dispassionate gaze to his friend. "Sir, I do not wish to imply in any manner that I will not soon be requesting a private audience with *you*."

Mrs Gardiner joined them at the coffee service. "Mr Bingley, I must apologize for disquieting you so. Mr Darcy, I fear Mr Bingley's and my conversation has revealed events surprising to him. We were discussing matters misrepresented to both my family and to Mr Bingley. I am mortified to unknowingly have spoiled this most charming evening." She caught Elizabeth's eye. "We should take our leave."

Elizabeth nodded and turned back to the pianoforte to make her excuses to Georgiana. Mrs Gardiner went to her husband, whispering in his ear. He nodded and arose.

Bingley's sisters still were unaware of the storm about to burst, but they were watching their brother warily.

Bingley spoke firmly. "Mrs Gardiner, you owe me no apology. In fact, I am very much in *your* debt. Mr Gardiner, I look forward to seeing you at the river tomorrow." Bingley bowed to the Gardiners. "Louisa, Caroline, come with me."

His sisters looked at him with alarmed surprise. "Charles, really!" chirped Louisa. Her brother fixed her with a gimlet eye, and her next words died on her lips. The three siblings exited the room.

Darcy looked woeful. "Must you all leave?" He knew it was unavoidable but could not resist speaking. His gaze turned to Elizabeth as she returned to the centre of the room, followed by Georgiana.

"May we assume, Aunt, Mr Bingley knows at last that Jane was in London for the winter?" Elizabeth asked.

Mrs Gardiner looked at Darcy with perceptive eyes. "He quite believed himself to be in the fairest way for happiness when he left Netherfield the day after the ball. Suddenly, he was beset by obstacles that made no sense to him. Imagine his confusion."

Darcy lowered his gaze, his face colouring. He turned away and went to pull the bell for a footman. He returned and looked at Elizabeth. "You know already, Miss Elizabeth, that I behaved without honour or probity in this matter, and you know why. I give you leave to tell your excellent aunt and uncle whatever you wish. I know you will be honest."

Georgiana looked from face to face, openly perplexed.

The footman entered, and Darcy ordered the Gardiner carriage brought around. "Mr Gardiner, you are still more than welcome to fish with us in the morning. If you do not arrive at eleven as we have planned, I shall understand completely." Darcy looked meaningfully at Elizabeth and her uncle.

The Gardiners and Elizabeth made their way to the entry hall, followed by Georgiana and Darcy, and they were met by the butler and footmen holding their outerwear. The study where Bingley was engaged in a rencontre with his sisters was just two doors down the hall, and as Elizabeth and her aunt were donning their pelisses, that door opened. Louisa Hurst emerged first, in tears, and ran to the stairway. A furious Caroline, red with rage, followed in long strides behind her sister. Bingley was behind Caroline and said in a low but audible voice, "This will be continued at breakfast."

Bingley joined the waiting group. "Mr Gardiner, may I have one quick, private word with your niece?"

"Yes, Mr Bingley, of course."

Bingley offered his arm to Elizabeth, who, carrying her bonnet and gloves in her other hand, went with him into the vacated drawing room. Darcy looked worried.

Bingley sighed and turned to Elizabeth. He patted her hand nervously and spoke in a low voice, as they had not closed the door behind them. "Lizzy...if I may call you so; I feel you are the sister I was meant to have. I

35

know you will tell me the truth. Was Jane at all partial to me at the time I left Netherfield?"

"Yes, yes, Mr. Bingley, she was. Jane was quite in love with you, but she is modest and we live in gossiping country. Those who do not know her nature would not have seen through her public equanimity. But I can tell you with every certainty that it would take very little effort on your part to encourage her. She still holds you in the highest possible regard."

Bingley looked down at Elizabeth's hand. "I do not deserve such forbearance." Looking back at her face, he asked, "Was Jane told by my sister I had formed an attachment to Miss Darcy—that Darcy was hoping to align me with his sister?"

"Yes, Caroline inferred as much in a letter and, when she called at my aunt's, said a betrothal was in the offing."

"And did Darcy know of this?"

"He knew Jane was in London and had seen your sisters, but he knew nothing of the lies concerning Georgiana. You must know, sir, after Georgiana's trying episode a year ago, Mr Darcy never would have agreed to even the suggestion of such an idea. Please absolve him of that at least. When we talked this morning, he was, I believe, genuinely displeased to learn of your sister's dissemblance. He has much to answer for, Mr. Bingley, but not for the involvement of his sister's name in Jane's deception."

Bingley nodded. It was all as he thought.

"Lizzy, if I were to write a letter to your father asking permission to court Jane when I return to Netherfield, do you think he would honour my suit?" Bingley looked intensely into Elizabeth's eyes.

Elizabeth's chest expanded as tears stung her eyes. "Yes, oh yes, sir… Mr Bingley! You do not know how happy you have made me." She laughed and hugged him.

Darcy stood with his sister and the Gardiners in the entry hall, looking into the open door of the drawing room and fearing the conversation progressing there. *Why did I not speak to Bingley sooner? What a coward! What word did Elizabeth use? Missish? I should have known Mrs Gardiner would have attended as hostess when Caroline called on Jane. I will lose them both… the perfect woman—my beloved—and my best friend. I am losing them both.* He wanted to walk out into the night and never return; he wanted to roar at the moon.

"…isn't that right, Brother?" Georgiana had asked him something and was looking at him. She was expecting some response, and her expression was concerned.

Darcy looked at her then back at the drawing room door. "I am sorry, Georgiana, I did not hear you."

"I was confirming with the Gardiners our plan to visit Arbor Low."

"Yes, yes, of course." He shook his head and smiled at the Gardiners. "There is no reason to think this fair weather will not hold. Mrs Gardiner, you know how beautiful the Derbyshire summer can be, and we shall have a wonderful time." He hoped he sounded more sociable than he felt.

In the drawing room, Bingley chuckled and offered Elizabeth his handkerchief. "I shall never understand the female tendency to cry when happy."

Elizabeth laughed through her tears. "Far lesser men than you have given up the effort as a hopeless case. I do think, Mr Bingley, you should tell my uncle of your intentions."

"Yes! I shall do so directly, before you leave, shall I?"

"Yes, you shall." Elizabeth looked down and smiled to herself. *How like Bingley to ask my permission! Well better mine than someone else's, concerning my own sister…*

They turned to leave the drawing room, but Elizabeth stopped him. "Mr Bingley?" she began.

Bingley stopped and smiled at her with a tilt of his head.

"I must beg you to forgive Mr Darcy. He knows he has stolen months of happiness from you and my sister, but I believe him to be filled with remorse. He can, at least in some measure, explain his actions if not excuse them. Please listen to him. Or if he happens to write you a letter, read it."

"I fully intend to forgive him, after a few hours and a few brandies…" Bingley chuckled, and Elizabeth joined him with a beaming smile. They started out of the room. "And you will come with your uncle in the morning?" Bingley whispered.

She raised her face to Bingley's and nodded. She would come.

The front door of Pemberley opened as the Gardiner's carriage rolled to a stop. Darcy turned in time to see Elizabeth and Bingley emerge from the drawing room. They were smiling, and she was nodding and dabbing at her eyes with Bingley's handkerchief.

"Now what is this?" Mr Gardiner asked. He was a calm man, not given to the enjoyment of emotional drama. He had experienced quite enough of it growing up with two silly sisters. Elizabeth flew to her uncle's arms and looked back at Mr Bingley.

"Mr Gardiner, Miss Elizabeth would have me inform you that, tomorrow morning, I intend to send an express to her father asking permission to court your niece, Miss Jane Bennet, upon my return to the Meryton neighbourhood."

Mrs Gardiner inhaled a happy gasp, and Elizabeth moved from her uncle's embrace to her aunt's as Bingley continued, "I have a matter, or perhaps three matters, to settle here"—he glared at Darcy—"and then I plan to remove myself to Hertfordshire with all possible speed."

Mr Gardiner held out his hand to Bingley, who wrung it with excessive enthusiasm. "I am most pleased, Mr Bingley, most pleased. We do not know each other well, but I believe you to be an excellent fisherman, which I think will carry some weight with my brother Bennet!"

Darcy stood back and followed behind with Georgiana as Bingley helped the Gardiners and Elizabeth into the carriage. Darcy and Georgiana took part in the general thanks and well-wishes, and Darcy received a nod from Mr Gardiner when he reminded that man, yet again, to come and fish at eleven.

Elizabeth was handed last into the carriage, and Darcy heard Bingley whisper, "Thank you, Lizzy," as she leaned out to return his handkerchief.

Lavender
"Faithfulness"

Chapter 3

The carriage bearing the Gardiners and their niece rolled to Lambton with a happy cadence, mimicking the mood of the people it carried. Elizabeth spoke excitedly about her encouragement of Bingley and explained more fully the visit she had from Mr. Darcy that morning. She was overjoyed that matters had progressed so rapidly, although in her heart, she was worried about the conversation she knew to be taking place in Darcy's study. Elizabeth hoped Bingley truly had the forgiving nature she believed of him. The Gardiners asked many questions about Bingley's temperament, concerned as they were by the ease with which he had been influenced by his sisters and his friend. Elizabeth was able to answer honestly; Bingley had a limit to his forbearance, as she had just discovered, and Darcy was deeply sorry for his part in separating two such well-suited lovers.

When they reached the inn, her aunt and uncle beckoned Elizabeth to join them in the public sitting room. It was empty and the fire was down to embers. Wine was ordered and delivered, and the fire revived.

"Elizabeth," Mrs Gardiner began, "it is obvious to your uncle and me that Mr Bingley is not the only gentleman at Pemberley who is in love. That Mr Darcy regards you with fond admiration has been clear since we arrived in the neighbourhood. Is there something you would like to tell us? Is there some understanding between you?"

Her aunt watched in gentle wonder as tears formed and silently spilled from her niece's eyes. Mr Gardiner produced a handkerchief, and when she could, Elizabeth responded, "I am sorry to be so foolish. I own it will be a relief to speak of it. Only Jane knows of this matter, but not all of it. I first learnt Mr Darcy had formed an attachment to me when I stayed with Charlotte in Hunsford and he was visiting his aunt at Rosings Park for Easter. You will think I am delusional, but the truth of it is, he proposed to me—there in Charlotte's little parlour—and I was completely shocked. I refused him." She shook her head. "I was caught utterly unawares. I thought he and I had resolved not to like each other.

"In a roundabout way, I had my suspicions confirmed earlier that same day, that he had played a principal role in separating Jane from Mr Bingley, and…oh, I am ashamed to speak of it, but my contempt rained upon him. His proposal was"—she paused to find the right word— "inelegant. He spoke at length of my lack of connections and the folly of my mother and sisters—not Jane, of course, but Mary, Kitty and Lydia. He said his admiration for me—perhaps he used the word desire—overcame his scruples, but he scarcely mentioned love nor did he compliment me in any way. But no matter what he might have said, once he did not deny or even defend, his treatment of Jane, I poured my venom upon him most copiously." She sniffled a moment then went on. "Without restraint, I eviscerated his character, enumerating every flaw I found there. Poor, poor man…"

The Gardiners looked at each other and waited for Elizabeth to continue. After drawing a deep breath, their niece explained the text of Darcy's letter and its effect upon her. "I did not know myself until I read his words. He explained his actions in the matter of Jane and Bingley very ill—although he and I both understand his actions better now—but in every other particular, I saw I had misread him.

"This is why I was so careful to determine whether or not he would be at Pemberley before consenting to a tour. I was certain he would cut me or believe I had come for some nefarious reason. Had we been told the family was in residence, I would have explained my difficult dealings with him. But we went…and there he appeared! And so changed. At first I could not accept that he would even be civil, but when he was *more* than civil—when he asked me to meet his sister and was so kind to you—I knew not what to think."

Her uncle asked kindly, "You did not? Surely you saw that he still has feelings for you?"

"How could he?" Elizabeth cried. "You have no idea the hiding I gave him. Even had I been more moderate in my choice of words, it was still a refusal." She took a swallow of wine and several deep breaths.

"Lizzy." Her uncle leaned forward and patted her hand. "He still loves you. I'd bet my future on it."

Her aunt nodded in agreement. "It is obvious; his improvements have been made because he thought your accusations just. Now that you have stumbled into his sphere again, he gives every indication of wanting you to know he has taken your words to heart and still cares for you."

Elizabeth shook her head. "He may still care and he *has* improved, but how could a man with such pride as he possesses possibly lower himself to renew his addresses where they were so ruinously met before? I cannot comprehend it." She shook her head again. "Indeed, I cannot."

"That," her aunt whispered, "is the depth of his love, Lizzy. He is restoring Bingley to Jane, both for his friend's sake and to please you. We are certain of it."

Elizabeth nodded. "Yes, in that I believe you are right. He wants to be forgiven, but I believe it is because, in truth, he is a good man. He does not want anyone, anywhere, thinking ill of him."

Her uncle caught her eye. "Least of all you."

After a few moments of silence, Mrs Gardiner asked, "May we take it as a given that you would not refuse him a second time?"

Elizabeth blushed deeply and looked down at the glass of wine in her hand. "I do not know," she murmured.

Mrs Gardiner took Elizabeth's hand in hers and tried to meet her eye. "When did *you* fall in love with *him*?"

Elizabeth's liquid eyes flew to her aunt's face with the utmost alarm and then looked away. "I do not know! I do not know what I feel! I do not understand myself at all. If only Jane were here, she would explain me to myself..."

"I think I can tell you, my love, what your dear sister would say. She knows what it is to love. She would say that you are indeed in love at last."

Elizabeth started to cry again, and Mr Gardiner decided it was quite time to excuse himself. Elizabeth had sunk from her chair and was sitting on the floor, crying into her aunt's knees as she had done as a child. Mr

Gardiner leaned over and kissed his wife's forehead. "I know you will sort this out, my dear. Take as long as you need." Madeline smiled and nodded.

"Lizzy?" Mr Gardiner gave her hand a gentle squeeze. "Your aunt is very wise, is she not?"

Elizabeth started to smile and gave a meek nod. She was reminded of prior times when staying with the Gardiners in London and she felt vexed or frustrated. She was now one and twenty, not ten or eleven, and yet she felt just the same.

"There's my girl. There is that beautiful smile. If you will smile just so for Mr Darcy, he cannot fail to propose again. Mr Bingley will not be the only one writing to your father. Good night, darling girl."

Smiling, Mr Gardiner took himself to bed.

"Now, sit beside me, Lizzy, or I shall have to write your father and tell him he has four silly daughters instead of only three."

Elizabeth stood and smoothed her gown, momentarily irked that she had set wrinkles into it.

"Oh, Aunt," she said, dropping onto the settee where her uncle had been. "I suppose I *may* be in love, but how do I know? When I first saw him again at Pemberley, my chest seemed to collapse; I could barely breathe. It was a most unpleasant sensation. But now it happens every time I see him, and it takes several minutes to compose myself. My heart beats so vigorously I feel my cross bounce upon my chest. I feel as if everyone can see it."

Mrs Gardiner put her arm around her niece's shoulder. "You only think that. For the most part, you have behaved very well—quite sensibly apart from the near-continuous blushing. However, Mr Darcy does not see you are in love with him. He is excessively worried you do not even like him."

"You are teasing me, Aunt."

"Yes, but that does not mean you should doubt me. What was all that business at dinner about lavender?"

"It is the scent I wear. He was letting me know he recognizes it. He was teasing me, too."

"He was letting you know, Lizzy, that he is still in love with you. Did he not say he is fonder of the scent now than in April? What more can he do? He is begging you to encourage him."

Elizabeth sat up to look at her aunt's face. "Tell me honestly. Do not answer as my dear aunt, but try to be impartial. Could he possibly think of renewing his addresses?"

"If you smiled at him with the warmth I see in your eyes right now, I do not think he could stop himself."

"Charlotte always said a lady should show more affection than she feels to secure a gentleman's regard. Were I to show Mr Darcy more affection than I feel...well, I do not see how I could without being improper." She said the words aloud for the first time, a revelation for herself and the world. "I love him."

As THE CARRIAGE BOUND FOR Lambton pulled away from Pemberley, Georgiana returned to the house, and Bingley turned to meet Darcy's anxious eyes. Darcy cocked his head to the left—the direction of his study—and raised his eyebrows. Bingley responded with a curt nod; he had much to ask his friend and imagined they might converse over Darcy's excellent brandy until well into the night.

Bingley preceded Darcy into the room.

"Fitzwilliam! Brother!" Georgiana hailed from the foot of the stairway.

Darcy halted and she ran to him. "I would speak with you, Brother. I have several questions, and they deserve answers."

"Bingley is waiting. His questions, I am afraid, are more pressing than yours. Let us breakfast together in the morning. Will that suit?"

Georgiana glared at her brother, just stopping herself from stamping a petulant foot. "What choice do I have? I will arrange for breakfast in my sitting room, shall I?"

"That will suit me admirably. I fear our breakfast room will host the battle of the Bingleys in the morning." Darcy kissed his sister's forehead absently and disappeared into his study. Just after closing the door, he immediately opened it again and walked back into the hall. Georgiana was at the top of the stairs, and he called after her. "Georgie, gosling, it occurs to me your questions will run in a similar bent to Bingley's. You are my friend as much as he, so I think I should treat you as more than merely my little sister. Will you join us?"

Georgiana's countenance transformed from annoyance to pleasure as she returned and followed him into the study.

"Bingley," Darcy said, as they entered, "do not think I am bringing Georgiana here to cause you to temper your completely justifiable anger

—far from it. You both have questions for me, and I suspect, in some cases, they are the same. To avoid repeating myself, I have asked her to join us."

Georgiana was not shy in front of Bingley as she regarded him as almost another brother. "You need not censor yourselves on my account. I have certainly heard you give vent to ungentlemanly language upon occasion, Brother."

Bingley nodded. "Well, Georgiana, if you're going to join us, would you prefer a splash of brandy or a finger of port?"

"Bingley!" Darcy snorted.

"Port, please," she responded. "I do not care much for brandy."

Bingley laughed.

Darcy stared at her. "When have you had enough of either to form a preference?"

"At our Uncle Matlock's. The ladies have port or brandy when they withdraw from the men, since that is what the men are taking." Georgiana raised her eyebrows, daring him to rebuke her.

Darcy flopped into a chair with an exasperated sigh. "Insolent gosling. Some guardian of your delicate sensibilities I am…"

Bingley handed Georgiana a modest portion of port and a tumbler of brandy to Darcy, and they each took a sip in silence.

"I am going to make the Spanish Inquisition look like a garden party, Georgiana, but if there is some line of inquiry you believe deserves a more thorough exploration, I pray you, jump in with your own questions."

Georgiana nodded to him with gracious condescension. "With your leave, Mr Bingley, I shall. Thank you."

"Just get on with it…" Darcy muttered.

Everyone sat up straight as if by design, and Bingley began. "I believe the following question will get us to the heart of the matter, so to speak… Darcy, how long have you been in love with Elizabeth Bennet?"

Georgiana nodded her approval of Bingley's tactics.

Darcy sighed. "I have been in love with Elizabeth Bennet for not much less time than you have been in love with Jane Bennet—perhaps as many as five days less but perhaps only five minutes. Maybe I did not know what it is to love until I had known her five months and was spurned in my addresses to her."

"Ah." Bingley nodded as if not at all surprised.

Georgiana, however, looked taken unawares. "Would you care to explain?"

"No," Darcy responded, brusquely, "but I shall. I believe, Bingley, your attraction to Jane Bennet might be described as love at first sight? Or very near it?"

Bingley smiled. "Yes, I'd say that sums it up nicely."

"I met Elizabeth, Georgiana, that same evening, and like a popinjay refused to dance with her, making idiotic comments, which she overheard. She laughed at me! She stood from her seat, went directly to her friend Mrs Collins and laughed at me. She stood across that damned assembly room and had a good joke at my expense. It was only then that I really studied her. She was taller than I thought and prettier than I thought and"—he glanced at his sister but continued— "had a better figure than I thought. She had a musical laugh, and it was directed at me!

"Then you danced with her, Bingley, and the look she gave me as the two of you skipped down the dance..." Darcy shook his head. "I shall never forget it. She was *still* laughing at me. I could have strangled her."

"You had insulted her?" Georgiana asked her brother.

Bingley chuckled. "Oh, do tell her what you said, Darcy. I remember it if you do not. This is priceless, Georgiana—Darcy at his petulant best. I told him he should dance with her, and he did everything but lie on the ground kicking and screaming like a spoilt five-year-old."

Darcy passed the back of his fingers over his lips glaring at them both.

"I'm waiting," Georgiana said, primly folding her hands in her lap.

Darcy fidgeted in his seat. "I told Bingley she was tolerable, but not handsome enough to tempt me, and I would not dance with a lady who had been slighted by other men. That is, more or less, the sum of it."

Georgiana shook her head. "Fitzwilliam Darcy, I am ashamed of you. This is how you behave out in the world, away from Pemberley?"

"Indeed, that is every inch how he behaves. There were far too many ladies than gentlemen that night, and ladies who wanted to dance could not. I believe even Jane stood idle during my dance with Miss Elizabeth."

"Must we dissect that evening so particularly?" Darcy asked.

"May I assume that when you had the earliest opportunity, you apologized to her? Once you understood fully that she had heard you?" Georgiana asked.

Bingley already knew the answer to this and started chuckling again.

Darcy looked down at his hands. "I am sorry to admit I have *never* apologized for those words in any specific way."

Georgiana looked at Bingley and rolled her eyes, "Oh my, such lovely manners...do go on with your tale, Brother."

"When we met the Bennet family again, it was at a party at Lucas Lodge. Elizabeth was in fine form. The militia had arrived, and she was witty and charming. We exchanged few words, but I found I could not take my eyes off her. She sang and played a little—very entertaining, as I told you in a letter, Georgie."

His sister nodded.

"And finally, the most singular thing happened. Sir William Lucas and I were speaking of dancing, and Elizabeth passed by. Knowing her as I do now, I believe she was on her way to censure her sister Lydia who was carrying on in a most boisterous manner. Sir William took up Elizabeth's hand and, insisting I dance with her, passed her hand to me. She snatched it away; she was vexed with him and tried to hide it, of course. I will say that I did, quite civilly I thought, ask her to dance, and she refused me. At heart, I was glad, as the dancing was very rag-tag, but to make amends for myself at the assembly, I would have danced with her. Looking back upon it, what I truly wanted was for her fine eyes to be trained upon me, and me alone, if only for the time it takes to dance a reel. She is the only woman who has ever refused to stand up with me."

"Did it occur to you, Darcy, she may have been getting back at you for your insult?" Bingley asked.

"Of course it did, and so I put 'paid' to that account. I was premature."

Everyone sighed.

"Would you care to explain your erratic behaviour towards her when she stayed at Netherfield tending Jane?" Bingley asked.

"What can I say? I found myself interested in her, and I did not wish to be. I could not will myself out of it. When she arrived, I happened to be crossing the hall, and the concern in her eyes was heartrending. Yet, she expected the disapprobation of the household, I'm sure she did, excepting yourself, Bingley, and the challenge in her eyes was thrilling to me. She had walked three miles, probably in a high lather, and had torn off her bonnet. Her hair..." Darcy took a deep breath. "It was just on the point of coming undone; she was glowing, her skirts spattered with mud. All she cared about was getting to her sister. She was...courageous, magnificent.

"When she joined us in the evenings, it was clear to me she wished to be anywhere else. Your sisters did not welcome her and made her uncomfortable with their civil disdain. Surely, you would not defend them, Bingley."

Bingley pursed his lips, allowing his annoyance to show. "Do not try to distract me with their actions, Darcy. I will settle with them. Let us concentrate upon you."

"Fine," Darcy huffed. "To my credit, I was moved to protective feelings for Elizabeth, but she would challenge every word I said. The verbal jousting was stimulating. How I laughed inside when she bested Caroline time after time. Were you in the room, Bingley, when Caroline was playing a Scottish air and I asked Elizabeth to dance a reel, and she refused me *again*?"

Bingley smirked. "I do not remember *that*, but I do know, at the ball, Jane was surprised to see her sister dance with you, for she had promised her mother never to do so."

"What? When did she...?" Darcy was shocked.

Bingley shook his head. "Jane said that after the Meryton assembly, when Mrs Bennet was telling Mr Bennet you had slighted his favourite daughter, Miss Elizabeth assured her parents she would never dance with you."

Georgiana turned to stare at her brother. "And you had no notion of Elizabeth's disliking you, did you?"

"God's blood..." Darcy muttered. His mind was propelled back to the last day the Bennet sisters were at Netherfield. *I ignored her so carefully. No woman was ever ignored so carefully, and she probably thought it a blessed relief. I was so sure she was aware of my softening feelings. This is awful. Bloody awful. What else does Bingley know that I should have understood?*

Bingley was back on the scent. "So you worked the whole time not to be in love with Elizabeth Bennet. You hid your tender regard uncommonly well, I must say. Jane and I had no idea of it. We thought the two of you were of the same mind—that neither liked the other." Bingley turned to Georgiana. "Yet, the most amazing revelation has not been exposed. Let me advance his story by telling you that your brother was held in esteem by no one in the Bennet family—no one except Jane." Bingley turned a glare at Darcy. "Ironic, isn't it?"

Darcy stood and turned to the fireplace, leaning on straight arms against the mantle. He stared at the fire until his eyes stung. Finally, he mastered his remorse, began pacing, and continued, "I have wronged that lady more than can or should be forgiven. At the Netherfield ball, Sir William interrupted

Elizabeth and me as we danced, and alluded to the expectation abroad in the neighbourhood that you and Jane were a fixed item. It alarmed me. I had promised myself one lovely dance with Elizabeth—a few smiles, charming talk about nothing, touching her hand—she was so elegantly dressed that night. But it was marred, first by her mention of her new acquaintance with Wickham then by the rumours of a connection between my best friend and her sister, which would make Elizabeth impossible to avoid were Sir William's rumours true. And for the rest of the evening, her family seemed to compete to see who could most thoroughly plumb the depths of impropriety and misbehaviour."

Bingley shook his head like a perturbed schoolmaster. "I left for London the next day, intending to return with all due haste. How long had I been gone before you convinced my sisters to decamp to *save* me?"

"It was but the work of an hour's conversation. Caroline and Louisa were concerned over the alliance with the Bennets. They had feigned friendship with Jane merely because they had nothing better to do, yet I still assumed they knew her better than I, who had never had a conversation with her. We were able to easily convince ourselves she was merely a mercenary with genteel manners, and that, on your side, Bingley, it was just another fleeting infatuation."

"And Caroline wrote to Jane that day as you prepared to follow me to London?" Bingley asked.

"Yes."

"It was that letter in which Caroline mentioned the notion of taking me away from Jane to align me with your sister." Bingley glanced at Georgiana, who was instantly incensed at having been so unkindly used by Caroline Bingley. "Jane had all of Caroline's correspondence with her in London and showed the letter to her aunt. It breaks my heart to think of her pining for me while I was mooning after her. Caroline developed the theme of marrying me off to Georgiana to increase the likelihood of ensnaring you for herself, Darcy."

Darcy nodded, a chagrined expression on his face. "Yes, so I gather."

Bingley turned to Georgiana. "I had not been in London two days when hither came Darcy and my family. They fell upon me like a flock of harpies, emphasizing the Bennet family's want of connections and fortune, and trying to convince me that Jane did not love me. And this is the responsibility *I* must accept. I did not have the confidence in myself to believe Jane *could* love me, and I had not the faith in my own observations, for I knew her better than anyone except Miss Elizabeth." Bingley hung his head.

Darcy added, "Even from the distance of Longbourn, Elizabeth saw through the whole affair. She said as much this morning."

Georgiana turned and took Bingley's hand, squeezing it sympathetically.

Bingley concurred. "Of course she did. There are only two failures of perception that I can detect her ever making, and they really amount to the same thing. She failed to see you falling in love with her, and she failed to see Wickham for a scheming rake. Sorry to speak of him, Georgiana," Bingley added quickly.

"It is of no consequence, Mr Bingley. It does me no harm."

"How do these failures amount to the same thing?" Darcy asked, annoyed with Bingley's logic.

"If you had not behaved as a complete clot from the very first, Miss Elizabeth would not have been inclined to believe Wickham's lies. She might have liked you and, having formed no ill opinion, might have seen your affection develop. Yes, her family lacks connections and some of them have little sense of decorum, but what of that? Really, Darcy, in the face of love, what matters the rest of it?"

Darcy stared into the fire. "As I have long expected, Bingley, it is finally revealed that you are a better man than I."

"Did you know, Darcy, it was Miss Elizabeth who suggested Jane stay with the Gardiners in London? She insisted. Mrs Gardiner told me so."

Darcy turned to Bingley from his contemplation of the fire. "I should not be at all surprised. I imagine she hoped the two of you would cross paths. She was pushing Jane after happiness, only to have your sister squash it flat with lies involving Georgie in the cruellest way. And me, I thwarted her hopes for Jane. It was wrong of me."

Bingley sighed. "How many times did I nearly saddle a horse and ride to Longbourn? Imagine if I had, only to find Jane gone to London..."

Georgiana rose, took the tumblers of brandy away from the men and tugged a bell pull. Darcy looked at her. "Heard enough of your brother and his best friend wallowing in self-pity?"

"Oh no, there is more to learn. I am ordering coffee. The brandy is making you both maudlin. *I* am having a little more port."

The butler tapped at the study door. Georgiana opened it to request coffee for the gentleman and then resettled herself upon the settee.

"If I may pursue my own line of inquiry, Mr Bingley?" Georgiana received a slight bow from him, yielding the floor. "At Easter, Fitzwilliam, you wrote to me twice, mentioning Miss Elizabeth Bennet was at the parsonage staying with Mr and Mrs Collins. The second letter was, if I may say, heavy with implication. I was certain, at that time or soon thereafter, I would meet Elizabeth, and she might be presumed to have agreed to take on the role of the sister I have always wanted by becoming your wife. You made it sound a certainty—that you were on the point of proposing…"

Bingley leaned forward, eyes attentive.

Darcy looked from one to the other. "There are only two people who know of what I am about to tell you: Colonel Fitzwilliam and Miss Jane Bennet. However, Elizabeth did not tell her sister the whole of it for reasons that will become obvious. We, Elizabeth and I, are not proud of what happened at Hunsford, but I have much more to answer for than she. I moved her to anger, and she duly expressed it. That is all. She gave me in abundance the setting down I had coming. I could not possibly have accepted it from anyone else."

Bingley and Georgiana were at the edge of their seats in anticipation of his next words.

"When the colonel and I arrived at Rosings, he wished to call at the parsonage right away as I had told him of my acquaintance with Elizabeth. I thought he would like her—who would not?—and felt my emotions were safe. We walked into the drawing room where I became every bit as stupid and sullen as I had been in Hertfordshire. She was lovelier than I remembered, and I was utterly tongue-tied. How it chafed to watch Fitzwilliam chatting so easily and she smiling and laughing with him. When I did manage to choke out the necessary formalities, the first thing she asked was whether I happened to see Jane in town." Darcy laughed abruptly at himself. "The knowing glint in her eye silenced me. And yet, I was oblivious…so overwrought in my own feelings. It never occurred to me that she knew me better than I knew myself and did not like at all what she saw. I look back on it now with utter self-loathing."

A servant entered with coffee, and Georgiana rose to serve her brother and Bingley.

Darcy sipped on his drink and continued. "Thank you, Georgie. Coffee was an excellent idea. So…the first week we were at Rosings, I did not call at the parsonage, and our aunt did not invite anyone to dine with us."

"How gruelling…" Georgiana murmured.

"Quite." Darcy smirked and nodded. "The colonel went out walking and, of course, encountered Elizabeth, who loves nothing better than a long ramble. He also called at the parsonage several times, while I stayed at Rosings for my sins, fighting with my demons. When at last the Hunsford household and their guests came for tea, I had become obsessed with her. Because of our aunt's fantasy that I am to marry our cousin Anne, Fitzwilliam was able to monopolize Elizabeth, and I had to sit and, yet again, watch him entertain her so easily. Then he asked her to play, and I wanted to strangle him—sitting next to her, turning her pages, smelling the scent of lavender."

Bingley nodded to himself. *Ah, lavender!*

"Lo and behold! I am a jealous creature," Darcy went on. "I had no notion. When I was able to escape Lady Catherine and approach the pianoforte, Elizabeth and Fitzwilliam tweaked me for being so taciturn in company. She teased me and alluded to my rudeness at the Meryton assembly. Had I not been a half-wit, I would have realized my insult had touched her deeply and was unforgiven. I was much more concerned that there seemed to be some partiality between her and our cousin.

"As soon as the Hunsford party departed for the evening, I warned Fitzwilliam about Elizabeth's lack of fortune and connection, knowing that as a second son, he must be circumspect as to marriage. He groused at me at first for my good fortune of not having to worry about such things but thanked me for the warning.

"The next day, I called at the parsonage, and finding Elizabeth alone, engaged her in an uncommonly awkward conversation, but by the end of it, I thought her friendlier. I started seeking her out, as if accidentally, on her morning rambles. The second time we met, she mentioned the grove we were in was her favourite in the park. She was trying to cry me off the place, I'm sure, to tell me where to avoid, but I was so conceited, I took her words as offering encouragement. When I met her there again, she was peevish at first… What a simpleton I was."

"You were a man in love, Darcy." Bingley looked kindly at his friend, even though reasons for anger were piling on by the minute. Darcy allowed himself what he would not allow Bingley.

"The next morning when I got to the grove, I found the colonel had preceded me. I heard their laughter, and I was instantly beset by the green-eyed monster. In all the time I had known Elizabeth, I had yet to say anything that made her laugh." Darcy sighed and stood, refilling his coffee, then continued his story while pacing and drinking. "I hung about in the shrubbery, and their conversation turned more serious. In what glimpses I could catch, I saw Elizabeth grow discomfited. She looked sad, and I thought she would cry. My cousin, damn his eyes, extended his arm to her, and they returned to Hunsford. How was I to ask him what had so suddenly changed her mood? I could not—not without admitting much about myself I was not ready to face."

Bingley and Georgiana looked sorry for him, but that changed as he went on. "That evening the parsonage crowd was to drink tea again at our aunt's invitation, but when they arrived, no Elizabeth. She had begged off, claiming a headache. In my arrogance, I assumed she stayed behind so I might find her alone. What an ass! Making some poor excuse, which Mrs Collins clearly saw through, I excused myself and went for a walk and—what a surprise—found myself ringing the bell at the parsonage. I was admitted, and she was in the sitting room with a pile of letters...Jane's letters as she later indicated."

Darcy took a deep breath. "The next thing I knew, I was proposing! I told her I admired and loved her, and then went on at great length and with exquisite eloquence on the want of connection of her family and the crude impropriety of their manners, and wasn't I a fine fellow to be praised for proposing to her anyway?"

Bingley snorted, trying to suppress outright laughter. "Darcy, you didn't!"

Georgiana hid a smile behind her hand.

"Oh, I most certainly did. I told her my feelings of repugnance were natural and just."

Georgiana spoke up, clearly confused. "Please speak plainly, Brother. You told her your love was natural and just?"

Darcy ruefully shook his head. "No, I meant my disapprobation of her family was natural and just."

Georgiana could not help giggling. "Oh my...the sweet words any lady longs to hear: I loathe your family; marry me anyway."

Bingley joined her. "Very smooth, Darcy, you silver-tongued devil..."

When his audience settled down, Darcy glared at them, setting off another minor round of hilarity. He waited until they stopped with obvious annoyance and then continued, "She refused me, of course, and I accused her of doing so with little attempt at civility. She was, at first, obviously shocked, but spoke quite evenly, stating that the feelings I had overcome to make the proposal would soothe me of the temporary discomfort caused by her refusing it."

"She didn't slap you?" Georgiana asked with wonder.

"Not with her hand, no, but she did it quite thoroughly with words. Not willing to leave a bad business from becoming worse, I insisted she tell me why she was refusing me. Immediately, she accused me of wilfully and wantonly separating her sister from you, Bingley, and motioned to her sister's letters as proof of Jane's attachment and heartbreak. I was so furious and self-righteous that I brushed this aside. Then she repeated the lies Wickham had told her about me, which fed my fury.

"I accused her of wanting flattery to cajole her acceptance, saying if I had spoken more prettily, these paltry considerations would have meant nothing to her."

Bingley had been silently laughing, but could stifle himself no longer. He guffawed, rolling in his chair.

"Bingley, stop it," Darcy seethed.

Bingley shook his head. "I cannot. Nor do I wish to." He finally gathered himself enough to say, "Darcy, you condescending son-of-a-bitch."

Georgiana gasped a little, sobered by the evidence of Bingley's emerging resentment.

"At what point did she skin you alive?" Bingley asked.

"Oh, that pretty much put the torch to her fuse. She barely raised her voice but I could see she was outraged. She accused me of making an ungentlemanlike proposal that did not require a ladylike response and spared her pitying me. She said I was conceited, disdainful of the feelings of others, and her dislike of me began after our first meeting. Within a month of knowing me, she had decided I was the last man in the world she could ever marry. Before separating you and Jane, before Wickham's lies, from the very start of our acquaintance, I had impressed her only with my arrogance and selfishness."

The room was quiet. Bingley rose and poured himself more brandy. He silently offered port to Georgiana, who accepted a drop more. Darcy turned away from them, breathing heavily. Bingley poured out more brandy, nudged Darcy's shoulder and handed it to him. Georgiana noticed her brother's posture was the same disheartened slouch he had exhibited for weeks after he returned from Rosings.

"At that time, by your estimation, I was a will-o'-the-wisp easily swayed in and out of love and Jane a lovely and well-mannered mercenary who would, with perfect equanimity, consider my defection with little more than a nothing-ventured, nothing-gained attitude?" Bingley asked with a tight voice.

"I told myself I did not wish to see you hurt by an unfortunate marriage. I told myself I needed to protect you," Darcy murmured. He humbly met his friend's eyes. "Can you forgive me, Charles?"

A sniffing sound alerted the men that Georgiana was crying. She was grieved to be complicit in causing her brother to relive what she could well imagine was a devastating sorrow. Darcy handed her his handkerchief. Bingley reached for his and it released the smell of lavender from the lady who had used it two hours before. It was still moist. The misery on Darcy's face was more than Bingley could bear. He handed the handkerchief to Darcy.

"I am not crying...yet." Darcy waved it away.

"Take it and smell it, you great pillock," Bingley responded. "I think you'll recognize the scent."

Darcy stroked the proffered fabric under his nose, then closed his eyes and inhaled. *She is right; it is soothing... She is always right.*

Georgiana dried her eyes, and after several great sighs, straightened herself and addressed her brother. "Not much is ever obvious to me, Fitzwilliam, but this much is: Elizabeth has forgiven you. How did you bring this about?"

Darcy looked incredulously at his sister. "Has she?"

Bingley agreed with Georgiana. "I would wager—and I do not say this as the hopeless romantic I know myself to be—she has a good deal more than forgiven you."

Darcy turned his wounded countenance upon Bingley. "Do not torture me, either of you. It is most unkind."

Bingley put his hand on Darcy's shoulder. "When I spoke with Miss Elizabeth in the drawing room, I asked her to confirm what I had learned from her aunt, and she did, very much to my satisfaction. Once I said I would write to her father, nothing would do but that I had to promise her I would forgive you. And she said the most curious thing. She said if you happened to write me a letter, I must read it."

Darcy continued to stare at the fire, barely breathing. The hankie was wadded in his hand. Bingley, who owed him nothing, had restored him to hope—a pure, naked, fragile hope to be sure, but for the moment, it was no small thing. "The morning after my ridiculous proposal to her, I gave her a letter. It took me all night to write it. I could not defend the flaws in my character but I tried to defend my actions in protection of you, and I explained *all* my dealings with Wickham."

Georgiana leaned forward to hear Darcy more particularly. *"All* of them?"

"Yes, little gosling, *all* of them. I had to, Georgie. I was fearful she had formed some attachment to him and felt she must know the truth." Darcy went to his sister, taking her into his arms. "I would trust her with any secret. I did fear she would not believe me, and advised her that the colonel could answer any doubts she might have of my veracity."

Georgiana shook her head, trying to arrange her thoughts. "She knows what a silly, foolish girl I have been. She knows I have been stupid. She knew it when we were introduced. You knew…that she knew. And yet, she still wished to meet me?"

"You see, Georgie? You are not so silly or foolish or stupid that a most intelligent and discerning lady would not wish to become your friend. When I asked her permission to make the introduction, she said yes without hesitation."

Georgiana burst into tears, sobbing onto her brother's shoulder.

Bingley began to feel superfluous. He caught Darcy's attention. "Just two more comments from me, and then I'm for bed. Tomorrow, I will ask Caroline and the Hursts to leave Pemberley and travel to Scarborough immediately. No argument from you, Darcy—none. It is a family matter, and you are better out of it. Secondly, Mr Gardiner asked leave to bring his wife's maid tomorrow"—Bingley winked at Darcy—"to make use of the Pemberley stillroom. I allowed it. I hope I have not overstepped my bounds as your guest?"

Darcy's heart leapt to his throat. "No, Bingley, it is no bother. I shall alert Mrs Reynolds in the morning. Thank you."

Bingley went to the study door and turned around. He could hear Georgiana softly crying. "And Darcy?"

"Yes, Bingley?" Darcy looked over his sister's head to see Bingley's face lit by the fire, much returned to its usual jovial countenance.

"I forgive you. I told Miss Elizabeth I would after drinking a good share of your brandy. You must tell her, when next you see her, that I have kept my word in every particular." Laughing, Bingley slipped out of the room.

Peppermint
"Warmth of feeling"

Chapter 4

Caroline Bingley, in a state of high dudgeon, stood at one of the long narrow windows in the Pemberley breakfast room, staring out on the beautiful summer morning with cold disdain. She despaired for the moment of arguing with her brother, and her sister Louisa entered the fray. Caroline had never seen Charles behave in such a recalcitrant manner. She assumed a little brandy and a talk with the sensible Darcy last evening would return Charles to his usual malleable amiability, but if anything, this morning he was cocky and imperious. He spoke of nothing but her alleged betrayal of his love for Jane Bennet. *I wish we never ventured to Hertfordshire. Why did I insist he take an estate?*

She saw Darcy and Georgiana emerge from the end of the house and enter the herb garden. They seemed in fine spirits, laughing and talking. The herb garden had a low hedge, and brother and sister could be seen moving from plant to plant, Darcy occasionally picking a leaf or flower to add to the bunch in his hand. Georgiana had a book, over which they consulted and laughed. Darcy was in shirtsleeves and waistcoat, without a frock coat or hat. Caroline snorted to herself. *Such country pastimes —Darcy loses all sense of himself when he comes here. His servants should not see him so unguarded.*

Bingley raised his voice, and Caroline turned to listen.

"Louisa, I have made up my mind, and for once, you and Caroline will not change it for me. In fact, you never shall again. You have, both of you, acted in your own interests with no thought to my happiness for the last time. Until you receive an invitation to my wedding, I have no wish to see you. You must give Miss Bennet time to convince me to forgive you. And please do not attend unless you can sincerely wish us well."

"What about *my* happiness, Charles? What about *my* hope of an advantageous marriage?" Caroline chided him.

"Caroline, I am firmly convinced you would not be happy if you were hanged with a new rope. Your careless disregard for my feelings in preference to your own was one thing when we were children, but now it is quite another. You have involved innocents in your lies, and Darcy is furious with you. Louisa, you are the older sister, yet you allow yourself to be drawn into Caroline's reprehensible plans without providing the least guidance or censure. After last night's performance and your contemptible behaviour to Jane, I cannot stomach either of you. Sorry, Hurst, but there it is."

Marcus Hurst had listened to the whole of the morning's dispute with cotton-headed wonder. He wanted to eat his fine Pemberley breakfast in peace but had given that up half an hour ago. Now he chewed sullenly, wishing everyone would lower their voices as he had a head that morning.

Bingley continued, "I sent an express to Scarborough to forward the rental period on the townhouse since our relations already have houses full of guests for Baby James's christening. There is no tenant, so I am sure the agents will oblige us quite willingly. So go. Go today."

Louisa sobbed and left the room. Hurst stood, finished his coffee, wiped his mouth, bowed briefly to his brother-in-law and followed her. Caroline looked daggers at her brother, and he reflected her countenance with every bit as much fury.

"Why have you never encouraged Darcy to court me? To marry me? I am your sister! What could make you happier than to be able to call your best friend 'brother'? I do not understand you, Charles."

"If Darcy wanted to marry for fortune and connection without love, he could have married his Cousin Anne years ago. I believe he has come to understand he will be a better man and have a happier life if he marries for love. I am sorry to say it, Caroline, but he does not love you, and neither he nor I believe you love him."

"You have ruined me, Brother," she hissed.

"You have ruined yourself. Return to Scarborough where you can still pass yourself off with some credit as a woman with a heart." Now it was Bingley's turn to leave the room. He did so with a spring in his step and a smile upon his lips. He could then concentrate on awaiting the arrival of Miss Elizabeth Bennet into the Pemberley stillroom, where he intended to return the favour that she had bestowed upon him the evening before. Prior to joining Darcy and Mr Gardiner at the river, Bingley planned to tell her that the man she loved—and he would brook no argument that she loved him, for he now felt confident he knew what a Bennet lady looked like when in love better than anyone else, certainly better than Fitzwilliam Darcy—was still passionately in love with her and very near the point of offering for her hand in marriage a second time.

WHEN DARCY LEFT HIS ROOM to join his sister, he heard raised voices coming from the breakfast room and was relieved he and Georgiana had made other arrangements for their morning meal. The clear weather bolstered the seedling of hope planted by Bingley the prior evening and further nurtured by Georgiana as they listened to his story. His sister believed Elizabeth must at least like him, from the becoming way she had of colouring whenever Georgiana repeated any of Darcy's compliments. Georgiana's last words to him were, "Instead of complimenting Elizabeth to me and to Mr Bingley, you really must try complimenting *her* to her face."

Darcy had chuckled all the way back to his bedchamber over this common sense suggestion from his seemingly naive sister. He dreamt of Elizabeth, and although this morning he could not recall the exact details, he awoke with embarrassing bedclothes, befouled by his ardour. He fervently wished he could remember some detail beyond the look of love and welcome in her beautiful eyes.

Over breakfast, Darcy told Georgiana of Bingley's intention to move his sisters and Mr Hurst on to Scarborough that very day. "I'm sorry, Fitzwilliam, mine are not the thoughts of a proper hostess, but what a relief! Miss Bingley is exhausting. The journey to Arbor Low will be much more amiable, and now we may invite Miss Bennet and her aunt and uncle to join us whenever they can spare the time. May I do so?"

Darcy hoped Georgiana would not take it upon herself to forward his suit in some clumsy way but said nothing of his concern. Instead, he said, "What if we send our own express to Longbourn and invite Miss Jane Bennet to join us? Perhaps, if she is able to arrive soon enough, we can ask both sisters to stay with us through August. Mrs Annesley will return in another fortnight from her family visit, so a chaperone will be in residence."

"Oh, Brother! What a delightful idea! I should love to have both sisters here. Then Mr Bingley will stay on. Maybe he will propose to Miss Bennet here, too."

"Too?"

"Will you not renew your suit with Elizabeth soon?"

"Not so soon as Bingley will propose to Jane. You forget, Jane is already in the practice of loving him. In Elizabeth's case, we can only hope she has forgiven me, has quit hating me, and may soon come like me. I have dug myself into a deep hole, Georgie."

"Harumpf," Georgiana murmured more to herself than her brother. "Well, at least we have persuaded you to stop digging further…"

Darcy narrowed his eyes at her. "Nasty little gosling… you should have been left out on the peaks to be raised by wolves. Sometimes, I think you were."

"How many allies do you have, exactly, that you can afford to alienate me?" She smiled impishly at him.

Brother and sister grinned and drank their coffee and tea in companionable silence until Darcy's heart became uneasy at the thought of Elizabeth's impending arrival. He could not immediately formulate a way to see her; he must play host to Mr Gardiner's fishing as Bingley, no doubt, would be involved with bustling his sisters off to Scarborough. As he contemplated this problem, his eyes fell on a little posy of flowers in a china vase on the mantle over the unlit fireplace.

"Georgie?" He broke her reverie. "How learned are you in the language of flowers?"

"I have studied it a little and have a thorough herbal that sets out the meanings of many plants. Are we to compose a message?" She was excited by the very notion.

"When Mr Gardiner arrives today, he is bringing his wife's maid. I am allowing her the use of the stillroom to concoct something or other needful to Mrs Gardiner. We could make up a floral message for her to take to

Elizabeth."

"How delightful! I have a little vase painted with iris, the flower of messages. Let me fetch it and my herbal. We should start in the herb garden."

Darcy finished his coffee, and presently, Georgiana returned wearing a bonnet. She looked out the window. "Hmmm, the herb garden is in the sun already and it is only nine o'clock. I do not think I need a spencer. Have you been outside?"

"Yes, I have. The day is warm."

Georgiana placed the little vase upon the table. It was not tall but the opening seemed generous enough to hold many stems. "Here, Fitzwilliam, you take the flower shears, pick what you like, and I shall carry the book and translate. We may be a bit limited by what is in bloom now. Some of the sweetest sentiments are expressed by the earliest spring flowers."

They walked out into the morning sun from Georgiana's sitting room, crossed a narrow terrace and descended the few steps to the herb garden. "What do you want to say?" Georgiana asked.

"I have taken your words of last night very much to heart. I would compliment her. She said something yesterday that rather disturbed me, along the line that she does not think herself beautiful. Her family always refers to Jane as the prettiest Bennet but Elizabeth has far more liveliness in her looks and those lovely eyes. Jane is fair and Elizabeth dark. Jane is a little taller, but Elizabeth's countenance overflows with an air of health and good humour."

"Oh my…well, you *can* be eloquent. Start showing me flowers and do not forget foliage, Brother, for leaves have meanings, too, and I will start looking through the book. Would you speak of love?"

"Will it not be obvious?"

"Why leave room for doubt?"

Darcy straightened from picking a flower and smiled at his sister. "When did you become so wise?"

Georgiana raised an eyebrow, clearly indicating she had merely been waiting for him to notice. She looked at the flower in his hand, a shaggy pink blossom, something that had seeded itself amongst the paving stones. "Ah! That is ragged-robin. It signifies wit."

"We want that," Darcy said. He then took a few steps further, looking around. "What is that plant with the very fine green leaves?"

"Southernwood. It signifies jest and banter."

"That is delightful. Our whole acquaintance is founded upon her propensity to jest and banter."

"Wait. It is also known as 'maiden's ruin'." Georgiana blushed and extended the book for Darcy to see.

"…'and lad's love… It increases…'" He stopped himself from speaking the word 'virility' and laughed. "Yes, we shan't alarm her."

They moved on.

"Here's a little garlic-chive already in bloom. That's for courage." Georgiana pointed to the plant with her toe.

Darcy picked its flowers, wrinkling his nose at the smell. "She is courageous. What is this frothy little white flower? It smells pretty. Perhaps it will counteract the smell of the garlic?"

"That is sweet alyssum." She flipped a page or two, looking for it. "How lovely! It means 'worth beyond beauty'."

They continued for some little time, both thoroughly entertained. The herb garden was not large and not all the plants flattering in connotation. At last, they stood before a patch of marjoram just running to flower. When Georgiana read its meaning, she insisted her brother pick several stems. She would not tell him what it meant and he snatched the herbal from her hand.

"'Blushes,'" he read and blushed himself.

"You may not have noticed, Brother, but she blushes a great deal when she is with you or when you are spoken of to her. I do not think she likes that her emotions are so revealed, but it is charming."

Darcy grew wistful but said nothing aloud. *Her blushes always leave me wishing to kiss her*, he thought as he stooped to harvest several more stems.

After briefly surveying the posy, Darcy sighed. "Our bouquet does not have roses. Might we have some?"

"Come to the rose garden with me. Some of the most specific may be finished blooming, but there are a few that bloom all summer or are later in their habit. We must be careful with roses, as not all are kindly in their meaning," Georgiana warned.

The walk to the rose garden followed a fence festooned with honeysuckle and Georgiana looked for it amongst the pages as they strolled. "Ah, honeysuckle," she said when she found it in the list.

"Even honeysuckle?" Darcy was amazed at the thoroughness of the book.

"'Generous and devoted affection.'" Georgiana read aloud. Darcy picked a large handful, making her laugh.

"Do you want to give her only that? You will not have room for roses."

Darcy laughed at himself. "Perhaps we can put a vase of this in the drawing room?" Georgiana smiled.

In the rose garden, Darcy gravitated to the last yellow blossoms on a large shrub. For this, Georgiana did not need the book. "No, Fitzwilliam, yellow roses signify the sender has a jealous nature."

He huffed a little to be so thwarted then chuckled at himself. "I own, it seems I do have a jealous nature, but we are finding *her* attributes, not mine."

The old velvet rose bush still carried some dark burgundy blossoms and Darcy was most pleased to learn the colour meant unconscious beauty, exclaiming it perfect for Elizabeth.

Georgiana read the list of rose meanings, one after the other. "'The bridal rose is happy love.' That puts the cart before the horse. 'The cabbage rose is the ambassador of love.'—which would be apt if they were still in bloom. 'The China Rose means beauty always new.'"

Darcy interrupted her. "Do we have that?"

"No, I do not believe we do."

"Have the gardeners find it and order two dozen."

Georgiana smiled and returned to her litany. "'The damask rose is brilliancy of complexion.'"

"Have we that?"

Georgiana went to where the bushes were. "No, they are finished."

"Damn."

She began again. "'The deep red rose is bashful shame. The dog rose is pleasure with pain. The hundred-petal rose is pride.'"

"Definitely not that."

"'The Rosa Mundi means variety. The musk rose means capricious beauty.' Oh! Oh, Fitzwilliam, the next is perfect! 'The open rose means I still love you.'"

"Which colour?"

"It does not say but let us find a red one, since red is love."

With two pairs of eyes scanning the bushes, it was quick work to find the most perfect, open red rose after comparing several specimens. Georgiana handed the book to Darcy and took the flowers and leaves from him, and as they walked back to the house, she began to arrange them in her hand. She placed the open red rose directly in the middle of the nosegay. Back in her sitting room, she poured water into the vase and finished the arrangement, tying it with a bit of string as Darcy watched. An unlucky thought crossed his mind.

"What if Miss Elizabeth does not know the language of flowers? How many ladies travel with an herbal?"

Georgiana stood, considering, leaving Darcy to wonder how much subterfuge could be borne until the secret of Elizabeth's coming and its reason would be revealed. He finally said, "Let me take the herbal, and I shall write a list of the contents of the vase with their meanings. I had intended to add a note in any case." His sister agreed, and he set off below stairs.

The housekeeper was in the stillroom when Darcy arrived. She eyed her master as he stood with vase and book in his hands.

"Mrs Reynolds!" Darcy was surprised to see her.

"No one uses the stillroom much, Mr Darcy. It was too dusty to receive a guest."

"Ah…good, yes." Darcy looked at the contents of his hands a little chagrined. "I appreciate that you have seen to it yourself."

"You have something there for the lady, sir? How very nice. We have some little cards if you want to place her name upon the flowers. You will want her to know who gives them to her."

Darcy seemed relieved, although he felt himself grow hot under his cravat, and Mrs Reynolds could be counted upon to notice. "Yes, a card. That will do nicely."

Mrs Reynolds stepped out to her workroom at the bottom of the stairs. She returned in a moment with a short stack of blank cards, a pen and some ink. "I am finished here, sir. If you have no need of me, I shall assist Mr Bingley's family as they prepare to leave."

Darcy met his housekeeper's eye with a smirk. "By all means, Mrs Reynolds. Extend them all the assistance they need."

She grinned and curtsied.

Darcy mused, *I shall wager my entire staff is relieved Caroline Bingley is quitting the place. I hope it will be years before they meet her again.*

He wrote on a card: "*To Miss Elizabeth Bennet, A bouquet of your admirable qualities, from F. Darcy,*" and tucked it carefully behind the open red rose in the posy. He placed the herbal next to the vase and smiled as he quitted the room.

WHEN MR GARDINER AND HIS niece rode from Lambton to Pemberley, the hood of the carriage remained up, though it was a fine day. It had taken nearly an hour for the inn to produce a cloak for Elizabeth's disguise, it being much the wrong season to easily locate such a garment. After depositing Mr Gardiner at Pemberley's front door, Elizabeth was driven to the servants' entrance.

She alighted from the carriage promptly at eleven o'clock, pleased to see a deep awning over the servant's door, evidence that the cloak was a formality only. Mrs Reynolds awaited Miss Bennet's arrival and showed her into the stillroom. "My workroom is just here, Miss Bennet." Mrs Reynolds indicated a room near the stairway up to the main floor with its half-windowed door ajar. "Once I have seen to the departure of some of the guests, I shall be there, and you may ask me for anything you need."

"You are very kind." Elizabeth untied the cloak and laid it over the back of a chair. "I may have need of this," she said when Mrs Reynolds moved to take it away.

The housekeeper smiled. "Oh yes, you might. I have been instructed you have leave to harvest anything you may find needful from the Pemberley gardens. We also have some very fragrant plants in the conservatory, such as jasmine and tuberose, but if secrecy is of the essence, you may need me to harvest them for you as the entrance is quite near Miss Georgiana's practice room."

The tiled counters and broad wooden table were clean and gleaming, but the bottles in the cabinets showed discoloured contents, bearing witness that the room was rarely used. On a long counter under a high window and against the far wall, stood a little vase of mixed flowers with a book bound in soft leather beside it. When Elizabeth saw it, she instantly felt a flush of warmth suffuse her cheeks. Mrs Reynolds, who made it a point to be observant, nodded to herself.

"Shall I leave you to it, ma'am?" she asked.

"Thank you so very much, Mrs Reynolds." Elizabeth smiled at her.

What a lovely young lady—such lovely manners. The housekeeper found herself humming as she returned to the departing guests and wondered at her behaviour. *I have not hummed for years...*

Mr Bingley passed her in the hall. "Mrs Reynolds, would you tell me where the stillroom is, please?"

As if it were the commonest thing in the world for a gentleman guest to ask, she replied, "At the bottom of the stairs to the kitchen, Mr Bingley. The second door on the left with mullioned glass on the upper half."

"Thank you, Mrs Reynolds," replied Mr Bingley, with a courteous brief bow.

ELIZABETH PICKED OUT THE CARD from the flowers and recognised the handwriting even before reading the words. Her chest expelled its air, just as if Darcy himself had stepped into the room. Her heart thumped so strongly, she felt as if she could hear it. She picked up the book, 'An Herbal and Legend to the Meaning of Flowers'. *I am meant to decipher this. Oh...!* Her knees grew unsteady. She moved the posy and book to the broad table in the middle of the room and sat in the chair where her cloak rested on the back.

She looked at the posy more particularly. Mrs Bennet had encouraged all her daughters to garden and know flowers. It pleased her to have guests see the girls dressed in summery gowns, discovered at work amongst the flowers at Longbourn. With her younger daughters, it was merely a pretty conceit, but Jane and Elizabeth truly loved the tasks inherent in gardening and flower arranging. Elizabeth understood the red rose meant love but knew not all herbals agreed as to meanings and opened the book.

Clematis, she turned the pages, *means 'cleverness'—yes, he thinks me clever; corncockle means 'gentility'—he thinks I have good manners, then, even if my family does not. Yarrow means 'healing' and heliotrope means 'devotion'—ah! These two refer to my attentions to Jane, I think.* Her fingers flew through the little book, her breathing becoming more shallow. *He thinks me witty and courageous, and oh, teasing man...he admires my blushes. What a rogue!* She saved the two roses for last. *Roses, hmmm, so many listed...burgundy means 'unconscious beauty'.* Elizabeth sat back. She held up the book, reading the words again. *He means I do not know I am beautiful but he must think me so. He never used to. Or did he?* She picked up the bouquet again, scanning the list of rose meanings. *An open rose means 'I still love you'.*

Elizabeth leaned her head forward and tears fell unbidden onto the flowers.

Bingley entered the room. "Lizzy? Are you unwell?"

She looked up at her beloved's best friend. "Can this be true?" she asked through her tears. She jumped to her feet and waved the posy at Bingley. She had taken it out of its vase and it was dripping on her gown, the table and the floor.

"What? Can what be true?" Bingley leaned solicitously over the table.

"I rely on your honesty, Mr Bingley. Has Mr Darcy told you he still loves me?"

Bingley smiled and straightened, happily full of himself. "That is *precisely* what I have come to tell you!" Bingley handed her a handkerchief and Elizabeth wiped her nose and cheeks. She returned the nosegay to its vase, dried her wet hands and sat down, the hand holding the handkerchief resting upon her bosom, and smiled.

"May I assume, once again, these are happy tears?"

She looked up at him with a little nod and then recalled Mrs Reynolds' words. "Mr Bingley, are you leaving for Netherfield *today*?"

"No, I am not quite so impetuous as that. I will wait for an answer to my express to Longbourn. Why do you ask?"

"Mrs Reynolds said some of the guests are leaving."

"Yes, so they are, thankfully."

Elizabeth grew serious. "You must know, sir, Jane will not be happy to believe she has caused you to break off relations with your family. Such a report will render her sad indeed."

Bingley continued to smile. "I very much look forward to your sister appealing to my better nature to reunite with my family, and I firmly intend to allow her to talk me into it whilst we prepare our wedding invitations."

Elizabeth started to laugh. "You think of everything!"

"It seems, in matters of love, I have rather more common sense than in other aspects of my life. I am learning to trust my inclinations." Bingley paused and fixed a friendly eye upon Elizabeth. He longed to ask her outright whether she was in love with Darcy but stopped himself. Although he had always felt a sisterly regard for Elizabeth Bennet, and now called her Lizzy as her family did, he felt such a question would be presuming too much. "I am trying to teach my betters to follow my example."

Elizabeth looked at the posy. "When you see him, please thank him for these on my behalf. After I blend the scent for Georgiana, I will contrive to respond to him in the same dialect."

"I must see my sisters off; then I shall join your uncle and Darcy at the river." Bingley picked up the now abandoned hankie, thinking what sport he would have in explaining to Darcy Lizzy's response to the flowers before giving him a second, tear-soaked handkerchief. With a slight bow and a wide smile, he left Elizabeth to her work.

Damask Rose
"Brilliancy of complexion"

Chapter 5

Half an hour later, Georgiana was interrupted at her practice by Bingley, who beckoned her into the hall. "May I impose upon you, Georgiana, to see my sisters on their way? Darcy, in his current mood, may be counted upon to be less than civil, which is all they deserve, but he will not want to part from Mr Gardiner."

"Of course, Mr Bingley. Has Mrs Gardiner's maid arrived?"

"Yes, I believe so." Bingley smiled to himself as he followed a pace or two behind Georgiana.

"My brother created a nosegay for the maid to take back to Miss Elizabeth. It describes the attributes he finds most admirable in her, and it most particularly says he still loves her. Isn't it romantic?"

"I'm certain it will have the desired effect. Miss Elizabeth is very partial to flowers, as is her sister. We must find out which flowers ask forgiveness. I shall heap them at Miss Bennet's feet the very next time I see her."

"About that, Mr Bingley…"

"Yes?"

"What would you say if Fitzwilliam and I asked Miss Bennet to spend August with us at Pemberley? And we will ask Miss Elizabeth to stay on after her aunt and uncle depart."

Bingley thought it the best idea he had ever heard. "How marvellous!

How delightful!"

They reached the entry hall. The front doors of Pemberley were open and the Hurst's carriage stood waiting. Caroline and the Hursts milled about awaiting their outerwear.

"What is so delightful, Brother?" Caroline asked scornfully, then turned to see Georgiana was with him. A creamy smile transformed her countenance. "Dear Georgiana! Is my brother not a brute to send us away? I do so apologise for any breach of manners you may have perceived in *me*."

Georgiana calmed herself. "Your apology is, of course, accepted, Miss Bingley. I wish you all a safe and easy journey to Scarborough." Georgiana began walking behind the guests as if to herd them forward. Bingley handed Caroline into the carriage without either saying a word; he stood back as Mr Hurst did the same for Louisa, and they were off. Bingley and Georgiana watched the departure without waving and then re-entered the house.

"Well, Georgiana, I suppose you will go back to your music room?"

"Yes, I shall. I have given an hour's annoyance to my pianoforte, and now I shall attack my harp."

Bingley laughed. "I'm for the trout stream. Shall we rescue your instruments from you when we have finished harassing the fish?"

"Yes, please!"

DARCY AND MR GARDINER STOOD some twenty yards apart on the spur of the river Derwent, which had been diverted to create a trout stream by the great gardener Lancelot 'Capability' Brown when Darcy's father had been still a young man. The present Mr Darcy and his guest spoke amiably on every topic except Mr Gardiner's two eldest nieces.

Mr Gardiner was reeling in yet another fine brook trout—his third —when he called to his host. "I say, Darcy!" They now considered each other as friends, and both had adopted the less formal mode of address.

"What? Another?" Darcy caught a fish on his first cast, but for the last three-quarters of an hour, his line had been quiet.

"I do not say this to be proud of my prowess," Mr Gardiner said, laughing. "But I *am* wondering if you would like to try this new rod of mine? Just for curiosity's sake?"

Darcy smiled and began to reel in his line. "I was hoping you would ask. Had you caught no fish and I twenty, I still hoped you would ask."

The two men approached each other upon the bank. In the distance, Darcy detected a movement upon the carriage road and watched briefly until the Hurst's carriage was lost in the trees again. "Well, Bingley's conniving sisters are off to Scarborough. I am sorry to speak so, but surely your niece has told you something of them."

"Yes, indeed. Let us just say Elizabeth told us many things when we returned to the inn last night."

Darcy was silenced, and a little embarrassed.

Mr Gardiner cleared his throat. "My wife was the only one who could handle Elizabeth when she was a girl. I think she was about eight and Jane ten or so when we married. Lizzy was too clever for her own good and such an energetic child. She ran circles around her mother, and indeed, she still does!"

Both men laughed. It delighted Darcy to hear of Elizabeth's girlhood. Mr Gardiner went on, "I went to bed before the ladies. It was all I could do to wait for my wife without falling asleep, and I, a night owl!"

"You wanted to know what she heard from your niece?"

Mr Gardiner looked down and abstractedly studied the reel on Darcy's pole, which he now held. "No, no, not necessarily. I heard the gist of Lizzy's tales before I went to bed. Let us simply say for the sake of delicacy that love was in the air at the Rose and Raindrop last night…"

Mr Gardiner turned away, returning to the place where he had been fishing. He thought his comment rather ingenious, and he was smiling to himself. Darcy gaped at his companion's back. It usually annoyed him when married men spoke, even so subtly, of conjugal relations, but the idea that Elizabeth had spoken of love in such a way as might inspire her uncle to lose a little sleep, confused and excited him.

"How is the fishing?" Bingley yelled down to them from the bridle path above. He had chosen to join them on horseback.

"Gardiner is cleaning out the stream again today, Bingley. I am now trying his new pole, hoping it changes my luck. Your sisters are off, I see."

"Yes, Georgiana did the necessaries and went back to practicing. And I looked in on the stillroom."

"You did?" Darcy was surprised and moved to join his friend while Bingley dismounted and arranged his tackle.

Bingley tried, and fairly well succeeded, in looking as superior as he possibly could. "I did. And what do you think I found there?"

"Bingley," Darcy lowered his voice, "you insolent pup. I will box your ears if you aren't careful. In the last twenty-four hours you have grown monstrously insufferable."

Bingley took a large step backward before replying, "If I did not know you were fond of me, I would be highly insulted. I know something you do not, and trust me: you wish to know it, so there will be no boxing of *my* ears, sir." With a flourish, Bingley produced a second, soggy handkerchief, redolent of lavender. "The lady in the stillroom was in a state of tearful astonishment at what she had just read in a bouquet of flowers—tears of joy if I am any judge, and I *am*."

"Bingley! I will not have you harassing Miss Bennet!" Darcy snatched the handkerchief and glared with a nod upstream towards Elizabeth's uncle.

"Someone has to provide a lady with a hankie when she needs one."

"Do not sport with me, Bingley, I pray you. Was she truly happy?"

"She had already sorted out the message when I arrived and asked me to verify her findings, which I happily did. She shed tears of joy, hence the hankie, and then laid her hand holding it very prettily upon her…" He thought better of saying bosom as Darcy seemed a trifle more tightly wound than usual. "…chest. It would have made a lovely miniature. She wishes me to tell you that she thanks you and will contrive a reply, in kind, before she leaves. You may now say, 'Thank you, Charles, you are a good and true friend.'"

Darcy smiled at Bingley. "You *are* a good and true friend. You are a better friend to me than I have been to you."

Bingley slapped Darcy on the arm. "Good man! Excellent response." Then Bingley dropped his voice. "When will you make her an offer?"

"If I am bold, I will assume she has left off loathing me and moved to, perhaps, a wary warming of her regard. I will not risk proposing until I know that she might, some day in the future, like me enough to be willing to try to love me."

Bingley rolled his eyes. "That's asking a lot of her."

Darcy's dark eyes narrowed. "Bingley…"

Bingley grew serious. "Darcy, listen to me. I am not joking and I am not wrong. She *already* loves you. You have given her no reason to, but there it is."

Darcy could see over Bingley's shoulder that Mr Gardiner was angling another fighting trout toward the bank, preparing to net it. He hissed in Bingley's ear, "Did she say so?"

"She did not have to."

"Did she *say* it?"

Bingley shook his head. "No."

Mr Gardiner called, "That's four! How many more do you want?" He was laughing with delight. He turned to look at Darcy and Bingley, and noticing them tarry, called out, "It has been my experience, gentlemen, that it is impossible to catch fish without putting a line in the water."

Bingley looked at Darcy with raised brows. "Truer words were never spoken, Darcy."

ELIZABETH MARSHALLED HER WITS AND began looking through the shelves and cupboards of the Pemberley stillroom. She found some attar of damask rose in a brown bottle that had not lost its perfume. Generally, the room was clean, but the cupboards were a fright with drawers housing broken shears as well as those still useful. Open shelves were full of dust and grimy bottles with contents no longer fresh, most with faded labels. One cupboard was devoted to vases of all shapes and sizes, and half a dozen were sparkling clean as though recently used. She developed an idea for a scent and started making a list of the items she would need just as the housekeeper returned to the stillroom.

"May I be of service, Miss Bennet?" she asked.

"Mrs Reynolds! Yes, I was just putting a short list together. I need an apron and some boiled water, and if I could impose upon you, is there Arabian jasmine in the conservatory?"

"Yes, ma'am, shall I pick some?"

"Yes, please. Just blossoms that are open, as one would use in tea." Mrs Reynolds nodded as Elisabeth continued, "And an empty bucket?"

Mrs Reynolds wanted to ask Elizabeth just how much scent she intended to make but knew such a question was impertinent. "And that is everything?"

"Yes, thank you. I am going to don my cloak of secrecy and venture out for some flowers whilst you are picking jasmine. Where is the cutting garden?"

"Are you sure you should, miss?" Mrs Reynolds was worried.

"I know what I want, and if the flowers I require are not there, I shall return directly." Elizabeth took up the herbal and found a pocket in the cloak for it.

Mrs Reynolds gave her directions to the garden. It was located off the southwest corner of the house in a walled area and she consoled herself that Miss Bennet would be on the opposite end of the house from any view to be had by the occupant of the music room.

Elizabeth walked down a long dark hall, past little pantries of jarred fruit and curing meats. She squinted at the bright sun upon exiting the house and waited a moment for her eyes to adjust. To her right, was a path lined with espaliered fruit trees; she had been told the cutting garden was at the end of it. She entered a walled garden and found Sweet William and scarlet lychnis growing there. She consulted the herbal. *How much do I wish to say? I would not have him think me forward, but Charlotte always said a lady should leave a gentleman in no doubt.*

Elizabeth found the first blossom on a clump of red chrysanthemums and snipped it. *Dare I say so much?* She walked back toward the house, feeling her nosegay would not be as eloquent as Darcy's had been. She saw a perfect peach hanging low over the stone path and stooped to pick it. It occurred to her that fruit might have meaning and she consulted the herbal. 'Your qualities, like your charms, are unequalled,' it read. *Hmm,* she thought, *I could leave the peach sitting with the vase and herbal. He would understand they are meant to be together.*

As she walked back to the house, she noticed a swath of viscaria had seeded itself at the edge of the paving stones. She stopped, turning pages. *It means 'Will you dance with me?' How marvellous! This is exactly what we should do! We should start over.* Elizabeth picked enough for a whole vase full.

Another path lined with garden plants beckoned to her left. She could not resist a little exploration. She found betony, the flower of surprise, and decided it would do quite well. Mr Darcy was now surprising her daily. Bearing an armful of flowers, she snuck back into the house.

GEORGIANA ATTENDED TO HER HARP in an unusually desultory manner. Her mind wandered back to the happy hour spent with her brother, picking flowers and crafting his message. She decided, since it would be just herself, her brother and Mr Bingley for dinner, it would not take much effort to contrive a vase of flowers for each place with a message of encouragement. Assuming Darcy had left the herbal in the stillroom, she descended the stairs thither and was perplexed to find evidence of activity, but the list of meanings for Elizabeth's flowers and the herbal were missing. Had her brother kept the book?

"Miss Georgiana!" Mrs Reynolds came into the stillroom behind her and placed a folded apron and empty bucket upon the table. "Oh! You have given me a fright. I did not expect to see you."

Georgiana looked askance at the housekeeper. "No...I suppose you thought me practicing. I thought my book of flower meanings might be here."

"Oh, oh yes, it was. I believe Mrs Gardiner's maid has borrowed it. She is gone outside." Mrs Reynolds was flustered, which Georgiana found uncommonly odd. A scullery maid entered with a deep soup kettle of freshly boiled water. "Just sit that on this big table, Sarah. Miss Georgiana, I shall bring your book to you as soon as the maid returns. Where will you be?"

"I shall return to my music room, I suppose." She took a last stealthy glance around the room. "Please see that anything my brother has written to go with the flowers for Miss Bennet is not forgotten."

"Oh, yes, I certainly shall ma'am."

Mrs Reynolds expelled a sigh of relief when she saw Georgiana's shoes go out of sight as she ascended the stairs to the main floor. It was some minutes before Elizabeth returned.

"Good heavens, Miss Bennet! Miss Darcy came looking for her book!"

"Oh dear! Are we found out?"

"I think not, or not yet, but I must take it to her soon or she will suspect."

Elizabeth laid the flowers and peach upon the table and handed the book to Mrs Reynolds. "Take it to her directly. The less time she waits for it, the better, I expect."

"Thank you, ma'am," Mrs Reynolds smiled and rolled her eyes most humorously.

Elizabeth laughed. "What a tangled web...!"

Elizabeth went to work. Mrs Reynolds had provided a small bowl of jasmine blossoms. Elizabeth selected and set aside the most perfect ones. She poured a little boiling water into the remaining jasmine, and mashing the flowers into the sides of the bowl with a pestle from the tool drawer, made a watery paste. She had found an attractive empty bottle and stopper in the cupboards, which she washed in the hot water. She strained the water from the mashed jasmine into the bottle with a funnel and cheesecloth, then added attar of damask rose to the jasmine water until she had what she thought a pleasing scent. The reserved whole jasmine blossoms were dipped in the rose oil and added to the bottle, and Elizabeth fixed the stopper. She set the bottle aside with a label written out in her most careful hand and adhered with mucilage from a little jar.

Elizabeth turned to the flowers she had picked. She slipped the nosegay from Darcy into her pocket. It would be wilting before she reached the inn but she intended to press the individual stems. *No matter what the future brings, I will have these flowers and his letter from Rosings to keep by me in my spinsterhood.*

Elizabeth composed a nosegay of plants representing Darcy's best qualities and placed it in the iris-painted china vase. She had withheld the red chrysanthemum, but at last tucked it into the middle of the posy, its stem too short to be securely bound into the twine. It was partially obscured by the other flowers. She opened the cupboard of vases and selected a taller one painted with a gentleman and lady dancing in the out-of-doors. She smiled to herself, arranging the viscaria in the vase. She had seen the little pile of cards with pen and ink on the long counter at the back of the room and created a little vignette similar to the one she had found upon her arrival. The tall vase had a card reading, *"May I have the honour of dancing the next with* you, *Mr Darcy? E. Bennet"*—these were similar to the words he had used to ask her to dance at Netherfield, as best she could remember. The nosegay note read the same as the card she had received, with sender and recipient reversed.

Now that her stated purpose, as well as her clandestine one, was complete, Elizabeth cut a square of cheesecloth to use as a cleaning rag and began dusting shelves. She poured stale vials of scented oils into the formerly empty bucket, using the hot water to peel off old labels so the bottles could be refreshed. As needed, she wrote new labels to replace faded ones. She tossed tired bunches of dried flowers into the waste bucket. The room wanted a thorough clearing and it made her feel happy and useful to be contributing something of her own interest to the smooth running of Pemberley.

Elizabeth had opened the tool drawers and started to make a tidy pile of broken tools on the big table when Mrs Reynolds announced her return with an alarmed gasp. She quickly grasped what had been keeping Miss Bennet so occupied. "Oh, Miss Bennet! Oh dear! I am mortified to find you toiling so. At Pemberley, we are *not* in the habit of putting our guests to work, I assure you."

Elizabeth turned to her with a laughing smile, revealing dust and smudges upon her apron and forehead. "You see before you no lady of leisure, Mrs Reynolds. Once I finished making the scent for Miss Darcy, which is here"—she handed the bottle to the housekeeper—"you should hide it —I could not sit idle, for I brought nothing to read and I could not go for a walk, given the nature of my visit. Organizing a stillroom is one of my few domestic talents."

"Oh, but Miss, I could have spared a maid to help you, to do the sorting and bottle washing under your direction. Mr Darcy will have me drawn and quartered should he learn of this."

"He shall not hear of it from me." Elizabeth's eyes twinkled.

"I could have ordered you refreshments, ma'am."

"I am not so frail as to need constant nourishment, Mrs Reynolds, and why disturb the kitchen staff unnecessarily? Pray, do not alarm yourself. Besides, I take no joy in drinking tea alone. Since my uncle is not yet returned, I have time to dust the cupboard of vases, and then, may I come and take tea with you in your room?" Elizabeth looked into the old woman's eyes with her best smile and a little nod of encouragement.

Mrs Reynolds shook her head in wonder and involuntarily returned the charming smile that was fixed upon hers. "I would be delighted, Miss Bennet. I shall order it now." She turned from the room feeling a little dumbfounded. *I have not had a lady take tea in my workroom since Lady Anne was alive. Could* this *be the next mistress of Pemberley?*

GEORGIANA SAT WITH HER HERBAL in the window seat of her sitting room, wondering at the strange behaviour of the rarely flustered Mrs Reynolds. Since Georgiana was now in possession of her book, it must mean the maid had returned to the stillroom. The whole affair smacked of secrecy. Georgiana decided to yield to curiosity and return to peek into the stillroom. If she was caught, she thought she could say she was returning the book in case it was needed again, that her research could wait until the Gardiner maid was gone.

On entering the marbled hallway, Georgiana heard the tapping of her heels and reversed direction to scamper to her dressing room. She quickly exchanged the low heels for soft-soled slippers and padded back downstairs.

She slipped past Mrs Reynolds's door, which was ajar, and looked into the stillroom through the glass door. The maid was half concealed by the open cupboard doors. An apron was tied behind her back, and her gown was of pale cream cotton printed with little bouquets of violets—rather nicer than a maid would wear. She was humming, a rich mezzo-soprano. The song was Mozart. Georgiana's eyes darted to the long counter at the back of the room. There were two vases of flowers, each with a note card, and a peach sat next to a nosegay, which had been situated in the iris-painted vase. *Why is the maid not taking the vase? It is part of the gift. Why are there new flowers? Surely, Elizabeth has not arranged with my brother to carry on a floral conversation through a maid. It only began this morning.*

Suddenly, Georgiana recognised the voice. It was Elizabeth. *Why is she here, and why has her presence been concealed?* Georgiana slipped away from the door, leaning against the wall. She was confused, to be sure, but also intrigued. She heard footsteps approaching and turned to skip silently up the stairs when she noticed a scullery maid with a china tea service set for two, emblazoned with the initials H. R.—Harriet Reynolds—enter the housekeeper's workroom. Georgiana could not hear what was said until the maid came out, turned and replied, "Yes, ma'am," and then crossed the hall and entered the stillroom.

"Excuse me, ma'am. Mrs Reynolds bids me tell you the tea is ready."

The response to this confirmed the speaker was Miss Elizabeth, both by the pleasing timbre of the voice and the kind words expressed to the maid. "Thank you…" Elizabeth paused, and must have nodded encouragement to the maid.

"I'm Sarah, ma'am. Sarah R. We have many Sarahs here."

"Thank you, Sarah R. If you have time and it is no imposition, this bucket should be taken away, dumped, and rinsed. Also, these tools are broken and should be removed."

Sarah picked up the bucket and tools. "I can do it now, ma'am." She curtsied and left the room.

Georgiana stepped up into the hall of the main floor before being seen.

Elizabeth bathed her hands in the cooled water and wiped them clean on the hem of the apron, which she folded and left upon the table. She picked up the hooded cloak and tapped on Mrs Reynolds' door.

There was a knock at the Pemberley front door as Georgiana passed through the entry hall, and Grayson, the butler, opened it. "From the Rose and Raindrop Inn, sir. I have a message for Mr Gardiner, sir."

"Does it require a response?"

"No sir, I was told I needn't wait."

"Thank you." Grayson slipped a shilling into the young man's hand and, with a precise bow, closed the door. Georgiana proceeded upstairs as a footman was sent to find the gentlemen and deliver the message.

The footman, in his elegant Pemberley livery, was more formally dressed than the fisherman he found a half mile up the trout stream. The day continued warm, and the men had removed their coats, angling in shirtsleeves. Mr Gardiner caught the most fish while Darcy managed to catch four fine trout. Bingley, being excitable and yanking his line about, brought in only two.

"It seems I am unable to think like a fish today," he complained.

The footman appeared, and Mr Gardiner read his note.

Dear Edward,

I am returned to the inn and await your arrival. Since we are very much a visit in debt to Mr Darcy and his sister, perhaps you would ask them and their guests to join us for dinner tomorrow afternoon after matins.

We have no fixed engagements until Monday dinner with the Aspinalls.

Yours, M.

Bingley, Darcy and Mr Gardiner repacked their tackle and combined their fish into one creel. The footman was dispatched to take the fish to the kitchen and order the Gardiner carriage, which he was told should call at the kitchen door to collect Mrs Gardiner's maid before meeting Mr Gardiner at the front door. They started back up the slope to the bridle path where Bingley's horse waited. Bingley mounted and rode to the stables.

Mr Gardiner cleared his throat. "My wife would have me invite you and Miss Darcy to join us for dinner after church tomorrow. You know, ladies are very much aware of these things, social debts and so on. Mr Bingley would be more than welcome to join us. My wife is not aware his family is gone."

"We would be delighted to join you after church, Gardiner, delighted. My sister and I have favoured the church at Kympton but merely because my parents started us in that habit. I have been thinking we should attend at St. Swithin's occasionally."

ELIZABETH WAS CONTEMPLATING A SECOND cup of tea as she sat companionably with Mrs Reynolds in the housekeeper's workroom. The two women engaged in a lively conversation about the youths of Fitzwilliam and Georgiana Darcy. Mrs Reynolds's opinion of Miss Elizabeth Bennet continued to rise, and it became increasingly apparent that this gently bred young lady, while evidencing no impropriety, had a ready wit and deep intuition, which would make her an ideal companion for Miss Georgiana. Elizabeth asked more about Darcy's sister than about the man himself, but had just determined to inquire further when Sarah R. tapped on the open workroom door.

"'Scuse me, miss, but the carriage is come for ye." She smiled with a curtsy.

Elizabeth sat her cup and saucer upon the tea tray with sigh. "Thank you, Sarah R. Just when I had talked myself into a second cup, Mrs Reynolds." Elizabeth stood and donned the cloak. "Please let Mr Darcy know my mission here has been accomplished and that you are in possession of Georgiana's gift. I hope they both like it. It should not be unsealed until her birthday; the scents must meld to form one perfume. And thank you, too, for your hospitality. You have been most gracious to have a stranger in your midst."

Mrs Reynolds stood and made a slight bow to Elizabeth. "It has been no inconvenience to me, ma'am, I'm sure. I have been delighted to get to know you. And I should be thanking *you* for setting our stillroom to rights."

"About that..." Elizabeth blushed a little and looked down. "There is a little vignette of flowers and fruit I should very much like Mr Darcy to see, if he will. If you have a chance for a private word with him, you might let him know it is there."

Mrs Reynolds smiled gently. "Yes, ma'am, I shall."

A little embarrassed, with nothing else to say, Elizabeth left the kitchen and had only to walk a few steps to her uncle's carriage. It stopped at the front entrance to Pemberley, and she overheard Mr Darcy's and her uncle's adieus. She was surprised and pleased to learn the Darcys and Mr Bingley would spend the afternoon and take dinner with them the next day.

DARCY WAS MET IN THE hall by Bingley. "I say, Darcy, we must rescue Georgiana from her instruments. I promised her."

Darcy laughed. "Let us have some refreshments. Grayson?"

The noble butler appeared quickly from a side hall. "Yes, sir, Mr Darcy?"

"Mr Bingley and I would like something cool to drink, and I'll wager my sister would like some tea. And whatever fruit and cheese and such as the kitchen staff have quickly to hand. They needn't cook; no sense heating up the kitchen until dinner on such a warm day. In my sister's music room, if you would, Grayson."

"Of course, sir." Grayson disappeared down the kitchen stairs.

The two men entered the music room laughing about the fishing prowess of Edward Gardiner. Georgiana was leaning against the windowsill, wondering how she could manoeuvre her brother to the topic of Elizabeth Bennet.

She turned and smiled at them. Perhaps Mr Bingley knew of Elizabeth's visit? "Mr Bingley! When do you suppose we will have the pleasure of seeing Miss Elizabeth Bennet again?"

Bingley blushed anxiously, which Georgiana took to be a statement of some secret closely held. "Not being the host, Georgiana, I am afraid I cannot say."

"I can," Darcy spoke up brightly to relieve his friend. "We have been invited to dine at the inn with the Gardiners and Miss Bennet tomorrow. I thought we might attend church in Lambton for a change. You are to be included, Bingley. I suspect the Gardiners want to give you a thorough looking over before any response arrives from Longbourn. They may be asked to render an opinion of you, you know, so you had better make the most of these opportunities to impress."

Bingley chuckled. "I will not have impressed Mr Gardiner with my fishing today."

"You were too nervous with your line, pulling and jerking. What was the matter with you?"

Bingley smiled absent-mindedly. "I believe, I *hope*, I am soon to be a very happy man, Darcy. Although I was furious with you last night, this morning I find myself comforted to know Jane's regard for me is as stout and enduring a thing as mine for her. Miss Elizabeth was kind enough to calm my concerns. Yet, I am agitated. I imagine where the express might be on its journey. I do hope Mr Bennet will send an express in return and not dawdle about making a reply."

"When did you speak with Miss Elizabeth?" Georgiana asked. She believed Bingley would be the weak link in the apparent conspiracy.

Bingley looked at her with a confused expression. "Last night, of course, when I asked for a moment in the drawing room, just as they were leaving."

Oh! Georgiana thought, *I had forgotten that.* "Oh, yes. Of course."

Darcy looked at his sister most particularly. *That was odd. Does she suspect something?*

Servants entered with refreshments. Nothing more was said until they left the room. Georgiana tried another tack. "I wonder how Mrs Gardiner's *maid* managed this morning. I believe the stillroom was in disarray."

Now, both Bingley and Darcy looked at her warily. The three were tense and silent until Georgiana sighed in frustration. "Really, Brother, I am ashamed of you—asking Miss Bennet to come here to clean our stillroom? Whatever were you thinking? I do hope she was compensated in *some* way. Or did you pay her like a common servant?"

Darcy stared at his sister. *What on earth?* Through a clenched jaw he hissed, "Infernal gosling...whatever do you mean? Cleaning the stillroom?"

Georgiana drew herself up. "I went to fetch my herbal, which, the last time I checked, is not illegal. There was Miss Elizabeth in an apron, giving the room a thorough clearing out. You obviously knew she was coming."

"Did she see you? Did you speak with her?" Darcy was most seriously displeased and would have been highly offended to know at that moment his inquiries made him a mimic of his aunt, Lady Catherine de Bourgh.

"No, she did not see me. But she did take tea with Mrs Reynolds. I overheard a maid tell her the tea was ready. Is she being interviewed?"

"Interviewed! I asked her to perform a special favour for me. That is all. I know nothing about any cleaning." Darcy did not know what to think. He was irked and confused. He strode to the door. "I will have Mrs Reynolds explain this for all of us."

Darcy returned with the housekeeper in a matter of moments. Bingley left the room rather than listen to Darcy upbraid a servant, especially one he liked so well as Mrs Reynolds.

"Mrs Reynolds, please sit down. Would you care to explain why Miss Elizabeth Bennet, here as a guest to do me a personal favour, came to be cleaning in the stillroom?"

Mrs Reynolds reddened. "The lady arrived and requested some items she would need to complete her project. I did not understand from the items requested that it was also her intention to reorganise. Since your mother's passing, there has been no one who cared much for using the stillroom. When the last stillroom maid left, she was never replaced. The room showed neglect."

"It looked fine to me when we were there this morning."

"The contents of the cupboards were most untidy, sir, which became apparent to Miss Bennet, and evidently, she is not a lady to sit idle if she can find occupation. I was most alarmed indeed when I caught her at her work, but she seemed happily entertained and *completely* unrepentant when I told her you would have me drawn and quartered, Mr Darcy. Might I ask, sir, how you came to hear of it? The lady said *she* would not tell, and *I* certainly would not have done so, and that leaves the scullery maid who served us tea. It is not like the family to listen to the gossip of servants."

Georgiana was blushing. "*I* saw her cleaning, Mrs Reynolds. I came again below stairs thinking Mrs Gardiner's maid might need the herbal. I saw only the back of her leaning out of a cupboard, but Miss Elizabeth was humming, and I recognised her voice. It has been my experience that scullery maids, however pleased with their work, do not hum Mozart, nor with so lovely a mezzo-soprano."

Darcy started to chuckle, which progressed to laughter. He could easily imagine Elizabeth jumping into the breach when she saw one. *She does not like to be bored any more than I do.*

Mrs Reynolds shook her head. "Miss Georgiana…*really.* Your curiosity will be the end of you one day, my girl. I should have known when you came downstairs the first time and gave me such a start that you would sneak back, though *why* you should, I am sure I do not know. Your tendency to inquisitiveness borders on the unnatural. *Never* have I seen such a one…" Mrs Reynolds was all ruffled feathers.

Darcy laughed still more. "This really is a very tiny house when it wants to be."

Suddenly, he stopped laughing. He remembered something Bingley had said. "Mrs Reynolds, did Miss Bennet happen to leave any flowers behind?"

His heart began to race as he asked the question.

"Oh, yes, sir. I was waiting to tell you. She asked me most particularly to mention what she had done. Fruit and flowers she said. I did not go to look."

Darcy bolted unceremoniously from the room with Georgiana hard upon his heels. When they arrived at the stillroom door, they skidded to a stop and looked inside as if the room might be haunted. In the shadows at the end of the room under the high window sat a nosegay in the iris vase with a peach and a tall vase of all one kind of flower. Darcy beamed. Georgiana looked at him and his expression made her smile.

"Are you so much in love as that?" she spoke in a low voice.

He looked fondly into her bright blue eyes. "Yes, dear little gosling, I fear it is true. Your brother is very much in love."

They entered the room together. Georgiana picked up the peach while Darcy slipped the cards from both vases into his waistcoat pocket and picked them up. In his excitement, he bumped the nosegay against the taller vase, and the posy tumbled to the floor.

"Oh! She cut those stems too short," Georgiana observed and she bent to pick up the flowers, not noticing the little red chrysanthemum had come loose. It lay, unseen, and the sweep of her skirt brushed it behind Darcy's feet, out of sight. "You will have to be careful carrying it."

Darcy concentrated on the flowers as they walked back to the music room. They heard balls clacking in the billiard room, and Darcy called Bingley to join in the deciphering of Elizabeth's response. There were cloth napkins on the food tray, and Georgiana employed one to wrap up the stems of the little nosegay to prevent drips. "I shall read off the flowers, Brother, and you may look them up."

Darcy picked up the herbal, ready to flip its pages. Georgiana began, "There is clematis again, which we put in her nosegay, so she thinks you are clever, as you think her clever. That is a good start. Here is scarlet lychnis."

Darcy found it in the book and blushed to read, "'Sunbeaming eyes.' How I wish we had found that for her. She likes my eyes?"

"So we may assume," said Georgiana, continuing to examine the flowers.

Bingley chuckled. "Will wonders never cease?"

"Sweet William," said Georgiana. "That's rather obvious."

Darcy looked it up anyway and read out, "'Gallantry.'"

Georgiana nodded. "Very good. Peppermint?"

After a moment Darcy responded, grinning, "'Warmth of feeling'".

"See? That's what I said," Bingley was adamant.

"No, Bingley, you said 'love,' which is not the same," Darcy corrected, "but this is good all the same."

"These are double china asters, I think," Georgiana continued.

"Double china asters," Darcy repeated. "'I partake of your sentiments.'" Darcy's excited voice was nearly a whisper.

"There!" Bingley said, as if his point surely must now be taken.

"She *still* is not explicit," Darcy murmured, but he was smiling.

Georgiana sniffed at the nosegay, rubbing foliage with her fingers. "Lemon Geranium."

"Hmmm... Ah! How acute she is. She found a plant that means 'unexpected meeting'. You see how exacting the flowers can be, Bingley?" Darcy was chuckling and stepped to his sister to look at the nosegay more particularly.

"There is one last type of leaf here; I call it lamb's ears."

Darcy looked for it in the lists. "Lamb's ears, 'see betony'. Betony...ah! It means surprise. She refers to our surprise meeting here. Let me see if I have this correct, Georgie. She likes my eyes. She thinks I am gallant and clever. She refers to our surprising meeting here, and clearly her feelings toward me have improved, and she would even say as much as they have warmed."

"She says more than that, Brother. She partakes of your sentiments. Your open rose clearly said you still love her. She is saying, in a refined way without being too forward, that she loves you, too. Were I you, Fitzwilliam, I would be immensely pleased."

Darcy looked at the nosegay. "Make no mistake. I *am* pleased. I am delighted! But she does not say she loves me, and I will not assume sentiments that are not obvious."

"Wait...the peach!" Georgiana set down the nosegay and took the herbal from her brother. "That is meant to be a part of the message." There was a breathless pause as Georgiana searched for the meaning. She sounded a trifle disappointed as she read, "'Your qualities, like your charms, are unequalled.'"

Darcy smiled.

"Now I am thinking Miss Elizabeth is losing her wits..." Bingley muttered good-naturedly.

"Tweak me all you like, Bingley." Darcy was feeling charitable. "I am pleased with her. I like her wits just as they are. I always have."

"Perhaps the big vase says what you are hoping for," Georgiana said. "It certainly makes an emphatic statement, being all one flower."

"What are they?" Darcy asked.

"Sticky Catch-fly?"

Darcy looked it up. "Sounds horrid for something so frothy. 'Sticky Catch-fly. See Viscaria.'" There was a pause. He started to laugh. "'Will you dance with me?'"

"That is what it means?" asked an incredulous Georgiana.

Darcy pulled the cards from his pocket. He did not wish to share them aloud but continued to chortle as he read to himself, *"May I have the honour of dancing the next with you, Mr Darcy? E. Bennet."* He looked at the vase with the happily dancing couple painted onto the porcelain. Georgiana and Bingley watched as Darcy's countenance took on an even more besotted expression.

"Come on, man, does she say she loves you?" Bingley was beside himself.

Darcy felt himself to be almost more elated than if she had expressed love. She was teasing him with memories only the two of them could share. He had first refused to ask her to dance; she had refused to dance with him—twice!—and the second time had accused him of asking only to find fault. She accepted his invitation to dance at the Netherfield ball but, he had to admit, rather reluctantly, and they sparred throughout their set. Certainly, the only permutation left was for *her* to ask *him*, and she knew a true gentleman would not say no to a lady willing to run such a daring risk against propriety.

"Alas, no, Bingley, but what she does say refers to memories only she and I would share. I am come to admit, she may like me..."

"Oh, bother, Darcy. I am going riding. Care to join me?"

Darcy sighed. "No, Bingley, not just now. You go. Enjoy yourself. Take the dogs for a romp." He was speaking absently. "Georgie, will you help me carry these to my room?"

GEORGIANA WITHDREW WITH A SMILE as her brother began moving the nosegay, peach and dancing vase about on the table where his brandy decanter stood until he was satisfied with the arrangement. Darcy read the cards again, noting that in describing the nosegay, she had repeated his words from the nosegay given to her. *She follows my lead.* At last, he picked up the peach, opened the doors to his balcony and sat in the sunshine, stroking the fruit with his thumbs as if it were Elizabeth's two blushing cheeks. He dozed and dreamt that the peach in his hand, plump, soft and rosy, was rather another part of that lady's anatomy and like her cheeks, of which there were two.

Peach
"Your qualities equal your charms"

Chapter 6

Letters To and Fro

Mr Bennet sat at the desk in his library reading the second letter that had arrived from his brother-in-law since the Gardiners absconded to the north with his dear Lizzy. He often mused on the topic of how such a pleasant, clever, steady man as Edward could have sprung from the same family that produced his silly wife and her vulgar elder sister, Mrs Phillips. Himself a lackadaisical correspondent, Mr Bennet did always enjoy a good letter with interesting particulars. He thought himself an excellent recipient. This letter contained stories of his favourite daughter and so was more highly valued.

Mr Gardiner had already written once, telling Mr Bennet of stops at the Oxford colleges, Blenheim and Chatsworth. Mr Bennet was not a man inclined to travel, but he knew Elizabeth enjoyed it and was just beginning to think that, perhaps, he would like to see the white cliffs of Dover whilst still able-bodied enough for travel. If he could take only Elizabeth, he would get pleasure from seeing this natural wonder. If he had to take his whole family, he would never go.

The travelling party had arrived in Derbyshire, and Mr Gardiner related the amusing story of Elizabeth scrambling over the Peaks—how no view was high enough to suit her and how Mrs Gardiner had, at last, become filled with panic and called her down in the name of her father. Mr Bennet chuckled. Had he been with them, he would have given Elizabeth free rein. He hoped he would have a letter soon, relating the same story through the eyes of dear Lizzy herself.

The last tale in the letter evoked a much different response. Edward told of a chance meeting with Mr Darcy at his estate, which Elizabeth seemed to like more than any other place she had been. Much to Mr Bennet's surprise, Mr Darcy, when introduced to the Gardiners, gave every appearance of easiness and hospitality and treated Elizabeth with a gentle deference, which indicated some tender regard as the Gardiners saw it. Mr Darcy called at the inn at Lambton at noon the day following to introduce Elizabeth to his sister, Miss Georgiana Darcy, a handsome, fair girl of nearly seventeen with friendly, if shy, manners. Edward and Madeleine noticed Miss Darcy studying Elizabeth carefully, and she was quick to return her smiles. Once Mr Darcy learnt Mrs Gardiner had spent much of her youth in Lambton, he began to treat her like a kinswoman and seemed delighted to babble with her for several minutes in the local dialect. Elizabeth appeared increasingly confused and blushed when Darcy smiled at her.

Mr Gardiner ended the letter with his observation that Elizabeth admitted Mr Darcy much—if not completely—improved in manners since last seeing him in Kent. To the Gardiners, he did not appear haughty or above his company, although, perhaps, a little reserved until he learnt of the Lambton connection. He gave every appearance of having some interest in Elizabeth, more than simply renewing a previous pleasant acquaintance. He often smiled when she was speaking with his sister and not looking at him. They were to dine at his estate in two days' time, and Mr Gardiner looked forward to fishing at Pemberley the very next day. He was quite certain Darcy's regard for Elizabeth drove the invitations forward.

Mr Bennet stared at the last paragraph and then reread it. He sat back in his seat, staring at nothing out the window. His dear daughter's face appeared in his mind's eye, rolling her twinkling eyes at some absurdity. Mr Bennet was so partial to her that he never could comprehend how a man of Darcy's alleged breeding and refinement could have slighted her and always looked upon her to find fault. Having rarely exchanged words with the man, Mr Bennet was now at something of a loss. *Perhaps absence had made his heart grow fonder?*

Mr Bennet longed for his dear Lizzy to materialise before him and debate the situation. There was no one with whom he could share the quandary. Perhaps Jane could tell more of her sister's heart. At last, he troubled himself to lean his head out into the hall.

"Jane? Mrs Bennet?"

Mrs Hill popped into the hallway from the breakfast room. "They are in the garden, sir, with the Gardiner children."

"Ah, thank you, Hill."

Mr Bennet drew on his linen summer coat to join his wife and eldest daughter. The children were capering around the lawn, chasing each other and kicking balls about, whilst Jane and her mother chatted on chairs in the shade. He sat on the adjoining bench.

"Jane, Mrs Bennet, I have had the most interesting letter from my brother Gardiner about his current travels. Have you had a letter from Lizzy, Jane?"

Jane smiled. "I have had one letter, full of details of gardens around great houses. Lizzy will return, she writes, with long lists of plants to find for our garden."

Mr Bennet nodded. "Yes, well, she has ample pocket money if she cares to bring any flowers back that can be had with ready cash. She has not written of visiting Pemberley, the estate of Mr Darcy?"

"Mr Darcy!" Mrs Bennet erupted. "Our Lizzy would go to great lengths to avoid that odious man, I should think."

"And so would I have said." Mr Bennet looked carefully at Jane, who never could be coy, as she avoided her father's gaze. *So! She knows something.* "It would appear, Mrs Bennet, that in order to raise himself in our Lizzy's estimation, no less a person than Mr Darcy is attempting to render himself agreeable to her. I have it in a letter from your brother that during their first days at Lambton, Mr Darcy has been their constant companion and pays our Lizzy every compliment.

"Our brother says further that Lizzy receives Mr Darcy's attentions with every appearance of good will. Although he reports he and Madeleine are not completely certain she is in love with him, they think she may want to be, and they suspect both Lizzy and Darcy of some slyness that has not been completely exposed."

Jane turned quite red. "What?"

Mrs Bennet sat up, alert. "Our Lizzy and Mr Darcy? I do not believe it. What nonsense. He is such a disagreeable man. Perhaps this is some other Darcy?"

Mr Bennet rolled his eyes and continued, "It appears they toured Pemberley thinking the master of the house was from home, but he appeared, and there was a terse but not uncivil exchange between Darcy and Lizzy. He reappeared some few minutes later in clean clothes and stayed by Lizzy's side as they toured the grounds. The next day, he appeared at the inn to introduce his sister, and gave the impression of wishing the two girls to form a friendship. He has invited Edward to go fishing on the estate, and tonight they will dine at Pemberley."

Jane and her mother stared at Mr Bennet as though he had lapsed into a foreign language, perhaps Arabic.

"Oh, Mr Bennet! Oh, Jane, can you imagine such a thing? Our Lizzy? Noticed by Mr Darcy? Lydia will find this most amusing. I am just on the point of writing her with birthday money. I must include this news! Mr Darcy is headed for quite a fall, I must say…" Mrs Bennet turned to the house at a respectable trot for a matron of her girth and years.

Mr Bennet eyed Jane throughout his wife's ravings. She rose slowly to her feet to follow her mother.

"Jane? Do you know something of this?"

"I am not sure what would be right for me to say, Papa. What I know, Lizzy has confided. I can say her feelings for Mr Darcy were unsettled, by my reckoning, when last we spoke of him. That was right after her return from Kent. She has not said anything of him since."

"But what of Mr Darcy's sentiments? Has she said?" Mr Bennet asked.

Jane's furious blush heightened further yet. "You would have me break her confidence?"

Mr Bennet looked quizzical and then shook his head. "No, Jane. I will not ask that of *you.*"

As Mr Bennet strolled back to the house, Kitty emerged from it to join the children. An hour later, Mrs Bennet sent a servant into Meryton to post the letter for Lydia.

AFTER SUPPER THE NEXT EVENING, a horse was heard at full gallop approaching the paddock. It was an express rider. The packet was addressed to Mr Thomas Bennet, Longbourn Manor House, Hertfordshire, from Mr Charles Bingley, care of F. Darcy, Pemberley, Derbyshire. Mrs Bennet was rushing down the stairs as Mr Bennet entered the house.

"Oh, how I hate expresses! They never bring good news! It is Lizzy, isn't it? She has died! Just to vex me, she *would* do it." Mrs Bennet was ever quick to assume the absolute worst, and all her meagre logic failed her when immediate news was at hand. Jane followed her mother down the stairs.

Mr Bennet, who was full of the most pleasant and forceful sensation of curiosity, put a hand up to silence his wife but looked up at Jane as he said, "Yes, it is from Pemberley, but I doubt it has news good or bad about our Lizzy. The sender is a certain Mr Charles Bingley." He smiled, and after enjoying the effect of this revelation upon his wife and daughter, turned and entered his library to read the contents of the express in private. Jane and her mother watched him closet himself in stunned silence.

When Mr Bennet opened the outer packet, he felt his own surprise. In addition to an envelope from Bingley, there was a second, thinner one addressed to him in a much different hand but with no indication of the sender. He opened the thicker letter first.

Pemberley, Derbyshire
25 July, 1812, midnight

My dear Mr Bennet,

"His dear Mr Bennet, am I?"

It has been my great luck to have the opportunity to reacquaint myself with your daughter, Miss Elizabeth, whilst I am a guest of Mr Darcy. She has given me to understand that, were I to return to the Meryton neighbourhood to enjoy some autumn shooting, I would not be unwelcome to your charming daughter, Miss Jane Bennet, much to my profound relief. It is of her that I write.

When I was last in Hertfordshire, your daughter impressed me as having every characteristic of manner that would suit me in a partner for my life—in addition, of course, to being the most beautiful creature I have ever beheld to this very day. When I left Netherfield, for what I had assumed to be a brief trip to London, I was convincing myself to approach you for permission to court her upon my return. My family, sadly, had other ideas, and because of Miss Jane's natural and proper habit of guarding her feelings in company, they were convinced—and I am sorry to say, they convinced me—that her regard was not out of the common way. Had I not been such a thundering lack-wit...

Here Mr Bennet laughed out loud.

...I would have trusted my own better knowledge of Miss Bennet. She and I shared enough candid, private conversation that I ought to have trusted I knew her heart. For this, I will forever remain apologetic. I should have followed my heart, of which I was certain, at any rate.

At this point Bingley proceeded with several paragraphs of ample compliments to Jane's manners and accomplishments with a carefully worded delineation of her physical attributes, none of which gave her father any concern other than amusement for the many scratchings-out. The word angelic was used extensively. *There is a whole sentence blotted! I shall always wonder what it said. Perhaps he judged himself too explicit. I do hope so.* Finally, Bingley came to the point.

When I clapped eyes on Miss Elizabeth some three days ago, the force of my affection for her elder sister was revisited upon me ten-fold. Miss Elizabeth and I sat next to each other at dinner at Pemberley tonight, and she was kind enough to assure me that her sister, quite miraculously, still has some remnant of tender regard for me, and so I am emboldened to produce this letter. I have informed Mr Gardiner of my intention to write you, and I hope he will vouch for my character if called upon to do so.

Will you do me the honour, sir, of allowing me to court your daughter, Miss Jane Bennet,

"As if I doubt of which daughter he speaks?"

...when I return to Netherfield for the shooting? I remain in the firmest belief that she is just the sort of woman who would be my first choice as an amiable wife. I would have you share with her any part of this letter, as I am sure, as her father, you will also require her assurances that she wishes to know me better.

"Probably no need for that, Mr Bingley. All seems visible enough from the surface."

I shall remain at Pemberley until I have your response, and if, as I pray, it is a positive one, I shall open Netherfield and will, no doubt, be in residence well before the first of September. Please respond as soon as possible with the expense of an express borne by myself upon its arrival at Pemberley.

Yours hopefully and faithfully,
Charles Bingley

Mr Bennet sat back and smiled, anticipating the opportunity to observe Jane's agitation as she read the letter. The whole tone of Bingley's remarks pleased him greatly, it making a nice variation from the obsequious missives from his cousin William Collins.

Before calling Jane to him, he decided to read the other letter. The hand-writing on the envelope, "Mr Thomas Bennet", was precise and decided, the hand of a man who had attended much more carefully to his penmanship instruction than had Charles Bingley. Mr Bennet opened the letter and glanced at the signature first, "Respectfully, F. Darcy". *Perhaps he writes to strengthen Bingley's hand.*

Pemberley, Derbyshire
25 July, 1812

Dear Mr Bennet,

It has been my privilege to renew my acquaintance with your daughter Miss Elizabeth Bennet during her present visit to Lambton. We had the good fortune to converse often during her stay at Hunsford last April, which served to increase my regard for her begun at Netherfield last autumn. Your daughter has made me perfectly aware that, at the earliest time of our acquaintance, she did not regard me in a favourable light, but I believe she has forgiven my initial unfortunate manners. I have seen to their improvement.

Mr Bennet dropped the hand bearing the letter to the arm of his chair and stared into space. He was dumbstruck. *Whatever does he mean? Has he had one of Lizzy's set-downs? And she didn't tell me?* He continued reading.

Although I am by no means certain of success, I humbly request permission to court Miss Elizabeth while she remains in Derbyshire, and longer if necessary. To this end, my sister, Georgiana, and I will invite her to stay on as our guest at Pemberley through the month of August if you are approving of my suit. My sister's companion, Mrs Annesley, will act as chaperone after the departure of the Gardiners.

It is the custom at this point for a gentleman to reiterate the estimable qualities of the lady he wishes to court. Because I know you to hold her close to your heart as your dearest daughter, I will only say my tender regard and admiration of her spring from the same lively wit and intelligence as do yours. She has compelling eyes, which I think chief amongst her ample charms. I am not ashamed to say I love her passionately. Her happiness will always be my first concern if I can convince her to accept me.

I would further request you keep this matter private—although I trust Miss Jane Bennet if you wish to consult her—until I can report I am making some progress. I shall inform her uncle of my intentions when I have received your response. I beseech you to include some reply to me under separate cover with your response to Mr Bingley.

Respectfully,
F. Darcy

Mr Bennet's head was spinning, and in an unprecedented display of action, he stood abruptly and marched up the stairs to his wife's sitting room, where she was composing a letter with Jane and chattering about Charles Bingley. He silently grabbed Jane by the hand and proceeded back down to his library. As they sat, he handed her Darcy's letter, saying only, "What can you tell me of this?"

Jane read the letter, although as her astonishment increased, her comprehension of the words diminished. She ceased reading at the word *passionately* and looked at her father. "I am all bewilderment, Father. I know not what to say."

"Did you finish the letter?"

"No, sir."

"Pray, do so, Jane, and then I expect you to tell me *everything* you know since you hereby have the permission of one of the parties involved. Do not deny you know more than you were willing to tell yesterday."

Jane finished reading, carefully folded the letter and handed it back to her father. Tears glistened at the corners of her eyes. "He writes a lovely letter."

Mr Bennet sighed. Jane was obviously prepared to be mawkish, and he would just have to bear it. "Yes, there is a pleasing aesthetic to his penmanship, but I doubt that is what you meant."

Jane gathered herself and explained what she had been told of Mr Darcy's proposal at Hunsford. She did not mention the particulars Elizabeth divulged regarding Wickham and Georgiana Darcy; it was misery enough to reveal Wickham as a dissembler. "By Lizzy's own description, Father, she gave Mr Darcy a blistering rebuke and rather regretted it, or at least regretted being so very vehement after reading his letter."

"Have you read that letter?"

"No, sir."

"Did she keep it, do you think? Should we search her room? He must have made quite an eloquent case for himself if it softened Lizzy's heart."

Jane's blue eyes widened with alarm. "Do you suspect any impropriety in the letter, Father?"

"You mean other than the impropriety of a single man writing to a single lady without so much as a by-your-leave from her father? No, I suppose not. He says here he loves her passionately. I always heard her claim to hate him passionately. The word is too much bandied about."

Jane and her father gazed at each other. "Are you asking my advice?" Jane asked after some moments of silence.

Mr Bennet's eyebrows raised in surprise. "Yes, Jane, I suppose I am."

"We have Uncle Gardiner's letter to assure us Mr Darcy is behaving with every civility. That Lizzy has not confided in me as to any alteration in her opinion of Mr Darcy leads me to believe her opinion *is* changing. You know Lizzy as well as I do. After making so public a display of her disgust with him, she will be embarrassed to admit her perceptions were at fault. She sets great store in her first impressions. His pride cannot be so very great if he would attempt to make his addresses a second time. He must be very much in love with her."

"You think I should encourage this man, Jane?"

"If he is to be discouraged, let it be Lizzy who does so."

"Very well. I shall take the unprecedented step of sending a response tomorrow after church."

Jane rose to leave.

"Where are you going?" her father asked with merriment returning to his eyes.

"To my mother. She was writing a letter to Lizzy about Mr Darcy."

Mr Bennet smiled. "Sit down, Jane. I believe we have the means at hand to very thoroughly distract your mother." He handed Bingley's letter to Jane. "This letter you will not find as aesthetically pleasing as the last, but neither is it to remain private. Let me know when you have finished it, and I will call your mother hither."

Tears of happiness were spilling over his eldest daughter's cheeks before she was halfway through, and her father's handkerchief was deployed as she finished. She held the pages to her chest and murmured, "I knew it. Lizzy was right."

"So you approve my favourable response to Mr Bingley? I am inclined to be positive." Jane nodded adamantly, too full of emotion for speech. "You may keep the letter, Jane. I believe ladies to be sentimental about such things. But your mother should read it, and I believe she will credit Lizzy with being friendly to Darcy for your sake. Are you ready for me to summon her? I believe myself to be as ready as I shall ever be."

Jane smiled through her tears and nodded again.

"Mrs Bennet!" Mr Bennet called as he opened the door. She nearly fell into the room.

THE MONDAY MORNING POST BROUGHT Jane a letter from her travelling sister. Her father gave an inquiring look, but Mrs Bennet took no notice of it, although she had been praising Elizabeth to the skies as the quick and devoted sister who secured Jane's happiness when presented with the chance of it. Had Elizabeth been at home, her mother would have kissed and petted her until she was quite overwhelmed with unquenchable affection from so unusual a source. "See, Jane? This is what comes of having such a clever sister. She thinks always of you, dear Jane. I know what our relatives say but I won't hear it; Lizzy really is a very good girl."

Upon returning to her bedchamber, Jane opened Elizabeth's letter.

The Rose and Raindrop Inn
Lambton, Derbyshire
25 July

My dearest Jane,

You will forgive me, I know, for not having been a more diligent correspondent, but the tour of Derbyshire has become something very different from what I expected. Certainly by the time you read this, an express from Pemberley will have arrived, and I smile as I imagine you smiling. I am certain our father has given consent to a courtship, which will commence with great haste once the response arrives here.

Although I have no direct knowledge of what Mr Bingley might have written to our father, I seriously doubt he has recounted the rencontre he had with his sisters when he learnt, quite by accident from our aunt, that you had been in London through the winter. I did not think him capable of such anger, and you will be distressed to hear he sent his sisters and Mr Hurst away to Scarborough when their deception was revealed, and he would not let Mr Darcy intervene. They abundantly deserve such censure, but I know you are too good to think so. Mr Bingley and I have spoken briefly about this, and he assures me that a family spat of this nature will in time be forgiven, but I believe you may need to do some persuading when you see him. However, I do not think that needs to be your first topic of conversation.

There is another person here about whom I must write. I believe my uncle has written to father that we have encountered Mr Darcy, and he beseeched me to make the acquaintance of his sister, Georgiana. She is a handsome girl with fair features and taller than you, even though not yet seventeen. She is not proud, as I was informed, but is shy and lacks confidence. However, it is not of her I wish to write, either.

You would be shocked, I think, pleasantly so, but shocked nonetheless, at the change in Mr Darcy since our last encounter in Kent. His acquaintance in Meryton would not recognise him for the proud, inconsiderate man he appeared then. His manners are so improved that, were his looks not as

handsome as ever, I would not know him myself. He is everything kind
and civil to our dear aunt and uncle, is a devoted brother, which of course
we suspected before, and has been almost gratuitously generous of his time
and the resources of Pemberley in entertaining us. I fear our aunt will
be vexed as he invites us so often to dine or make some little trip to see
the wonders of the area, that she cannot spend the time she would like
renewing acquaintances from her youth. My aunt and uncle believe he is
exerting himself to secure my good opinion, and I must confess, dear Jane,
he has come a fair way to succeeding. He still studies me a good deal when
we are in company, but I see now it is with admiration, rather than to find
blemish. While I cannot argue with his taste, I find his approval somehow
more disquieting than his assumed disapprobation.

Pemberley is a very grand estate; the manor house is everything elegant
with none of the ornate frippery of Rosings Park. The grounds and
parkland are, likewise, everything anyone could wish for who enjoys the
open air, flowers and birds. Jane, just think of it. Before I had even seen
his home, he had determined to his satisfaction that I should be a suitable
mistress of this place. And it is clear from his every word and look that he
still finds me so. I believe he still loves me, and Mr Bingley believes it, too.

My feelings about the man are so changed that I find nothing but
mortification in my previous sentiments, and I am heartily sorry I was
so vociferous and so mistaken. That he might forgive all I have said is
astonishing. I cannot allow myself to hope he will ever pay his addresses to
me again. Jane, I was far too unkind and so wretchedly wrong.

And yet, I do hope. Oh! How I wish you were here, that you could be
with your Mr Bingley and see this beautiful Pemberley. I long for you
to observe Mr Darcy for yourself and tell me if there might be any way I
could encourage him to trust me again. Whenever he enters a room, or
when I know I am about to see him, I feel a constriction in my chest that
admits to the gravest vulnerability, such as I have never experienced before.
Then he smiles at me, and my concerns are vanished. Jane, I believe I am
quite in love with him and feel every portion of the bitter irony of it. Now
that I would not hesitate to accept him, he will never dare to ask again,
even though he treats me with kindness and is obliging in all things. He
even finds ways to tease me, which must be the most improbable part of
the business.

Seven letters such as this could not begin to relate the particulars of all that has happened. I will have so much to tell you, when next we meet, and so much to describe, especially my witnessing of the reawakening of Mr Bingley's love for you. It pleases me to know your future will be so very happy.

With every affection,
Elizabeth

Jane smiled down upon the pages. She arose from her window seat and crept downstairs, suspecting she would find her father in his library. She tapped and was admitted.

"You should read Lizzy's letter, Father."

She handed the missive to him. As he read, he smiled and chuckled several times. "So, Jane, it appears we did the right thing, offering Darcy a little encouragement. He means to nurture her affections and propose again; she is convinced he will not. Oh! What I would not give to be a flea in the ear of either of them!" He handed the letter back to her. If he had to lose Lizzy, how delightful for there to be some amusing drama in the case.

Sunday, 26 July

ALTHOUGH ELIZABETH EXPECTED TO SEE Darcy, Georgiana and Mr Bingley at the Rose and Raindrop Inn for Sunday dinner, she had no notion of meeting them at St. Swithin's Church for matins. A phaeton drawn by two shining roan ponies drew up to the little church as she and the Gardiners strolled High Street. Elizabeth took no notice until her uncle said, "Ah! So Darcy *does* choose to worship in Lambton instead of Kympton this morning." He smiled slyly at his niece, who glanced briefly at her uncle's face before looking towards the church doors. When the phaeton pulled away, Elizabeth could see the party from Pemberley approach the vicar and Darcy greeting him.

Elizabeth was struggling to regain her breath when her aunt whispered, "You know, Lizzy, the Darcy family has the living of Lambton in their gift as well as Kympton."

"Yet, you did not know them when you lived here?" Elizabeth asked with her eyes down. She had seen Darcy turn and search High Street, but she was not ready to meet his gaze in so public a place as the street now filled with the citizens of Lambton making their way to church.

"We knew Mr Darcy and Lady Anne by sight. They did come here to worship but not often."

Bingley caught sight of Mr Gardiner and waved. Mr Gardiner picked up his pace, but Elizabeth lagged behind. *What must he think of me with my brazen flowers? Will he believe me or have I reduced myself to a mere flirt? Why was I so impetuous? Once again, I have let my high spirits run away with my good sense. I had such a lovely time yesterday; anything seemed possible.*

She and the Gardiners reached the church, and Elizabeth was able to say good morning to Bingley and Georgiana with some semblance of composure. Then the world seemed to stand still. Having greeted everyone else, Elizabeth and Darcy were left standing face to face. Darcy was smiling just enough to show his delight; he could not help himself even though he knew he was being scrutinised.

"Good morning, Miss Bennet!" He bowed slightly.

Elizabeth felt herself colouring but could do nothing to stop it. She curtsied and murmured, "Good morning, Mr Darcy."

"May I ask you and your aunt and uncle to join us in our family's pew?" he asked. She felt his eyes on her, as intense as when he was in Meryton.

Elizabeth could not gather her wits. Her eyes stayed downcast. She was honoured and mortified.

"Why thank you, Mr Darcy," her aunt spoke. "How very welcoming you are."

Darcy lead the way up the aisle of the church attended by whispers —"There's not been a Darcy in't pew for ten yer!" "'At's the Miss Darcy, isn't she a pretty sight…"— and somehow Elizabeth found herself seated between Darcy and her uncle. She was quite sure everyone was staring. *In their place, I would certainly be doing so myself,* she silently admitted.

The vicar of Lambton reminded her of the minister at Longbourn, a jovial older gentleman with a mass of white hair, and eyes made kind by years of smiling. This was not one of those aesthetic spiritualists, such as the vicar Darcy had chosen for Kympton, nor a man beset with the confused piety of her cousin William Collins who worshipped his patroness rather more than he sought oneness with the Holy Spirit.

As they sang the opening hymn, Elizabeth heard Darcy's untrained but pleasing baritone at her ear. She had to pause to catch her breath, although she knew the song by heart. She noticed Darcy glance at her when her voice stopped mid-phrase, but a deep breath renewed her song.

She seems unsettled this morning, Darcy pondered. *Perhaps she is regretting what she said with her flowers. She is used to assuming I disapprove. I shall show her I do not.*

As the congregation stood for the opening prayers, Darcy held his own prayer book, bound in fine leather with his name inscribed in worn gold on the cover. It was a gift from his mother and had seen much use. He opened it to a flattened sprig of viscaria, which he had placed between the pages that morning. He lowered his hands and moved one elbow to brush Elizabeth's arm. She looked over in silent surprise, her eyes landing on the flower lying on the open page.

"Yes, Miss Bennet," Darcy murmured. Without venturing to move his head, he slid his eyes toward her face.

He is saying he will dance with me! She did not look at him but let him see her suppress a smile and gave one slow nod of her head indicating she had heard him.

Elizabeth was pleased he had chosen to be amused by her floral jest rather than affronted. For the present, she was oddly relieved it was not the little red chrysanthemum in his prayer book. The rest of the service was without incident.

THE DARCY PHAETON HAD BEEN taken to the inn's stable yard. The party took a leisurely walk back down High Street. The shops were not open, but Georgiana and Elizabeth walked together and remarked on items in the windows. They stood for the longest time at the display of Peaks Outfitters, purveyors of goods and supplies for touring the Peak district. Elizabeth remarked upon a flower press with binding straps holding layers of thin wood and blotter paper. It came with a satchel worked with vines stained green on a brown leather background. Elizabeth mentioned she had some flowers she wished to press but was reluctant to use her aunt's, fearing she would take up space her aunt wanted to use for Derbyshire wildflowers.

"My aunt loves drawing flowers and amuses herself in the winter by making pictures from the wildflowers she presses in the summer," Elizabeth explained.

Georgiana did not acknowledge she knew of Elizabeth's nosegay from her brother but determined to tell him Elizabeth's admiration for the press. As she considered the matter further, she decided such a gift from her brother would be improper, but she was free to do as she pleased for her new, and already dear, friend.

The private dining room was on the second story of the inn, across the hall from the guests' sitting room. It was not made for large parties, but six people fitted comfortably. The meal would not be served until two o'clock; however, coffee, tea, and cider were brought immediately as they entered the room, and a settee and chairs near the fireplace allowed for conversation.

Bingley could not contain himself and kept nodding at Darcy as if to prompt him. When all were seated and comfortable, Darcy spoke.

"Mrs Gardiner, I feel we have, perhaps, kept you from paying all the social calls and taking in all the sights you have wished to revisit."

"The fault is not yours, Mr Darcy, nor would I have you believe I have found my time ill spent. It has been delightful to visit Pemberley again and make the acquaintance of you and your sister."

"But would you stay longer if you could? I know Mr Gardiner must return to town but Georgiana and I would like to invite you to stay on after Thursday"—he glanced quickly at Elizabeth—"with Miss Elizabeth at Pemberley."

The Gardiners were too astonished to respond. Elizabeth smiled nervously and looked at her hands.

Bingley would not be repressed. "We were talking yesterday at dinner and thought it would be a great treat if Jane, er, Miss Bennet brought your children here, and then we could all stay together through August. Mrs Annesley returns in five days. There will be ample chaperonage." His blue eyes beseeched both Gardiners.

Darcy spoke again. "Bingley has invited me to shoot at Netherfield this autumn, and Georgiana will join us." He made a furtive glance at Elizabeth, who was blushing furiously and keeping her eyes down. "Miss Bennet and Miss Elizabeth could travel back to Longbourn with Georgiana and Mrs Annesley, and I can travel with Bingley. As we will need two carriages anyway, they may as well be full of friends."

The Gardiners were not at all surprised that Darcy looked every bit as anxious as Bingley. "My chaise and four could see you and your children to Oxford, Mrs Gardiner, with whatever nurses and footmen you might need if perhaps Mr Gardiner could meet you there?"

Mr Gardiner looked quizzically at his wife. London in August was a trial, and although he would rattle around their house alone, he thought the opportunity for his family too important to deny. "I have no objection. What say you, my dear?"

Mrs Gardiner was quietly pleased for Elizabeth. "You are kind to brave my children, Mr Darcy. I would so enjoy my Lambton friends having the opportunity to meet them. And I am sure Mr and Mrs Bennet would spare Jane. We have only to ask Elizabeth." She turned and looked at her niece. "Well, Lizzy? The plan hinges on you."

Elizabeth was so thrilled, embarrassed and astonished she hardly knew what to say. Her eyes bounced from Bingley to Georgiana, both of whom looked sincerely hopeful. She then looked at Darcy. His eyes were on his coffee, his cheeks aflame. For Jane's sake alone, she would have said yes, but the racing of her heart told the truth: it was for herself she had hope.

Still looking at Darcy, she answered in a low voice, "This is very generous of you, sir, and Miss Darcy." Both brother and sister looked at her with some surprise at the uncharacteristic shyness of her address. "I can answer for Jane, I think; she and I would be most pleased to stay at Pemberley for the month of August."

"How delightful! We shall send an express directly!" Bingley smiled.

Elizabeth and Darcy surveyed each other in unrestrained wonder. It was obvious to everyone, except themselves, that each was deeply in love and the affection was mutual. Although both were abundantly endowed with self-confidence, when they thought of each other, it failed them completely.

Monday, 27 July, 1812

WHEN THE EXPRESS FROM LONGBOURN arrived at Pemberley late Monday night, Darcy was still awake, pacing in his study. The next day Mr Gardiner was coming to fish, with Elizabeth along to observe. Mrs Gardiner would arrive for dinner after visiting several friends to let them know she would not be leaving the area as soon as planned. Darcy was relieved the express was presented without Elizabeth or the Gardiners being about the place. If it was bad news, as Darcy half expected it to be, he could share his sorrow with Bingley and have the night to recover before having to face the others. As the express was addressed to Bingley, Darcy asked Grayson to rouse him. He also requested a bottle of champagne from the cellars, assuming Bingley, at least, would have reason to celebrate.

Bingley was in his dressing gown reading before the fire and joined Darcy without dressing. Darcy had opened the packet and held the letter addressed to him. The thinner letter for Bingley, just one sheet, he laid upon the desk. He observed Mr Bennet's handwriting, and his stomach lurched into his throat.

As Bingley entered, Darcy indicated the letter on the desk. "Now, Bingley, we shall see where we stand."

Bingley looked around. "You have not called Georgiana? That does seem hard. She will be cross."

"I suppose you are dressed enough." Bingley was in his stocking feet, and wore only a shirt, but his dressing gown was more modest than any Darcy owned. "Can you wait whilst I fetch her?"

Bingley smiled. "It only seems fair."

Darcy finally made his revelation. "Bingley, you were not the only one to request permission to court a Bennet daughter." Darcy could see Bingley inhaling to produce some manner of loud and festive noise, but Darcy held up a hand to quiet him. "Unlike you, I have requested to keep it private. You know, and Georgie shall know..."

"Know what?" his sister asked as she entered the room.

"Where have you come from? Did Grayson alert you?"

"I was coming out of the library when I saw Charles. So my question remains: what shall I know?"

"There may be a response here to your brother's request to court Lizzy." Bingley supplied her answer.

"Court Lizzy? Does *Lizzy* know?" Georgiana gaped at her brother.

"No, nor do I wish her to. I will not make my addresses until I am certain of Elizabeth's affections and after Bingley and Jane are betrothed. I suspect that once they are reunited, Elizabeth will look upon me more favourably."

Bingley and Georgiana both began shaking their heads, telling him he was steering a wrong course and should tell Elizabeth of his request to her father, but Darcy was adamant.

"...in any case, we have Mr Bennet's letters before us. Open yours, Bingley." Darcy wanted to hear what he was sure was good news.

Bingley read aloud:

"Dear Mr Bingley, May I say that the entire Bennet family is delighted, no —that does not seem a strong enough word—elated, yes, that is more accurate, to be hearing from you and upon such a happy subject. I have consulted the

daughter in question—Jane, was it?—and her regard for you is as steady as one would expect from such a steady young woman. Her smile, which I have always thought quite remarkable, has taken on a radiance with which I believe you will be most pleased when next you see her. However you choose to proceed, you have the abundant blessings of her mother and myself.

"*Please write straight away if we have connected you with the wrong daughter!*

"*Regards, T. Bennet.*"

Darcy sighed with relief. "Well, Bingley. That's your future settled." He turned and smiled at his friend.

Bingley was grinning. Georgiana squealed and hugged Bingley.

Darcy looked at his sister with mild disapproval. "I am most alarmed to learn you can produce such a sound, gosling. What a disturbing noise."

"Wait until Darcy reads his. We might all be making disturbing noises," Bingley said, laughing. They quieted, and suddenly, there was not a breath to be heard in the world.

Darcy began as Bingley had done, reading the letter aloud, but his voice was barely above a murmur.

"*Dear Mr Darcy,*

"*To say your request comes as a surprise is, you will understand, an understatement of vast and epic proportion. That you would undertake to court a woman who has been known to express a spitting contempt for you seems reckless at the very least. You have never given the appearance of being inbred, nor do I have reports that insanity runs in your family.*"

Georgiana began to giggle nervously. A strange huffing sound could be heard from Bingley, who was attempting to suppress his mirth.

"*I have consulted Jane, as you suggested, and we agree that if you wish to undertake a courtship of our Lizzy without certain knowledge of the outcome, after failing quite miserably once before, then we must consider it seriously. Jane says you felt such a strong need to correct Lizzy's false impressions of you that, without a thought to propriety, you wrote her a letter, which, with a similar lack of propriety and her typical curiosity, my daughter read. Let that be your first warning as to her character. For the moment, I shall set that fatherly complaint aside and return to the home question.*"

Darcy glanced at his companions, chagrined, then continued.

"*Jane and I can only assume that your love for my best and most brilliant daughter has made you courageous or foolhardy, and possibly both. We can, neither of us, claim to know Elizabeth's current sentiments about you. She has kept her own counsel since divulging to Jane the contents of your letter in April, so we have decided we simply must leave you to make your own way. Jane wisely says, 'If he is to be discouraged, let Lizzy be the one to do so.'"*

Darcy's voice grew stronger, and he smiled as he read:

"Howsoever, if you are able to secure Miss Elizabeth Bennet's respect and affection, then I will consent to the marriage. If she cannot love and respect you, you are better to give her up. Be forewarned, for I believe Lizzy will surely destroy whatever peace of mind your bachelor life has allowed you. Lizzy is remarkable indeed, but I fear she will not make anyone a tranquil or amiable wife. She has too much of my nature.

"I marvel at your bravery, I admire your persistence, and I applaud your good taste. I wish you the best of luck, for you shall certainly need it. Jane and I will, as requested, keep the matter between us. Rest assured, in any case, but most especially if you succeed, I shall pray daily for your immortal soul.

"Respectfully,

"T. Bennet."

Darcy started to laugh, a rumbling chuckle that built to a level of boisterous hysteria. In a moment, they were all laughing, and when the footman entered the study behind Grayson with the tray of flutes and champagne, he stopped and stared. The footman had never seen the master or his sister overcome with joy.

Iris
"Messages"

Chapter 7

When Mr Gardiner and Elizabeth arrived at Pemberley at eleven o'clock for fishing, they were surprised that Darcy was easier with them than he had ever been before. He lead them to the phaeton, which he drove to a fishing spot further into the Pemberley woods than Mr Gardiner had yet been. He informed them Bingley would ride out to join them shortly and Georgiana would come in a curricle with a picnic in a few hours. Darcy was smiling with every sentence he uttered as if possessed by the highest spirits.

Elizabeth wore a pale pink walking gown with leaves and vines printed on cotton and her ankle boots. She had a large reticule with tools for gathering wildflowers for her aunt. It was a warm day; her spencer was lightweight and her bonnet a simple straw affair with green satin ribbons. She could see from his every expression that Darcy was pleased with her.

Elizabeth settled on a mossy log at the edge of the stream whilst the men dawdled over their tackle and lines. The water was flowing so rapidly that Elizabeth could not hear their conversation.

"The fishing here must be excellent, Darcy, for you seem in hopeful spirits." Mr Gardiner smiled as he selected a lure for his line.

"Hopeful spirits," Darcy repeated the older man's words. "Yes, indeed. I have something I must tell you, and I believe it will please you. We have had a response from Longbourn to the express Bingley sent Saturday. It arrived last evening with good news."

Mr Gardiner smiled. "I am not at all surprised, except that my brother Bennet was prevailed upon to make a suitably hasty reply. He is usually a desultory correspondent."

"He may have been prompt because there was more to respond to than you presently know. Along with Bingley's request to court Miss Bennet, I sent a request of my own to court Miss Elizabeth." Darcy was facing away from her lest she should look up the bank and see his irrepressible joy. "Mr Bennet does us the honour of allowing *both* our suits."

Mr Gardiner was startled into delighted laughter and clapped Darcy on the back. Darcy's voice dropped. "I would rather she not know about my intentions until matters are settled with Bingley and Miss Bennet. But I want you, and Mrs Gardiner, too, to know I love your niece and want nothing more than to share Pemberley with her for the rest of my life."

Mr Gardiner whispered, "Madeleine and I believed something like this might be afoot. My advice to you, sir, is not to wait too long to declare your intentions to Lizzy. She is not known for her patience. She does not expect you to renew your addresses, you know. But neither will she refuse you."

Darcy shook his head. "I feel I should wait until Miss Bennet and Bingley are a settled thing. It is my fault they are not already married, and Miss Elizabeth will think better of me when they are betrothed. Then I shall not hold back in any way."

Both men turned and looked back at Elizabeth. She had drawn her legs up on the broad log, and her arms were wrapped around her knees. She was watching a wren hopping over her head and whistling to it.

Mr Gardiner smiled with approval as Darcy whispered, "See? She looks like she belongs here."

Elizabeth moved her gaze to her uncle and Darcy. "You are both jolly fellows!" she exclaimed.

"It is Bingley's news to tell, but I cannot wait," Darcy said to Mr Gardiner and then called out to Elizabeth, "We have had word from your father. He has given Charles leave to court your sister."

"Oh!" Elizabeth's joy propelled her off the log and up to her uncle and Darcy. "What happy, happy news! No wonder you seem so full of yourself today, Mr Darcy!" The men were standing close enough together that she made to embrace them both at once, but her uncle bore the brunt of her exuberance as she threw an arm around him and kissed his cheek. Her other hand grasped Darcy's arm, and just as quickly as she touched him, she realised the impropriety of her action and pulled away. "Excuse me, sir! I am too happy."

Darcy reached for the hand that had so briefly caressed his upper arm, squeezed it and let it go. "You may be as happy as you like, Miss Elizabeth. I do not think your uncle will mind in such circumstances."

Elizabeth blushed. Darcy's touch warmed all of her, and she glanced nervously at her uncle. His smile was indulgent.

Wednesday, 29 July

AT TEN O'CLOCK THE FOLLOWING morning, the Darcy barouche with its hood down—for the weather was as fine as all had anticipated—pulled to a stop in front of the Rose and Raindrop Inn in Lambton. The townspeople watched with undisguised interest as Fitzwilliam Darcy alighted. Within a moment of his entering the inn, he came out again, followed by the Gardiners and their niece. Mr Gardiner handed his wife into the carriage and climbed in, leaving Darcy to see to Elizabeth before boarding the carriage, and away they went.

Georgiana carried a parasol and used it to shield herself as best she could from the well-meaning curiosity of onlookers. Darcy would have shown more reserve, but having received an express to say Jane was on her way with the Gardiner children and would arrive on Friday, he had every reason to be happy and no reason to hide it. Merriment illuminated his countenance, and he looked as amiable as the other two gentlemen in the party. He gazed on Elizabeth with a contented expression, proud of himself for finessing her ten days in Lambton into an entire month at Pemberley. Their eyes met, and hers questioned his obvious levity.

As soon as the carriage left High Street and was on the road to Bakewell, Darcy answered Elizabeth's unspoken query. "Miss Elizabeth, Mrs Gardiner, we have had word from Longbourn. Miss Bennet and the children are on their way to us. We are to expect them Friday."

Elizabeth leaned a little forward, the better to see Bingley. He was beaming.

"Miss Elizabeth, I shall want your advice," he began when he noticed she was watching him, "and Miss Darcy, too. What are Miss Bennet's favourite flowers? Which flowers represent apology? And gratitude? I shall shower her with petals of gratitude as soon as she arrives."

The ladies laughed. "You will overwhelm her, Mr Bingley," Mrs Gardiner said, smiling.

"Yes. Precisely. She shall never have reason to doubt my affection again."

When Mr and Mrs Gardiner had questions about the countryside as the carriage travelled beyond Bakewell and turned south at Monyash, Georgiana, who was now more used to their company, answered as best she could. Elizabeth and Darcy gazed at each other, unabashedly oblivious to their company and the surroundings.

The carriage drew up to the broad field in which the Arbor Low was situated. Elizabeth was surprised to enter it from between its surrounding berms and a little disappointed to see the stones were lying down with no imposing height or massive lintels as at Stonehenge. The men stood about, admiring the effort that had brought the stones to the place and positioned them for marking each solstice. The ladies scampered around, with Mrs Gardiner and Georgiana making rubbings of the rock surfaces using charcoal and paper from Mrs Gardiner's satchel of art supplies. The field was scattered with thistle and church-steeples, making a random violet and yellow tapestry in the pasture grass.

"Mr Darcy?" Elizabeth beckoned.

He walked over to her. "Miss Elizabeth?"

"Why are the stones not standing? Were they knocked down by misguided religious zealots during the reformation? Or by the Romans?"

"No, Miss Elizabeth. To anyone's certain knowledge, they have never stood upright."

"So perhaps Arbor Low was left unfinished?"

"Perhaps." Darcy was amused by her curiosity and that she expected him to have all the knowledge of a tour guide.

"Do the Druids still come?"

"Yes, at each solstice and equinox. We still have a few wild folk about in Derbyshire."

She walked by him closely, looked at him appraisingly and murmured for his ears only, "That much I knew."

He laughed. *I believe she is flirting with me!*

Mrs Gardiner called for Elizabeth's attention and bid her sit on one of the stones. Within a few minutes, she had drawn her niece's likeness, sitting amidst Arbor Low with the thistles and church-steeples against her skirts.

Georgiana watched and admired the quick sure strokes of the pencils. "How clever you are, Mrs Gardiner. I wish I could draw."

"It is my one lady-like accomplishment, Miss Darcy, since I do not play music as you do. I can scarce plunk out a tune on our pianoforte, although my daughters have started lessons."

"How delightful! May I give them a lesson or two while they visit here? You would not think me interfering?"

"Far from it. I am certain Alyse and Louise will enjoy it." Mrs Gardiner smiled at Georgiana's burgeoning confidence.

The men approached, led by Darcy, to see Mrs Gardiner's drawing. "There!" she said. "Now that I have the outlines, I might add some tints or perhaps just some shading with charcoal or pen and ink."

"It is lovely as it is." Georgiana was enthusiastic.

Elizabeth stood, and the admirers parted so she could see her aunt's work. "Oh!" She blushed and wondered if she were truly as appealing as her aunt made her appear.

"You have captured Miss Elizabeth's smile remarkably well," Bingley commented.

Darcy looked over Bingley's shoulder, raised his eyebrows and turned away. Clearly, Mrs Gardiner had talent. *If I owned that drawing, I would never get a wink of sleep again.* He noticed the subject of the sketch had wandered away and was atop one arc of the Arbor Low barrows.

"Mr Darcy?" she asked as he approached, "What is that distinct rise of ground just beyond the next field?"

"You must be seeing Gib Hill. It is an easy walk. Shall we?" He held out his arm and turned to the rest of the party. "Miss Elizabeth and I will walk to Gib Hill. Who will join us?"

Bingley answered with a knowing look. "I shall be along in a moment. You two start."

"I shall go along with Mr Bingley," Georgiana added, hoping to slow Bingley's pace.

Elizabeth came down from the berm and carefully tucked her gloved hand into Darcy's elbow.

"Miss Elizabeth, what do you think of your likeness? You seemed unsettled by it." He spoke in a low voice when they were a little distance from Arbor Low.

"I am always surprised at how my aunt renders me."

"How so?"

Elizabeth looked away with a rueful smile and then shook her head, "It is not for me to direct how others perceive me. I am what I am, and others see what they will. I fear she tends to heighten what few attractions I have."

"Why do you always disparage your looks, Elizabeth?" Darcy spoke without thinking. He drew in his breath. He had used her given name as if he were speaking to her in one of his dreams. "Excuse me, *Miss* Elizabeth."

She did not meet his eyes but nodded. "No offense is taken, Mr Darcy."

"I thank you." There was a pause. "But my question stands unanswered."

The corners of her mouth twitched up, and she turned away from him, the brim of her bonnet hiding her face. "So it does." She let go of his arm and increased her stride. Darcy knew she would have sprinted the distance had she been alone.

They reached the top of Gib Hill and looked at the view all around and back toward Arbor Low. They could see that Bingley and Georgiana were halfway to them. Darcy stepped away from Elizabeth and admired her as she admired the view.

"You called this a tumulus, Mr Darcy. As in a tomb?"

"That is the local assumption, Miss Elizabeth, but no one has gone digging for bones. I hope dancing on someone's grave does not make you uneasy."

I am more uneasy being here with a living man than with dead ones, she mused, turning partly away as if to regard a different prospect. "Indeed, Mr Darcy, you will not find me superstitious. Those buried here have such beauty around them; I cannot think them spiteful. If only there were music, I would have my dance of you, sir."

Darcy stepped closer and would have taken her in his arms for a waltz had Bingley not called, "Darcy, Miss Elizabeth! You will never guess. Georgiana brought her herbal, and we found the flower of forgiveness growing all around us here! The church-steeples!"

Elizabeth saw Darcy lifting his arms with an odd look in his eyes and became breathless. However, he immediately recovered himself when Bingley climbed the rise and joined him to look at the pages of the herbal, which explained that the botanical name of church-steeples was agrimony.

Elizabeth descended the hill alone. Something had been about to happen, but she was not certain what. *Did he take my jest seriously? Was he going to dance with me? Where everyone could see?*

Darcy was discomfited by his near breach of conduct. He was certain, from the glimpse she had into his unguarded eyes, that she had read his thoughtless impulse. *How in God's name shall I get through a month with her under my roof?*

WHEN SHE WAS BACK ON the roadside of Arbor Low, Elizabeth saw Mr Gardiner lifting a picnic hamper from the carriage. She returned to help her aunt set out the midday repast. A blanket was laid on the ground, but when the others returned, no one was inclined to sit.

For his part, Darcy pursued Mrs Gardiner, who had found a tree stump in the shade. "Mrs Gardiner, I am intrigued with your portrait of your niece. What is your intention for it?"

"It is the second in a series of three. I took a likeness of Lizzy along the banks of your trout stream yesterday."

"And the third?"

Mrs Gardiner became enigmatic. "I do have an idea for it, sir, but more I will not say."

Darcy was fixed with a desire to obtain the drawings but it would be an insult to Mrs Gardiner to offer for their purchase, and he suspected she would judge him both condescending and improper. Indeed, he saw himself so, but he coveted them nonetheless.

Mrs Gardiner watched Darcy with a keen interpretation of his thoughts. She took pity on him a little. "I have not really answered your home question, have I, Mr Darcy? Because Elizabeth and I shall be at Pemberley for your sister's birthday, we have decided to give her the triptych if you will direct me to a framer when the works are ready. I have until the seventeenth of the month?"

"Yes, madam, that is correct. I can supply you with the name of an excellent craftsman just outside Lambton. He is a young man but quite adept —keeps the trumpery to a minimum."

"I thank you, sir." Mrs Gardiner nodded as Darcy turned away. She smiled to herself. If the brother wheedled one of the pictures from the sister, it was no concern of *hers*.

The party grew drowsy as they returned to Pemberley with full bellies and their minds occupied with ancient ceremonies and rituals imagined at Arbor Low. They were assorted in the carriage in an order different than they had entered it, and although Darcy and Elizabeth were again seated opposite each other, they were away from the door side of the box. Darcy stretched his long legs as far as he could as he fell into a doze. His crossed ankles tucked amongst Elizabeth's boots. She was already nodding and did not consciously notice the intimacy.

Mr Gardiner awoke as the carriage made the wide turn onto the Pemberley carriage road. It was he who first noticed the position of Darcy's ankles against those of his niece. He leaned across a slightly snoring Bingley—with stems of agrimony in his lap—and lightly tapped Darcy upon his knee. Darcy started and opened his eyes, which happened to be positioned at the precise angle to see immediately where his feet were. He then glanced at Mr Gardiner, blushed, and set about untangling his feet from Elizabeth's. The toes of his boots caught in her hem and she awoke to a tugging of the petticoat under her gown. There was coolness on her calves as a mortified Darcy struggled to pull his feet back and sit up straight. He had a pleasing glimpse of pale pink stockings and looked shyly at her.

Mr Gardiner chuckled silently. Darcy leaned to give him a look of apology. The awakened Elizabeth kept her eyes turned towards the woods. The warm impression of Darcy's ankles against hers remained for several minutes after the offending appendages were removed. Her heart was thundering in her chest, and she found that, once again, he had stolen her breath. *How shall I survive a month here? It is too much folly. Even his most accidental touch burns me. Why does he not acknowledge my statement of love with the flowers? It is surely because he cannot propose again and will not give me false hope. Nothing makes sense between us.*

THE CARRIAGE ARRIVED AT PEMBERLEY's front door. Evening clothes had been delivered for the Gardiners and Elizabeth from the inn, and the ladies were shown the rooms they would inhabit when they arrived the next day. Georgiana's maid entered to help Elizabeth dress for dinner. Bingley and Georgiana went outside to search for more agrimony now that they knew what it signified. Assuming the ladies would rest and dress, Darcy went to the stables to see the two colts born the week before.

Elizabeth's hair was being styled when she heard a tap at the door. It was her aunt, who had not yet donned her evening gown. "Lizzy, I have had it from the housekeeper that we are two hours from dinner. We are meant to be resting because we are dainty." Her eyes danced with mischief. "I have a very particular idea for your last portrait and I would steal you away when you are ready."

The maid stepped away from the dressing table, revealing Elizabeth's hair beautifully dressed with fresh flowers—tufts of honeysuckle the maid used under orders from Georgiana—with three glossy ringlets left loose that bounced as she turned to her aunt. Elizabeth seemed aglow, almost bridal in her radiance.

"Lizzy, child! I have *never* seen you lovelier. Hold that expression if ever you can!"

Mrs Gardiner led her niece to the portrait gallery. There she positioned Elizabeth turned at profile toward the picture of Darcy.

"Aunt, might I hold some flowers?" Elizabeth asked when she saw what Mrs Gardiner was about.

"That is a happy thought, my love. You know a little of the gardens here. What would suit you?"

"Red chrysanthemums. They are in the cutting garden. Mrs Reynolds will know where." *I will try once more.*

Mrs Gardiner disappeared, giving Elizabeth the opportunity to picture Darcy's reaction to seeing so explicit an expression of the depth of her regard when the portrait was unwrapped. *This exceeds dignity, but what else am I to do? This will be a most artless work of art.* Her aunt returned, having encountered Grayson who would pass the request to Mrs Reynolds.

A quarter of an hour later, when Mrs Reynolds took the half dozen stems to the gallery, she found Mrs Gardiner seated on one of the tufted benches with her drawing board upon her knee. Before her stood Elizabeth in her pale yellow evening gown, perfectly still and lost in admiration of the painting labelled *Fitzwilliam George Darcy, 1805.* The flowers were handed to Elizabeth, who unselfconsciously brought them to her bosom. Mrs Reynolds looked over Mrs Gardiner's shoulder.

"May I?" she asked.

"Certainly. With four children and an inquisitive husband, I am now quite accustomed to an audience as I work." Mrs Gardiner's eyes did not leave her subject.

Mrs Reynolds gasped, "How beautiful!" The angle caught Elizabeth's profile, chin up, gazing at Mr Darcy. Enough of his portrait was included as to leave no doubt of what it was by the stance of his legs and riding boots. As Mrs Reynolds watched, Mrs Gardiner made a rough addition of Elizabeth's hands and flowers.

"You work wonderful quick, ma'am," Mrs Reynolds remarked. "Is this picture for my master?"

"Oh no!" exclaimed Mrs Gardiner. "It is for Miss Darcy. For her birthday."

Mrs Reynolds blushed a little, vexed with herself for her initial assumption. "Of course. Presumptuous of me." She muttered under her breath in the local Derbyshire dialect, "Art a balmpot—tow'd woman…" ("Silly old woman.")

Without a turn of her head but with an indulgent smile, Mrs Gardiner replied in the same vernacular, "Thad no need to bother thysen." ("Do not trouble yourself.")

Elizabeth turned to look at them.

Mrs Reynolds was surprised. "You're from county Derby, ma'am?"

"Indeed, yes, Mrs Reynolds. I had the good fortune to live in Lambton from the ages of four to eighteen. Very happy years. I was sorry to leave, but of course, if my family had not flit to London, I would not have met my dear husband."

Mrs Reynolds chuckled. "Well then, I had best mind my mutterings during your visit since another besides the master will be able to decipher me." She smiled and gave a bobbed curtsy of respect, as much as her old knees would allow, and left the gallery humming.

"Isn't she marvellous, Aunt?" Elizabeth sighed as she returned to her pose.

"A treasure. The new mistress of Pemberley will be lucky to have her and to be already so well ensconced in her good graces." Mrs Gardiner let the implication of her words sink in without further comment.

Elizabeth slowly met her aunt's eyes with a glowing smile. "Now hold that smile, Lizzy, and turn it to the portrait."

Thursday, 30 July

THE DARCY CHAISE AND FOUR collected Elizabeth and Mrs Gardiner from the Rose and Raindrop Inn the next day at noon. Mr Gardiner had departed for London two hours earlier in his own coach after a jovial and fond farewell. In a month's time, he would meet the Darcy coach in Oxford and transport his family home.

As the chaise was loaded, Darcy arrived on horseback and rode escort to the guests. Georgiana met the coach as it arrived. Darcy excused himself to meet with his steward, and Georgiana took Elizabeth on a more detailed tour of the house as Mrs Gardiner rested. Her weariness was a ruse to return to the portrait gallery to improve her reproduction of the lower left corner of the painting of Darcy.

Elizabeth stepped briefly into the bedchamber that was to be hers. An addition had been made to it. The table next to the window with the wonderful view now held a bowl of fresh roses of mixed colours, all of them open. She stared at it. *Did Mr Darcy place those here? Surely not. He would not make such a presumption. Perhaps he would. It is his house. Has he been in this room where I have dressed? The notion seems so intimate.* She grew flustered. She never would forget the meaning of open roses. *He still loves me, but what does he mean by it?*

A tap on the door made her jump as she heard Georgiana call, "Elizabeth?"

Elizabeth was blushing as she turned, and Georgiana realised the cause. "Aren't they lovely? That is every open rose my brother could find on the whole estate. Come, I want to show you around the house."

Georgiana shared with Elizabeth her favourite rooms of Pemberley. Elizabeth wandered in awe through the conservatory of tropical flowers, which had been tended by Lady Anne Darcy. They looked into the first floor music room where Georgiana spent hours at practice. Elizabeth asked to see the library, which was entered down the hall from Darcy's study.

It was a perfect summer day, and Elizabeth asked if they might walk outside. Georgiana suggested they visit the stables and kennels. Elizabeth was delighted. She loved dogs and always thought it hard Mrs Bennet would not allow them into the house as other neighbourhood gentry did. Georgiana informed her that Darcy was forever bringing members of his hunting pack inside to sit with him in the evenings. She suspected, but could not confirm, that he even allowed a favoured bitch to sleep on his bed, as she had once overheard chambermaids complaining of dog hair on the master's winter counterpane.

Although Elizabeth could barely sit a horse, it was a pleasure to feed them treats, and she was charmed by the two colts born just the week before to different mares on the same day.

When they returned to the house, they were met by Darcy dressed for dinner. Georgiana checked her little pocket watch with alarm. "I am so sorry, Brother. I was having such a good time with Lizzy! We went to the stables and kennels. I showed her where the library is, and we spent a long while in the conservatory." Georgiana endeavoured to cast Elizabeth a sidelong glance. "She loved it so much; I thought I might have to drag her out of it." Elizabeth smiled at her attempt to be teasing, much to Georgiana's relief.

Darcy had longed to show Elizabeth the library himself and could not mask his annoyance. He took in a deep breath as he attempted to alter his grumpy-brother face, reminding himself that, in the eyes of the world, Elizabeth was Georgiana's guest, not his. "Cook will not be happy, Georgie, unless you can dress in fifteen minutes. I know for a fact, you cannot."

Georgiana grabbed Elizabeth's hand. "He has thrown down the gauntlet, Lizzy!" They ran down the hall, with Georgiana giggling like a mad thing.

After dinner and a harp recital by Georgiana, the ladies withdrew to their bedchambers. Darcy and Bingley sat in the study. Bingley was unusually quiet, although he fidgeted over the book he was reading. Darcy did not pretend to any concentration of attention and gave himself over to musing as he stared at the fire. Sometime the next day, Jane Bennet would arrive, and knowing Bingley's impulsiveness, Darcy assumed a proposal could happen anytime thereafter. Once Bingley and Jane were betrothed, Darcy could see no impediment, other than Elizabeth's reticence, to renewing his addresses or at least making it known to her that he considered their acquaintance to have progressed to a courtship.

Darcy reviewed Elizabeth's behaviour since their exchange of flowers. Clearly, she was pleased when they met at the church in Lambton. She seemed to respond best when his actions differed from her expectations. He was reminded of her flirtatious behaviour at Arbor Low, which had very nearly made him forget himself. Those closest to her believed her to be in love with him or at least disposed to now think well of him, and yet she held back.

It is true, I have not said *I still love her, but the flowers were explicit. Even*

today, she finds a bouquet of open roses in her bedchamber. Her bedchamber.
She is here. Elizabeth Bennet is my guest. She sleeps next door to Georgie. Does
she read herself to sleep? Yes, she would. Did I tell her she might use the library?
Oh, yes, I did, at dinner. Anytime…I told her to use it anytime, day or night.
What if I found her there? Would she make a confession to me? No, I must say
it. I must speak the words first before she will. There is some lack of faith in me
that I must overcome before she will speak. Elizabeth is more like Jane than she
thinks. When it comes to the point, she does not wish to be caught vulnerable,
so I must not be missish.

Bingley stood. "I am too excited for anything, Darcy, even to be good
company. I shall take a little port and go to bed."

Darcy glanced up. "Tomorrow night you will be in my shoes, Bingley:
under the same roof as the woman you love."

"You forget Netherfield when Jane was ill. I have faced these demons before."

Darcy was annoyed with himself to be selfishly mired in his own turmoil
once again. "Of course, Bingley. Stupid of me… Perhaps tomorrow night I
will be too exhausted not to sleep, but I will sleep very ill tonight."

"Darcy! You hound! Is the temptation so great? This does not bode well
for your gentlemanly reputation." Bingley slapped Darcy upon the shoulder
as he turned to leave.

Darcy stood and chuckled. "I am a pitiful thing, Bingley. When I am
realistic, I hold onto a tremulous hope, but with her here, my fancy runs
away with me."

"Steady on, Darcy!" Bingley laughed as he left.

Darcy paced slowly in front of the fire. He knew the view from the windows of the room assigned to Elizabeth. She would see down to the river,
beyond the formal watercourse near the house. Would the river's wildness
call to her in the morning? Or would she climb the hill behind the house to
take in the view? In Hertfordshire, she wandered farmland and lanes, but
at Rosings Park, she had chosen the shaded glades rather than traversing
the open meadows. *But of course, that was to avoid the prying eyes of my aunt.*
He could imagine her wandering his walled gardens, the kitchen gardens,
the herbs and roses, and his mother's flowers. Perhaps she would find the
Arboretum planted by his father with its rare trees and odd foreign shrubs.
The point is, if I do not see her leave in the morning, how will I find her? "God
in heaven," he muttered aloud. *Why does Pemberley have to be so damn big?*

he wondered for the first time in his life.

Darcy exited his study and looked beyond the entrances to the largest drawing room and dining room, past the music room used for entertaining. The hall extended to Georgiana's end of the house, where he, too, had slept before becoming master. He had thought to put Elizabeth in his old room but decided it would be better to house her in a room closer to Georgiana. He told himself the two new friends might sit up late chatting as ladies liked to do, and it would not be wise to have Elizabeth wandering Pemberley late at night trying to find Georgiana's room.

His feet, unbidden, guided Darcy down Georgiana's hall. There was candlelight under his sister's door at the far end. He stopped some feet from Elizabeth's room and crossed the hall to view the space under the door. Yes, candlelight. As he watched, the door opened, and he held his breath. He tucked himself into a doorway insufficient to the task of hiding him. *What if she makes for the library? She will certainly see me.*

It was Georgiana. She closed Elizabeth's door, glanced down the hall absently and turned towards her room. Suddenly, she stopped, turned back and, without looking at her brother's face, approached him and took his arm. Saying nothing, with only a sardonic smile upon her lips, Georgiana escorted him to the end of the hall and the stairway landing that led to the public rooms. He did not resist.

"Thank you, Georgie," Darcy whispered when she released his arm. "Thank you for protecting my virtue." He smiled and kissed her forehead.

"Hmm, yes, well…and Lizzy's. It is going to be a long month if you cannot control yourself on the first night."

"I only came to see her door—to make sure nothing was amiss." Darcy's whisper was distinctly defensive.

"Perhaps we would have done better to put her on the guest floor, but we cannot make the change now. How would it look?"

"You are perfectly right. I shall regulate myself better, Georgie; really, I shall."

"See that you do, or neither of us will get a wink of sleep the entirety of August."

Georgie had turned away when Darcy blurted, "Are you not at least going to tell me what you were speaking of together?"

His sister turned back with a withering stare. She accompanied the expression with a stern shake of her head.

Chastened, Darcy walked to his dressing room.

ELIZABETH SPENT A FITFUL NIGHT but put it down to the first attempt at sleep in a different bed and her excitement over Jane's pending arrival. She awoke early and dressed quickly, foregoing a corset and donning a light cotton walking gown with her boots. She pinned her night braid upon her head and fluffed the curls around her face before tying a bonnet in place. She carried a little watch borrowed from Georgiana, so she would know when to return for a bath and breakfast.

Although the whole of Pemberley's woods was a wonderful mystery to be solved in the coming month, Elizabeth set out to find a few paths Jane might enjoy. Jane was not so prodigious a walker as her sister, but Elizabeth entertained the fanciful notion that she might find some romantic wayside where Bingley would be moved to propose if Jane would steer him thence. Wondering whether there was a path through the woods to the spot where she had first seen Pemberley, Elizabeth headed Northwest, passing over the lawn where she and Darcy had unexpectedly met ten days earlier.

Her thoughts of that happy meeting, or so it now seemed in hindsight, caused her to begin humming and increase her pace. That the meeting had been alarming and awkward was something she meant to forget as soon as possible. If she and Darcy ever did unite in marriage, that day would always be a holiday in her heart.

By the time she disappeared into the shrubbery, she was skipping and soon was running along a gently rising path. It forked downward to the stable yard, but she continued upward until she was above a hidden pond and could look back at Pemberley awakening. She stopped to gather her breath, and as she watched, a handsome riding horse was led towards the house. Georgiana mentioned she might ride early. Two gardeners with tools in their carts laughed along the path bordering the watercourse and disappeared to the south. A young man with a pack of foxhounds following him ran out to exercise them. Georgiana emerged in her riding habit, and she was helped onto the horse. She rode away, disappearing around the far end of the manor. Two chatting kitchen maids entered the house with baskets of freshly gathered eggs. Men on foot emerged and receded.

Pemberley was a veritable beehive. Elizabeth was fascinated. Of all this she might have been mistress.

DARCY STOOD WITH HIS MORNING coffee in hand. The night had offered him little sleep. Elizabeth's nearness would be a trial. It was vexing that she could exit to the outside from any of ten doors, only three of which Darcy could see from his balcony. He believed he was dressed early enough to intercept Elizabeth's walk and was thus dismayed when he looked to the north and saw a flash of pale green gown and bonnet plunging out of sight. *So early!* "Damn!" he cursed aloud.

"Sir?" His valet stepped towards him.

"It is nothing, just an opportunity I let slip. It is nothing."

Darcy's valet knew full well when the master said, "It is nothing," twice —or more—the issue at hand was not nothing.

"May I be of any assistance, sir?"

Darcy handed him his empty cup. "No. No, thank you. It is an opportunity that will likely present itself again."

"Very good, Mr Darcy." Garrick left the room.

Where is she going? Maybe she will find the pond, but it is not far, and she would not tarry there if she means to exercise. He smiled to himself. *She is no doubt running by now.*

WHEN DARCY JOINED HIS GUESTS in the breakfast room, Elizabeth was wearing a fresh gown, and Georgiana's maid had dressed her hair. The tantalizing clean scent of lavender floated to Darcy's nose as he asked, "You have already walked this morning, Miss Elizabeth? What did you see?"

They were standing side-by-side at the breakfast arrayed on a sideboard. She lowered her voice. "You will think I am a foolish creature, Mr Darcy, and I daresay not for the first time, but I went in search of a romantic place where a gentleman might propose if a lady were to lead him there." Her sidelong glance was full of merriment.

Darcy inhaled sharply. His heart gave one strong beat and seemed to stop. *She is speaking of Bingley and Jane. You know she is, Darcy. She is not speaking of you.* He swallowed and replied, "And you were successful?"

"Oh, indeed. I am quite spoilt for choice."

Darcy watched as Elizabeth helped herself to several kinds of fruit, bread and jam.

"But I own, I was more intrigued by watching the big house awaken. It was a remarkable sight to see everyone going about their tasks. Other than as regards a certain man whom I shall not name, your father must have been a keen judge of character, Mr Darcy, and so must you be."

"Am I?"

"You must be. You do not supervise each task directly. That is not possible. You must have entrusted authority very well to overseers who organise the work. Everyone I saw seemed purposeful, some even quite happy—not a querulous face in the crowd. It does you credit." She smiled up at him and turned away, seating herself at the table.

Darcy stared after her. Was there ever a visitor to Pemberley who would notice such a thing? No woman guest setting foot on the estate gave consideration to its efficient function. Darcy was used to compliments on the beauty of the house, his possessions and the grounds, but never had he been extolled as the master who chose the staff who had the running of it as their charge. He was flattered for his looks and fashionable dress, for his dry wit and generosity. Never had a lady praised him as an able manager of a complex estate, let alone made a careful observation of its workings.

Bingley looked up to see the strange aspect of Darcy's face. The man looked as if he had been slapped with a cold fish, but then broke into a wide grin as he gazed adoringly at the back of Elizabeth's head. Bingley smiled and tucked into his ham.

THE HOUSE WAS IN A nervous state for the rest of the morning. Outriders would arrive half an hour before the carriage bearing Miss Jane Bennet and the Gardiner children, but the Darcys and their guests found themselves at the north windows of the public rooms, peeking up the entry drive. A basket of agrimony was waiting for Bingley to strew at Jane's feet as she alit from the carriage. Elizabeth stole into the library but found herself pacing. She smiled, and had Darcy approached her then, she would have thanked him again and again for, as he had said, "righting a very great wrong."

At about three o'clock, she heard Darcy and Georgiana calling her name somewhat frantically. She stepped into the hall and could see Georgiana. "I am here! Is Jane arrived?"

"Oh, Lizzy!" Georgiana rushed to her and took her hands. "The outriders have come." The two friends ran to the front entrance of the house and crossed Darcy's path as he came up the kitchen stairs.

"I thought you might be with Mrs Reynolds. We could not find you, Miss Elizabeth!" Darcy's voice was nearly scolding.

"She was in the library, Brother, which is allowed our guests, is it not?" Georgiana explained before Elizabeth could defend herself.

Darcy pulled himself up straight. *Of course, she would go there! She does not have to tell us where she goes every minute. What is it about her that always makes me look ridiculous? You love her,* he answered himself. "I apologise, Miss Bennet. I must be as excited as everyone else." He bowed in a curt manner.

Elizabeth met his eyes and looked away with a vague smile. "There is no need to explain yourself, Mr Darcy. I understand you." She found herself wishing she had spent the time waiting with him. "You would not wish me to miss this arrival."

They emerged from the house to find Bingley and Mrs Gardiner already in attendance. It was only a few moments before they heard the carriage approach. Once it stopped, a footman opened the door, and the Gardiner children exited the coach in ascending order of age with the two little boys bursting in the direction of their mother, where they were embraced into her skirts. The second eldest daughter, Louise, bounced lightly down the step, joining her brothers in accepting a motherly hug. The last child, Alyse, now eleven years old, was becoming aware of her station as the eldest, and took her cousin Jane as her model in social deportment. Before joining her mother, she smiled at the other adults, hoping to give the appearance of a calm she did not feel.

Elizabeth watched the inside of the carriage as Bingley approached it. She could see Jane gathering toys and gloves and nervously avoiding looking out to those awaiting her. After spreading the yellow flowers of agrimony at the bottom of the carriage step, Bingley reached his hand into the carriage and murmured, "Miss Bennet?"

Jane looked at the hand waiting for hers. She had already been blushing for some miles, but now allowed herself a pleased smile. When she stepped from the carriage and looked into Bingley's face, Darcy repented again his stupidity. *Jane Bennet is radiant,* he observed. *How could I not have seen her affection for him? Is Bingley going to propose right here?* He glanced at Elizabeth, who was smiling knowingly at her sister. She turned to Darcy and raised an eyebrow as if to say, "See?" Darcy caught her gaze, closed his eyes and opened them again, shaking his head. *Yes, I was blind*, his look spoke to her. Elizabeth chuckled at him and turned to her aunt.

Bingley held Jane's gloved hand, blissfully unaware that she now stood on terra firma and no longer needed his assistance. "Why have you spread church-steeples at my feet, Mr Bingley?" Jane whispered.

"They are agrimony, the flowers that ask forgiveness, Miss Bennet. I have much for which to be forgiven." Bingley grew serious, and his eyes did not allow her gaze to wander from his.

"Do you? I am not aware of it, sir."

"Jane," Bingley breathed, and raised her hand to his lips.

Mrs Gardiner decided the lovers should have their necessary moment and herded her children to where Darcy stood with Georgiana. When Alyse looked into Mr Darcy's face as he stooped to be introduced, she became tongue-tied and giddy. She executed an unnecessarily deep curtsy and then wobbled upright. He was the handsomest man she had ever seen. "Why are you not married, sir?" she blurted.

"Oh, Alyse!" her mother cried in mortification. Georgiana giggled behind her hand.

"A truly discerning woman will not take me, Miss Gardiner." Darcy smiled. "I *have* tried."

"She must be abominably silly," Alyse pronounced scornfully, condemning Darcy's unknown deliverer of a refusal.

"And infernally correct in her judgment." He laughed at his own joke and did not see Elizabeth's look of alarm as she turned away.

Jane and Bingley became aware that the rest of the world existed. Jane saw her sister's face briefly etched in painful memory. "Lizzy?"

Elizabeth's countenance returned to a beaming welcome for her sister. They hugged for a long moment and then Elizabeth took Jane's hand to introduce her to Georgiana.

The attention of the Gardiner children moved en masse to their adored cousin Elizabeth, the boys pulling at her skirts and each girl taking a hand. Thus burdened, Elizabeth was the first to re-enter the house.

Darcy watched, his heart pounding, as Elizabeth disappeared from sight. *How at ease she looks, how natural with children.* He sighed, unaware that he had been observed by the ladies. Georgiana and Mrs Gardiner smiled to themselves.

Yes, he does *love her*, Jane Bennet confirmed, and she smiled, too.

Agrimony
"Gratitude, forgiveness"

Chapter 8

Elizabeth stood at the window of the second story dining room of Pemberley. She could hear Georgiana practicing her harp in the adjoining music room, but her manner of playing was haphazard for so accomplished a musician as if something was distracting her. The window where Elizabeth stood had been recommended during her first visit to Pemberley as having a lovely prospect, and indeed, she found it so on visiting it again. On this occasion, however, two people in the foreground gave the scene its interest.

Darcy strode up the corridor, following the sound of his sister's playing. *Where is everyone?* The footman at breakfast said Mr Bingley, Miss Jane Bennet and Miss Darcy had breakfasted early and gone walking, but clearly, from the sounds coming from the music room, Georgiana had returned. *Where is Elizabeth?* The footman further stated he had overheard Miss Darcy and Miss Elizabeth Bennet agree to practice duets in the morning, but Darcy heard only a harp. He peeked into the music room to see his sister finish a melody and set the sheet music aside. She half stood and looked out the nearest window. Sitting again, she began another piece. Darcy looked around —*no Elizabeth*. He withdrew without speaking.

Continuing up the hall, Darcy passed the next door, which opened into the formal dining room. It was decorated in shades of green and cream so the flash of pink he glimpsed arrested him. There, by the window, stood Elizabeth, lost in contemplation of the view.

She was wearing a new pink walking gown, a shade Darcy thought particularly flattering. It had arrived with Jane from Longbourn. Darcy did not know that it was two years old and much worn. Her mother had used fresh ribbon to rebind the neckline and cuffs of the pleated short sleeves, and inserted panels of lace under the raised waistline down over the skirt and attached at the hem. Mrs Bennet, although having an erratic and frivolous nature, and her housekeeper, Mrs Hill, were accomplished seamstresses and enjoyed the challenge of freshening the girls' gowns. It had distressed Mrs Bennet to think Elizabeth would be staying at Pemberley wearing nothing but gowns Mr Darcy had seen numerous times before.

Darcy stepped silently into the dining room. He gazed at her, marvelling again that she was there in his house, staying as his guest. She toyed with the garnet cross at her neck, and the corner of her bottom lip was caught by her teeth in a considering pose. *She is lovely*, he sighed to himself. He took a deep breath and went to her.

Elizabeth heard footfalls when Darcy's booted feet stepped off the carpet and onto the wooden floor. She glanced at him, blushed and smiled, nodding toward the window. "Look," she whispered, although the people she was watching were in no danger of hearing anything she said. Darcy stood next to her and followed her gaze.

Bingley and Jane were standing nearly toe-to-toe, profiled on the path next to the long watercourse some 50 feet from the house. Jane was looking into Bingley's face and he was speaking most earnestly. Darcy glanced at Elizabeth. She was luminous; her eyes alight with hope and love for her sister.

"Could he be proposing?" Elizabeth murmured excitedly.

"How long have they been there?" Darcy asked. He filled his lungs with the scent of lavender as he stood next to her, longing to take her hand at that tender moment.

"I have utterly lost track of the time. I even have to remind myself to breathe," she said in a lowered voice. She chuckled at herself and looked up at Darcy. *Perhaps this will prod you, sir...* she mused. *But how could it? Even with his improvements in civility, that is asking too much of any man's pride. Now that I love him, I must accept how I have insulted and hurt him in a way quite likely to persist, even if he professes with flowers some fondness for me still.*

Her smile faded as she acknowledged the regard she now had could never to be returned in equal measure, and she looked away.

Darcy noticed this change in demeanour and misread her emotions. "I cannot help but apologize again, Miss Elizabeth. It was my selfish action that caused this much-hoped-for event to occur months later than it should have done."

Elizabeth's eyes returned to her sister and Bingley. She did not respond to Darcy's apology. In truth, she wished he would cease apologizing. He was now making amends for his prior actions, which bespoke his regrets well enough, and she wished to dwell on the past only as it gave her comfort. Nothing she had ever said to Fitzwilliam Darcy prior to her present visit to Derbyshire gave her any pleasure in remembrance. *Now I am in love with him when he can no longer be in love with me. Oh, what a foolish business love is.*

Darcy and Elizabeth stood side-by-side, not speaking, until Bingley took one step back from Jane, held out his hand and fixed upon her a luminous smile full of relief and joy.

How easy it must be to propose when one knows one will be accepted, Darcy thought. He refrained from snorting derisively at himself, *perhaps as easy as blindly assuming acceptance where failure would be obvious to a less arrogant man.*

Jane took Bingley's hand. It was clear to Elizabeth and Darcy that she was nodding, grinning and saying, "Yes!" repeatedly.

An "Oh!" escaped Elizabeth, her rapid breathing audible to Darcy.

They watched as Bingley lovingly held Jane's hand to his chest and embraced her with his other arm. "Oh, my! Jane!" Elizabeth looked down, blushing.

Darcy was dumbfounded at his own response. His eyes stung. Never had he been more desirous of taking Elizabeth into his arms, yet he could not look away from Jane and Bingley.

Elizabeth took a deep breath to steady herself. She felt as though heat were pouring off Darcy and washing over her. She was aware of the tension in the air. As she and Darcy watched, Bingley bent his head and kissed a suddenly solemn Jane. The kiss lasted only a few seconds; then they smiled at each other and were soon laughing and talking again.

Elizabeth drew in another deep breath. She turned to Darcy, tears poised in the corners of her eyes. "Thank you, Mr Darcy. Thank you."

He smiled crookedly and pulled a handkerchief from his pocket. "I believe you are about to need this," he whispered tightly, handing it to her. She took it, nodding. Darcy expected her to dab at the corners of her eyes but instead she pressed the white handkerchief with the Darcy crest against her chest.

Elizabeth still held his eyes. They looked at each other without reserve for a long moment. She seemed about to say something, hesitated, then bravely continued, "I am proud of you, Fitzwilliam Darcy. I do not care what they say; you are no Charles Bingley to be sure, but nonetheless you are a very good sort of man."

A single tear crept down her cheek, yet she still teased him. He closed his eyes, lowering his face, ready to meet the lips that so bewitched him. But with a whisper of slippered feet, she was gone.

"They are coming in! I must go to my sister..." Her words trailed behind as she ran from the room.

Darcy straightened, releasing a deep sigh—*that could have been another disaster!* He followed her from the room and down the hall to the stairs leading to the doors closest to Jane and Bingley, who were now walking hand in hand to the house. Darcy caught up to Elizabeth, and the sound of steps behind them announced Georgiana was following to congratulate them, wearing a jubilant smile.

Darcy flung open the doors, and Elizabeth burst across the path. Jane braced for the impact, but it was to Bingley that Elizabeth rushed, hugging him and kissing his cheek. She was laughing and in tears. "Thank you, Charles!" She had never called him by his first name before. "Thank you for loving my sister!" Elizabeth said the words softly, so only he and Jane could hear.

"What? Were you *all* watching?" Bingley laughed.

Darcy stood back and suffered, although a half smile emphasized his dimples. Georgiana danced past him to greet the newly betrothed couple. Elizabeth turned her affections to Jane. Darcy stayed withdrawn, watching. *If she will never have me, I shall never wed. I cannot imagine loving another like this.*

The Bennet sisters laughed and cried together with Bingley remaining in the thick of it. Darcy saw Elizabeth still held his handkerchief. Jane reached for it but Elizabeth stopped her.

"No, dear Jane, Mr Bingley must provide your hankies now. He keeps a pocketful. You shall not steal mine ever again!" Elizabeth chuckled and turned to catch Darcy's eye with an expression he had never seen her wear before. He thought it could be shyness.

She has forgiven me, to be sure, but can she ever love me? He returned her smile with one of equal warmth, nodded and then looked away.

"Did I not manage that rather well, Brother?" asked Georgiana as she took Darcy's arm. They turned back to the house. Ahead of them was Bingley with a joyful Bennet sister on either arm.

"*You* managed it? Impudent little gosling! How is it you deserve such praise?"

They stopped, and Darcy called ahead, "Bingley! Find Grayson and tell him to bring up a bottle or two of champagne. It is not too early in the day, is it?"

"Ha! Thank you, Darcy! I shall."

Georgiana leaned to her brother. "Yesterday afternoon, I suggested Mrs Gardiner take the children in the phaeton today to look at the upper lake. I told her, quite rightly as you will agree, that early in the day, the wading birds feed there and would be a delightful sight for the children. Then last evening, I invited Mr Bingley and Miss Bennet to walk with me early this morning to visit the stables and see the two new colts. Once we were walking, I remembered my engagement to practice duets with Elizabeth, although in truth, she and I had not fixed a time to meet. Thus were Mr Bingley and Miss Bennet finally left alone." Georgiana fixed her brother with a self-satisfied smile imparting her sense of accomplishment.

Darcy had to laugh. "My dear sister...I had no idea you had formed an interest in matchmaking."

"I seem to have a talent for it, although I do say it myself."

Elizabeth looked outside the receiving room where she stood with Jane to see Darcy laughing at his sister and giving her a genial hug with one arm about her shoulders. Georgiana was laughing, too, and Elizabeth smiled to see brother and sister so happy and at ease.

Darcy took his sister's hand and dragged her to the house, announcing as they entered, "Bingley, do you know my impudent—dare I say, impertinent —sister is taking the entire credit for this morning's achievements?"

Georgiana blushed.

"Is she? I do not recall her taking any part in my proposal. I spoke extemporaneously, and quite eloquently I thought—given that I met with success..." Here he took Jane's hand and tucked it into the crook of his elbow. Darcy marvelled; *Jane Bennet appears utterly besotted.* "…and was not prompted by Georgiana in any way."

"That is the point, Bingley." Darcy smiled. "She contrived *not* to be with you."

Bingley feigned surprise at Georgiana. "Did you? Are you so little to be trusted as a chaperone?"

"I fear it is true." Georgiana maintained a blushing smile. "When I think two people belong together, it appears I have it in me to become very helpful." Georgiana then fixed a meaningful look at her brother and stepped away so she was no longer standing between him and Elizabeth.

Elizabeth was now the one blushing. She and Darcy smiled tentatively at each other. *There is that delightful shy smile again. Does Georgiana know something I do not?*

Servants entered with champagne and glasses, and Georgiana purposefully picked up the bottle and began removing the muselet. Darcy went to assist her and found she needed no aid. "What a day of discovery this is! My sister is revealed as a matchmaker, and now I find she has a more than passing familiarity with the workings of a champagne bottle."

The bottle exhaled its cork with a throaty pop into Georgiana's hand. Her incredulous brother asked, "Where did you learn this skill?"

"Whilst staying with our uncle at Matlock House when you were at Netherfield last autumn. Cousin Richard taught me. I can open champagne with his sword, too." She raised her brows at her brother.

"Some guardian he is. First my aunt is feeding ladies port, and now I learn my cousin is teaching you such skills—my own sister, not yet seventeen —as to make you proficient at uncorking champagne. And am I to suppose you have tasted it?" Darcy laughed.

"Trust me, Brother; I would not have been prevailed upon to master the technique without reaping the rewards."

Elizabeth, Bingley and Jane formed a festive group around the Darcys until each had a full flute of champagne. Darcy cleared his throat in preparation for a toast.

"First, of course, I should like to raise my glass to the future Mr and Mrs Bingley, but, more importantly, I drink to the man himself, my friend, Charles Bingley, who knows a great deal more about love than I do. Miss Bennet, I believe you will never want for a better husband." He smiled and lifted his glass, but his voice contained a strain of melancholy quite plainly heard by everyone.

The morning was fair, and the little group wandered out to the lawn and back in again. A second bottle was at the ready, but Darcy did not let it be opened as he did not want to encourage Georgiana. Elizabeth and Jane watched anxiously for the return of their aunt and little cousins. They were overflowing with desire to share the good news.

Darcy and Georgiana left the party to find Mrs Reynolds to order a fine repast for dinner. When they returned to Jane and Bingley, Elizabeth was gone. Jane saw Darcy's eyes searching the room. "Lizzy feels ready for a walk. Too much excitement, I think. She has gone for her bonnet and spencer, but she will return here before going out."

"So this is her regular habit, Miss Bennet?" asked Georgiana. "She takes a long walk every day?"

"Oh, yes. Lizzy always has from the age of twelve or so. The exercise seems to soothe her," Jane replied.

"I have heard rumours, Miss Bennet, that your sister has been known to run, just for the exertion of it. Do you know if it is true?" Darcy asked with a twinkle in his eye.

Jane gave him an appraising look before answering, "Indeed, sir, I have heard those rumours myself." More she would not say, but she directed at Darcy a rather sly smile that made Bingley laugh.

"Surely, Darcy, you must know these two sisters will never betray each other," Bingley said.

"No, and I would not have it any other way, but please, Miss Bennet, do not assume any disapprobation on my part. I find your sister uniquely fascinating; that is all. She is a most interesting creature."

"Where is Elizabeth?" Georgiana asked, entering the room.

Jane answered, "She is fetching a bonnet and putting on her walking boots, I expect. She is missing her daily walk."

"Perhaps I should join her, and then she and I can practice our music when we return."

"Perhaps Miss Elizabeth wishes to stroll alone, gosling." Darcy smiled.

Georgiana smiled enigmatically. "Perhaps...but perhaps I might come upon her unexpectedly if I take a walk. Perhaps my brother might join me?"

"Georgie..." Her brother used his grumpy-brother face.

Ignoring him, Georgiana said merely, "I shall await her pleasure here, then decide if I want a walk or not."

Chinese aster
"I partake of your sentiments"

Chapter 9

Grayson, the Pemberley butler, noticed Miss Elizabeth Bennet ascending the stairs to the guest rooms with her usual skipping step. She always had a smile for him, and he relished the lightness of heart that attended her and those in her company, most notably his master and Miss Darcy. Even Mrs Reynolds seemed to like her—not, of course, that it mattered a jot what the opinions of the servants were. Still, Grayson felt a pleasant air of expectancy throughout Pemberley since the arrival of Miss Elizabeth in the neighbourhood, as if a question was about to be settled very much to Pemberley's benefit. As he stood musing in the entry hall, he heard the approach of a rider at the front door and so was not surprised to hear a knock.

An express letter was presented to him from Miss Mary Bennet of Longbourn, addressed to both Miss Bennets. He stood a moment and decided to take it to Miss Elizabeth in her room since he was not precisely certain where Miss Jane could be found. Just as he started up the stairs, he heard rapid light steps descending, and Elizabeth reappeared.

Grayson turned with her, clearing his throat, and addressed her when they reached the marble entry floor. "Ahem, Miss Bennet. An express has just arrived for you and your sister from Miss Mary Bennet. I was just coming up to deliver it."

"Oh! You are very kind, Grayson. Thank you." Elizabeth stepped to the square table at the centre of the hall, carved from the swirling burl of oak taken from a fallen tree in the Pemberley woods at the time the house was built. She laid down her summer gloves and parasol. Grayson withdrew, and Elizabeth tore open the letter, already feeling some disquiet. She was right to feel the stirrings of alarm as she read:

30 July, 1812

To my dear sisters,

Our father has asked me to write with haste, and we are certain what must be reported will cause you great shock and distress, but it cannot be helped nor delayed until your return. I shall write it all as quickly as I can, and we can more thoroughly discuss the moral and ethical implications of what has occurred when you return home, which we bid you do with all possible speed.

Very early yesterday morning, we were the recipients of an express from Colonel Forster, followed some hours later by the arrival of the man himself. The news was of such an alarming nature that our mother has taken to her bed, and my father has left for London this morning to enlist the assistance of our uncle.

It appears our sister Lydia has either been abducted by, but more likely has eloped with, George Wickham. Most alarming, there is no evidence of them having gone to Scotland. Their trail stops in London, hence our father's haste to get there and begin a search. Lydia left a letter for Mrs Forster, which our father has allowed me to see, and I trust, like me, the two of you will be most shocked when you read it. Her waywardness is appalling to say the least.

The facts, as we know them, are that they left Brighton in the dead of night Tuesday, and when Lydia was discovered missing yesterday morning, The colonel was able to track them as far as Clapham but no further. They travelled by post from there into London, but the post made many stops in town, and the colonel was not successful in finding where they had disembarked before he continued on to Longbourn. He found no evidence they have married, and Mr Denny, when asked about the matter, said he never heard Wickham utter a flattering word towards Lydia nor mention any special regard for her, saying only that she was the kind of girl it would "not be necessary to marry to obtain her charms, meagre as they may be." Is this not deplorable?

Mr Denny said Wickham showed no interest in Lydia until she bragged at a card party one evening that her sister Elizabeth was visiting Lambton, and Uncle Gardiner suspected Mr Darcy of some partiality for her. The news quite captured Wickham's attention, and he set about, to use Mr Denny's dangerous word, "seducing" our poor sister.

There is much more to tell, but the particulars can surely wait until your arrival. Please encourage our Aunt Gardiner to come with you as Mama is a trial, and Kitty does not have the patience to sit with her much.

Please send an express when you leave Derbyshire, letting us know when we may expect you, although I know travelling with the children may slow your pace.

Praying for your safe journey,

Your loving sister,
Mary Bennet

Elizabeth stared at the letter—*Lydia, Wickham, not necessary to marry, no evidence they have married, seducing*—until her eyes burned. She leaned heavily with one arm on the table, trying not to shed tears caused by the perfidy of George Wickham. She was livid, seeing quite clearly Wickham's actions as an attack on Darcy, and perhaps even herself, for what he would selfishly see as her defection. The leaves of the letter fluttered to the table. Elizabeth's right hand shaded her eyes.

"Elizabeth?"

It was the startled and concerned voice of Darcy, who had been looking for her, hoping he might join in her walk with Georgiana. He had reason to think Georgiana would mysteriously vanish, leaving him alone with his love on the paths of Pemberley. His little hope had been rekindled by Elizabeth's shy smiles. He prayed one accepted proposal might encourage the furtherance of another.

Elizabeth lowered her hand from her eyes and turned to him. Upon seeing his face, now so dear to her, the tears gave way, and other ramifications of the present calamity crowded her mind. *Lydia is in the most dire straits, and all I can think is I have lost him...poor stupid Lydia, a pawn in a game not of her making.* Elizabeth had tucked Darcy's handkerchief up the wrist cuff of her spencer and she now made use of it, turning from him.

"Elizabeth! What has happened?" Darcy's voice was quiet and earnest. He longed to touch her, to turn her around to face him. *If only I could embrace her and absorb whatever is causing this anguish.*

"An express has arrived from Longbourn with the most dreadful news. I cannot imagine anything worse." She managed to choke out the words. "Jane and I and our aunt must leave at once." She finally turned and looked at Darcy. "Could you send a footman to retrieve my aunt and the children? Mary asks particularly that my aunt travel with Jane and me."

"Grayson!" Darcy called.

In scarcely a moment, the butler was in the hall. "Please send a footman to find Mrs Gardiner and the children."

"I have just seen them, sir. The phaeton is approaching on the lower river bridle path. They shall be here in a matter of minutes."

Darcy looked at Elizabeth to see if she had heard; she nodded.

"Meet the phaeton, will you? Servants can see to the children, but you must bring Mrs Gardiner here to Miss Elizabeth. And ask Miss Jane Bennet to join us. She is in the receiving room with my sister and Mr Bingley. Thank you, Grayson." Darcy spoke decisively, his eyes never leaving Elizabeth's face.

"Yes, sir." Grayson was gone in an instant.

"What has happened?" Darcy said the words again in a low voice.

Hanging her head, Elizabeth picked up the letter and handed it to him. "You and I know each other too well for me to keep this a secret, Mr Darcy. Please read it."

Darcy took the letter. She knew he had finished when he looked at her incredulously. "I am shocked, grieved."

"You asked me to keep your dealings with Wickham secret, and I have, but I should have spoken against him to my father when Lydia was invited to Brighton. I could have prevented this—I, who knew what he was. I warned father she was too impetuous and too young to take such a trip, but I was not explicit enough. Father would not have spread your business about, but he would have kept Lydia at home." Elizabeth started to cry again.

Darcy laid the letter upon the table and turned away. When he could manage his anger at Wickham, he said, "This is not your fault, Miss Bennet."

So now I am Miss Bennet again. This ends it. The love of my life ends here. Unaware of doing so, Elizabeth sank to the floor, her head resting on the barley twisted leg of the table. Her anger at her youngest sister and George Wickham, while profound, was undone by the depth of her own despair. She quietly sobbed into the handkerchief. It smelled mildly of sandalwood. *It is all of him I am ever to have.*

Darcy whirled around at the sound of her collapse. "Elizabeth!" He knelt next to her, taking her free hand. "This is an attack upon me by Wickham, nothing more. Surely you see that?" Her vacant nod did not reassure him. "You must not take the burden of this upon yourself. You will make yourself ill, and then what use will you be to your family? They need you."

And you, most certainly, do not. She looked at him with abject misery and whispered brokenly, "It seems I bring nothing but vexation to you, Mr Darcy."

His throat tightened, and he, too, could only whisper, "Elizabeth...I would not have you think so." *If only I could embrace her, I could drive away her fear, but it would be seen as taking an advantage. Even just saying her name is wrong of me. If Wickham walked through that door right now, I would cheerfully run him through.*

They heard footsteps. Elizabeth looked over Darcy's shoulder and saw Georgiana approach.

Elizabeth's eyes were wild when they returned to Darcy. "Please do not speak of this to Georgiana," she begged. "You must protect her from me, from my family. Take her away to her room until I am gone."

Darcy felt his heart break. *She still expects me to put my pride first, but I will not let George Wickham destroy my chance for love.* Darcy inhaled and gathered himself, shaking his head. "Protect her from *you*? Georgiana is strong. She can help you, Elizabeth."

Elizabeth looked into his eyes. *How many times must I ask his forgiveness before the well dries?* She looked down. Her head ached, and her only solace was the release of tears.

"Lizzy!" Georgiana reached them, and without hesitation, knelt beside her new friend and embraced her. "Lizzy, my god! What has happened?"

Darcy stood. *At least one Darcy is in a position to comfort her. Bless you, little gosling.*

"Help me get her to her feet," Georgiana ordered her brother.

Darcy bent, took Elizabeth's arm and reached behind her back, lifting her shoulders as Georgiana assisted him.

"Georgiana...I am sorry to be so silly. I am quite ashamed of myself."

Darcy picked up the letter. "Miss Elizabeth," he whispered, "I must tell her if you will not."

Elizabeth sniffed and straightened. She was clearing her throat to speak when Jane and Bingley entered the entry hall. Seeing them was another twist to her insides. Elizabeth gathered the pages of the letter and handed them to Jane. "Mr Darcy, may I speak privately to Georgiana in the drawing room?" Elizabeth asked.

"We shall all meet there, but I will await your aunt here and join you with her."

A gasp escaped Jane as she read, and she clutched Bingley's forearm. "Oh, my. Oh, no..." Jane sighed. She looked from Elizabeth's tearstained face to Bingley's concerned eyes and returned to Mary's words.

Georgiana offered her arm to Elizabeth, and they proceeded to the drawing room ahead of the others. "Lizzy, I heard you say I should be protected from you. How can that be?"

With a deep breath, Elizabeth gathered her strength to repeat the horrible news. "It seems Mr Wickham convinced my youngest sister, who is just turned sixteen, that he wished to elope with her. Of course, he wishes nothing of the kind. They are gone to London—are quite vanished—and have not married. Now my whole family must partake of her ruin. Oh Georgiana... even a man as good as your brother could not possibly countenance this." Elizabeth's eyes searched Georgiana's, fearing to witness the first signs of disapprobation and rejection. Instead, she saw concern and courage, and for the first time, she could see the strength of the brother in the set of the sister's jaw.

"I am shocked but somehow not surprised. It seems George Wickham will try anything to insult my brother. So he heard the news from your sister that you are here and attacks us again. Fitzwilliam said he tried to make an ally of you, and in addition to punishing my brother for his very existence, he strikes at you for what he sees as a betrayal. Oh yes, I can easily guess how he thinks—wretched man." Georgiana squared her shoulders. "What is being done?"

Elizabeth and Georgiana heard approaching voices from the hall. Darcy, Mrs Gardiner, Bingley and Jane entered the drawing room. Jane was crying quietly, but Mrs Gardiner was seething.

Elizabeth raised her voice a little so all could hear the answer to Georgiana's question. "My father is gone to London. He and Uncle Gardiner are to begin a search, although how they are to be found and how such a man is to be worked on, I hardly know."

Georgiana said aloud what Darcy was thinking, "Money."

Elizabeth looked alarmed, as did Jane, and their eyes met. "We have little in the way of financial benefit to offer a man of Wickham's vanity," Elizabeth spoke with irritation. "One might think our circumstances would have rendered Lydia safe. To say nothing of the fact she was staying in Colonel Forster's household. Oh, why did I not speak more forcefully to our father?" Elizabeth asked her sister.

"Because *I* advised you not to when you asked me, Lizzy. This is my fault," Jane said as if it should be obvious.

Darcy quietly marvelled at the ability of the two best Bennet sisters to play tug-of-war with blame that very clearly lay with him. It was then he determined to travel to London, and he would send an express immediately to Colonel Fitzwilliam, asking him to make inquiries in Brighton and meet at Darcy House as quickly as possible. Georgiana could see her brother's mind working and, if asked, would have explained his thoughts. Her blue eyes nodded into his brown ones, approving his unspoken plans.

"No, Jane. I *did* speak to our father, and I could and should have said more than I did." A new thought occurred to Elizabeth, and tears formed in her eyes as she turned to Bingley. "Charles," she stepped to him and took his free hand in hers. "I have no right to ask this of you, but you will honour your proposal to Jane, will you not? Please do not forsake her. You have only let Netherfield and so may let another house, far away, and take her where she is not known, where her sister's folly will not be so talked of." Elizabeth spoke slowly, fighting tears again. "Please."

Darcy had never felt more powerless. Had the letter arrived a few hours —or even a day—later, he, too, might be betrothed to a Bennet, and it would be his place to protect her. *Elizabeth is assuming the worst of me. She assumes I will forsake her. Does she truly know me so little, or is she merely too alarmed for reason?*

"Lizzy!" Both Bingley and Mrs Gardiner sought to quiet her. Bingley continued, "This nonsense of Wickham's does not prevent our wedding, and as soon as he has been apprehended and brought to whatever justice is appropriate, I will have the honour of marrying Miss Jane Bennet. I think I have amply proven my patient devotion." He smiled down upon Jane.

Georgiana extricated the Bennet sisters from Bingley's arms. "Come, I will help you prepare and gather the servants we need. My maid is an excellent packer." She looked over her shoulder at her brother. "Fitzwilliam, when I have the packing underway, I would speak with you."

Darcy nodded absently. "Yes, Georgie, at your service." He turned. "Mrs Gardiner, Bingley, might I have a word with you?"

Darcy's eyes followed Elizabeth's retreating form, his longing apparent. He hoped Elizabeth would turn back to him that he might nod encouragingly at her, but she did not. She exited the room with her head bowed, his handkerchief at her cheek. Was there any way to capture even a brief moment alone with her in the next fleeting hours as the Bennet sisters prepared to leave Pemberley?

Georgiana herded Jane and Elizabeth upstairs to their adjoining rooms, shouting orders to footmen and maids as if she were her brother. When Elizabeth and Jane's trunks were brought and they bent to their work, Georgiana excused herself. She had a suggestion about where Darcy should begin his search.

DARCY URGED MRS GARDINER AND Bingley to sit, but was himself too agitated for anything but pacing. "Mrs Gardiner, it is my intention to leave for London tomorrow and conduct my own search for Wickham. Sadly, I know him well enough to understand his ways. Lydia Bennet is not the docile little heiress about which his schemes usually pivot. To make such a grave step as to abduct her is a clear strike at me and also a certain declaration of his need to escape Brighton with debts heaped in his wake. If Lydia was in possession of sufficient pin money to afford their journey, it would have greatly enhanced her appeal, if only temporarily. When I am known to be in town, he will try to touch me for as much money as possible to buy Lydia's reputation.

"I also believe he feels some great defection by Miss Elizabeth and seeks to punish her. He will think if I am partial to her, the degradation of one Bennet will lower my estimation of all of them, and I will end my acquaintance with her. I fear Miss Elizabeth thinks the same."

Mrs Gardiner was quick to respond. "Mr Darcy, you are very kind to give such attention to a family to whom you owe nothing. If you do not involve yourself, perhaps this matter might be settled with less cost and in Lydia's favour. Perhaps it would be more prudent of you to send what information you have as to their whereabouts to my husband rather than proceed to London yourself."

"I am determined, Mrs Gardiner. I will contact my cousin Colonel Fitzwilliam. His regiment is also in Brighton, and he can make inquiries. Indeed, if he has heard of the matter, he will be doing so already. We will then meet at Darcy House, so any negotiation with Wickham may take place with as much foreknowledge as possible. Had I followed Bingley's excellent advice and exposed the man when he first arrived in Meryton, all this calamity would have been avoided."

"Mr Darcy, we must make allowances for the wickedness of Mr Wickham and the foolishness of Lydia. Let us put the responsibility where it belongs. This is their doing, not yours, sir."

"Of course, I cannot speak for your niece, ma'am, but I have known of Wickham's evil temperament since we were boys. He uses his false charm to draw people in until he either finds a way they may be of use or drops them as unimportant. No, Mrs Gardiner, I must put myself forward in this. I must make right where I have been wrong."

Mrs Gardiner looked into his eyes, observing his disquiet. Was his love for Elizabeth so profound that he would bear these mortifications to protect her and her family from disaster? She believed it was. "You will have to make this argument again, Mr Darcy, when you meet my husband and Mr Bennet in London. If you will pardon my saying it, I believe it is your regard for Elizabeth that forms some part of your motive here, and for that, let me express my gratitude."

Darcy started to speak, but Mrs Gardiner put up a hand. "Do not deny it, sir. I speak as I find."

Darcy was silenced.

Bingley spoke up. "How may I be of help, Darcy?"

"Bingley, do I presume too much to ask you to ride to Hertfordshire with the ladies? I would have them travel with the security of your presence. Elizabeth and Jane can ride in your carriage, and Mrs Gardiner and the children may go in one of mine. Let it be known Miss Bennet has accepted you, and you only await the settling of Lydia's affairs to begin your wedding plans. Jane will certainly need your support. Until matters are settled, both sisters may need some place to receive consolation, which you could provide at Netherfield."

Bingley nodded. "You are quite sure you will need no assistance in London?"

"I think you will better serve the Bennets in Meryton. Let something good be said of the family, not just vile gossip, which is, no doubt, already circulating." Darcy looked into the faces of Bingley and Mrs Gardiner. "And if you would both say nothing of my plans in London, I would be most grateful."

Both Bingley and Mrs Gardiner protested.

"No, no, I must insist." Darcy pursued his reasons aloud. "I do not wish to inspire hope as it may come to nothing. I cannot promise what may transpire with Wickham or even that I can find him. And more importantly, even should I succeed, I do not wish a certain lady's regard to be influenced by gratitude."

Mrs Gardiner said only, "I understand not wishing to stir unfounded hopes. I do *not* understand adding gratitude to 'a certain lady's regard.' I trust we shall have the opportunity to debate this further, Mr Darcy. For now, I must pack." She smiled knowingly into Darcy's eyes and dropped a quick curtsy, to which he responded with a respectful bow.

"Of course, Mrs Gardiner. Eh, Bingley," Darcy said, catching his friend's sleeve as he seemed inclined to follow Mrs Gardiner from the room. Bingley stopped and looked questioningly at Darcy. "You should send an express with Elizabeth's to get the servants into Netherfield. And I must ask a favour. I know Elizabeth is in a state of shock now. It had been my intention to propose to her once you and Jane were betrothed. I had even thought I might do so this afternoon. But it seems as if this catastrophe causes Elizabeth to question my regard. Could you, if the moment comes aright, perhaps let her know my feelings for her are as they have always been? I cannot imagine not loving her, Bingley. I have been at it nearly a year now and it has become my way of life. Keep me in her mind, won't you? I shall write you often. Please let her know you are getting word from me, and that

I mention her constantly, for I shall."

Georgiana entered the room in time to hear his last few sentences. "What nonsense you do talk! Of course she loves you."

"Georgie, you should know our plans. Bingley will depart today with Mrs Gardiner and the Bennets. I will leave tomorrow, so the Bennets will not know I am going to London."

"Mrs Younge!" Georgiana blurted and looked quite triumphant. "If you can take up her trail, I am sure she will lead you to Wickham, Brother."

"Of course! What a stroke of genius, Georgie! Last season, I heard she was keeping a boarding house and making every attempt at respectability. She should be easy to find."

"Shall I tell Jane and Elizabeth?" Bingley asked.

"No. She has no reason to help us and may prove recalcitrant. I pray you, Bingley, let the Bennets think me here. I could not bear to engender false hope in those tender hearts. But I have a little hope myself, at least." Darcy smiled at his sister.

Bingley winked and nodded. "I must pack." He left brother and sister alone.

"Georgie, since inspiration visits you today, can you contrive a way for me to see Elizabeth alone one more time before they leave? I...I would speak with her, to let her know my regard will not falter during this calamity."

"She will need someplace quiet to write her express to Longbourn. I shall suggest the library. If she is found there..." Georgiana did not need to finish. Her brother thanked her.

"Am I to accompany you to London? Since my suggestions prove of value?" Georgiana asked with enthusiasm.

"No, gosling, you must be kept well out of this. Mrs Annesley returns in a few days, you shall not be alone for long." Darcy's grumpy-brother face told her not to push the point.

"May I at least write to Elizabeth?" Georgiana asked.

Darcy considered this and then nodded. "You overflow with fine ideas today, Georgie. Please do write to her. She will be in turmoil, and it would be a good thing to remind her of her time here and to let her know she may always come back to Pemberley. You can keep the old place alive for her."

"You mean I will keep *you* alive for her. Of course, I will. She belongs here with you. But I do not understand why you will not tell her you intend to help."

"Georgie, it may take a great deal of money to settle this affair. Wickham strikes at us, but money will soothe him. There will be debts to be settled and perhaps a husband to be purchased for Lydia if Wickham will not have her, for who knows what we will find when they are discovered? The Bennets and Gardiners combined would be much stretched to meet such expenses, but for you and me, it is merely an annoyance and a few less Christmas presents. The harvest looks to be a good one, the sheep look well, and there are plenty of deer in the woods for our tenants, should the winter prove difficult. But I would not have a certain lady's acceptance of me proceed from gratitude. I would not have Elizabeth think I am buying her favour along with Lydia Bennet's reputation."

Georgiana mused a moment. "I have known Lizzy scarcely a fortnight, Fitzwilliam, but I believe you are in error about her feelings."

"I will know after I speak with her again."

Georgiana's face lit up. "Will you propose?"

"This is not a romance novel, Georgie. Now is not the time. But she needs to hear this affair is merely a trifling concern to me. It is her happiness that matters. I need to say it, to know I have said it, and hope she is not too distraught to listen."

THE LIBRARY AT PEMBERLEY STARTED its life as one large room with shelf-lined walls and broad windows along one side, looking into the cool forests stretching up the hills behind the manor. Stacks filled the open space. In old Mr Darcy's time, the books then overflowed into the small sitting room adjoining the original chamber. In the current Mr Darcy's relatively brief tenure as master, another spate of acquisition caused the library to spread further, and just the year before, modern titles insinuated themselves into a larger drawing room, which was now also lined with shelves. Taken en masse, it was quite possible for several people at a time to enter the library from any of six entrances, peruse the stacks, sit and read, write letters at one of a half dozen escritoires, and exit again without encountering one's fellows. At this time, however, such was not likely to be the case. Darcy knew Elizabeth was there, somewhere.

"Miss Elizabeth," Darcy began when he found her in front of a window, writing the express to Longbourn. He did not feign surprise, but she looked at him with some amazement.

She started to rise. "Mr Darcy!"

"Please, do not trouble yourself." He drew up an armchair and seated himself as she returned to a sitting position. She had been crying and looked as if, at the least agitation, she would do so again. "I will not distract you—I know you write to your family. Georgiana has told you we will write to Colonel Fitzwilliam to obtain more information if he can uncover anything we do not already know. If this concerns you, this spread of the terrible news, you must understand how the militia operates. Our cousin is a commanding officer equal to Colonel Forster. Aside from disgracing a young lady—which, sadly, soldiers sometimes do—Wickham has greatly dishonoured his commanding officer by ruining a lady of his household, and I will be very much surprised if he has not left a packet of debts of honour behind him."

"He is a gamester?" Elizabeth looked shocked.

"Oh, yes, to excess. So you see, all of the highest officers at Brighton will have been informed of his actions. We will not be telling our cousin anything he does not know. We only ask him to dig deeper and present anything he learns to your father and uncle in London." Darcy watched Elizabeth's face.

She nodded. "Then I thank you, sir, and Miss Darcy for your effort. Any little thing may help." She smiled at him all too briefly.

Darcy continued, "Georgiana has asked to be allowed to correspond with you, and of course, I approve. It is my wish that she continue to profit by her friendship with you."

Elizabeth was so astonished she could not speak. A tear slid down her cheek. Darcy, unthinking, gently brushed it away with his thumb, then remembered he was not connected to her in any proper way that would forbear such a liberty and withdrew his hand. "Excuse me, Miss Bennet," he whispered. "I forget myself."

Elizabeth was too abashed to look away. Darcy spoke again, barely above a murmur, "You have strengthened my sister, Miss Bennet. From the time of your attendance to your sister at Netherfield, I have known your influence over Georgiana would be a welcome thing—that she would benefit from having a friend like you. Let her perform the same service for you."

Darcy paused and then continued in a slightly louder voice, deeply in earnest. "Elizabeth…I pray you will not let this break your spirit. You are everything a gentlewoman should be, and you will always be welcome here."

Elizabeth pulled Darcy's handkerchief from her pocket. When she could, she gathered in a deep breath and replied, "Mr Darcy, these events have reminded me keenly of certain comments you made to me last April, comments about my family…what you said then and in your letter."

Darcy sat up straighter, his chest emptied. Elizabeth held up a hand to silence anything he might be ready to say. "Comments that, once I reflected upon them, I had to own were wholly valid. No matter Lydia's motives or Wickham's, she has acted in a way that brings ruin upon all of us. Let us not try to pretend otherwise."

This is intolerable. Darcy looked out the window. He longed to take her hand and force her to run with him through the park until all their frustrations were spent. Then they could have a reasonable conversation.

He finally turned to her. "When matters are settled for Lydia, no matter the nature of the settlement, I am certain Georgiana will invite you to Pemberley for an uninterrupted visit. Will you come?"

Elizabeth looked at him through a sudden flood of tears. "I cannot imagine such a time. It would be selfish of me to do so."

Darcy's throat tightened, but he persisted. "When Bingley and Jane marry, *they* will be invited here. Will you not come, even then?"

Why does he not speak of love? Dear Jane…will she allow herself to be happy in the midst of this misfortune? Should I? "I cannot say, Mr Darcy."

Damn it, man, say it. "Elizabeth. You belong here. Do not let a foolish sister and a scoundrel ruin *your* life. What are they to you, or to me, if you could be here?" He whispered as if praying, "Choose to love." Darcy realised this was something like a proposal.

Elizabeth hung her head, sobbing quietly. *He does not know I love him?* When she did at last look up, she met his gaze. "I must see to my family, Mr Darcy. I will never forgive myself if I do not. Surely, you know that?

"As for love…I shall always love Pemberley and all the people in it. Tell Georgiana, I will appreciate receiving her letters with any news of this beloved place. Have her write to me through Mr Bingley, so my mother will not boast of the connection."

"But you will not come back?"

"I do not know, Mr Darcy. I cannot say now. I shall always *want* to come back. But I will not do so if it brings dishonour upon what I love." Elizabeth stood abruptly. Darcy stood as well. She briskly folded the letter to

Longbourn and handed it to him. "Please see that it is posted?"

Darcy nodded dumbly, and she was gone, leaving behind only the scent of lavender.

WHEN ELIZABETH STARTED TO CROSS the entry hall on her way to the stillroom, her Aunt Gardiner's voice gently hailed her from the stairs. "Oh, Lizzy! I was just looking for you. Is the letter written?"

"Yes, Aunt. Mr Darcy has it, and it will be sent as soon as the footman reaches Lambton."

"It is taking us some time to get the children organised. Can you perhaps distract them while Jane and the maids and I gather their things? How can they have made such a commotion? They have only been here one night!"

"I was just going to the stillroom to make sure I have left nothing behind, and then I shall come directly. Entertaining the children will be a pleasant diversion for me."

"Lovely, dear. Thank you." Her aunt nodded and turned to climb the stairs.

Elizabeth stepped into the stillroom, which had not been entered by anyone since the day she had created Georgiana's scent. It was still tidy, although a new layer of dust was beginning to form. She was relieved to see the little stack of cards, pen and ink remained upon the narrow counter on the far wall as she took a bottle of lavender water from her pocket. She brought two for the journey and one was still sealed. As she was packing, she decided to leave a bottle of her scent for *him*. Even in her present confusion, it was something she was compelled to do.

She looked around. It was another summery day and the sunlight warmed the air, which had taken on the scents of many flowers combined into a fragrance unique to the room. Elizabeth smiled a little, seeing her careful writing on the labels of bottles in the glass-fronted cupboards. She had been happy here in the stillroom, creating a scent for Georgiana, pondering the implications of the nosegay from Mr Darcy—letting herself hope. Organising the disorder, she felt a part of the big machine that was Pemberley.

Elizabeth shook her head. *Yes, he still loves me in his way. He loves the idea he has of me, for he does not really know any true good of me. And what would our life be like here if we could never leave? Other than Jane, my family could never visit. Would he know any of them in London? I cannot imagine his visiting Longbourn ever again, not even for me—not with Wickham attached to my family.*

She stepped around the end of the large worktable and happened to glance at the floor. There, shrivelled and faded, lay the remains of the red chrysanthemum. Her eyes instantly began to blink. *Oh great god! He does not know. He truly does not know. The stem was too short. He does not know...I love him, and he does not know it. He must think I am heartless.* She picked up the tiny blossom with its insufficient stem. Placing it carefully upon the table with the lavender water, she selected two cards. Sitting at the worktable, she wrote the first:

"Dear Mr Darcy,

"You are fond of lavender. This is not rosemary for remembrance, but I trust it will remind you of me just the same. Thank you for allowing me to spend the happiest hours of my life in the Pemberley stillroom.

"E. Bennet"

Elizabeth leaned the card against the bottle and wrote the second:

"Here lie the remains of a red chrysanthemum, dislodged from a nosegay for F. Darcy, given to him by E. Bennet."

She sat crying for a moment, when a gentle hand tapped her shoulder. Elizabeth turned to see Mrs Reynolds.

"I understand you are leaving us, Miss Bennet." Mrs Reynolds looked sad and old.

"I am sorry to say it, but it is so. You have been most kind to me, Mrs Reynolds. I shall never forget you or Pemberley. I do not want to go."

Mrs Reynolds looked seriously into Elizabeth's upturned, tear-stained face. "Then do not go. In spite of his wealth, my master has not had an easy life. He lost his mother young and worried always that his very own father might prefer another boy—a most unworthy boy—to himself. He does not trust women, other than his sister. I think his father warned him to hold himself back. But with you, he is easy; he laughs; he is relaxed and happy. You are so lovely, so gracious. You do not put on airs, and you seem to appreciate Pemberley in a way few women do. You understand it as a place, not a possession. I am afraid for him if you leave him without hope. You will return?"

"The situation calling me and my family so urgently away may resolve in such a manner, it might be best for Mr Darcy and his sister that I do not return. If you knew the particulars, you would understand."

"I am an old woman, Miss Bennet. Life has taught me things. One of them is to trust love. It will find a way."

Elizabeth burst into sobs, grasping the old housekeeper around the waist. Mrs Reynolds shushed and patted her until Elizabeth's breath returned somewhere near normal. When she was able, she said with a shaky chuckle, "I cannot *believe* myself today. I have never cried this much in the whole of my life. I am so sorry."

"I have no place to ask this, Miss Bennet, but do you love my master?"

Elizabeth knew she could not lie. She responded in a strong voice, "Indeed, I do, Mrs Reynolds. I love him. With my whole heart, I love him."

"I know you do, my dear. I just wanted to hear you say it. I believe you will come back to us. I feel it."

The two women smiled at each other, then impulsively as she stood to leave, Elizabeth kissed the old woman's forehead and whispered, "Thank you."

WITH A HEAVY HEART, DARCY emerged from the library and saw Elizabeth disappear down the kitchen stairs. *How typical of her...she goes to say good-bye to Mrs Reynolds.*

"Darcy!" Bingley approached, waving a letter. "Here is my express to Netherfield." Bingley looked closely at Darcy's strained face. "Good god, man! You look awful. What is wrong?"

Darcy gave him a tight smile. "I have Elizabeth's letter to Longbourn here. I'll just fetch a footman to take them down to Kympton; it is faster."

A concerned yet knowing look covered Bingley's face. "You have just seen her?"

"She is in a bad way, Bingley. Why is she so ready to assume the worst of me?"

"Why are *you* so ready to hide yourself from her? Darcy, if you were to tell her you leave for London tomorrow, that you make no promises but you intend to try to help her family, it would mean everything to her. You think it would only confer a burden of gratitude, but I think you mistake the matter entirely. Give her *some* credit."

Darcy studied his friend. *If only I knew she loves me. If she does, why is she coy? Why say she loves Pemberley and everyone in it, and not say she loves me?*

Bingley saw his words were being considered and grew bolder. "Darcy, have you *told* her you love her? Have you said the words instead of letting flowers speak for you? As lively as Elizabeth can be, she is not frivolous. She is no idle flirt. She would never dream of revealing her heart if she felt it would be improper. She is like Jane that way. Charlotte Collins used to tell them a lady should show more than she feels and leave a man in no doubt, even express *more* than she feels. Jane told me that she and Elizabeth do not agree. They think it dishonest."

"She says she does not know whether she will ever come back to Pemberley—that if matters with Wickham and her sister are as she fears, it would bring dishonour upon Georgie and me to even know her. Can you imagine?"

"Then *you*, sir, will have to go to *her*. When we know how this charade is to be played, if Wickham can be found and made to do the right thing, or even if we discover Lydia abandoned, when the dust has settled, you must come to Netherfield immediately."

"Of course, you are right, Bingley. You are absolutely right. You are a good and true friend."

Bingley laughed. "There! You said it without being prompted. Good man!"

They turned and proceeded to find a footman to ride into Kympton. As they walked, Darcy explained to Bingley there would be letters for Elizabeth arriving at Netherfield from Georgiana.

"You see, Darcy? That is precisely my point. That is just the sort of little consideration Elizabeth or Jane make by instinct. They are aware of their precarious connections and the impression their family makes upon the world."

"Elizabeth insists on this nicety because the present situation reminds her of the ill-judged remarks I made last April. There I was, telling of her family's improprieties, when she had just spent six weeks listening to the appalling incivilities of my aunt. Was there ever such a hypocrite as Fitzwilliam Darcy?"

"If Elizabeth is comforted by secrecy, she shall have it," Bingley confirmed. "It will give me a chance to speak to her of you, and if you will make the most of the opportunity, you may include a few words of your own from time to time in Georgie's letters. It would forward your suit."

"Perhaps I *shall* drag Georgiana to London when Mrs Annesley returns. That way, Georgie would not have to spend her seventeenth birthday alone."

"There you are!" Bingley chuckled. "A perfect plan."

Sweet William
"Gallantry"

Chapter 10

At two o'clock, the Darcy carriage carrying the Bennet sisters, and the Bingley carriage with Mrs Gardiner and her four children, left Pemberley with Bingley riding on horseback alongside. Elizabeth's eyes were red but dry; she felt herself to be cried out.

Darcy quietly instructed the drivers to exit the Pemberley area through Lambton. He did not want Elizabeth to see or know she had been through Kympton, since the little town was now associated in everyone's mind with George Wickham. The travellers would spend two nights at inns along their route and arrive at Longbourn three days hence.

Darcy had stopped to watch from a window as Elizabeth played with her little cousins for half an hour upon the lawn where, not two weeks before, he met her by surprise—of course, he now called it fate. Although the Gardiner children were fair and their cousin Elizabeth dark, Darcy could easily imagine sometime in the future when it would be his children playing with this woman, their mother, Elizabeth Darcy, on the lawn. He closed his eyes. When he opened them again, Elizabeth had been joined by Bingley and Jane, who helped gather the children and bring them to the house. *It must mean they are ready to leave. Then I will prepare to leave myself.* Darcy sighed, not for the first time.

After the carriages were gone and Darcy's own packing had begun, he slipped away to wander idly through the halls of his home. He leaned for a few moments against the door of the music room, remembering Elizabeth's voice. He lingered in the dining room, staring at the chair to his right where Elizabeth had been habitually seated during her stay. He stood behind his chair, looking to the end of the long table where she would sit as his wife, and dreamt of exchanging looks with her over some guest's absurdities. *This house will never be right again without her. Bingley is correct. If she will not come back, I must go to her and bring her back. This is her home. With me.*

Darcy went down the formal staircase to the receiving room, where at about ten o'clock that morning they had all been so very joyful. At least Bingley had made his case to Jane Bennet and was accepted. There would be a wedding, for Charles Bingley was no longer a man to let the nefarious actions of strangers, the selfish conspiracies of his sisters, or the well-meaning but ridiculous interference of friends stand in the way of his own happiness. Even though his engagement, sure to be sanctioned since his request to court Jane had been thoroughly endorsed by her father, was only an hour old when the horrible letter from Longbourn arrived, he would not betray Jane's unfading love.

Why cannot Elizabeth have faith in me? I had permission to court her, why did I never tell her I love her? Even in the library, I said everything except that. Why was I missish? He huffed with exasperation at himself. *I need a walk.*

Darcy proceeded outside and strode to the kennels. He ordered the dog runs opened, and his pack of foxhounds burst out toward the stables, thinking they would run with the horses. Darcy whistled and the dozen dogs wheeled around excitedly, then followed him as he made long strides up the hills into the woods, where the paths were mere trails and the hiking would be strenuous.

When he re-entered Pemberley an hour later, he brought his favourite bitch, Hermia, with him. He entered by the kitchen door and walked up the pantry hall towards the stairs. When he passed the stillroom, he stopped. He regretted never being in the room with Elizabeth. *How charming she must have looked, working away like a little gipsy at her potions.* His eyes went immediately to the bottle on the table and he stepped quickly into the room. When he read the card, he slid, disheartened, into a chair. *Remind me of her, remind me of her! She does not know her cruelty. But she was happy here…* It was too much. Darcy's eyes stung and were blurry when he saw the second card with its little brown flower. He did not know the significance of a red chrysanthemum, but his heart sank when he realised his own clumsiness had caused the blossom to be upset. Clearly, the flower held significance for Elizabeth. He felt the tears spill onto his cheeks, his mouth forming a grimace to keep from audibly sobbing. Finally he emitted a low growling moan and a very alarmed Hermia stood her front legs upon his thigh and began baying, a deep carrying howl, which he was sure would bring servants running. He had no handkerchief. He had not taken up another to replace that which had gone to Elizabeth. The dog began licking him and Darcy had to smile. This would explain his wet face at least.

"Mr Darcy! What a commotion!" Mrs Reynolds was the first to reach the room. She turned back and held up a hand to the two approaching scullery maids. "It is nothing, girls, just the master. He's brought a dog in…"

Mrs Reynolds closed the door behind her and stood at her master's shoulder. She saw what Elizabeth left behind and reckoned Darcy had been crying. "That dog slobber does not fool *me*, sir."

He turned his head and shoulders to embrace Mrs Reynolds around her waist, shaken by fresh grief. Through his coughed sobs, he thought he could smell lavender on her apron. When he could, he said, "Mrs Reynolds, dear old thing, have you been making lavender biscuits?"

She looked at him oddly, "No sir." Then she remembered Miss Elizabeth Bennet wore that scent. "You are not the first person today to cry into my apron." She dried his tears with the apron, thinking it might have been over twenty years since the last time she had done so.

Darcy was astonished. "You were in here, today, when Elizabeth was? I saw her come down the stairs. I thought she had done so to extend her gratitude."

"She did, Mr Darcy, but came in here first. I found her crying over that little flower in this very chair. You are quite a pair, you and she." Mrs Reynolds smiled.

"It is a red chrysanthemum, or was, do you know what it signifies? Should I fetch Georgie's herbal?"

"I have my own, sir." Mrs Reynolds slipped from the room and returned a moment later.

"It is a different edition from Miss Georgiana's but quite thorough."

Darcy took the book and read '*Chrysanthemum, red — I love*'. "Oh god," he handed the book opened to the pertinent page to Mrs Reynolds. "She took the risk and I bungled it." He lowered his head. He inhaled. He exhaled.

Mrs Reynolds said, "Yes, she told me she loves you."

"What? When?"

"Just now, here, in the stillroom before she left. I asked her, and she paused. I do not think she *wanted* to tell me, but I can be a charming old lady sometimes, and she could not lie." Her eyes twinkled at her master. "She said she loves you with her whole heart, Mr Darcy. How you get her back here, I do not know, but just see that you do."

Darcy chuckled, and his dog took the opportunity to crawl halfway onto his lap and lick his face again.

"When she was here, I found myself humming, Mr Darcy, *humming*. As I worked, I was like a songbird and have been since she came that morning. I have not done that since your mother was alive. I found myself hoping..."

"Had I seen this in the nosegay as she intended it, had I not been a clumsy oaf, I would not have waited for Miss Jane to arrive, let alone for Bingley to propose. I would be a betrothed man by now. I could have offered her some proper comfort today instead of standing around like a dead stick. Bingley and Georgiana are sure she loves me, but I would not believe it. I thought she would say it if she felt so, but she must have thought I knew her feelings and was ignoring the chance she took in revealing herself. I have committed a deadly sin, Mrs Reynolds; I have been missish. Elizabeth must think me spoiled and heartless."

"She found the flower, Mr Darcy, and left it for you particularly. She did not have to do it; you must not lose sight of that. She could only think you sadly uninformed."

"True enough." Darcy toyed with the dried blossom in his hand, and two petals fell onto the table. "Oh! Have we mucilage? I shall affix this to the card she wrote before I ruin it altogether."

Mrs Reynolds found the pot and noticed the refreshed label. "Do you recognise this writing, sir?" She smiled.

Darcy dabbed the sticky paste onto the card and gently tapped the flower into it. He carefully laid it aside then stood. "Is there more of her writing?"

"Look for it in the cupboard with the glass front, sir," Mrs Reynolds instructed.

Darcy opened the doors and began moving bottles until every one with a label written by Elizabeth was gathered on a shelf. He liked her handwriting: clear, legible, simple, feminine to be sure, yet precise.

Mrs Reynolds watched him touching the things Elizabeth had touched. The housekeeper cleared her throat. "Mr Darcy, Miss Elizabeth said some things that indicate she believes, because of her family's troubles, that she will not be coming back to Pemberley. I do not know what those troubles are, but they are nothing to us, are they?"

Darcy smiled and shook his head. "No, Mrs Reynolds, they are nothing to us. Nothing can change that I love her and that she will be an ideal mistress for Pemberley."

"Then, with all due respect, Mr Darcy, may I suggest, if she will not come back here to you, go where she is and convince her."

Darcy started to laugh. "It appears you share the prevailing wisdom on the matter, Mrs Reynolds. I am for London tomorrow to see if I can assist her family from there, then I shall go to Netherfield, and I shall stay in the neighbourhood until she is convinced. I will not return without her. The next time you see Miss Elizabeth Bennet, she will be Mrs Elizabeth Darcy. Will that suit?"

"Yes, sir. Thank you, sir."

DARCY AND GEORGIANA TOOK THEIR dinner in the stillroom that evening. "I hope you do not mind all the scents, Georgie. She was happy in this room; therefore, so am I, or as happy as I can be…"

"…Under the circumstances. Yes, I know. Now what is this piffle about your going to town without me? I may be of some assistance, you know."

"I told Elizabeth you have my permission to correspond with her, and it suits my purpose that she receive a letter or two from Pemberley. Let her think, for a fortnight, that we are both here. Then, when Mrs Annesley has returned, come to London in time for your birthday. I would not have you turn seventeen without me."

"Why so secret, Brother?"

"To raise the hopes of Elizabeth and her family, and perhaps fail, would be devastating, both to them and to myself. And if I succeed, although I am not sure what form success will take, exactly, I would not have Elizabeth accept me on the pretext of gratitude. If her family were to know they are under some obligation to me, they might push her into a marriage she would not otherwise choose."

"But she loves you! We have ample proof. I shall invite her to return for a nice long visit once the present storm has passed. Every report I hear of you says you are seen to much better advantage here than in Hertfordshire."

"What about inviting her to Darcy House once you are there?"

Georgiana brightened. "An excellent plan. I shall find some pretext for being in London and send her an invitation. I shall write the first letter tonight, so you can have a look at it in the morning before you leave."

"I intend to leave very early; it will interfere with your beauty sleep," he warned. Darcy often chided his sister for sleeping later than he thought seemly.

"In matters of the heart, especially my dear brother's heart, I am happy to sacrifice a little sleep and a good deal more if need be." Georgiana smiled coaxingly at her brother, and he at last reluctantly smiled in return. "Elizabeth told me she finds your smile charming. 'Irresistible' is, I believe, the exact word she used. I cannot think why. But you will do well to remember it as an asset."

"Dear gosling. You always have the knack for turning happy information into a backhanded compliment. You need not worry. Elizabeth has taught me not to be vain." He paused, becoming wistful. "You know, she did once tell me she admired my smile, but she had never complimented me before, and I took it for teasing."

"You do so often deserve to be teased that I can understand your confusion."

Darcy gave Georgiana his best grumpy-brother look, but it was no longer taken as censure. She laughed at him as Elizabeth had taught her to do.

From Pemberley

Dear Elizabeth,

Pemberley is not the same with you gone away. Everything seems subdued and muffled, even the birdsong by the lake. My brother is dismal company, and I await the return of Mrs Annesley in a few days for a change of conversation and lively companionship.

In a few weeks' time, you will see my letters come from London. I abhor the summer weather in town, but as part of my birthday gift of the pianoforte, which you were able to try while here, my brother has paid for private lessons with a master from Vienna visiting England for a limited time. It would please me for you to join me in London then with Mrs Annesley as our chaperone. I cannot offer the further inducement of my brother's presence as he has not expressed an idea of travelling with me. Perhaps, if he knows you will join us, he might be tempted. I fully comprehend that, if matters are not settled with your family, you may not wish to visit me in town, so do not feel compelled to give an answer to this invitation now. Let us consider this an open thing—respond when you know more.

As for my brother, I would wish you to know I was with him when he gathered the flowers and fruit you left him in the stillroom. I still do not know why you were there or why I was not told, but that is a discussion for another time. He tried to carry too much—a constant metaphor we may apply to his life in general, I fear—and I was the one who picked up the nosegay when it tumbled from its vase. Do not cut the stems so short in future, I pray you!—and it was I who failed to notice the little red chrysanthemum had come loose. Do not assume he was unobservant; that prize goes to me. I am doubly sad for it as he repeatedly expresses the mortification he feels since you must have been confused by his actions —or their lack—once you knew he had received the nosegay. I must apologise, too, to both of you. And here, I had just been preening over my fine matchmaking success with Charles and your sister. Now I know better. Please extend my fondest regards to dear Jane.

I expect you will have news from Colonel Fitzwilliam as soon as, if not sooner than, we will here at Pemberley. I do so hope anything he learns will be of material use to help your family.

I am writing this from the stillroom, and Mrs Reynolds, who just looked in, asks to be remembered to you. How singular! She has never asked after any of our guests before—not ever. My brother and I linger in the stillroom often since you are gone and have even taken a meal here. You are very much in our prayers.

Your dear friend,
Georgiana Darcy

Darcy read the letter early the next morning as he shared breakfast with his sister before departing. "Did you truly write it in the stillroom?"

"I did, indeed, and Mrs Reynolds saw my candles."

"You write a fine letter, Georgie. Thank you."

"You needn't thank me, Brother. I will do whatever I can to persuade her back to Pemberley. Perhaps I should propose to her myself?"

Darcy was not in a mood to laugh, but he did smile. "Silly goose. You are no longer my little gosling. You are now a full grown goose."

Georgiana patted his arm. When the meal was completed, they rose to part. "I shall post this tomorrow, and in my next letter, I will tell her when I will leave for London. Be careful on your way, Fitzwilliam. I love you and God speed."

"I love you, too, and I will take care, Georgie. I'll send an express when I arrive with any news from our cousin."

Darcy left in a carriage, taking a different route than that of Bingley and the ladies. On the morrow, he would proceed on horseback to shave precious hours from his time. Efficiency would at least allow some semblance of being productive.

AN EXPRESS TO GEORGIANA REPORTED that he had arrived unscathed and their cousin Fitzwilliam had come to Darcy House several hours later. As Darcy feared, the colonel reported that Wickham paid Lydia Bennet no special attention, nor she him, until she had a letter from her mother with tidings of Elizabeth being in Lambton.

The letter from Mrs Bennet was found amongst the haphazard jumble of clothes and personal effects left behind in the bedchamber Lydia occupied at Colonel Forster's lodgings. Mrs Bennet revealed the early surmises of her brother as he observed Darcy's very particular civility to Elizabeth, paraphrasing the letter Mr Gardiner had written to Mr Bennet. After Lydia made a joke of this to Wickham whilst they were at a party—stating she thought Mr Darcy ridiculous to pursue the sister who liked him least—all of that vicious man's attention focused on the hapless youngest Bennet.

Lydia Bennet was no match for the insinuations of George Wickham. Unbeknownst to her, he was in debt, and she made no secret of the gift of funds sent by her mother in celebration of her sixteenth birthday. Wickham was truly intrigued by Elizabeth, even though he found that lady's interest had cooled after she returned from six weeks in Kent. That Elizabeth might develop a better regard for Fitzwilliam Darcy was seen as a betrayal worthy of punishment, which could easily be carried out by ruining Lydia. Darcy's infinite pride, as Wickham saw it, would demand an end to all contact with Elizabeth when he saw her family brought to disgrace. If Darcy was in love with Elizabeth, so much the better for Wickham to dash his hopes by blackening the name of Bennet. Thus were the assumptions of Colonel Richard Fitzwilliam, and he was correct in every part.

It had taken only a few days of concerted flattery to ensnare Lydia. She knew nothing of Wickham's debts of honour, debts to tradesmen and the sullied reputation of another officer's sister. She only knew Wickham had fallen violently in love with her and was generous with his affection. It mattered not to her that, when he suggested elopement, she must pay their way. She was thoroughly deceived.

Wickham let it be known, when in his cups amidst his fellows, that he had no intention of marrying Lydia Bennet. He would enjoy her favours until he had spent her little money, grew tired of her or got her with child —then he would disappear. That all the Bennet sisters would suffer from the ruination of one was rather more his point than not. They served merely as his means to exact revenge upon the Darcys.

This, Colonel Fitzwilliam related to Darcy with brandy in the Darcy House study. Over dinner, taken in that same room, the cousins composed a letter to Mr Gardiner explaining the situation in its plain truth with the final draft written in the colonel's legible military hand and signed by him alone. He told Mr Gardiner he could be reached through messages sent to Darcy House and he would gladly call on Mr Gardiner and Mr Bennet at Gracechurch Street, should they so wish. He apologised for not having any clues as to Wickham and Lydia's whereabouts. The letter brought its recipients no comfort but let them know exactly the sort of man with whom they were dealing and confirmed their worst fears. A brief note of thanks was sent by return post.

The first morning in London saw Colonel Fitzwilliam chasing leads given him by officers to whom Wickham owed money. Darcy learnt through his butler, who seemed, at times, as much a spy for the family's interests as a majordomo, that Mrs Younge had lately been given management of a boarding house in a not wholly reputable part of town. With his father's miniature likeness of Wickham in his pocket, Darcy made inquiries in that neighbourhood and was able to obtain an address. He had confirmation from a wine merchant that Wickham attempted to establish an account, appearing first in his regimentals and returning later the same day dressed as a gentleman. The wine merchant was not as gullible as Lydia Bennet.

Of Lydia, Darcy was able to learn little except that Wickham had a young woman, well-cloaked, with him at an inn near to Mrs Younge's establishment. Clearly, Lydia and Wickham were not lodging at Mrs Younge's but were in the area.

On the second morning, Darcy and Fitzwilliam set themselves up in an alehouse that afforded a view of Mrs Younge's front door, and they took turns nursing flagons of ale, eating coarse bread and cheese, and watching her lodgers come and go. These were men on the rough end of respectability, probably new to the city and working in the trades. It was Darcy's hope they might intercept Wickham without having to apply to Mrs Younge, who would exact a toll for any information. The day was wasted, but during his turn at the table by the window, Darcy wrote to Georgiana, letting her know of the progress and asking whether she and Elizabeth had ever spoken of Wickham. It would help in his possible negotiations to know whether Elizabeth had been truly smitten as much as it would hurt Darcy to know that particular truth. He also entreated his sister's silence about the worst details of the affair; if Elizabeth was to know the depths of Wickham's evil and the desperation of Lydia's plight, let the information come to her through her relatives and not from a Darcy. He sent the letter by express and asked Georgiana to respond as soon as possible.

When the sun set with no sign of Wickham, Darcy at last and very grudgingly approached the boarding house of Mrs Younge. A servant girl answered his knock, and he stepped inside the vestibule to await the servant's mistress rather than wait upon the step outside.

"A gentleman to see me?" Darcy heard Mrs Younge ask. "Why did you not tell him we have no rooms to let at present?"

"He didn't ask for no rooms, ma'am. He asked to see you."

The servant was shocked at the wrath Darcy's appearance produced on the face of her mistress, and the girl ran crying from Mrs Younge's glare. Darcy was not surprised that Mrs Younge had a vindictive reputation amongst the servants. She was a mean and weak-willed woman, but her nature could be used to his advantage.

Mrs Younge was no actress and did not try to hide that Wickham, with a girl, had applied to her for rooms. Darcy suspected there was something of a woman scorned in Mrs Younge, and she held an unrequited tenderness for Wickham, which often gave distress with every fresh evidence of his preference for very young maidens—a description she could not claim, although she was not ill-favoured. Yes, Wickham had asked for rooms as a favour! The girl with him seemed in no state of alarm, looked about the place curiously, and produced giggles at anything Wickham said that might be construed in the least bit as humorous, especially if it was vulgar.

"She seems a silly, vacant little chit, and in spite of her fine figure, Wickham won't keep her long. He prefers sleighs with new runners," Mrs Younge stated, giving her embittered view of the matter.

"Her family is known to me, and they are respectable people. They do not deserve to be at Wickham's mercy for their honourable name. If you know where they have gone, I would appreciate the information." Darcy eyed Mrs Younge carefully, wondering how much loyalty she might extend to Wickham, and if she had lent him any money.

"You might as well know, Mr Darcy," she began, pronouncing "mister" in a highly insolent manner, "Wickham and I had words. I do not know where he went after they left here."

Darcy could see she was lying. "If you do not know, then I have no use for you." He rose to leave. "I would just mention; I hope you have not lent him any money. He left Brighton owing nearly £1,000 to his fellow officers. They will not like to be left with debts of honour and will be paid before you ever will, madam."

Mrs Younge was genuinely surprised. "As much as that?"

"I hope you have not depleted your savings or dipped into the income of the one who owns this establishment on a promise of rapid repayment." Darcy thought the last very likely, given the woman's character and history.

Mrs Younge lowered her gaze. "He intends to sell his commission, and he always pays me first." She was a little too strident.

"Then your best hope, Mrs Younge, is that peace with France does not break out anytime soon, or Wickham will find his commission difficult to sell. But this is nothing to me. His lady's family can offer him little monetary inducement to make her an honest woman, so you mustn't expect remuneration of his loan from that quarter."

Mrs Younge grumbled, "He never succeeds half so well with the rich ones as the poor ones."

"I will take my leave, Mrs Younge, since you have no knowledge of their whereabouts, and that is the only information of any consequence to me. You know where I can be found should you learn anything I might *value*." Darcy stressed the last word and saw a glimmer in Mrs Younge's eye.

The wretched woman would have the last word. "You will wait a very long time, sir, if you think I will sink so low as to betray a friend."

Darcy turned his back to hide his smirk. "Let us hope in matters of loan repayment your friend is as kind as you."

Darcy reunited with his cousin at Darcy House and related his evening's activities. "I expect to have a note from Mrs Younge requesting I visit again within 24 hours, Richard, for I am sure she has lent him more than she should—probably out of the accounts of the lodging house. She must hope the owner does not audit her soon."

"I have found the record of who owns the building, Darcy. Sadly it is no one we know, but you might let slip the name if it would be helpful."

"Richard, you are a brilliant fellow to think of it. If I do not hear from her tomorrow, I shall seek her out armed with that knowledge."

As DARCY ASSUMED, A SCRUFFY young lad knocked with great trepidation on the door of Darcy House as they sat down to breakfast at eight-thirty the next morning. Mrs Younge would see him at ten o'clock if he could spare the time.

Heliotrope
"Devotion"

Chapter 11

By noon, without having to mention the building owner but after lining Mrs Younge's pocket with £50, Darcy was in possession of the name of the sordid inn where Wickham and Lydia were lodged. It was in a part of town where even the confident Darcy was loath to travel without an armed escort. Rather than proceed there immediately, he returned to Darcy House to ask his cousin to join him. The colonel agreed to stay with the carriage, along with one of the larger Darcy footmen.

Darcy stepped to the desk of the inn and noticed a public house adjoined the vestibule. He enquired whether George Wickham was in residence and whether there was a private place they might have a conversation. The innkeeper informed Darcy the use of a private room would add to Wickham's bill, but a bright sovereign erased the innkeeper's cares. Darcy wondered whether the innkeeper already suspected Wickham was the sort to steal away in the night, leaving behind an unpaid bill and possibly a young, foolish country girl. Wickham was fetched.

"Darcy! I wondered whether you might come looking for me. Tell me, do I have something you want?" His manner was as overly familiar and insinuating as ever.

Darcy found it in himself to smile a little. "Indeed, you do, Wickham. Something that is of no real value to you: the Bennet family honour."

"Ah…honour. Intimate acquaintance with the youngest Miss Bennet has taught me there is not much honour to be protected there, Darcy."

Darcy looked away. "Nonetheless, that is why I am here."

"I was not aware you had any friends amongst the Bennets. There is one lady of the family who thinks nothing of disparaging you. She has been very"—Wickham smirked—"shall we say 'candid' with me."

"Yes, I know perfectly well of whom you speak, and she did not scruple to disparage me to my face when I gave her the chance of it. You are producing nothing that is news to me."

"But now you entertain her at Pemberley?" Wickham raised his brows with leering mock surprise.

"Do not assume I entertain her as you are entertaining her youngest sister, here in one of London's *finest* establishments."

"Believe me, I do not." Wickham laughed at Darcy derisively.

Darcy would not be ruffled. "May I ask what your intentions are to-wards Lydia Bennet? She left a letter implying a wedding between you is imminent. Is it?"

Wickham scoffed. "It most decidedly is not. I needed to leave Brighton on urgent business matters, and she was ripe for adventure with birthday money burning a hole in her pocket. So you see—we were of one mind about leaving Brighton."

"That I do doubt. I would speak with her."

"What? With Lydia? Why?"

"If she can be convinced to leave you, I shall take her away at once, and that will be an end to it unless she is with child already."

Wickham started to make a caustic reply, but paled and was silenced by Colonel Fitzwilliam's entrance into the room.

Darcy was surprised. "Who guards the carriage, Cousin?" he asked.

"The burly footman your butler sent to add to the one we brought. I am glad we told Mr Lesley where we were going as he has forwarded orders to me from General Bagbey, endorsed by Colonel Forster." Fitzwilliam held out a document. "It seems I am empowered to take one George Wickham into custody should I deem it necessary or advisable." The colonel caught Wickham's eye with a malevolent nod that nearly sent him scampering back up the stairs to Lydia's arms. "He is charged with desertion, dishonouring a superior officer and owing debts of honour to fellow officers in excess of

£800. I thought you would like to know, Darcy. If you see fit, he will start out in a stockade, and when the military sentence is served, he can then move on to a debtors' prison to repay the tradesmen he owes."

Darcy raised his eyebrows and smiled a little. "Happy news, Cousin, happy news." He turned back to Wickham. "Back to the matter at hand then, Wickham. If Lydia Bennet can be convinced to leave you, I shall take her to her aunt and uncle straight away and my cousin may do as he likes. If she thinks she must marry you, then we shall have a further conversation."

Wickham sneered. "I have no intention of saddling myself with Lydia Bennet. Absolutely not. There is *another* Bennet I would consider, but never Lydia. Had I been able to secure the little heiress, Mary King, as my bride, I surely would have returned to Hertfordshire to make a mistress of Elizabeth Bennet. Now *there* is a Bennet worth some effort."

Instantly furious, Darcy turned away, but Wickham continued, "Such a challenge but *such* a potential reward. Lively, buxom—I'm a tit man, you know, Darcy, always have been. Oh, Elizabeth will be a delight for the mind *and* body. You prefer a well-turned leg, do you not? I would be a happy man, indeed, if I could report to you on that score. Would you let me trade Lydia for her, do you think?"

Darcy's blood was pounding in his ears, but over it, he heard a sound very much like a sledgehammer hitting a melon. He turned to see Wickham's stunned face, his nose flattened against his right cheek, and then a spurt and flow of blood. The colonel had done what Darcy had wanted to do.

"Son-of-a-bitch!" screamed Wickham, holding his face.

Darcy sighed. "Thank you, Cousin, for doing what I should have done. But a broken nose presents its own problems."

"Fitzwilliam, you bastard!" Wickham sat and rocked from side to side with his bleeding face in his hands.

"Oh? I fail to see any problem," the colonel replied equably.

"Well, for one thing, we must now involve a doctor who will report Wickham was attacked," Darcy explained.

"I think you mistake the matter, Cousin. This man was resisting arrest."

Darcy smiled. "Of course. Silly of me." He bowed to his cousin and then stepped out to the hallway, sending the first servant he saw for a physician. He re-entered the sitting room and approached Wickham. "I wonder how Lydia Bennet will like being married to a man who wears the scars of a pugilist. That nose is broken unless I am very much mistaken."

"Damn you, Darcy!" was Wickham's next coherent comment.

"Me?" Darcy chuckled. "I did not strike you. I ought to have, and I might yet, but I did not break your nose, sir." He turned to his cousin. "Fitzwilliam, I will seek Miss Lydia now if you will await the doctor. I shall return directly."

Darcy took his hat and left them. He found a maid to take him up a frail flight of stairs to Wickham's room. He tapped upon the door and bid the maid enter before him to ascertain Miss Lydia Bennet was at least in a dressing gown, but she was fully dressed.

"Mr Darcy! La! What are *you* doing here?" Lydia snorted in alarm.

"Good afternoon, Miss Bennet. I am happy to see you, too. Your family sends their regards, and I can report that, other than being worried for your safety, they are well."

Lydia looked quite vexed. "They know I am with Wickham and shortly to be married? Oh! I so particularly asked Mrs Forster to keep this to herself until I could write to my sisters and surprise them!"

Darcy unconsciously shook his head. "Surely, you must realise an escapade such as this would be widely reported and alarms sounded. Think of the dishonour you bring upon your generous hosts—Wickham's colonel, no less—and the position of your sisters now that you are shamed."

Lydia laughed. "What shame? It is *their* shame that I shall be the first of my sisters married as Jane becomes an old maid! Is it not a wonderful joke? I married! And to the handsome George Wickham, Lizzy's particular favourite."

"But you are *not* married, are you?"

Lydia pouted. "No, not yet, but I shall be." No unpleasantness was a match for Lydia's ignorant optimism.

"Why are you not yet married?"

"Oh, la, it is all so tiresome. Wickham has told me…some business of his being owed for debts. He is too generous lending the other officers money. He said something about selling his commission, and then we shall be wed. I am sorry he will no longer be in regimentals, but it does not signify. Oh! I had *so* wanted to be the one to write to my mother and sisters as Mrs Wickham. The youngest, the first married! Imagine it!"

"Imagining this ambition is all you may ever do, Miss Bennet. You have not heard the latest news. Your eldest sister will be no spinster. She has lately become engaged to Charles Bingley."

The turn of Lydia's countenance changed in a heartbeat from blissful to tearful. "What? Oh, no! Is a date set? Oh, Lord…"

Darcy closed his eyes. *What a loathsome, useless creature. How is it possible she and Elizabeth are sisters?* He opened his eyes. "You are not happy for her?" There was a pause and no response but sniffles from Lydia. "In truth, I have not heard a date is set. The betrothal is recent. If you wish to be the first Bennet to marry, you must not allow Wickham to dawdle about his business."

"Indeed, I shall not allow it."

Lovely thought, Darcy mused, *now Lydia will become a scold.* "You do have another option, Miss Lydia. If you now think better of marrying Wickham, I will transport you to your uncle's house immediately, where your father awaits. If you have any doubts or wish to preserve your honour, it is not too late."

"Leave Wickham and break his heart? He dotes on me and will make me a jolly husband. We are already having such a merry time. What call have I to leave my handsome Wickham?"

Darcy looked around the squalid room. "As to Wickham being handsome, you may have to get used to some alteration, madam. He has run afoul of a superior officer just now, and you might find him less charming when next you see him. But he may heal well…who can say? It depends on the skill of the physician at setting his nose."

Lydia met this report with obvious confusion. Without waiting for further remarks, Darcy tipped his hat and left the room.

A doctor was attending a cursing Wickham when Darcy returned to the sitting room. He pulled his highly diverted cousin away from overseeing the ministrations to Wickham's nose and the screams at every attempt to correct its displacement.

Darcy whispered, "Miss Lydia is unashamed of her actions. The only thing to give her upset is learning, unless matters speed up mightily, Jane Bennet will be married before she is, and *that*, of all things, is Lydia's chief concern."

Fitzwilliam chuckled softly.

Darcy pursued another thought. "I would like to set a guard upon this place, Cousin, to watch Wickham's every movement. Can you manage it? I fear we must go forward with a marriage negotiation, loathsome as that will be for all concerned. It would be like Wickham to attempt an escape."

"I know some men, Darcy. This can be easily done."

Wickham created a louder uproar as his head was tipped back and a squishing sound announced the realignment of his nose upon its under-pinnings. He spat blood as cotton was stuffed into his nostrils. When he looked down again, Fitzwilliam and Darcy laughed.

"Isn't there a creature from the New World that looks like that?" Colonel Fitzwilliam asked.

The doctor looked at his patient. "Yes, the Americans call it a raccoon. It has a mask of dark fur around its eyes. This gentleman is quick to bruise."

"He is *not* a gentleman, which may account for it," Darcy observed. As the physician cleaned and repacked his bag, Darcy handed him several coins. "You understand he was resisting arrest?"

"Yes, sir. I have seen the colonel's document."

"Fine. We have an understanding," Darcy confirmed.

"If you have any inclination to mercy, sir, you might stand the patient to a bottle of brandy," the physician suggested as he took his leave.

Darcy smiled. "What say you, Cousin? Brandy?"

Fitzwilliam laughed. "I doubt what they serve here is drinkable, but we will never know if we do not try."

Darcy stepped into the hall, and with ready money, the proprietress was delighted to provide a dusty, unopened bottle of brandy and three tumblers of dubious cleanliness.

"I would not worry about the smears on the glasses, Darcy," Fitzwilliam said when he noticed the scepticism in his cousin's eyes. "This alcohol should kill anything living." The two gentlemen drank to each other's health and noted the liquor was not so vile after all. "I believe we are to apportion the lion's share to Mr Wickham, Darcy."

"Oh, right. Right." Darcy poured a glass and handed it to Wickham. "Now," Darcy said, drawing up a straight chair and turning it to sit leaning his elbows on the back, "Wickham. I would be inclined to hold your debts, those in Brighton and Meryton, if you will consider yourself betrothed to Miss Lydia Bennet. I shall settle some little money upon her, and I am sure Mr Bennet will do for her what he would have planned to do for any of his daughters under more honourable circumstances. I can prevail upon my cousin to assist with selling your commission. That is the offer. Think upon it, and I shall return tomorrow."

"Bastard, I owe you nothing." Wickham spat in his face.

"If I might amend, Darcy," Colonel Fitzwilliam spoke as Darcy wiped his face without emotion. "This document I possess indicates Wickham's commission now has no value since he has dishonoured it, and he may now only resign. He can make no profit from it. This was not a well-thought scheme, Wickham. However much you may dislike it, marriage to Lydia Bennet is the only option that maintains you outside a stockade."

Wickham viewed his tormentors with narrowed, aching eyes. "You always get your way, do you not, Darcy? Make no mistake: someday I shall best you."

Darcy's countenance was implacable. "My money is on your dying before I do, most likely of the French pox; in *that* you shall best me. Do be aware you are being watched, Wickham. You will *never* go anywhere *ever* again that I do not know. *Forever.*" Darcy stood, and his cousin preceded him from the room. Darcy shut the door behind Fitzwilliam and turned back to Wickham, who was now standing.

"As for owing me nothing, you owe me a great deal, Wickham. Had I denounced you in Meryton as I should have, you never would have had the opportunity to trifle with *any* Bennet daughter." He turned his back to leave.

"Then I should have got my leg over Elizabeth Bennet whilst I had my chance, with her consent or no."

Wickham never saw the blow coming that sent two of his teeth across the room—where they bounced neatly onto an ancient doily decorating a dusty table—and dislocated his jaw.

When Darcy quitted the inn, he saw the physician standing on the corner counting the money in his hand. Darcy approached to hand him several more coins, and the doctor returned to the inn.

Fitzwilliam cocked his head quizzically as he held the carriage door open for his cousin. "Would you believe he attempted to resist arrest *again?*" Darcy asked mildly as he climbed into the coach.

The colonel snickered. "He did, did he?" He noticed Darcy was rubbing the knuckles of his right hand, which were beginning to swell. "Some things are better left to professionals, Darcy."

"I expect you are right, but it felt grand at the time." Darcy smiled.

UPON RETURNING TO DARCY HOUSE, he found an express awaiting from Georgiana:

Pemberley
4 August, 1812

Dearest Gander, (if I am now a goose, you see what it makes of you),

Mrs Annesley has returned, looks well and had a fine visit with her family. My report to her of your affection for Elizabeth comes as no surprise, as she observed it herself when Elizabeth and her aunt called on the day before Mrs A. departed. We shall be ready to leave for London whenever you bid us come.

As to what Elizabeth has said to me about Wickham prior to this present predicament, it was what we talked of on her first night here, when I had to lead you away from lurking outside her door, you shameful thing. She thinks ill of him. She knew early in their acquaintance he would be a highly imprudent choice but felt sorry for him. She said her father and Mrs Gardiner found his tales unseemly, to be saying what he did amongst relative strangers, which stole the ring of truth from their telling. Her own interest took the form of pity, as I see it, for she has a kind heart, and you had not exactly set yourself up as a paragon of civility. She said when she left for Kent in March that he was pursuing an heiress in her neighbourhood—she said this to comfort me, to let me know he is making a career of deceiving heiresses and I was merely one of many. She would not have me think ill of men and reminded me how good you are. If Wickham thinks he had a great ally in Elizabeth Bennet, we can put it down to vanity and predilection for self-deception.

The regiment left Meryton less than a fortnight after Elizabeth's return, and she said she was heartily glad to see the back of Wickham and all the officers. She did laugh and say our cousin is the only officer she has ever liked, who has manners she does not have to fear every minute will veer off to indecency. I have not yet received a response to my first letter as I only dated it and put it in the post to Netherfield yesterday. You and my cousin are in my constant prayers. I worry, and hope you will keep me well apprised.

Yours as ever,
The Goose

DARCY REREAD THE LETTER DURING his hot bath before dinner. He must trust Georgiana's assessment of Elizabeth's feelings, knowing ladies have more insight into each other. Everyone he knew seemed to read Elizabeth better than he did. He remembered the heated exchange of words during his regrettable proposal in April, which convinced him to share Georgiana's opinion. In defending Wickham, Elizabeth spoke only of pity, and it was Darcy's actions that owned the responsibility of making Wickham appear pitiable. But in Darcy's experience, pity was a far cry from love.

He found Elizabeth's appraisal of Colonel Fitzwilliam somewhat more unsettling. He had seen his cousin amidst drunken revels where he treated women very indecently indeed, but Richard was the second son of an earl and knew how to appear gentlemanly. Elizabeth instantly sparked his cousin's interest in a way that was more serious and respectful, even though after ten minutes conversation, they were playful and lively with each other. And then, there was the matter of the colonel's unhesitating defence of Elizabeth's honour when it was denigrated by Wickham today. *My cousin seems to have formed his own attachment. His actions speak volumes.* Darcy considered this as he soaked.

Before dinner, he managed to write a response to Georgiana, noting all the progress being made—minus the details of her brother and cousin acting impulsively—although it made his hand ache to hold the pen. He encouraged her to proceed to London and to send another express upon leaving Pemberley.

Over dinner, Darcy and his cousin discussed the future of George Wickham and Lydia Bennet. In practical terms, they decided it would be best for Wickham to take a commission in the regulars somewhere far away from Hertfordshire, and they hoped he would land in a regiment with a likelihood of seeing action in France. Fitzwilliam spoke of a general in that branch of the army, a man he considered the strictest disciplinarian of any general of his acquaintance. He knew not where that general's regiment was currently billeted, but it was information easy to obtain. They decided to appear at the war office together when it opened in the morning, and then Fitzwilliam would proceed to Brighton and his duties. Darcy could easily finish the contract with Wickham on his own.

While the cousins lingered over fruit and cheese, the butler brought an express from Bingley, written earlier that afternoon. They withdrew to the library, and Darcy perused his letter as his cousin read a book.

Netherfield Park, Hertfordshire
5 August, 1812

Dear Darcy,

The journey to Hertfordshire was without incident, and I must say, the Gardiner children are very well behaved. Howsoever, by the end of the trip, my dear Jane and her aunt had become deeply concerned for Lizzy.

Bingley had written Lizzy, crossed it out and written Elizabeth, crossed *that* out and written Lizzy again. Darcy scanned ahead to see the whole letter was similarly chaotic.

We reached Longbourn Tuesday afternoon, and between the two of them, they could not recall seeing her eat more than one mouthful of food at any meal. I joined the family for breakfast this morning, and I did not see her take more than a piece of bread with jam, and this she did not finish.

Mrs Bennet is keeping above stairs but did come down to the drawing room to receive me and drink tea last night. Her despair over Lydia overcomes her happiness for Jane and me. She spoke of visiting the neighbours to brag me up, but Lizzy and Jane talked her out of it. They fear their mother rattling on about Lydia outside the family. Lizzy feels her father's absence from home keenly, and Jane feels it all the more since she must see to his correspondence and business in his absence. Lizzy helps her in this. Makes me wish I knew more about running an estate. You would be more help to them than I am.

This morning, Lizzy announced she would take up the tenant visits, which had not been done since her leaving home in July. Her mother has long left this chore to her. I asked how she liked visiting the tenants as we three were the last at breakfast and she is always so frank. She says she enjoys it, and with only six tenant families, she can have a round of calls completed in two days' time. I told her she has had excellent preparation for being the mistress of a larger estate, and she blushed very nicely but made no other remark. Jane said afterward that Lizzy looks for every excuse to get away from the house, and who can blame her?

Of my own family, I can only report they are in Scarborough still. Hurst's last letter was full of hints to shoot here in September. My letters from Louisa and Caroline do not incline me to issue an invitation yet. I have sent them an announcement of my betrothal and move to Netherfield, no time for a response.

Do send me news when you have any to share, and anything you say will be kept confidential. Is Georgiana in London? Please extend my good wishes upon her birthday.

Best regards and faithfully,
C. Bingley

Darcy stood and paced. His cousin looked up and watched him for a moment before suggesting, "Brandy?"

"Yes, thanks, if you're pouring." After his first swallow, Darcy asked, "Fitzwilliam, were you ever in danger from Elizabeth Bennet?" Darcy looked at his cousin intently.

"Because I hit Wickham for insulting a lady whom you love and I rather like?"

"What did you feel in April?"

"Why ever does it matter now?"

"In April she liked you better than she did me, and if you had asked her to marry you, she might have said yes."

"Darcy...why this torture?"

"I know you have more means to support a wife than you say you do. I *know* you have put money by and could certainly make a wife with Elizabeth's prudent expectations quite comfortable, but you let me warn you off."

"Cousin, I do not understand you, but I will tell you what transpired. I did feel an attraction, although I cannot say what Elizabeth might have felt. When you explained the Bennet family circumstances, and after seeing you with her, I realised you were warning me for two reasons: one acknowledged, that I must be circumspect in my choice of wife, and the second, that you were utterly obsessed with her. When I explained I was merely the second son of an earl, she understood my meaning immediately. She is a clever girl and made a good joke of it. She reckons I ought not sell myself for anything less than £50,000."

Darcy pondered this. "You would make a better husband for her than I, Richard," he finally muttered through a clenched jaw.

Colonel Fitzwilliam stared at his cousin in disbelief. "You cannot be serious, Darcy. Please sit down. What troubles you? Something in Bingley's letter? Or in Georgiana's?"

"Elizabeth is making herself unwell. She is not eating. She is despairing, and I am to blame. From what she said when we parted, and from Bingley's report, I believe she feels she has lost me. She does not trust my affection."

"You make no sense. What has any of this to do with any short-lived inclination I might have had? As for not trusting your affection, you must strive to relieve her mind, and not just by securing Wickham for her sister without taking the credit of it. Have you any way to communicate with her?"

"Georgiana writes to her through Bingley."

"There you are! When Georgie gets here, include a few lines in one of her letters. Whatever you think you need to be forgiven for, ask it of her. Consider her situation, Darcy. In spite of Jane and Bingley's happy news, her family exists under a cloud of disgrace. She must have convinced herself you will not renew your addresses because of the association with Wickham. And why does she feel that way? It began before she ever met Wickham when you so carelessly and publicly insulted her at the Meryton assembly, for which you have never asked forgiveness, have you?"

Darcy shook his head as his cousin continued, "That rude beginning left the field ploughed for Wickham to sow his lies. He appeared amiable when you did not. You blame yourself for the current situation, and so you should, but not because you did not expose Wickham when you had the chance, rather because the person in the best position of influence in the neighbourhood—a lady known for her sensible opinions—was the person you thoughtlessly insulted at your first meeting. Darcy, this is all quite clear to Georgiana. Bingley explained his observations to her, and she to me. I have nothing to do with Elizabeth's current sadness or future happiness. She can have no regrets of me. It is all down to you. Accept it. Correct it."

Darcy was lost in reverie, and although he heard his cousin and agreed with him, he made no response for several minutes. At last he said, "Bingley wrote of something I had not even considered, which adds materially to

Elizabeth's already extensive virtues. She is the one of her family to undertake the visiting and administering of aid to the Longbourn tenants. It is a mere handful compared with the number at Pemberley, but Bingley and Jane say she enjoys the work." Darcy slumped down into a chair. "Richard...cannot you imagine her, smiling and charmingly officious, winding her way around Pemberley's farms in a curricle with children waving at her approach?" His strained voice lowered to a whisper. "Was ever a woman more perfect for me than Miss Elizabeth Bennet?"

Colonel Fitzwilliam stood and patted his cousin's shoulder as he left the room. "You know what you must do. Communicate with her however you can, as soon as may be, and get this mess with Wickham mopped up as quickly as possible. Goodnight, Darcy. Mind your hand; it will pain you in the morning."

Thursday, 6 August, 1812

THE NEXT DAY'S BUSINESS TOOK up much of Darcy's time. With his cousin, he obtained the documents for Wickham to resign his present commission. A commission in the regulars under a General Steveton was purchased in its stead. The general's brigade was stationed in Newcastle. Darcy was pleased with the arrangement of Wickham's immediate future.

When Darcy visited Wickham in the afternoon, Wickham would not come down until he was assured Colonel Fitzwilliam was not in attendance. Once calmed on this account, he attended Darcy in the sitting room used the day before but kept himself an arm's length away throughout their interview. His face, Darcy was happy to see, was a wreck. Although the doctor had successfully realigned his jaw, the bruising was extensive. Wickham recounted the lies he told Lydia about how he came to appear so beaten, but to this, Darcy paid no heed. He was only quietly pleased that an exceedingly vain and immoral man with only his looks to recommend him would now be less appealing to the fair sex, and Lydia's triumph in securing him must be much diminished.

After a few hours, all-important papers were signed for the army, a monetary agreement was reached—which amounted to less than Darcy had expected to spend—and Lydia was consulted about a date for a wedding to be held under special license to speed the arrangement of the ceremony. All was dependent upon the approval of Lydia's family, and this, Darcy hoped to secure through Mr Gardiner the next day.

As Darcy left the inn, he was approached by two young toughs who made themselves known as respectfully as they were able. They introduced themselves as two of a band of watchers who had been recruited and paid their first wages by Colonel Fitzwilliam. Darcy said he was glad to know them and they would have three to four weeks employment. He asked them to consider moving north to Newcastle in the autumn to continue their task and to ask the same of their fellows.

Late that evening, another express arrived from Georgiana. She had a letter from Elizabeth, which she would bring with her to London. Georgiana said only that the tone of the letter seemed sad, but Elizabeth was comforted to have returned to her regular responsibilities at home. There was no good news at Longbourn concerning Lydia, and the family had just received word that, barring some swiftly proceeding development, Mr Bennet would return home the following Saturday morning. Mrs Gardiner would return to London that afternoon. Elizabeth did ask to be remembered to her brother, which Georgiana made much of to offer encouragement.

Darcy's encouragement was slight, but he was happy to have word of Mr Bennet's whereabouts and put off his visit to Mr Gardiner until Saturday. He sent word to Wickham and Lydia to expect a visit from himself and Mr Gardiner on Saturday afternoon. He mulled over how to explain Wickham's altered looks to Mr Gardiner and decided, after the meeting of the parties, he would tell the truth of Wickham's injuries to Elizabeth's uncle.

Sunday, 9 August, 1812

THE DINNER WITH THE GARDINERS became tense when they realised, from the direction of his comments on the Wickham matter, that Mr Darcy intended his effort and expense on behalf of the couple to go unsung and without reimbursement. Mr Gardiner saw it as a presumption on their burgeoning friendship that he was forced to receive accolades due to Darcy's action and could not accept that so much goodness should go misdirected and un-praised. Darcy was adamant, and after a tortured hour of talking at cross-purposes with nearly raised voices, Mrs Gardiner put a stop to it by laying a gentle hand on her husband's knee and meeting his eye with a nod of her head.

She said, "Mr Darcy, I see your purpose has not changed from what you expressed as I left Pemberley. I had hoped you would change your mind. There is one person whom you would not wish to feel obliged to you. We shall keep your secret for her sake, but should she learn of it from some other source and ask me the particulars, she will be told everything. You would not wish to establish a more permanent arrangement with Elizabeth under a cloud of dissemblance, I think."

Darcy started to argue, but Mrs Gardiner held up a staying hand. "Someday you shall know my niece as well as I do. She is the very definition of curiosity and is too inventive by half. If she does not know the facts, she will fill the vacancy with her own assumptions. It will be better, if she does learn of this, that she know all, and accurately."

Mrs Gardiner rather liked the look of Darcy's smile as he chuckled and said, "Yes, I am sure you are correct there."

Mrs Gardiner looked directly into Darcy's eyes. "You must not keep from Elizabeth the opportunity to be proud of you, sir. For that is what she will feel. She will be proud of you when she learns all you have done. Do not deny her that."

When Darcy arrived home at nightfall, he found his sister and Mrs Annesley had arrived, and they were finishing a light meal. Georgiana showed him Elizabeth's letters. They held no revelations, but he was comforted to see her handwriting again.

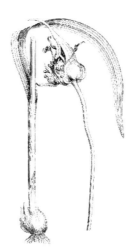

Garlic
"Courage"

Chapter 12

Monday, 17 August, 1812

Georgiana Darcy's seventeenth birthday dawned excessively warm. The morning post brought a letter from her cousin Anne and another from Lady Catherine. The former was full of warmth and good wishes, and Anne continued her praise of Georgiana for pushing Darcy toward Elizabeth.

Lady Catherine's letter was as unkind and absurd as ever. Without having seen her niece in a year, Lady Catherine, in her infinite and benevolent condescension, decided Georgiana was not practicing enough at her music, and therefore, she had been surpassed by the non-musical Anne in both musicality and expression. She further instructed Georgiana to come out during the next season lest the difficult truth about an improper relationship the previous summer become generally known, and she must also encourage her brother to make a formal proposal of marriage to Anne.

Hence, Georgiana was vexed when she emerged from her room for a late breakfast. Darcy had been up several hours and joined her to take another cup of coffee as his sister ate her usual morning meal.

"Dear Goose, what has made you so unhappy on your birthday? You look exceedingly cross," Darcy observed.

"I have had a lovely note from Anne and an annoying letter from Aunt Catherine. What a hoyden she is, Brother. I am more sorry for Anne with each passing year. But Anne does cheer me, and I ought to concentrate on what *she* said rather than being disturbed by her mother."

"What does our cousin say?"

"She wishes me to keep pushing you at Elizabeth Bennet, if you must know."

Darcy tried not to show his foreboding. It would be a fearsome thing if Lady Catherine learnt of his affection for anyone other than Anne, whatever Anne's wishes might be. If letters should fall into Aunt Catherine's hands or first drafts tossed carelessly aside, the whole country would hear of her displeasure. She was not a woman to be gainsaid.

Georgiana read her brother's thoughts easily. "I do not mention your lady by name, Brother. It is not necessary. We have been at the topic long enough that our cousin understands of whom I write."

Darcy smiled a little and produced an ornate brown bottle from his pocket, seeking to steer the subject away from Lady Catherine. "I have a gift for you, Georgie, which is utterly unique to you, and its existence will explain a mystery of which you have not lately spoken." He laid the bottle on his arm imitating a sommelier in Paris presenting a fine vintage.

Georgiana read the label. "It is from Elizabeth?" she asked, recognising the writing.

"She made it for you at my request. That is why she was in the Pemberley stillroom. We had made the assignation the evening before, so this would be ready in time for your birthday. She makes perfume for all her family, including her own scent."

"Which, I take it, is lavender?"

Darcy smiled. "It is."

Georgiana read the label aloud. "Arabian Jasmine for Amiability, Damask Rose for Brilliancy of Complexion." She looked at her brother. "Did you request this combination?"

"I left it entirely to Elizabeth."

Georgiana pierced the wax over the stopper with a fingernail, opened the bottle and inhaled the scent. "I love it!" she said instantly.

Darcy leaned over to smell the stopper. "Very pretty!" he agreed. Darcy smiled at his sister, but in truth, he was smiling at a lady who was not in the room, or even in the city. He had hoped to arrange for the Gardiners to dine at Darcy House as a further surprise for Georgiana. However, because of the unruly and ungrateful niece currently burdening their household

—who was noisily chafing at the restrictions placed upon her behaviour by her all-seeing and all-knowing aunt—the Gardiners felt they could not get away from home, much as they wished to.

After breakfast, Darcy and Georgiana spent an hour in the library, where Darcy presented her with a selection of novels and poetry. They were later joined by Colonel Fitzwilliam, who would stay for dinner. He had just settled himself to join them in reading when the butler entered, followed by a footman carrying a large, somewhat flat, wooden crate. The butler handed Georgiana a card.

"It is from Mrs Gardiner and Elizabeth! What can it be?"

Darcy took the small hammer from the footman and began prying the slats apart. He believed the portraits of Elizabeth on the banks of his fishing stream and at Arbor Low would be inside. His expectation was incomplete.

The pencil sketches of Elizabeth *en plein air* had been elegantly framed and hinged together so they might sit on a table. The three stood and admired them. "I had no idea Mrs Gardiner and Elizabeth intended these for me," Georgiana said. She paused. "I thought them spoken for..." She looked at her brother.

"I knew they were for you, Georgie, but assumed they would be presented at Pemberley. I have been on my best behaviour that you would part with one for me, but they are hinged together. Mrs Gardiner is the very soul of propriety. I'm glad she and the subject sent them here, even if they could not enjoy the fulfilment of seeing you open their gift."

"But there is another picture in the crate," their cousin observed.

Darcy was surprised but then remembered Mrs Gardiner had planned a triptych. He assumed, events unfolding as they had, that Elizabeth's aunt had not the time to complete the third image. He lifted a larger picture from the box, wrapped in a layer of chamois cloth. It was facing his sister and the colonel when he pulled the covering away. They both looked startled and then smiled. A note in Mrs Gardiner's hand fluttered to the floor. Georgiana picked it up as Darcy leaned the picture in a chair and stepped around to see the image.

Clearly the ambition of the composition was more complicated than Mrs Gardiner's gifted but amateur talent could capture fully, but Elizabeth's face was luminously rendered, and it was clear enough she was looking at Darcy's portrait at Pemberley, mainly because Mrs Gardiner included just the first few letters of the name plate on the frame: "Fitzw..."

Darcy could not breathe. Although Elizabeth was in profile, even he understood the expression in her eye and the set of her mouth, as if caught on the very point of smiling. "Are those red chrysanthemums in her hands, Georgie?" he whispered.

"I believe they are," Georgiana replied and grasped her brother's arm as if he needed steadying.

"Read the note, gosling," urged their cousin.

Georgiana huffed. "Really, Cousin, you must try to keep up with the times. My brother has decided I am adult now and pronounced me a goose full grown before he left Pemberley. Make a note of it, I pray you." She opened the paper and read aloud:

"From Mrs Madeleine Gardiner

"Gracechurch Street, London

"17 August, 1812

"Dear Miss Darcy,

"Perhaps this painting has asked more of me than my poor talents can master, but my intent was to capture our dear Elizabeth at the moment we saw her fall in love with your brother."

Darcy looked down, blushing, at the floor.

"Her uncle, Mrs Reynolds and I were the only witnesses, and having seen this picture in various stages of completion, those two will vouch for the accuracy of the fondness of her gaze, and the look of realization that overspread her then. We can thank Mrs Reynolds for supplying the flowers at Lizzy's particular request."

At this, Darcy stepped in front of his sister and cousin to look at the painting more particularly. His eyes were burning, and he feared he might cry, so he squinted.

"It is my fond wish, dear Georgiana, that someday soon I will have the opportunity to make more of that day known to you—the day my niece first came to Pemberley. What you see here is my testimonial that she was in love with your brother even before she met him by chance outside the house. I am not the romantic many women are, but I believe, in some way, her heart called to Mr Darcy that day.

"Please accept my very best wishes for your birthday and those of my niece as well,

"M. Gardiner"

It was Georgiana who cried, and handkerchiefs from both men in the room were proffered for her use.

Darcy avoided tears but was grinning stupidly. His cousin could not resist tweaking him. "I say, Darcy, I have never seen you look more like Charles Bingley. Are you as besotted as you look?"

Darcy could not be perturbed and nodded. "This waiting for Wickham's wedding grows more tedious by the minute. How gratified he would be to know I am tortured by impatience. I shall be fifty times as happy on the day I wed as he shall ever be on his, and I want my happiness to start right this minute."

Fitzwilliam murmured, "I am sure I should feel the same if so beautiful and fine a woman ever once looked at me that way."

Darcy turned to meet his cousin's eyes. "You did love her?"

"No, Darcy, truly, I did not. When I saw how you looked at her in the Hunsford parsonage, *I* knew she stirred you, even if *she* did not. I would have asked your feelings were mine growing serious, although you might have tried to prevaricate. And you did put me off with the reminder of my being a second son. I guessed what you were about, you know.

"Did you ever write her that apology I suggested? Have you written to her at all?"

Georgiana asked, "What apology?"

"After our first finding Wickham and Lydia, Darcy had a letter from Bingley full of worry. He thought Elizabeth pining for the loss of this great lout here. I told him he still needed to apologise for his misstep on the night he met her, that he had thus set this calamity in motion."

"Oh for heaven's sake…" With two handkerchiefs wadded in her hand, Georgiana went to the nearest desk. She dropped the hankies as she put the desk in order for writing; putting pen, ink, and paper upon it. She stood and said, "It is you, Brother, who has no more sense than a feather pillow. Write her the apology. Cheer her. Strengthen her. Let her know the time is as interminable for you as it is for her. At least you are with people who know your heart. She can say nothing except perhaps to Jane when they are alone. And what can Jane say to her of real encouragement since she appears to be keeping the secret that you have Mr Bennet's permission to court Elizabeth? Write to her and leave her in no doubt. Do it as a gift to me."

Darcy walked to the desk, gave his sister a last grumpy-brother look since that visage now seemed to have completely lost whatever effect it had ever commanded, and sat.

Picking up the pencil drawings, Georgiana took her cousin's arm, and they started to leave the room. She stopped at the door. "Gander, you may have the loan of that painting until you are in possession of its subject. Then you must return it to me."

Darcy looked up, reappraising Georgiana yet again. "Georgie, I think it would be a fine thing if you made me a present of it when I marry."

Georgiana rolled her eyes. "Well! There's another surprise ruined. You really are impossible, Brother."

The colonel was laughing as they closed the library door on Darcy, whose head was now bent to his task.

Thursday, 20 August, 1812

ELIZABETH'S NERVES WERE STRAINED AS she awoke just before dawn from another night of poor sleep. Jane stirred as Elizabeth dressed for a vigorous walk before breakfast.

"Lizzy? You are going out early again? Dearest, you overdo. You walk too far and you eat too little. I am despairing of you."

"I am apprehensive, Jane. The cursed wedding nears, and for no good reason, I fear it will never take place. Let me work out my ill humours. I will be back for breakfast this time; I promise."

"Of what good is it to join us at breakfast if you will not eat it?"

Lizzy smiled. "I shall wander through the orchard and eat an apple. At least the family can claim a handsome crop this year; we have so little else of which to boast. Except for you, dear Jane, there is little to make us happy. Let me at least take pride in our apples and pears."

"Just eat them; that is all I ask." Jane smiled at her sister and took her hand for a moment before Elizabeth went out the door.

As she returned to Longbourn from the orchard with a gathering basket of apples, Elizabeth was overtaken by Charles Bingley on horseback. He was joining the Bennets for breakfast. He dismounted and exchanged a bow and curtsy with Elizabeth.

"Good morning, Lizzy! I hope you are well?"

"Perhaps a little more cheerful than I have been." She held up an apple core. "When you get to the house, please let Jane know I have eaten an apple." She smiled.

"She will be pleased." Bingley laughed and reached into the pocket of his riding coat, producing a letter. "Your post, madam!"

Elizabeth glanced at the direction on the letter and her breath left her as she recognised the handwriting. It was from Darcy. The stamp of his signet ring on the seal confirmed it. Bingley was pleased that the mere sight of his friend's handwriting left her blushing.

"Do not worry. It came to Netherfield inside a letter addressed to me. Darcy is in London for Georgiana's birthday. He tells me they will invite the Gardiners to visit at Darcy House after Lydia is married and gone. Frankly, Lizzy, I am surprised he did not write to you sooner."

"Oh!" Elizabeth did not know where to look or what to say. "Thank you, Charles. I…I was turning for home, but I will stay here and read it, although I know it is improper."

"Some weeks ago, you told me that if Darcy should write me a letter, I should read it. Take your own advice." Bingley nodded at her with his habitual smile.

"I remember. That was the night before one of the happiest times of my life. You wrote to my father, and I was full of anticipation on Jane's behalf. I believed Mr Darcy still in love with me, and I had a wonderful time in the Pemberley stillroom. When I am your children's old maid aunt, it will be one of my fondest memories."

Bingley shook his head. "You are stubborn in your belief that Darcy will not propose again?"

Elizabeth blushed, looked down and shook her head. "I have not the smallest hope."

Bingley remounted. "You know, Lizzy, I used to tell Darcy how sensible you are, for all your liveliness and wit. But about him, you are not so sensible. In fact, if I may speak plainly as one who will soon be a brother, when it comes to Fitzwilliam Darcy, you have no more sense than a pot of soup." He turned upon his horse and proceeded to Longbourn as Elizabeth opened her letter.

Darcy House, London
Tuesday, 18 August, 1812

Dearest Miss Elizabeth,

Since you left Pemberley, I have thought and spoken of little except you. I cannot comprehend how we let the present circumstances ruin what could have been, and could still be, the happiest possible future for us both.

Elizabeth stared at the words and then repeated them aloud.

At last, I have reckoned the source of the complications existing between us, and now that I understand it, I can at least try for a remedy. On our very first meeting, I insulted you. It was public, it was petulant, and I regretted it nearly instantly. Within ten minutes, I knew I had made a most grievous mistake, but my pride, as it was then, would not allow me to make amends. You were right to laugh at me.

I see now that those dreadful words have continued to hurt you, and I have not been forgiven them because they were too cruel, and idiot that I am, for all the self-improvements I have made, I have yet to ask forgiveness for that first misstep. And so, dear Elizabeth, for that deplorable display of bad manners and childish temper, let me, at long last, beg your leniency. Forgive me. It was my first and greatest sin against you and set in terrible motion your distrust of me. Every sorry thing that has happened since has sprouted from that bad seed. To think I planted it myself, in the heart dearest in the world to me, makes me wretched.

Elizabeth inhaled, feeling his words squeezing her chest.

That you ever overcame your justifiable dislike enough to include a red chrysanthemum in a bouquet meant for me, speaks to your generosity, kindness, goodness, and perhaps, a sadly questionable taste in men, for which I am in no position to fault you. You are, and have always been, a woman without fault. Everything I learn of you confirms this. No matter what you may now think of me, you are my idea of feminine perfection.

Please say you will allow me to call upon you when I am next in Hertfordshire. I expect to arrive sometime in September, and I will stay as long as it takes to secure your good opinion, shoot a few birds, and see Bingley and your sister safely wed. That first thing is the most important, and henceforth, Georgiana will write to you at Longbourn. Let your mother say what she will; I am done with the pretence that there is no connection between yourself and those named Darcy.

With deepest affection,
F. Darcy

Elizabeth was so stunned by what she read that she sat on the nearest seat she could find, the muddy tread of a stile. She read the letter twice before feeling the telltale ache of approaching tears. Perturbed to be yet again on the verge of crying, she burst into movement, racing to the Longbourn garden. She did not have to look far to find a red chrysanthemum, and she carried it into the house. After taking the flower and letter to her room, she joined her family for breakfast. That her skirt was muddy brought her sisters into an uproar, and Jane accompanied Elizabeth back up the stairs to help her change her gown. She showed Jane her letter, and they both had a good cry. With Jane in the room, Elizabeth wrote out a quick note and enclosed the chrysanthemum in it. Jane took the lumpy envelope and passed it to Bingley when no one was looking.

Bingley and Jane were most pleased to watch as Elizabeth ate all her bread and jam, another apple and a slice of ham for her breakfast.

Saturday, 22 August, 1812

DARCY AROSE EARLY AS USUAL, his first thoughts wondering whether Elizabeth had his letter. After breakfast, as Garrick dressed Darcy for a stroll with his sister, the butler brought in the post with a letter from Bingley. The packet contained a single sheet in a beloved hand, preceded from its envelope by a flattened and tired, but recognizable, red chrysanthemum. Still in his shirtsleeves, Darcy scattered the servants from the dressing room, entered his bedchamber and stood reading at the window.

Longbourn, Hertfordshire
Thursday, 20 August, 1812

Dear Mr Darcy,

Your letter leaves me in the firmest understanding that you have become well aware of the meaning of a red chrysanthemum. If what you say is true and I have questionable taste in men, I can only reply, you are a lucky fellow, for I am so very sensible in every other way. Mr Bingley told me this morning, as regards you, I have "no more sense than a pot of soup." Now that he is to be my brother, I suppose there will be many similar drolleries aimed at myself in the future.

*Be assured, I shall always forgive you anything and have forgiven you
everything in the past, even that early offense against my pride of which
you particularly wrote. Please, let us forget the incident.*

*I will welcome your next visit to Hertfordshire by promising your
luck will persist, and in the meantime, I will continue to question and
misunderstand you in as ridiculous a manner as possible—since doing so
entertains Mr Bingley—until you are here to speak for yourself.*

With deepest affection,
E. Bennet

After reading his letter, Darcy needed to sit, and after tucking the wilted
flower in a book of Shakespeare's sonnets on his night table, he sat on the
edge of his bed, rereading the brief missive. *She follows my lead still; she
will not say she loves me—as I did not do—but she sends me her flower. She
signs herself as I signed my letter to her, just as she mimicked the card with my
flowers. I think I may now hope.* It was clear to Darcy that, when he feared
for Bingley's reception in Meryton, it was his own acceptance of which he
was uncertain. Now the one source of disapprobation he most feared was
disposed to forgive and welcome him.

He laughed. *To Bingley she is a pot of soup, and to Georgie, I am a feather
pillow. Together we are a fine kettle of fish—two objects that do not appear to
belong together, and yet we do.*

Darcy crossed the hall to his study to consult a calendar. He groaned
as he saw it was another five days until the Wickham wedding. There was
some hope Mr Bennet would not receive the newlyweds at Longbourn, but
Darcy was uncertain of it. How long would Lydia and Wickham stay if they
were allowed? *A fortnight? Surely not longer than that. A fortnight! I cannot
go to her for over a fortnight, at least.* "Damn!" he cursed aloud.

"Ahem." Darcy looked up from his desk at Garrick clearing his throat.
"Bad news, Mr Darcy?"

"No, not at all. Very good news. Wonderful news, which, alas, I cannot act
upon as speedily as I would wish." He paused, greeted by a happy thought.
"Garrick, I will be writing to Mrs Reynolds. Please tell Mr Lesley not to
let a packet of correspondence leave for home until you know my letter is
included." His valet nodded, bowed and left the room.

As HE WALKED WITH HIS sister in Hyde Park, Darcy mulled over changes to his sleeping arrangements at Pemberley, and a freshening of the mistress's adjoining apartment.

"Georgie, do you owe Miss Elizabeth a letter?"

"No, Brother, we are at evens now. I suppose either of us may write when we have anything particular to say. Mr Bingley has been an excellent postman."

"As to that, I would have you write her directly at Longbourn in the future. We shall have no more disguises."

"You have had a response? She has forgiven you?"

The turn of her brother's countenance answered her question before his words did. "She informs me I am a lucky man, and she expects my luck will persist."

Georgiana laughed aloud and in public, amongst strangers in the park.

When they returned to Darcy House, he walked into his bedchamber, surprising the young chambermaids. "Do not trouble yourselves," he ordered as he passed them and unlocked the door into the adjoining bedchamber, which he had not entered since his mother's death. Everything was concealed by dust covers and sheeting. He turned back to the chambermaids.

"Ladies?"

Both women stood and curtsied to him.

"Please prepare this room; dust it and open the balcony doors, that my sister and I may see its present condition in a cleaned state. It is high time it was made habitable again. Tell Mrs Knightley what you are about; you will need the housekeeper's direction."

The maids blushed and curtsied again, "Yes, sir. Yes, Mr Darcy."

Darcy asked Georgiana to help him prepare Pemberley and Darcy House to welcome a new mistress. They were both quite giddy and wrote to Mrs Reynolds together.

That night, Darcy slept with the door to the mistress's bedroom open, and he fell into an agitated slumber, anticipating a future when Mrs Elizabeth Darcy would come to him through it, laughing at him.

Thursday, 27 August, 1812

IT WAS FORTUNATE FOR GEORGE Wickham—although he did not know it —that Mrs Gardiner had written to the Bennet family a week prior to his wedding. Although he did not deserve it, she had taken pity on his vanity and sent a letter in advance of his arrival with his bride, advising the Bennets to prepare themselves for his somewhat altered looks. The glibness of Wickham's story about being beset by officers from his former regiment —who just happened to wander into the low establishment where he and Lydia first stayed and just happened to find him at the bar—was too much coincidence for that sagacious lady to bear. It all seemed as highly unlikely as the tale of a gentleman of Fitzwilliam Darcy's reputation oversetting his father's will to deny Wickham a life in the church. No, Mrs Gardiner had another theory and no proper way to ascertain its value.

In any case, as the Wickhams' carriage rolled into the paddock at Longbourn, he did not have to encounter mocking giggles and sly glances. Lydia Wickham, as undaunted by the obvious as ever, introduced him to her family as the handsomest husband ever seen, and her mother squealed in agreement and gingerly kissed him on each cheek. She did notice the distinctly green cast to the skin masking his eyes when at close range—the bruising having faded that much—but was not inclined to comment. Although Mrs Bennet was solicitous of men generally after having lived with an independently minded husband for nearly 25 years, she was not disposed to baby them.

In the days that passed, waiting for his wedding, Wickham spent no little time practicing a warm and obliging closed-mouth smile. With a front tooth and its canine neighbour missing, and Lydia's hectoring about his inclination to stretch his upper lip on one side to cover the gap, he was moved to spend hours in front of the looking glass in his rooms—rehearsing. His nose had not healed altogether straight, but if he turned his head down and slightly tilted, its slant was not so noticeable. He fancied—as so vain a man would—that looking up from thus lowered eyes and smiling with a closed mouth gave him an enigmatic air that suited him. Lydia agreed, as he had tried his new mannerisms on the lady who would have to endure them more than any other.

Far from putting herself forward to greet her sister and new brother, Elizabeth hung back with her father and observed. Lydia was unchanged, but Wickham was somehow a little humbled, a little more aware of the situation and the Bennet family's true feelings about it. When he finally bowed briefly over her hand, she saw the bruising on his jaw, more blue than the green around his eyes. Elizabeth was indifferent to the story of how he received his injuries; she would rather pretend Darcy had done the damage. That her own imagined version of events brought her so near the truth was something she would not know for the present.

For his own part, Mr Bennet said as little as possible and less still that was truly civil. He found himself wishing he had been the one to inflict such damage to Wickham's formerly handsome features. He was as aware as Elizabeth that her value in the eyes of the man she loved may have diminished, for all of Jane's protests to the contrary. Jane was so disposed to see the best in everyone and Bingley was so like her that, when the couple implored him privately to have no doubts of Darcy's continued affection for Elizabeth, he remained dubious.

Upon entering the drawing room, Lydia gathered her mother and sisters around to share every particular of her wedding. Elizabeth detached herself even before the wedding gown was fully described and sneaked into the garden. She knew she was leaving her father alone to attempt conversation with Wickham, but she could not stomach the man. It was all she could do to steel herself for sitting at the same table with him for dinner.

The next morning, Elizabeth and Jane were lingering at the breakfast table when Lydia joined them. "Lizzy! I believe you did not hear when I was telling my sisters of my wedding. Are you not curious about how it was managed?"

"I think there cannot be too little said on the subject," Elizabeth replied.

But Lydia was too full of herself to think her sister anything but strange, and she prattled away about lace choices and the search for proper slippers, finally coming to the point: the ceremony. "My uncle was called away on business and I was frightened of his being too late, but then I recalled that Mr Darcy would be there as groomsman and could have given me away when my aunt and I arrived if my uncle was unable to."

Elizabeth directed an alarmed look at Jane. "Mr Darcy?" She was utterly amazed.

Jane looked at Lydia with surprise. "You did not mention him yesterday, Lydia."

"Gracious me! I quite forgot! I ought not to have said a word. I promised to keep the secret so faithfully. What will Wickham say?"

"If it was to be a secret," said Jane, "say not another word about it. I will not ask further."

Elizabeth burned with curiosity and felt—what with gaping between one sister and the other—that she might have looked like a confused fish. "Oh, certainly! We shall ask you no questions." *But I must know all! How could this be? And Jane did not know? Our aunt must know more.*

"Thank you!" Lydia giggled like the naughty child she was. "For if you did ask, I should certainly tell you all, and then Wickham would be angry." Lydia spoke as if drawing Wickham's disapprobation did not concern her in the least.

In a typical fit of agitation, Elizabeth bolted from the room and stood panting in the hallway. There was nothing for it but to write to her aunt immediately, applying to know why, of all men, Fitzwilliam Darcy would stand up with Wickham. Her letter to Aunt Gardiner was brief and to the point.

By contrast, the letter Elizabeth received in response was lengthy and bearing every particular of Darcy's involvement in the finding, negotiation, and marrying of George Wickham to Lydia Bennet. Mrs Gardiner alluded to some early assistance from Colonel Fitzwilliam, but the far greater share of credit belonged to Darcy, and he alone bore the monetary expense. Only Mrs Gardiner's conjectures about Wickham's injuries were withheld.

Even in the face of the evidence presented to her, Elizabeth was stupefied. She had taken herself into a remote part of the garden to read the letter. Now she wandered amongst the flowers noticing nothing, being otherwise occupied with feelings of mortification on Darcy's behalf, remorse that her family needed to be the unwitting recipients of such generosity, and astonishment that it was generally assumed he had taken on these burdens because of his regard for her. Astonishment gave way to a tender sort of satisfaction, and she was well on her way to being justifiably proud of Darcy when she heard someone approaching. She turned to see Wickham, wearing his closed-mouth grin.

"Dear Sister, I hope I am not an unwelcome interruption."

Instantly on her guard, Elizabeth smiled warily, and without giving the appearance of wanting to run away—although she did—her feet turned back to the house, slowly, giving the impression that he might walk with her, but the conversation would be brief. She could end it on some pretext when they reached the front door.

"We were always good friends," Wickham stated hopefully.

"Yes, of course we *were*. Are the others coming out?" Elizabeth did not wish to be alone with him.

"Lydia and Mrs Bennet are taking the carriage into Meryton. I believe they are to visit Lucas Lodge."

Elizabeth looked away. The volume of gossip such a visit would produce was beyond measure. That some secret from Lydia would become generally known, or some conjecture of her mother's about herself and Darcy would be spread across the countryside as fact, was inescapable. And now she had to bear the company of Wickham by herself.

He cleared his throat before saying, "Do I understand correctly from your aunt and uncle that you have seen Pemberley?"

Ah! So you wish to know how much of the truth I have been told, do you? Is it even in you, George Wickham, to be embarrassed? "Yes, indeed, I have. It was everything you described and more."

"I envy you the pleasure. It would be too much for me to visit again or I would take it in for Lydia's sake on the way to Newcastle."

Elizabeth could not look at him.

"You saw the old housekeeper, dear Mrs Reynolds? She was always fond of me. But now I am sure she would not mention my name."

"Oh, but she did. She heard you were making your career in the military. She said she was afraid"—Elizabeth paused for effect—"you had not turned out well. At such a distance, well, facts may get strangely misrepresented." *But not in this case.* Elizabeth gave Wickham a knowing glance and looked away again.

Wickham was silenced only momentarily. "I was surprised to see Darcy in town last month. We passed several times, and it left me wondering what he was doing there at this time of year."

Are you worried your new wife has not kept your secrets? And so, you should be. Or do you wish to know the depth of my acquaintance with the Darcys? "Perhaps he was on some business for his aunt or preparing for his betrothal to Miss de Bourgh."

Wickham reminded Elizabeth of a small boy with a skinned knee, worrying a scab. He asked whether she had seen Darcy in Lambton and what she thought of Georgiana. He wondered whether she had seen the parsonage at Kympton. *If it is blood he wants, he shall get it.*

"No, Mr Wickham, I never did visit Kympton. But I was given to understand that there was a time when settling there and making sermons was not so palatable to you. In fact, you declared you would never take orders and were compensated from the estate in a manner more agreeable to you."

"Oh! Um...well. That is not wholly without foundation. You may remember I told you something of that when we first met."

She met his eyes implacably. *You liar! Such a man! I would slap you, had not someone stronger beaten me to it recently. You think my memory both short and faulty?* Wickham saw the flash of anger and flinched; at last he looked away.

Knowing he would now comprehend she had made more honest allegiances, she smiled a little. "Oh come, Mr Wickham. As you like to remind me, we are brother and sister now. Do not let us quarrel about the past."

They were at the door of the house, and Elizabeth held out her hand. He kissed it, glad to be looking at her hand rather than her piercing eyes. The two former friends exchanged barely half a dozen words together over the remainder of the visit.

With the Longbourn small parlour to herself, Elizabeth decided she must write to Georgiana to let her know that she was aware of Darcy's secret and, once again, had misjudged him.

Longbourn, Hertfordshire
Friday, 28 August, 1812

Dear Georgiana,

Lately I have heard a report of your brother, which fills me with astonishment. My youngest sister is visiting—for ten very long days—and as she described her wedding to me, she let slip that your brother, of all people, attended the ceremony. Before checking herself, she said he stood as groomsman. I was amazed to hear it. Lydia then admitted she had been sworn to secrecy and said no more. Not wanting to appear interested in such a loathsome but necessary event, I did not inquire of her further —it must be admitted I ran from her presence rather than give her the satisfaction of observing my overwhelming curiosity—but I can own it to you that I am not disinterested.

Perhaps you know me well enough to realise I am an unusually —my mother says disturbingly—inquisitive creature, and so I applied to my Aunt Gardiner to learn how Mr Darcy came to be involved in the wedding. Her response is before me, and has set down such a tale as has my head spinning.

I can only assume that, like Lydia, you have been sworn to an oath

197

of silence on the subject, and I would not break a sacred bond between a brother and sister I have come to admire so well. Having said that, I will quote here a few particulars from my aunt's letter, asking only that you vouch for them. A simple yes or no will do; I shan't trouble you for more.

Here Elizabeth inserted several sentences from her aunt's letter, hoping she had quoted enough to assure a response from Georgiana.

Now I must ask you to do for me what I must assume you have done for your brother. I bid you keep my present inquiry secret since it is abundantly clear that Mr Darcy does not wish for my family or me to know any of the particulars of the settlement with the person whose name I cannot at this moment bear to write. That your dear brother is deserving of a vast deal of gratitude—but would have the acknowledgement of it bestowed on my uncle instead—is yet another grander example of the depth of his goodness. He is the best man I have ever known.

Am I safe to assume that not only yourself, but also Mr Bingley, is aware of your brother's generosity to all my family? Jane has said there is a prodigious quantity of correspondence between the two friends, and Bingley says only that he will have no secrets from Jane once they are married, meaning he will tell her nothing now. If Bingley has not done so, you might inform your brother that the couple now about to settle in Newcastle will not be returning to Hertfordshire for at least two years and likely longer. I am happy to report that Mr Bingley has begun the marriage settlement discussion with my father, and then a date will be set.

Do not attribute to gratitude the fact that your brother is dearer to me than he ever was before. My feelings are more complicated than that. My appreciation of his attention to my poor sister is only the smallest part of my regard for him.

In reviewing this letter, I see I have declared my affection for your brother. I will not change what I have written. Please be honest with me, Georgiana, and tell me whether I have no hope of his forgiving my own past missteps and those of my family. He may have told you that I have forgiven him any slights or errors in manners he thinks he may have committed against me. Indeed, I think I did so when we came upon each other accidentally at Pemberley. It was a numinous moment, and I believe it worked a change in us both.

Yours truly,
Elizabeth Bennet

꜅

Darcy House, London
31 August, 1812

Dear Elizabeth,

The account of my brother's involvement regarding the Wickhams' nuptials and financial settlement, as stated by your aunt, is true in every part as quoted. My situation is as you suspect, and I will say no more on the topic.

Your letter fills me with delight. Please keep me apprised of the plans for Jane and Bingley's wedding. I intend to be there.

But what pleased me most about your letter, dearest Lizzy, is that you have, for the first time, freely admitted your fond regard for my brother. How very vexing you are to bind me in an oath to seal my lips, but sealed they shall be since you wish it. I would not make a similar sacrifice for anyone excepting you, dear friend.

As for your closing comments about your affections and those of my brother: once the unfortunate couple are gone, I daresay he will be at your side in a thrice. There has indeed been an increase of correspondence betwixt my brother and Mr Bingley. Make of it what you will, but I believe Charles wishes my brother to come to Netherfield. I shall push for this from my end. Of course, with one of our foxhound bitches just delivered of a fine litter, perhaps Charles is only trying to procure the pick of it, but I think there is more to it than that!

Your dear friend,
Georgiana

When Mrs Bennet saw the letter from Darcy House amongst the family post, she erupted with unrestrained glee.

"Oh, Lizzy, it is good you have attracted such a highly placed connection. When Miss Darcy comes out, she will want a friend to accompany her to all the society to-doings and may well invite you to town for a season. Make of it what you can, dear." Mrs Bennet paused and looked lovingly at her second eldest daughter. "Do not think I will ever forget, dearest girl, how kind you were to encourage Mr Darcy for Jane's sake. I know it was against your inclination. Since we have heard nothing of him, we must assume Mr Darcy has better manners when at home than he does in society. But if he attends Jane's wedding, we shall be more than civil to him, for he has, through you, Lizzy, influenced his friend for Jane. I like him more already than ever I did. That you have made a friend of his sister is well deserved and may be the making of you in society, Lizzy. It may well be."

Lydia overheard her mother. The whole turn of events made her quite cross. It was not enough to be the only Bennet sister married, she wanted also to be the only Bennet sister to be happy. Since his bludgeoning by angry officers in London, Wickham was less tender towards her and less susceptible to her attempts to lure him into marital relations. Their noisy congress during their first night at Longbourn was not to be repeated, and Lydia was not at all confident about the healing of his face. She would need to be a scold to keep him from appearing lopsided. Her handsome Wickham was no more.

Netherfield Park, Hertfordshire
5 September, 1812

Dear Darcy,

The newly married couple, with whom you have lately spent far too much time, has this morning quitted the neighbourhood. Please come to Netherfield with all possible haste. You must assist me with wedding plans, and please, dear friend, you will stand up with me, won't you? It only seems right that you see the thing through.

Mr Bennet invited me for some shooting yesterday, and I have never seen so many partridges as they have at Longbourn. You must come.

You must see for yourself—great blind clodpoll that you are—how Jane is more affectionate to me in looks and speech than ever. Now that the above-mentioned couple has vacated the county and we become the sole object of local attention, I must have my second by me.

As for my future sister, Elizabeth Bennet, come directly and tell her you love her. I observe her appetite improved after receiving your letter. I will not have a dour bridesmaid, so again you must come.

Lizzy has said to Jane that she cannot believe you or any man could master his pride enough to offer for her a second time. She has not forgiven herself for mistaking your character. She thinks you would be loath to align yourself with her because of the man she must now call brother. By her consideration, the matter has ended as well as it could for Lydia and the Bennet family but as badly as possible for herself.

In short, I need you, the shooting is excellent, the unfortunate newlyweds are gone, and the favourite of my future Bennet sisters is ready to be courted if you can overcome those objections she believes to be in your mind but I know are not in your heart. Prove to Lizzy that you are the man I know you to be.

Regards and faithfully,
Charles

Yarrow
"Healing"

Chapter 13

As the ladies of the Bennet family sat down to breakfast at Longbourn three days after the departure of the Wickhams, they were not aware that Fitzwilliam Darcy had returned to Netherfield the previous evening. Mr Bennet received a letter from Darcy stating he would return to the neighbourhood with the intention of renewing his courtship of Elizabeth. Darcy wrote that he now enjoyed some hope of securing her hand, and he would endeavour to manage the Herculean task in a manner that would not too much damage his reputation as a proud and disagreeable man.

Thus it was that Mr Bennet joined his family with more than his usual air of self-satisfaction. Mrs Bennet was oblivious, prattling on to Jane about Mr Bingley's expected arrival for dinner to schedule a date for the wedding and to debate the relative merits of holding the wedding breakfast at Longbourn versus Netherfield if Mrs Hurst could be prevailed upon to act as hostess.

Elizabeth eyed her father carefully, suspecting something from his occasional sly smiles. It was not her habit to quiz him when he behaved in such a manner. That his furtive looks were aimed at her rather than her mother or sisters gave her pause. Keeping an alert eye upon him throughout the meal, Elizabeth determined that she would speak with him alone in his library when they left the table.

To that end, Elizabeth followed her father into the hall when a commotion at the front door halted them.

"I am Lady Catherine de Bourgh. I would like to speak with Miss Elizabeth Bennet if she is not out upon one of her interminable walks in the countryside. Will you take me to her?"

Lady Catherine swept past Mrs Hill and looked about the entry hall as if she were lost and hoping for direction.

Mrs Hill curtsied to the grand lady's back and sputtered, "Yes, ma'am, of course, your ladyship, I shall find her at once."

"Is that not Miss Bennet...?" Lady Catherine's eyes had fallen upon Elizabeth and her father down the hall but then remembered there were an inordinate number of "Miss Bennets" and she had better be specific. "... Miss *Elizabeth* Bennet, before me?"

Elizabeth dipped a curtsy as Lady Catherine approached.

"This, I suppose, is your father?"

"Yes, ma'am. May I present my father to you, ma'am, Mr Thomas Bennet? Father, this is Lady Catherine de Bourgh."

Mr Bennet bowed creditably, and Lady Catherine bestowed a grudging nod. "Mr Bennet, at some other time I would speak with you on the proper upbringing of daughters, as I am given to believe you have not gone about it properly. But today, I have not the time or inclination. I am here to speak with Miss Elizabeth Bennet. I saw a prettyish kind of little wilderness to one side of the garden. Miss Bennet, will you condescend to take a turn with me?"

"Certainly, your ladyship." Elizabeth skipped quickly to the closet under the stairway to obtain a spencer and bonnet, but Lady Catherine was already at the open front door, and Elizabeth hurried behind.

Like an ornate ship in full sail, Lady Catherine crossed the broadest sweep of the Longbourn lawn and passed up a short flight of stone steps leading through an arch in the wall into what Mrs Bennet referred to as the hermitage and Mr Bennet called his Arboretum. As soon as they were out of sight of the house, Lady Catherine rounded on Elizabeth.

"Miss Bennet, I am sure you can be at no loss as to why I have come."

"Indeed, madam, I am all amazement. To what does my family owe the honour of your ladyship's visit?"

"Certainly you must know, Miss Bennet, what you have done to render me so alarmed. Have you not taken advantage of your slight acquaintance with my niece Georgiana Darcy, which ought not to have been allowed to develop, to put yourself forward as the likeliest candidate to enter into a state of matrimony with my nephew Fitzwilliam Darcy? Have you not been spreading vile rumours of an engagement between yourselves to all of your friends and relations?"

"Indeed, Lady Catherine, I most certainly have not. It is evidence of how slight *our* acquaintance is that you have no better expectation of me than to make such an assumption of my motives."

"Do not be rude to one who is your superior, Miss Bennet. You do not know the influence I hold with those whom you are trying to coerce into intimacy with your arts and allurements. I am the nearest relation they have. Of course, Georgiana is an innocent and likely to make foolish decisions about where to allow friendly affection to develop, especially when her brother allows a correspondence between you."

"My acquaintance with Mr Darcy is a year old, Lady Catherine, as you are perfectly well aware, during which time he mentioned me to his sister on numerous occasions. He introduced me to Miss Darcy this summer while I was visiting in Lambton with my aunt and uncle, and after spending some time together, we suited each other well enough for her to invite me to spend the month of August at Pemberley. Georgiana asked her brother if she might correspond with me. I did not initiate the communication."

Much of this was news to Lady Catherine, and she turned white with fury. "Yes, but you did not stay the entirety of the month, did you? Or anywhere near it! I know it all! That you had to leave to address the waywardness of your youngest sister, that she was interrupted in an elopement with the nefarious George Wickham. Their marriage has been a patched up business, handled by your uncle in trade. How is this to be borne? Could the son of a steward come to be called brother by Fitzwilliam and Georgiana Darcy?"

Elizabeth was seething but relieved that Lady Catherine, in fact, did not "know it all." However, she raised a question Elizabeth had been privately considering. *How can Mr Darcy, no matter the degree of his inclination for me, reconcile himself to Wickham's attachment to my family? How could he countenance it? His consideration towards my family has been generous indeed, but surely he will balk at making a more intimate connection.* It was not a subject Elizabeth cared to debate with Lady Catherine.

That her ladyship was so visibly and loudly angry helped Elizabeth to maintain her equanimity, and she drew in a deep, calming breath.

Lady Catherine continued. "It astounds me that Fitzwilliam has gone against my wishes to enter into an engagement with you and has not sought my council. He forgets he is already engaged to *my* daughter."

"Mr Darcy has always behaved as a man of honour with complete, if sometimes uncomfortable, honesty. If he believed himself engaged to your daughter, he would never make an offer to me."

"Their engagement is of a peculiar kind. It was the fondest wish of his mother and me that they should marry. We spoke of it from Anne's infancy. You should be ashamed to break not only Anne's heart but mine, too; I was your generous hostess in the spring, *and* you defile the memory of Darcy's sainted mother."

"You bring up a subject that was of some concern to Miss Darcy, Lady Catherine. She applied to Colonel Fitzwilliam for the particulars, and he wrote that Mr Darcy's *father* was adamantly against the match because of Anne's poor health. Before her father died, Georgiana overheard him warning the younger Mr Darcy against it. The colonel also informed Miss Darcy that your daughter would not look favourably upon a proposal but did not tell you because she never believed it would occur and wished to avoid conflict. She does not love her Cousin Darcy, it seems."

"Insolent girl! That *you* should presume to know my daughter's heart better than I! This is not to be tolerated."

"Surely, even you must own you are not a lady with whom anyone would care to disagree if avoiding a dispute were at all possible."

"Hold your tongue, girl. I will not be distracted from my purpose. I give you no permission to marry my nephew and would have you renounce him and end your engagement. *My* character is not at issue here."

"Oh, yes, it most certainly is, Lady Catherine. You have done nothing to entice me to confide in you. You are everything that is irrational. You may not realize you have lessened your influence by appearing so continually unreasonable. But your behaviour to Mr Darcy is a family matter and none of *my* concern. If Mr Darcy is accustomed to your meddling in his life; that is *his* choice, but you have no connection to *me*."

"Miss Bennet, I find you obstinate and ungrateful. You will never make any man a proper wife by being so outspoken."

"Ungrateful? You were thanked amply and properly for your kindness to me in Kent. By dining several times at Rosings, I had no notion of being made permanently beholden to you, or I would most certainly have declined the invitations. I am sorry to speak so, but there it is."

"Cease this impertinence, Miss Bennet, for I have met with your type before. You have seduced him. His sense of honour demands he marry you. Are you with child?" Lady Catherine lowered her voice and hissed the final question like a stage villain.

Elizabeth stared. She narrowed her eyes as she lifted her chin and set her shoulders. Her voice stayed even, her elocution precise. "You have insulted me in every possible way. I am a gentleman's daughter and a maiden. If it will comfort you, let me say I have reason to believe that whatever his feelings for me may be, Mr Darcy is not likely to propose." Elizabeth just stopped herself from saying, "propose again."

Lady Catherine closed her eyes and yielded a great sigh. "You are not engaged to him?" Her angry eyes brightened.

"No, I am not."

"And will you agree never to enter into such an engagement? Should his senses utterly abandon him—should he make his addresses to you—will you promise me to refuse him?"

"I shall not. I shall make no promise of the kind to someone so wholly unconnected to me."

"You are resolved to have him?"

"I have said no such thing. *You* are not entitled to know *my* heart, and all your attempts to intimidate me will not induce me to be explicit. I am confirmed to act only in a manner which, in my opinion, will contribute to my future happiness."

"You leave me no choice, Miss Bennet, but to appeal to my nephew in your stead. He left London yesterday afternoon, and I was told he has arrived at an estate near here, a place called Netherfield. It is let to his friend Bingley. Do you know of it?"

The news that Darcy was in the neighbourhood caused Elizabeth's colour to rise from pale resentment to embarrassed blush. It was too much. Exasperation erupted as self-control failed her with this fresh evidence of Lady Catherine's absurdity. "Of course I do! It is the next estate north. Have your coachman receive directions from our housekeeper. *Our* conversation is finished, Lady Catherine."

"That will be utterly satisfying to me, Miss Bennet. I want nothing more than to remove myself from your company with all possible haste. You are headstrong, unfeeling and imprudent. If I can prevail upon my nephew to make the promises you will not, I shall take him back to Darcy House this very afternoon."

"If your nephew can be swayed by your ridiculous pride and boundless prejudice, by your conceit and your uncivil manners, then he is not the man I thought him, and he will be no loss to me. But I have come to trust he is a better man than *you* believe him to be. Indeed, your ladyship, Fitzwilliam Darcy is the best man I have ever known."

Lady Catherine gave Elizabeth one last haughty look from head to toe. "I am most seriously displeased. You may be assured you will receive no further invitations from the Hunsford vicarage."

"I shall bear the deprivation tolerably well, I expect. Art a balmpot —tow'd woman!"

Both women turned to the stone arch with the intention of quitting the walled garden as quickly as possible, only to see the silhouette of a tall, well-formed gentleman in riding attire giving the appearance of being possessed by a towering rage, which, upon translating Elizabeth's last words, turned to laughter.

Elizabeth froze. *How long has he been there? What has he heard? I should not have retaliated. He will never forgive me for insulting his aunt.*

Lady Catherine's response was quite the opposite of Elizabeth's upon seeing her nephew. She sallied past her opponent, flying to Darcy as if to attack him. He stepped forward and harshly grasped his aunt's elbow, catching her by surprise and wheeling her around. He nearly dragged her the ten feet to the nearest bench and pushed her down upon it as if she were a child caught in the midst of a tantrum. Darcy moved to place himself between his aunt and Elizabeth. Lady Catherine started to open her mouth but Darcy silenced her with a warning finger and a threatening glare. He turned to Elizabeth. He was trying to quell his amusement. *Where did she learn the Derby dialect?*

"Please excuse me, Miss Bennet. I once accused you of having unfortunate relations without acknowledging the considerable defects of members of my own family. You owe me no such favour, but please forgive my aunt for her uncivil behaviour. I know how it offends you. It offends *me*. One would think a lady of her rank would not importune a gentlewoman under any circumstances, let alone to accost her in the bosom of her own family. I am appalled to think of those things of which she has accused you."

Elizabeth's chest constricted as it always did whenever Darcy appeared. She could not properly take in all she heard, so surprised was she at the direction of Darcy's speech. His reference to the accusation of seduction sank in, and she coloured rather more profusely and felt a little dizzy.

"Nephew…" Lady Catherine's voice sputtered back to life.

Darcy turned to her. "I have heard quite enough from you, Lady Catherine. Quite enough."

He turned back to Elizabeth. "I ask your forbearance, Miss Bennet; would you be so kind as to give my aunt and me a private moment? It pains me as a nephew to address my aunt as I must do, but I would not risk *your* having to hear anything further she may say, and I mean to defend you as I should have done the moment I heard so much as a syllable of this exchange."

Elizabeth lifted her chin and met his eyes. "I am completely capable, Mr Darcy, of defending myself—and *you*—if need be. Indeed, sir, I have rarely met anyone as easy to best in an argument as your aunt."

Darcy was facing Elizabeth and she again appeared as the majestic she-wolf who had defended Jane in Lambton. What thrilled him now was her defence of *him* and that she was willing to take *his* part. In a quieter situation, he would thoroughly consider the implications of her statement to Lady Catherine that he was the best man she had ever known—quite a pleasing change from her opinion in April. He smiled into her eyes.

Elizabeth was ready to continue the argument with Lady Catherine or to storm away in a state of high dudgeon or even to yield the field of battle to him and watch them joust, but she was not prepared for Darcy's smile. The charming dimples and warmth of his deep brown eyes dispelled her wrath and filled her with feelings of wonderment. *He is not displeased with me. His looks admit that his regard is still in my favour. Has he come back for me? Is that why he is here?*

Elizabeth looked down at her hands for a long moment. "I find your forbearance with my behaviour towards your aunt quite miraculous, sir," she said in a quieter voice. She curtsied to him, saying, "I shall leave you to it, Mr Darcy," and left the garden with as much appearance of calm as she could summon.

Once on the lawn, Elizabeth stopped. Her sense of propriety told her she ought to keep walking, but her heart was not so governable a creature. She stole to her right into the shrubbery of Lauristinus, thus skirting the lawn until she was at the arch between the dense leafy hedge and the wall.

Darcy and his aunt were already engaged in their skirmish.

"…and you have no right to say with whom Georgiana may correspond. And lastly, you have no influence over whom I shall marry."

"Darcy, you forget yourself, your position, your connections and the family. Think of the reckoning you will face."

"My family… Georgiana and Richard realize I must have a wife who will make me happy. They love me and are determined to be pleased by whoever pleases me. You appear to have no such regard for my future happiness."

"Could you be happy with a woman of such low connections, such little fortune and so many impertinent opinions? Please, Nephew, vow to me what she would not. Promise me you will never propose to Miss Elizabeth Bennet."

Elizabeth's breathing stopped.

Darcy glanced at the stone arch. Elizabeth could easily be just outside it, listening as he had done. *It would serve me right if she is.* Darcy levelled an implacable gaze upon his aunt and raised his voice so he would be heard without sounding heated. "I will not. I shall make no such promise." He paused. "Lady Catherine, you have no idea how perfectly suited Miss Elizabeth Bennet is to be mistress of Pemberley. I myself have only recently learned how perfect. But I had been in love with her for quite some time before I knew that, in addition to being ideally suited to me, she is ideal for Pemberley."

Elizabeth's head dropped, tears stinging her eyes. *He is defending me. His aunt is right; I have been an ungrateful girl, but not to her, to* him!

"Darcy! I am ashamed of you. What of Anne?"

"You are frank, Aunt; I shall join you. What of Anne? She should not be shackled with a husband who cannot love her, whose heart is forever lodged elsewhere. And I believe her affections lie with quite a different cousin."

"What nonsense is this?"

"She has been quietly in love with Richard for many years. He cuts a much more dashing figure than I."

Lady Catherine sucked in her breath. "Why would she not confide in me? Her own mother?"

"Why *would* she? You are not affectionate, you attribute to her talents she herself does not claim, and you have crushed any independence to which she ever aspired. She cannot trust her own mother to be kind."

Lady Catherine glared at him, the bile rising in her throat. "I am not here to speak of Anne. I am here to stop *you* from making a grave mistake, which you will rue for the rest of your life. How could such a one ever make you happy?"

"Miss Elizabeth Bennet is the only woman who ever *has* made me happy. She laughs at me. She has an independence of mind that is pleasing. She is intelligent, and although her education has not been conventional, it is extensive. I am convinced the tenants of Pemberley will love her, and while *you* may think yourself vastly superior to your own tenants at Rosings, the approbation of *my* tenants matters a great deal to *me*. If I do not marry Elizabeth Bennet, I will never marry."

Elizabeth blinked back tears.

"And you were calling here today to pay her your addresses? On this very day?" Lady Catherine appeared flabbergasted.

Darcy did not wish to speak so candidly. "I came to call upon her, to let her know I am returned to Netherfield and Georgiana will be joining me soon. I must let her know I now have her father's permission to call upon her." He smiled to himself.

"Clearly her arts and allurements have rendered you addlepated. She is a schemer, Darcy. Can you not see it? She is a mercenary of the worst type."

"Arts and allurements? Elizabeth Bennet? Mercenary? No, Lady Catherine, no. I have ample evidence, the nature of which I am *not* willing to confide, that Miss Elizabeth Bennet will not marry except for love. I am not wholly certain she loves me…" Elizabeth inhaled sharply behind her leafy screen. "…but I have reason to hope."

The day was breezy enough that Darcy did not hear the swish of leaves as Elizabeth, incapable of listening to anything more, made her way to the footpath leading south of Longbourn, skirting the holdings of its tenants. She began running, unable to contain her disturbance of mind. As she bolted down the lane, heedless of the workers in the fields scything hay and watching her progress, Charlotte's long ago advice was hammering in her ears, *"Leave him in no doubt, leave him in no doubt, leave him in no doubt…"*

Darcy continued. "You must leave, Lady Catherine. You have insulted Miss Bennet and angered me. You will not change her mind, nor have you any influence over mine. Return to Rosings and see to your daughter."

Darcy walked to the arch, peeking outside between the shrubs and the wall, expecting to see Elizabeth. On one side were his footprints. On the other, the damp earth revealed the fresh prints of petite boots. Darcy followed the evidence until it blended into dryer ground and was plain for only a few feet more.

Lady Catherine came behind Darcy, watching him disappear into the hedge. She 'tsked' in disapproval and proceeded to her chaise and four. Faces bright with astonishment watched from the drawing room windows as Jane and Kitty saw Lady Catherine depart. Mr Bennet had retired to his bedroom above stairs, and although knowing nothing of what was said, was nonetheless highly diverted by what he could see, for he had the better view.

Darcy thought it auspicious that, as he emerged onto the lane, the sun came out from behind the grey clouds that had been gathering. To the south in the distance across a field, the flash of a pink gown was sprinting down a slope. Elizabeth's arms were flung above and behind her; her bonnet flew from its ribbons behind her raised hand.

One of the men in the field spied Darcy, stood up and motioned in the direction Elizabeth had run. The Longbourn tenants were quite accustomed to seeing the second eldest Miss Bennet dashing down the lanes. Darcy chuckled and waved in thanks. He began running. He was not used to that form of exercise, but his facility with swordplay gave him endurance.

At the end of a full quarter mile, Elizabeth's disquieted spirits had dissipated, and she slowed. Soon she heard Darcy's rapid steps behind her. *Has he followed me?* She swirled around. She laughed and gasped for breath, her eyes sparkling and turning quite amber in the autumn sun.

Darcy's inclination was to sweep her into his arms. Although her laughter encouraged him, he instead stopped before her and executed a deep formal bow. "Miss Bennet," he huffed and laughed. "You have led me a merry chase, madam." He thought her more beautiful than ever.

She curtsied gracefully. "It was not my intention, Mr Darcy."

Elizabeth straightened, and they met each other's eyes. Slowly, as they recalled all that had been said to Lady Catherine and realized what the other had likely overheard, both experienced the unusual sensation of timidity. Elizabeth looked down whilst Darcy's eyes travelled across the fields.

Elizabeth remembered the topic she most particularly wished to speak of with Mr Darcy, the topic that so occupied her thoughts since Lydia's slip of the tongue.

"Mr Darcy, I comprehend what I am about to say may disturb you, but it must be said. *I* consider it would be highly discourteous of me to know of the great service you have done my family as regards my poor sister and not express my gratitude. *You* do not wish it spoken of, but I am a selfish creature. For the sake of giving relief to my own feelings, I am willing to risk wounding yours. Ever since I have known of it, I have been most anxious to acknowledge how grateful I am. I have not told anyone else in the family, and so I must extend their gratitude for them." Her courage ran out, silencing her.

So this is why I am the best man she has ever known...it is gratitude. She would marry me out of gratitude. Darcy scowled a little. "I am exceedingly sorry you have been informed. I did not think Mrs Gardiner was so little to be trusted."

This incorrect accusation stirred Elizabeth to speak further. "You must not blame my aunt. Lydia made a thoughtless comment that first betrayed your involvement. You cannot be surprised that I would not rest until I knew all the particulars. My aunt wrote, and I also prevailed upon your sister for confirmation. Georgiana explained that you had extracted a promise of silence from her, but she went so far as to say she could find no fault with anything Aunt Gardiner had written.

"Please let me thank you again, in the name of all of my family, for the generous compassion that induced you to take so much trouble and bear such deplorable mortification for the sake of two people so wholly without merit."

Darcy looked at her imploring eyes. She obviously hoped she was not angering him. He began, "If you *will* thank me, let it be for yourself alone. That the wish of giving relief to your distress, of restoring happiness to you, led me on, I shall not attempt to deny. But your *family* owes me nothing. It was *your* tears that haunted me through the whole negotiation. Much as I respect your family, I thought only of *you*."

Her eyes held his face; she became more wondering than worried. "Let me ease your mind then, if my feeling gratitude is unacceptable to you, and say that when I first learnt of your many kindnesses in the matter, gratitude was not my first thought. In the moments after reading my aunt's letter, I was proud of you, Mr Darcy. It must be admitted, I borrowed some of that pride; I was proud of myself, that a man such as you should think me worth knowing. That such a man once held me in so high a regard as to... Yes, of that I am proud."

Darcy realized the full force of all she was implying. She had now admitted feelings for him of a sort he could more willingly appreciate than gratitude.

212

"You are too generous to trifle with me. If your feelings are not sufficiently changed from what they were last April, tell me so at once. My affections and wishes are unchanged. No, I cannot say that honestly. My affections are far greater than they were. Only my wishes remain the same. I still love you. If you cannot love me, one word from you will silence me on the subject forever."

Elizabeth smiled fleetingly and looked away. She nodded her head with a little bob, swallowing with a suddenly dry mouth. She glanced at him and then into the distance, and cleared her throat. "You did not see it... It was too short and fell out—in the posy, the red chrysanthemum. All that week when I was in Derbyshire, I thought you knew my heart but would not speak. Before I left, I learnt you did not know. Some things should not be left to flowers. I..."—*Leave him in no doubt*—"My feelings...my feelings are completely the opposite from what they were." Never had she believed herself to be expressing her thoughts in a more awkward manner. "I *can* love you, I *do* love you. I love you." She stated it earnestly, with intense conviction. "Now. I mean already, and for some weeks, since receiving your flowers, since seeing you so unexpectedly at Pemberley, since seeing your portrait. Since Lambton, when you spoke of Jane. Never think I am accepting you out of gratitude—far from it. Your efforts on Lydia's behalf merely confirmed that I have indeed fallen in love with a man in whom I can, with confidence, place my most tender regard and deepest respect...affection...trust..." Her words of praise reached diminuendo and her eyes flickered to his face.

"You are consenting to be my wife? You will give me your hand?" he asked gently and held out his bare hand.

She looked down. "I am as you represented me to your aunt. I will never marry where I do not love." She raised her chin and cocked her head as if stubbornness were somehow preferable to vulnerability. "So, yes, sir, I love you and I am consenting to be your wife." She put her hand into his.

Darcy broke into a grin expressive of such joy that he tossed his head and turned his face to the sun, dislodging his hat. He took in a great breath and fought light-headedness. When he could speak, he said with some mirth, "I am glad neither of us made any hasty promises to Lady Catherine today, which would thus already be broken."

Elizabeth smiled as she released his hand and bent to pick up his hat; he lowered his brow as she replaced it. Their eyes met. He thought of kissing her, and she thought of being kissed, but they stepped apart. Darcy took her bonnet and placed it over her hair, gently tying it under her chin. The feeling of his fingers brushing upon her skin brought the roses to her cheeks, and her old friend, the constriction of her chest, seized her. He noticed her blushing breathlessness and was as pleased as if admiring her for the first time. *She will be mine. This beautiful elusive creature loves me. How?* Darcy held out his arm; she tucked her hand in the crook of his elbow and they continued walking.

"I am sure, sir, however seriously displeased your aunt may be at this moment, it would feed her ire even further to know her appearance provided me the courage to address my thanks to you. But how did you come to be here?"

"It was as I told Lady Catherine. You may imagine my surprise to see my aunt's carriage outside Longbourn. Upon hearing me enter the house, your father emerged from his library to inform me where you and my aunt had gone, and understanding rightly her motive for calling, I made my way to you as quickly as possible. When I approached the arch, I could hear her quite plainly tell you 'I know it all.'"

"You heard the greater part of the battle, then."

"Yes, but I am ashamed to say so. I should have interrupted her. You should not have been left at her mercy since she has none. You did say something at the end that confused me. Why did you say that whatever my feelings might be, you did not expect me to propose?"

"I omitted a word, and that word was 'again.' I did not expect you, even with your fine character, to propose again. After the unkind and unjustified setting-down I gave you at Hunsford, I could form no reasonable expectation. Bingley and Georgiana assured me your love was constant, but it was my assumption that no man could forgive what I said, even a man as saintly as yourself." She glanced at him, teasing a little.

"What did you say of me that was not true? I needed to be humbled. I *was* conceited. I *was* arrogant. It did not occur to me I would be found wanting by a woman worthy of pleasing. Now I know better."

"And there was that other detail of my youngest sister's situation. The one thing your aunt said that rang true was the injustice you take on of having to call that couple, 'brother and sister.' I cannot fathom why you will do it."

"You cannot? Have I not stated my affections with enough conviction even yet? I have chosen to honour love, now that it has bested fate's many attempts to thwart it, over every other consideration. When I saw you in the hall at Pemberley with Mary's letter, my only thought was for you—to rid you of the burden of grief and shame, which, because of your kind nature, you took upon yourself. That Lydia was let anywhere near Wickham was more my fault than yours, but neither of us should take on the responsibility for his wickedness and her wildness. *I* am not wicked, and *you* are not wild."

Elizabeth had to laugh at this. "You have just caught me making a mad career through the countryside; if *that* is not wild, sir, then I am mistaken in the word."

"It was of short duration and led to a calming of your temper. You are not *so* very wild." Darcy's eyes softened as he looked into hers and then quickly looked away. His fancy formed an image of Elizabeth running down the paths of Pemberley to one particular secluded bower of willows near the pond where he liked to swim. That he would soon have leave to capture her there brought an arousal to his loins that took several deep breaths to quell. *I hope she does not favour a long engagement.*

Elizabeth looked away. She was concerned about her inclinations now they had declared themselves and were wandering away from Longbourn. *Now he has seen for himself that I run to ease my spirits; I hope he is not too disapproving.* She tugged on their linked arms to propel them forward. "I think, sir, we should turn back. My father will be wondering where we have got to when he sees Lady Catherine has gone."

They retraced their steps, each a little more silent, and both deeply relieved.

They reached the entrance to the lawn, just in sight of the house, when Darcy stopped their progress. "Elizabeth," he whispered. "There *are* two people in your family who can keep a confidence uncommonly well."

She chuckled. "I am surprised to hear it. What is the secret, and who has kept it?"

"In the express Bingley sent your father from Pemberley requesting permission to court Jane, I sent a similar letter of my own. I was determined to inform him of my honourable intentions. After consulting Jane, he granted me permission. My plan was that, once Bingley had proposed to Jane, whether at Pemberley or in Hertfordshire, and was accepted, I hoped I would have improved your opinion enough to accept my proposal. Had I not bumbled the nosegay, I promise you I would have put the impulsiveness of Bingley to shame and declared myself sooner. I asked your father to keep my intentions secret, in part because I feared angering you should my attentions still prove unwelcome. I sent him another letter three days ago, informing him that I was returning to stay with Bingley and again take up my suit. Are you angry with my presumption?"

"You were not presumptuous at all by my reckoning. You saw hope and took a risk. Although, had I known, I might have been emboldened to follow Charlotte Collins's advice and declare my heart more directly. Instead, I left it to a flower. When I found it on the floor, it broke my heart to know you did not understand me. You saw the card?"

"Yes, I saw the flower on the table after you had gone, and Mrs Reynolds loaned me her herbal."

"The red chrysanthemum; I had picked the first open blossom of the season and did not want to deface the plant by taking a longer length and remove the buds to come."

"But then you sent me another. And you held them in your aunt's portrait. She is a poet, your aunt. How could I stay away?" Darcy looked into her eyes for several long moments. Yielding to impulse, he lowered his lips to hers, raising her face with one finger under her chin. He turned his head to spare them the embarrassment of bumping hats and their lips met in a pleasing alignment.

Elizabeth felt her heart leap to her throat at the approach of his face and closed her eyes, which she believed to be the common practice. She felt a little giddiness when, just before their lips separated, Darcy's tongue took the briefest taste of the point of her upper lip.

"Oh!" she cried softly.

"Elizabeth, have I alarmed you?"

"You surprised me, I think"—She paused then smiled a little impishly —"and pleased me, I am sure."

Darcy could only respond by chuckling. He tucked her hand into his elbow again and placed his over it as they proceeded to the house.

MRS BENNET WAS INFORMED THAT much had happened whilst she dawdled over bathing before paying an afternoon call. As she changed from morning dress to an overly decorated walking gown and matching pelisse, a person of great importance had arrived. Mr Darcy followed shortly thereafter and ran out to find Lizzy and his aunt. Then that lady, quite alone, crossed the lawn in a state of pronounced disapprobation and departed. Now Lizzy and Mr Darcy were nowhere to be seen. Mrs Bennet at first implored Mr Bennet to find them but then saw her husband and Jane exchange a look of conspiracy. The implications of it, combined with their immediate withdrawal to his library, left Mrs Bennet fluttering about the drawing room windows like a giant moth, more than usually agitated. So it was that she was the sole witness to the couple's first kiss. The remarkable nature of such an event left her entirely speechless.

When Elizabeth and Darcy burst into the drawing room, Mrs Bennet gaped like a gaudy trout. Her eyes fell upon her second eldest child and the heretofore-unpleasant friend of Jane's intended as if she had never seen these two people before in the whole of her life.

"Mama! Where is my father? Is he in his library?" Elizabeth asked.

Mrs Bennet flapped an arm in a manner more affirmative than not, and managed to nod. Darcy smiled into Elizabeth's eyes, bowed respectfully to his prospective mother-in-law and left the room. He approached the closed door and knocked, hearing the quiet laughter of Jane and her father from within. "Come," said Mr Bennet.

Darcy entered to find Jane in a rosy humour and Mr Bennet mirthful. Darcy glanced briefly at Jane with a quick bow and said, "Might I have a moment of your time, Mr Bennet, if I am not interrupting?"

"Indeed, you may. Proceed," Mr Bennet replied. He pointed to a chair.

Darcy looked at Jane more particularly, and said, "A *private* moment?"

Jane blushed and stood. Her smile was more than usually enigmatic.

"What have you to say to me, Mr Darcy, that my eldest daughter should not hear?" Mr Bennet asked and took a sip of lemon water to keep from smiling.

"Miss Bennet, you may wish to assist Miss Elizabeth with your mother in the drawing room," Darcy said as he turned to Jane. It was now his turn to suppress a smile. "It appears your mother is in some sort of fit, the power of speech having quite left her. Perhaps she witnessed something shocking. Her silence is the most remarkable thing I have ever seen."

"Well, you are a young man yet, Mr Darcy, and I daresay more of the world's wonders await you, but my wife speechless is indeed a very rare thing and to be much enjoyed whilst it lasts." Mr Bennet smiled. "Go along, Jane. I am sure Mr Darcy and I will know when your mother is recovered. You needn't return to inform us."

Mr Bennet and Darcy took a moment, once they were alone, to regard one another. Darcy felt it his place to speak. "My first purpose, Mr Bennet, is to thank you for admirably keeping the contents of our correspondence a thorough secret."

"You asked it of me, Mr Darcy, and as it posed no hardship or expense, I was glad to do it. I was surprised, to be sure, but I saw the possibility for future amusement in it and I do like to be amused."

"So I have been told."

"And how does your courtship proceed, sir? I assume you will not think me presumptuous to ask since its object is my favourite daughter. In my response, I warned you of losing your wits should you not overcome her objections, which at the time I believed to be numerous and tightly held. Since I have been at home with her, I have come to be more concerned for *her* heart than yours. She has not confided in me—in such matters, she never has—nor has she done so in Jane. They have been as close as two coats of paint these many years, but lately Lizzy has been reticent. I put it down to her being lovelorn and not wishing to cast a shadow upon Jane's happiness. Have you any news?"

Mr Darcy drew himself upright in his chair and leaned a little forward. "Indeed, Mr Bennet, I do have news. In the last hour, I proposed to Miss Elizabeth and she has accepted me. My most important reason to be seated before you is to ask for your consent."

Mr Bennet's mouth turned up at the corners, and his eyes twinkled with merriment.

She is her father's daughter, Darcy thought to himself. *She gets her expressions from him.*

"You are not the sort of man to whom I would refuse anything, Mr Darcy. You should know you have been endorsed by my brother Gardiner and his wife, who are the most sensible people in the family, perhaps even more so than Elizabeth and myself."

Darcy smiled. Mr Bennet smiled. Darcy started to rise, but Mr Bennet motioned for him to sit. "In the interest of instructing you a little in the art of self-defence, Mr Darcy, I would have you stay a moment. You are, I trust, becoming accustomed to my daughter's teasing? For I do not imagine she would marry a man she could not pester with impunity."

Darcy chuckled. "Yes, sir."

"Ah, well then. Let us sit and converse for a little, and draw this out for her sake. We shall not raise our voices, but let us have Lizzy wondering whether this interview and its outcome have been a close run thing, shall we?"

Darcy laughed. "What a splendid idea!"

"No laughing, Mr Darcy. She, or Kitty, may be outside the door listening." Mr Bennet lowered his voice. "Would you like a glass of wine? Is it too early? I have been taking my daily lemon-water. I read years ago that it sharpens the mind. It has not hurt me any, but I will not offer it to you; you seem alert enough."

"Life with your daughter will require a ready wit of me, sir. That much I understood after knowing her only a month." Having spoken, Darcy recalled being told by Elizabeth, during his first proposal, she "had not known you a month before I decided you were the last man in the world I could ever be prevailed on to marry." He was a happy man to his very soul now and felt uncharacteristically jolly.

"If it is not too intimate a question, Mr Darcy, may I ask how you came to find yourself in love with *my* daughter? Anyone would surmise a gentleman of your rank would have the pick of every fine daughter in the land. How did you fall victim to a country girl with pretty looks and an agile wit, but with low connections and little wealth? I know you slighted her the first night you met, you bounder. I would have lambasted you, had I been there."

Darcy looked down with a smile, and his cheeks reddened. "Your daughter defended herself eloquently enough, sir, as she spent the rest of the evening laughing at me. I was used to deference, sir. Miss Elizabeth was not inclined to extend it to me, and as I have come to judge myself through her eyes, I had done nothing to earn it—far from it. I would not dance with her; she heard me say so to Bingley, and her response was to laugh at me and show herself to be the best partner in the room.

"The next time I saw her was at Lucas Lodge and I observed her closely…"

"As many noticed, Mr Darcy," Mr Bennet interrupted.

Darcy nodded. "I was looking for some flaw to fix upon as a reason to stop my developing interest. Unfortunately, I found none. And *she* refused to dance with *me* that night. It undid me, although I would not acknowledge it at the time. I spent the rest of my visit to Netherfield falling more in love and trying to cajole myself out of it."

Mr Bennet was utterly delighted. "My Lizzy laughed at you and refused to stand up with you. Such treatment bewitched you?"

"Thoroughly. The more I learnt of her, the more she suited me."

"You are aware you are not marrying the most amiable of my daughters,

Mr Darcy? Bingley has spoken for Jane."

Darcy smiled. "As it happens, I have come to believe an amiable wife would bore me senseless. I wish to challenge and be challenged. My hope is your daughter will continue to improve me."

"Continue?"

"Yes, Mr Bennet, continue. She has already made a proper gentleman of me in the year since we met."

Both men were suddenly aware of murmurs and whisperings outside the library door. Ladies proceeding up a stairway and failing to preserve the secrecy of their actions was a familiar sound to Mr Bennet. Mr Darcy looked at him in enquiry.

Mr Bennet whispered, "That is the sound of Jane and Lizzy attempting to get their mother above stairs to her sitting room before she explodes in a glass-shattering display of hysteria, whether delighted or distressed. I have heard it many times."

"If I may say, sir—poor Jane and Elizabeth."

"Indeed."

Darcy and Mr Bennet listened at the door. "Oh, Lizzy! Lizzy! I knew you could not be so clever for nothing!" Mrs Bennet's eruption began. Her sitting room door slamming shut muffled—but did not mute—her further happy ravings.

Both men laughed. The upstairs door opened and closed again, and light steps were heard descending the stairs.

"That might be Lizzy returning to the parlour," Mr Bennet whispered. "Perhaps you should go to her now. She will be nervous enough. Please send her to me. Try not to look too pleased with yourself. It will ruin your reputation—and mine."

Mr Darcy bowed over a handshake with his future father-in-law and paused at the door. "Do not sport with her too much, please, sir. My aunt has made her a little anxious, I think."

"Will your aunt be a problem for Lizzy and you?"

"No sir. She was, in her absurd way, most helpful."

Mr Bennet raised an eyebrow, much as his second daughter often did. "I would hear more of that interview at some later time. It sounds like a fine story. Now get along with you…" Mr Bennet shooed Darcy from the room.

Elizabeth had indeed returned to the parlour, feeling a little flustered by her mother's effusion of joy. Darcy entered nearly upon her heels. She looked at him expectantly. She had never felt so nervous, but she was radiant in her happiness. Darcy was no actor, however much he might have wished to appear disquieted for Mr Bennet's sake. When faced with his bride-to-be looking completely beatific, he could do nothing except respond in kind. They stood smiling at each other.

"Please tell me you did not hear my mother when she regained her voice, sir." Elizabeth blushed.

Darcy took her hand. "*I* know why you are so clever, Elizabeth, and it was not for nothing; it was for *me*." He kissed her hand.

"And what of my father?"

"He has consented, but he is not sanguine, I fear. He would see you."

"What? Now?" She looked up at him, the corner of her lower lip becoming stitched by her upper teeth. Elizabeth was not expecting this.

Darcy bent and kissed her, gently nibbling her lip free of her teeth as he had so often longed to do. Once their lips met, she seemed to return his ardency.

Darcy released her. "No, *now*. Now that I have kissed you."

Elizabeth raised her brows. "He did not tell you to kiss me."

"That part was my idea. Now go to him." Darcy stepped aside, and she left the room.

When Elizabeth was admitted into her father's sanctuary, Mr Bennet glimpsed the lovely smile on his daughter's face. Moved to return it, he turned abruptly away to gaze out the window. He stood up straighter than he had in years, marshalling all his skills as an actor and father of five daughters, which some will see as a redundancy of terms. He began pacing, attempting to work himself into a fit of pique. Finally, as Elizabeth's eyes grew wider, he found the right tone.

"Are you out of your senses to be accepting this man, Lizzy?"

Her shock was immediate. "But he said you have given your consent!"

Darcy is no actor, poor soul, thought Mr Bennet. *He will never be able to retaliate when she teases.* "Indeed, I have. He is the sort of man one cannot deny. It would be unwise. But *you* should deny him if you do not love him. With Jane happily situated, you need not marry for money, Lizzy. I would not have you do it. He is a dour disagreeable man. Can you live with that?" Mr Bennet continued to pace rather than see Elizabeth's distressed face.

"Father, I should not have spoken so forcefully against him from the first.

There were reasons I rushed to misjudge him, which do me no credit."

"You mean now that you know his side of the story, you see where your bread is buttered?"

"Father! You know me better than that, I think."

"Then explain yourself, Lizzy. I will not have you marry a man you cannot love and respect. You would place yourself in the greatest danger in an unequal marriage."

"Is this your objection? You think I do not love him?"

Her father met her gaze with narrowed eyes. "Yes."

"But I do! I *do* love him. He has proved the quality of his character and the durability of his affection. I find myself deeply in love with him. It will be a surprise to some, of that I am sure. But I must tell you, Father, he is the best man I have ever known."

Mr Bennet was all astonishment. He had not expected Elizabeth to take the bait so thoroughly. "Is this true?"

"He is kind, he is clever, and he has no improper pride. He is generosity itself. You do not know how generous."

Mr Bennet looked at his daughter closely—there was something unexpressed in her manner. "Would you care to enlighten me?"

Elizabeth lifted her chin. "He would have you believe you owe a heavy debt to my Uncle Gardiner for the salvation of Lydia and our family name, but it was Mr Darcy who found Lydia and Wickham. He negotiated the settlement of the entire affair, including Wickham's debts, before letting Uncle Gardiner know they were found. He waited until you were returning home so you and I would not know of it. He did not wish to have me or my family feel under obligation to him."

Now it was Mr Bennet who expressed surprise at the turn of the conversation. "How did you learn of it?"

"Mr Darcy did not trust Wickham to go through with the wedding. He stood up as groomsman and only then presented Wickham with a statement to sign and his money. Lydia has an amount held in trust in her name, which will not be hers until she is 21. Mr Darcy purchased Wickham's commission in the regulars. Lydia was told some of this, and she probably understood none of it. When she visited us, she could not hold her tongue; she would gloat, and as we well know, a vow of secrecy means nothing to her. Then I had to know more, so wrote to my aunt and to Miss Darcy."

"Does he know you know?"

"Yes, I have thanked him on our behalf."

"And his response?"

Elizabeth's cheeks coloured, but she said earnestly, "He said he did it for my sake. All of the vexing meetings with Wickham and Lydia, the expense of her wedding clothes, everything. He bore it all for me, because he would not have me believe myself dishonoured. And he will bear calling those two 'brother and sister' for love of me." Her eyes filled with tears.

Mr Bennet slowly shook his head in amazement. Elizabeth stood before him, drawn to her full height, chin lifted in defiance, tears dancing upon her lashes—she had never looked more magnificent. That Fitzwilliam Darcy, of all men, had inspired this display of fierce loyalty and affection in his beloved Lizzy was no laughing matter. He placed his hands upon her shoulders and kissed her forehead as he had done many times.

"I am proud of you both, Lizzy—you and Mr Darcy. I could not have parted with you to a lesser man."

"You will like him very much, I think, when you get to know him." Elizabeth hugged her father.

"I already do. I like still waters that run deep." *He is of sterner stuff than I suspected. Good man!*

Arm-in-arm, father and daughter joined Darcy in the parlour, and Elizabeth revealed to them that she and Jane intended to be wed in a double ceremony. Darcy and Mr Bennet were delighted, each for their own separate reasons.

Lemon Geranium
"Unexpected meeting"

Chapter 14

The cares falling upon a newly betrothed, gently bred maiden as she prepares for her wedding are numerous and varied. Clothes and flowers, guests and their lodging, menus and decorations—of all these particulars were Elizabeth and Jane Bennet expected to have an informed opinion. The sisters were consulted about every nuance of their nuptials to the point of maddening exactitude and then often found, that although their wishes were duly solicited, their mother had already made many final decisions.

The letter from her brother announcing Darcy's betrothal had cast Caroline Bingley into the depths of despair. She was not truly heartbroken —for that would presume she had a heart to break—merely thwarted and angry, but she did her best to convince herself she had been wronged. Her sister Louisa was more circumspect. She wrote Elizabeth a cordial letter of congratulations that the recipient suspected was at least partially sincere. When it became apparent Longbourn would be too small for the number of guests invited to the wedding breakfast, Bingley appealed to his elder sister and her husband to return from Scarborough that Louisa could act as hostess at Netherfield. The Hursts returned to Hertfordshire without Caroline, and it was still unknown whether Bingley's younger sister would attend the wedding. Jane was pleased that Bingley was reconciled with at least one of his sisters and that Louisa arrived with the desire to behave in a manner most helpful.

GENTLEMEN APPROACH THEIR WEDDINGS WITH many fewer facets of the event to consider, and so they may be accused of pondering with greater concern the night and weeks immediately following the ceremony and celebration. Bingley repeatedly expressed his worries on the matter of the wedding night to Darcy, who could not be said to be any more tranquil on the subject than his friend, despite his somewhat more thorough education on the arts of conjugal commingling, seven years ago though it was. Neither had yet faced the responsibility for the deflowering of a specimen of the fairer sex, and each felt a growing sense of alarm in different ways.

Bingley knew his bride-to-be was all things calm and generous and was loath to believe he might do anything to perturb her typical aplomb. If he could discern a method of consummating their marriage in such a way that Jane would not notice it happening, he would be most relieved. That Jane might harbour a desire to express any physical affection towards him at such an intimate time was more than Bingley dared hope, although she seemed to like being kissed well enough.

Darcy, at rather the opposite end of that particular spectrum, was engrossed in the contemplation of awakening in Elizabeth the passion he was certain resided within her and, had he but known it, was the bedrock of his initial attraction. It was abundantly plain that his satisfaction in their conjugal relations was bound inextricably to hers. Could he enable her to reach that peak of sensation he had heard—and had overheard—a truly aroused woman could summit? His cousin Fitzwilliam was always a gentleman, but with that, a far more accomplished sampler of women—especially young widows. He had some years ago outlined for Darcy the instructions he followed for raising the ardour of a woman who was predisposed—through her nature or the skill of her lover—to enjoy the act of love as thoroughly as a man and much oftener once she got the knack of it. Fitzwilliam assured Darcy that a woman in the throes of love could be made to feel the ultimate joy without penetration, which Darcy recalled with some comfort. But at some point, the deed of relieving Elizabeth of her maidenhead would have to be done, and even Colonel Fitzwilliam, for all his campaigns in foreign lands, had never accepted the burden of taking a virgin.

Darcy could not even decide where to spend the wedding night. Bingley, out of friendship, had invited Elizabeth and Darcy to stay on at Netherfield, but Darcy could not imagine sitting across a breakfast table from anyone other than Elizabeth on his first morning as a married man, however much it might comfort her to have Jane near.

Darcy had the option of taking his bride to his London home, but Elizabeth had never been there, and he did not want to start their life together amid the society in town. Even though he had spent weeks and months dreaming of her joining him in his bed in the master's chamber of Darcy House, and even though the carriage ride from Netherfield to London would take at most only a few hours, he could not countenance it. Darcy understood that, by the spring season when Elizabeth felt secure in her place as Mrs Darcy, wife, helpmate, and lover, she would be confident enough to endure the *ton* for a few weeks.

Darcy awoke at Netherfield some three weeks before the wedding realizing he wanted more than anything to take Elizabeth back to Pemberley. It was the only alternative that would allow him to feel all was as it should be. Pemberley was home. When there, he felt life presented him to best advantage. Elizabeth owned to everyone who asked that Pemberley was where she first comprehended the depth of Darcy's regard for her and where she admitted to herself that she loved him. The very moment seemed to be captured in Mrs Gardiner's painting of her, which now resided upon the mantle in his bedchamber at Netherfield.

But Pemberley was nearly 150 miles away. There would be at least two days of very determined travel between Netherfield and Derbyshire. The wedding was to be at ten o'clock, with no possibility of escaping the following breakfast festivities before noon at best. Darcy built up the pillows under his head and shoulders and continued his ruminations. Their first night together would be spent on the road, and although there were many suitable inns along the route, Darcy could not reconcile taking Elizabeth the first time in a strange bed. And if she bled, for he knew virgins often did, what would become of her maiden blood, the proof of their consummation? Would their bedding be displayed on the wall of some tawdry alehouse? There was nothing for it but to wait. They would make for Pemberley with all possible speed, riding in his lightest, quickest carriage with teams of fresh horses at the ready along their path. If they followed the most direct route with the best roads, it could just be done. He and Elizabeth would wait one night. *Even if we roll into Pemberley in the middle of the second night, we will not spend two nights on the road. We will wait to consummate our love—and begin our married life—until we are home.*

Can I do it? Can I wait, knowing she will be mine for the taking even as we travel? I must and I will. I will promise her we will be at home.

Darcy bounded from his bed and stepped to the washstand to sprinkle water on his face. He willed a morning erection to subside. Garrick heard his master's tread and the water splash; it had been thus every morning since their return to Netherfield. Darcy dressed for riding.

Galloping across the countryside as the sun rose, Darcy made for the back boundary of Longbourn, hoping Elizabeth would emerge. Darcy smiled as he slowed to a cantor along the lane where he had proposed to Elizabeth, and where they so often walked with Bingley and Jane. It was a chilly morning, but the clouds were few, and Darcy knew Elizabeth needed the morning activity to dispel the vexation of wedding details. Although the many evening social gatherings meant Darcy and Elizabeth spent their time together, often by supper she was at her wits' end. She regaled him with amusing tales of lace decisions made and changed, and her mother's endless lists, but beneath her merry loquacity was a coiled tension he knew was distressing her sleep and shortening her temper. If she could take a brisk walk in the morning, her humour, at least for a time, would be refreshed.

The kitchen door of Longbourn opened, and Darcy was surprised to see Jane venture out with Elizabeth. They were talking animatedly, although their expressions were not happy. Darcy had to chuckle. Had the ceaseless hectoring at last discomposed both Elizabeth *and* Jane? He had seen his beloved marching along exorcising her demons many times. This was the first instance of Jane joining her, keeping up with her sister's torrid pace and simultaneously ranting away; someone was being castigated mightily, by Jane as well as Elizabeth.

The ladies heard Darcy's horse and looked up, startled, from their heated discourse. They stopped and curtsied as Darcy slipped from his mount. He tipped his hat with a brief bow and could not help dimpling as he said, "Good morning, Miss Bennet and Miss Elizabeth. Do I interrupt important schemes?"

Elizabeth cast him a sceptical sidelong glance while Jane smiled tightly and blushed. Darcy laughed. "Miss Bennet, I have seen Miss Elizabeth out of temper many times and will continue my days enjoying the spectacle, but to see *you* out of humour is something I *never* expected to see. What can possibly be the cause?"

As if rehearsed, they responded in unison, "Aunt Phillips."

"Oh, dear," said Darcy, attempting to appear serious.

"Mr Darcy, I am pleased to see *you* at least are in fine fettle this morning." So saying, Elizabeth at last produced a smile.

"I am indeed, my dearest. I think that, compared to you, my tasks are light and my decisions few as regards the wedding. But I have mastered one of the most important questions before me, and Miss Elizabeth, I would speak of it with you when we may have a private word."

Both Jane and Elizabeth sighed heavily and exchanged brief sisterly glances.

Elizabeth spoke. "Mr Darcy, if I may extend a word of warning, let me beseech you to make sure the decision you would address truly does need my attention. I am, er, *we* are so beset by niggling, inconsequential details, which others can and should spare us; I fear my patience is not what it ought to be.

"Even your sister, sir, torments us. Dear Georgiana has very graciously offered to create our bridal bouquets, but she *will* quiz us as to every detail. All I want is for her to hand me the silly thing as I take Father's arm."

Jane nodded, "And you will not believe it, but I feel the same as my sister. I am to take breakfast at Netherfield this morning with Louisa. Lizzy has wisely suggested I walk to Netherfield and consented to join me for the journey. But she does not stay to breakfast since *she* will not soon be mistress of that house."

Darcy bowed. "I shall continue my exercise, and if I may, Miss Elizabeth, I shall join you when you have left Miss Bennet at Netherfield."

Elizabeth executed a gracious bow in return. "I will endeavour to regain my civility by then."

The two sisters continued on their way as Darcy mounted his horse. Elizabeth turned to watch her betrothed riding away. *He is a fine specimen of a man,* she mused. "What Aunt Phillips says of him cannot possibly be true, Jane," she said aloud. "She paints all men with the same brush, I fear. I know not how she comes by her information."

Jane shook her head and rolled her eyes. "A fertile imagination and too much elderberry wine."

Elizabeth took her sister's arm as they walked. "Oh, Jane, I fear the trials of the wedding preparations are turning you into me!"

"Oh, yes. You will get no defence of her from me, Lizzy. Even our mother seemed shocked at the depths of her vulgarity."

"The things she says about Mr Darcy do not shock me in the least. She means to scare me and titillate herself. I plan to avoid her assiduously from now until the wedding."

"She does seem to take some strange thrill from talking of marital relations, Lizzy. It is unseemly. I shall follow your lead. We shall avoid her, or at least avoid being alone with her."

DARCY RETURNED HIS HORSE TO the Netherfield stable and found Elizabeth awaiting him behind a hedgerow. He thought it might be the same place he had come upon her as she approached Netherfield to attend Jane almost a year earlier. Her skin was similarly aglow, but he was more entranced now as Elizabeth smiled and held out her hand. She was holding the ribbons of her winter bonnet in her other hand. The sisters had warmed themselves quite thoroughly with the pace of their walking, and Elizabeth had removed her gloves and bonnet when they were still a mile from Netherfield.

Upon one of Elizabeth's fingers was the simple emerald ring set in gold he had given her a week after their betrothal. It was her birthstone.

"Feeling better?" Darcy asked, then bent over her extended hand, turned it over and gave her palm a reverent kiss. He felt the response he desired when she cupped her hand against his mouth with a throaty chuckle and stroked his cheek as he stood upright again. He held her hand at his face. Her eyes had the intelligent merriness that always left him enthralled. "Yes, I can see that you are."

"After you and Mr Bingley departed last night, Jane and I found ourselves left alone with our Aunt Phillips. We have resolved between us not to allow such a circumstance to happen again before the wedding—or *ever*, as far as *I* am concerned."

Darcy laughed. "I shall not quiz you as to the topic of her discourse. I can guess it easily enough."

"Thank you, Mr Darcy." They turned to begin their walk, and Darcy allowed Elizabeth's hand to slip down his arm and rest in the crook of his elbow. "I think you and I might walk at a more leisurely pace than Jane and I set." They strolled for some distance without speaking. Elizabeth was indeed returned to her usual equable spirits, ready to be pleased with Darcy and anything he might choose to say.

Darcy was lost in imagining the ribald tales and lurid speculations Elizabeth's aunt must have imparted to most thoroughly discompose both Elizabeth and Jane. It would make the subject current in his own mind much more difficult to raise at present. He looked out over the brittle, cold fields of corn stubble, lately harvested for hay, musing over how he should approach the topic of their wedding night.

Elizabeth remembered Darcy mentioning a matter upon which he wished to consult her. "Mr Darcy, if I might interrupt your apparent reverie, I am reminded there was a subject you wished to speak of this morning."

Darcy sighed heavily. *She never forgets a thing...*

His sigh was Elizabeth's first clue that her betrothed was not in the same mood as she. She glanced up to his face, reading his countenance. "If you have changed your mind, sir, it is of no particular importance to me, what-ever it was." She tried to comfort him by embracing his arm more tightly, which, unbeknownst to her, had the opposite effect of the one she intended. The nearness of her body disquieted Darcy further.

"Elizabeth..." he began but then went silent, not knowing how to proceed.

"Yes?" Elizabeth grew concerned. She stopped and willed his eyes to meet hers. She tried a new tactic. "Yes, Fitzwilliam?" She addressed him by his given name for the first time and saw his eyes instantly soften.

He smiled. "Elizabeth. At last you are comfortable enough to speak my name? I am most pleased."

Darcy bent his head to Elizabeth's upturned face. Her lips were parted, and she closed her eyes as their mouths joined. But unlike their previous kisses, Darcy embraced her and clasped her acquiescent body completely against his. The evidence of his strength made Elizabeth dizzy. She raised her hands to his neck, in part to steady herself, and itched to run her hands through his hair, but his hat interfered. She firmly held his face to hers as her tongue sought his. She had been practicing such a manoeuvre in her mind, working up her courage to respond to him as she had longed to do since their betrothal. She pressed her bosom against his layers of coats. When the kiss ended, the embrace did not.

She smiled at him. *He is very handsome*, she mused to herself, but decided she would not say so. *He looks as if he knows it well enough.* She whispered instead, "If this is my reward for pleasing you, Fitzwilliam, I will be distracted for the rest of our walk with finding more ways to do so. My skills as a conversationalist will suffer."

Darcy smiled, kissed her nose, chuckled, and kissed her lips again, even more ardently than before. Elizabeth felt the constriction in her chest she had come to equate with some manner of attachment to Darcy. The sensation caused her breathing to grow rapid and her bosom to ache in an odd combination of yearning and pleasure; in the present instance, a previously unfelt tension arose in the very pit of her stomach—or perhaps lower. The strength of her body's response surprised her, and she ended the kiss gently and began to step backwards to create some distance between them.

As his hands withdrew from her back and waist, they hugged her ribs, and brushed the sides of her bosom with some pressure before dropping to his side. *Will she chide me?* Darcy wondered. *How can I help but try her forbearance when I desire her so desperately? It is becoming more difficult to resist my inclinations. I must remind myself that she does not mean to be tempting; she simply is.* He could not apprehend his impulses to both protect her innocence and discard it utterly at the same time.

Elizabeth's eyes widened that such a liberty was attempted, her mouth forming an unspoken "oh!" of unguarded wonder. She most decidedly had *not* disliked the sensation of his hands near her breasts. She blushed and looked away, not daring to meet his eyes. *He reads me too well. He will see that I am...what am I? Is this love? Please*, she prayed, *do not let him try my virtue. I do not trust myself.*

"Elizabeth?" Darcy lowered his head and attempted to meet her gaze. "I love you. I hope you know that, if we are alone and you show me such affection as you have now, I will show mine for you in return. It is not my intention to try your goodness, but you may as well know the depth of my desire. It is no very great secret, is it?"

She shook her head, her cheeks infused with a deeper shade of rose. "No," she answered him quietly. "You are a man in love. You, I understand. It is myself I cannot follow."

"And that, dearest Elizabeth, is why I will hold myself in check. I would have you come to understand this aspect of love once we are husband and wife, that there will be nothing to concern you. After we are wed, we will both be free to concentrate upon your feelings…sensations, on…" Darcy stammered, realizing the nature of the conversation aroused him even as he sought to calm her. He understood the folly of trying to explain what she was experiencing; the effort was enticing to him and confusing to her.

"Pleasing you?" She was embarrassed but not so much as to not take pity on his agitation. Just last night, Aunt Phillips admonished Elizabeth and Jane to make every attempt to learn what was pleasing to their husbands, but could expect no pleasure themselves. She said ladies ought not to show physical enjoyment to their husbands as it only increased their demands. "If they have lascivious tendencies or attempt to be at you all the time, discourage them and let them take mistresses," she cautioned. Even Mrs Bennet could not listen to such notions and mentioned the lateness of the hour, calling, a little more shrilly than usual, for her sister's carriage to be brought.

"Pleasing *yourself*, Elizabeth. If you are well pleased, then you will always welcome me, and *then* I will be pleased."

His eyes were gentle and concerned. She believed him to be completely sincere. She had never heard him speak to her in so earnest a tone. *Surely, Aunt Phillips is wrong. What does she know of the heart of Fitzwilliam Darcy? That mystery is for me to solve and me alone.* Elizabeth smiled wanly. "I do not understand except that you love me, and I expect I *will* understand after we are married."

"Ah," Darcy sighed. He took her arm and they started walking. "That leads me to the topic on my mind this morning. Have you given any thought to where we should go after the wedding? Let me acquaint you with our several choices. I know you love travel, and it is my fondest wish to take you on a grand tour and show you the Lakes as the Gardiners, thankfully, could not. But this is not the season for travel. Prudence dictates a proper honeymoon should wait until spring. So what should we do?"

Elizabeth's blushes grew fierce. She thought her cheeks and chest would ignite. "I am sorry to admit, sir, I have given the matter little thought."

Darcy glanced down at her nervously and noted the colour of her right cheek, which was all he could see. Elizabeth abruptly donned her bonnet, tied it securely under her chin before he could do it for her and quickened her pace.

"Bingley has invited us to stay on at Netherfield, at least for the first night. That would not be my preference, but if you would be comforted to be near Jane, I will, of course, acquiesce."

Elizabeth thought she would not be comforted in that instance but said nothing.

A little daunted by her silence, Darcy continued. "We might go to the house in London, but you have not been there before, and if we stayed longer than a week, we would be in danger of having to make and receive calls, which would not please me. I own I do not expect to be willing to share my Mrs Darcy with the world quite so soon. We have been too much in company already."

Elizabeth still said nothing, although she agreed with him.

"The last choice is to make for Pemberley as soon as may be after the wedding. I will not lie: I long to take you home as my wife more than anything I have ever wanted in my whole life. But that would mean our first night, our wedding night, would be spent at an inn. Have you any thoughts on the matter?"

Elizabeth kept her eyes on the path ahead, but lowered her chin in an involuntary show of diffidence. "I did not know it to be common practice, sir, for brides to be consulted on such matters."

"Perhaps I have learnt better than other bridegrooms, Elizabeth. I would not presume to decide this alone, although in April, I might have done."

She nodded. "No, you are not like other men, or I would not love you, and we would certainly not be betrothed." Darcy chuckled. She continued, musing aloud, "At least if we go to London, it is Darcy House, and not an inn...but I *would* like to get to Pemberley." She stumbled and reached for Darcy's arm, which quickly encircled her waist to steady her. He pulled her to him. *I find myself in his arms again.* She paused, trying without much success to catch her breath. She gave great study to the button of his great coat at the middle of his chest.

Darcy found himself speaking to her bonnet. "This morning, I had an idea that might serve us well, but it will require your agreement. What if we postpone the..." *How do I say this to her?* "...union of, uh, the consummation..." *Just get on with it, man. Say it with conviction.* "...consummation until our second night together once we have reached Pemberley? It makes the travel arduous, with few stops except to change horses. It will mean even more to *me* if we are ensconced at home. Would it be too odd? I would not have you think I do not desire you; it is your comfort I would ensure."

Elizabeth's first response was relief. Unlike Jane, she would have a day to adjust to having a husband without the pressure of what most maidens approach with a sense of impending dread. She did not fancy beginning their intimate relations in a strange place. *What if he means to unclothe me? What if the event is noisy, as with my sister and Wickham? Better to be at Pemberley. What if the roads are in poor condition and it takes more than one night to reach home?*

"Home," she murmured as she pondered the implications of his suggestion. *He seems more impatient in his demands today. Will he be able to wait?*

Darcy smiled a little, deepening his dimples. "Home, is it? Are you decided?"

"You are willing to wait for my sake?" Her eyes met his, all seriousness.

Darcy could read her relief immediately in her now upturned face. He smiled more fully. "I promise you I will wait one night, but one night only, Elizabeth. It may be we reach Pemberley in the middle of the second night, and if that is the case, you will not have been home two hours before we are truly made husband and wife." He noticed Elizabeth eyes widen and her colour deepen. "If the weather turns against us and the roads are bad, I will not wait further. If we find ourselves at an inn on our second night, I cannot vouch for my character."

"Then I shall begin praying for calm weather, sir, and swift horses." She smiled a little.

Darcy kissed her nose and inhaled the scent of lavender as she looked up. "It delights me that you speak of Pemberley as home," he murmured.

They turned and continued their walk, returning to Longbourn.

Thursday, 26 November, 1812

ELIZABETH AWOKE ON THE MORNING of her wedding with fluttering in her stomach, the existence of which she would have been loath to admit. She rolled to face the other bed in the room, and from across the length of a yard separating them, saw her sister's blue eyes blink open. Jane immediately blushed.

"Did you sleep?" Elizabeth whispered.

"I think I did a little, just now. And you, Lizzy?"

"The same for me. I could not will myself to sleep by any means. I hope my eyes will not have circles."

Jane smiled. "You will be beautiful, Lizzy. Everyone remarks on how pretty you are now that you are in love."

Elizabeth sat up, dubious. "Do they? I find it hard to believe."

"You never could take a compliment to your looks with any grace, you know," Jane chided her gently. "What do you say when Mr Darcy compliments you?"

"I say nothing. In fact, I usually kiss him to stop him speaking such nonsense."

"Lizzy!" Jane laughed nervously, but was not as shocked as she sounded. She was in the habit of kissing Bingley and believed Elizabeth allowed Darcy the same liberty. Jane smiled.

Her outburst alerted their maid, Sarah, that the brides were awake, and she entered the room. On this most special morning, the sisters were allowed to bathe in their bedchamber, the metal tub having been brought up the night before, and Jane, as the eldest, was to be first. She had just settled into the water when Mrs Hill tapped on their door. Elizabeth peeked out and then admitted her.

Mrs Hill was as radiant as any bride, so delighted was she with the happy turn of events. "Two packages from Netherfield for you."

Elizabeth took them and bid Mrs Hill, who had turned to leave, to stay and see them opened.

Jane leaned her arms out of the tub and dried her hands on some towelling. Elizabeth handed her the one addressed by Bingley's sloppy hand. Elizabeth's was addressed by the strong precise letters of Fitzwilliam Darcy, and saying his name to herself caused the jolt in her chest that still surprised her with its violence.

Inside both packages were smaller parcels. Jane's contained a simple pair of coral and pearl earrings to match the coral beads she would wear with her gown. Elizabeth's gift from Darcy was similar to Jane's, but the pearls were set with garnets, to match the garnet cross her father had given her when she turned sixteen. This had been her only piece of jewellery until the emerald ring from Darcy.

The sisters smiled. "We are well matched, Jane," Elizabeth chuckled, "in every particular. I see Georgiana's hand in this. These are exactly the sort of little details she would notice."

In spite of the dithering and fluster of Mrs Bennet, Mr Bennet and his two eldest daughters left for the Longbourn church precisely on time. The trip was less than two hundred yards on foot, but was made longer by Mrs Bennet insisting father and daughters arrive at the church in a carriage, which could not follow the footpath. Elizabeth would have preferred the walk but made no argument.

After the ceremony, Elizabeth had little memory of what transpired. As she sat at the wedding breakfast, she could recall her father's kiss on her forehead as he arranged himself between his daughters for the processional. She could remember the solemnity in Darcy's eyes as he turned to face her, which he seemed to do more slowly than Bingley did to Jane. Elizabeth felt herself grow solemn, but just as they were turning away from each other towards the minister, Darcy winked ever so slightly. Elizabeth smiled, and smiled throughout the remainder of the ceremony. She remembered hoping she looked serene; she remembered the fragrance of the white jasmine sent from the Pemberley glass houses for her to carry; she remembered the sound of Darcy's voice as he said, "I will," in a way that made her heart race. When they reached the vestibule of the church, Darcy stopped their forward progress behind Jane and Bingley to take some leaves of lavender and a red chrysanthemum from his pocket and tuck them into the corner of her neckline with a soft caress, saying only, "From me." As they signed the registry, she could barely breathe.

Now they sat beside each other in the Netherfield dining room amid a crush of people. Darcy leaned to her ear. "You look beautiful."

Recalling Jane's comment about her lack of grace when complimented, Elizabeth vowed to improve herself. "Thank you," she whispered. What would she do without Jane nearby to guide her?

"Oh god," Darcy murmured. "I believe Mr Collins is attempting to capture my notice."

Elizabeth looked up, following Darcy's eyes. Her cousin William Collins was indeed trying to attract their attention and, having secured it, began an odd nodding and bobbing of his head toward his wife, Charlotte. "His ministrations are on Charlotte's behalf, my dear," Elizabeth whispered to Darcy while smiling politely at her cousin. "I am the victim, not you."

Darcy snickered. "You had better see to Charlotte before someone assumes your cousin is having a fit."

Elizabeth could not suppress a chuckle and turned to give Darcy an amused but scolding look. "You will get me into trouble, making me laugh at such things. Jane would not approve, and my character is in *your* hands now." She rose to her feet, but Darcy stayed her a moment with his hand holding hers.

"Then we are both in trouble, Mrs Darcy." He smiled up into her eyes with a smouldering look. "My dearest, loveliest Mrs Darcy." He kissed her hand.

Elizabeth was utterly breathless as Charlotte approached. "Oh, Lizzy!" Charlotte's voice dropped so only Elizabeth could hear it. "There is a gift I must put into your hands before you depart."

"But we have opened the beautiful bible from you and my cousin, Charlotte. You needn't give us anything more."

"In this case I am merely the bearer, Lizzy. It is from Rosings Park."

Darcy could tell from the look on Elizabeth's face that Charlotte had murmured something sensational, and he rose to his feet. Charlotte led Elizabeth to the small sitting room the female guests were using for refreshing themselves. Darcy awaited them in the hall.

Charlotte handed Elizabeth a wrapped box with a card attached. Elizabeth read the card:

To my new cousin, Elizabeth Darcy,

Please accept this gift with wishes as warm as the gift itself. You have done me a great service by securing the affections of my Cousin Darcy. I am forever in your debt for freeing us both from an obligation neither of us sought. I wish you every joy.

Your devoted cousin,
Anne

Well I'll be...! Elizabeth thought. She said, "Could you bring Mr Darcy to me, Charlotte?"

He entered when Charlotte opened the door and, seeing Elizabeth's astonishment, started to ask, "What on earth...?" She passed him the card.

Elizabeth opened the wrapping that covered a thin-sided cedar box. Removing its lid, she pulled out an exquisite wool shawl in muted shades of blue, rust and deep green, softer than anything she had ever felt. Elizabeth looked at Charlotte with wonder. "Did you help her? What wool is this? How...?"

Charlotte started to laugh. "Steady on, Lizzy!"

Darcy touched the shawl. "Cashmere! I am impressed."

Charlotte explained, "As soon as your aunt received your letter, Mr Darcy, Anne came to the parsonage. She was quite transformed. She was ripe for conspiracy, and the parsonage was the centre of it. I do not think your aunt suspects a thing. But Anne wanted me to wait until today, before you leave, so you could wear it on your journey, Lizzy. She always does worry lest anyone suffer from the cold as she does. I think she will always be fragile, but there is a light of defiance in her eyes now that I think quite healthy. Perhaps it will spread."

"How will we thank her?" Elizabeth embraced herself with the shawl.

Darcy looked about the room and seeing no materials for writing, excused himself and went down the hall to Bingley's study. He returned in a few moments to show Elizabeth the quick note he had penned and signed from them both.

Dearest Cousin Anne,

We thank you as much for your kind words as for the glorious shawl. We hope our appreciation of it will warm you from afar. When next we meet, we shall have so much to tell you. Be well.

Your loving cousins,
Elizabeth and Fitzwilliam Darcy

Charlotte folded the letter into her reticule. "It is killing Mr Collins to keep this from Lady Catherine. He expects thunderbolts at any moment, but he is truly on your side, Lizzy, however it may appear."

"Oh, Charlotte!" Elizabeth gave Charlotte a long embrace.

"Now might be a good time to sneak away, Elizabeth," Darcy said as they left the sitting room behind Charlotte. He was carrying the shawl in its box and handed it to a footman to place in their carriage.

Elizabeth waited for him in the entry but knew their leave-taking could not be as stealthy as Darcy hoped. Jane suspected such subterfuge, and soon the portico of Netherfield was teaming with friends and family. It took another half hour before they were truly away.

Scarlet Lychnis
"Sunbeaming eyes"

Chapter 15

Longbourn to Coventry

Fitzwilliam Darcy stayed on the gentlemen's side of the carriage, sitting across from Elizabeth, as the smallest Darcy barouche rolled away from the environs of Meryton. He gazed at his bride fondly as she watched familiar terrain recede. She had removed her wedding bonnet, and it sat on the seat next to Darcy. The colours Anne chose for the shawl accented the russet highlights of Elizabeth's hair. Even in the dark coach, she seemed illuminated by the late autumn sunshine. She was still as radiant as she had been in the church.

Elizabeth smiled as she finally settled her eyes upon her husband. "If you would not be too scandalized, Fitzwilliam, I would have you join me when we get beyond the Meryton neighbourhood. We will be taking a different route to Derbyshire than I have been before, I think?"

"You now present me with a quandary, Elizabeth." His voice was low and gentle. "Do I stay here where I can admire how lovely you are, or do I take you in my arms as we ride along and tell you what we are seeing? I own I cannot decide which I prefer more."

"How can you form an opinion when you have never ridden with me in your arms?"

He laughed. "You are quite right. And I have a well-witnessed history of gazing upon you." With a quick lithe movement, Darcy sat next to Eliza-

240

beth. "How capacious is that lap robe?"

She chuckled. "Ample enough."

Darcy opened his great coat and extended his arm so Elizabeth could lean next to him inside it. She covered his legs with the lap robe, tucking it under his thigh as if she were ministering to one of the Gardiner children. She settled under the shawl, and Darcy's other arm soon snuggled under it, on top of her arms. The scent of lavender wafting from her hair tickled his nose.

"Mrs Darcy, this is, in every way, better than sitting by myself." He kissed her temple.

She turned her head away with a smile, giving his lips access to her ear and neck. Darcy leaned to kiss the little earring perched upon her earlobe, then the smooth bare skin of her neck. Elizabeth shivered in his arms. "Are you chilled?" he whispered, although he knew from the temperature of her skin against his lips that she was enticingly warm.

"No, sir, I am…" Elizabeth started to reply. His kisses upon her neck were causing her heart to pound and produced the frisson of pleasure that inspired Darcy's question.

"You are…" he coaxed.

"I believe, sir, I am happy."

Darcy's chest swelled and he embraced her more tightly. "Elizabeth," he murmured. She turned her head and leaned against his shoulder. He rested his cheek upon her coiffed hair.

"We do not go into Oxfordshire, sir?"

"We will make for Coventry and spend the night, although it will be well after dark before we arrive. The inn there is comfortable. In the morning, we will enter the main road to Derby, and you will start to remember the country. Coventry to Derby to Bakewell, through Kympton to home. It will be a long day tomorrow."

Elizabeth blushed to think just how very long the day would be, and what was in store at the end of it. She was glad Darcy could not see her face. She swallowed. "So at last I shall see Kympton!"

"Indeed, but there is no great charm in it. It serves as the market town for Pemberley. Lambton is the prettier village, for it has cultivated its character to appeal to visitors of the Peaks. It is something of a gateway to and fro for the tourists—well, of course, this you know. My family has had more occasion to come and go through Kympton, but we encourage our guests to approach Pemberley from Lambton as you did."

Their conversation continued for some miles until there was a silence, and Darcy realized Elizabeth was napping. *Elizabeth Bennet is asleep in my arms,* he mused, smiling to himself. *And we are married.* Soon he was asleep, too.

Darcy returned to awareness; he noticed the darkening, cloudy sky. He could not consult his pocket watch without disturbing the still-dozing Elizabeth but thought he had not been asleep for too long and sensed the loss of light was the result of travelling into a storm. He straightened his neck, which had a crick, and suddenly realized the hand under Elizabeth's cosy shawl was reposing upon her breast, albeit over her pelisse. *Darcy! What a rake you are when you sleep!* Slowly and carefully, he lifted his hand and returned it to lie on her arms, which were crossed at her waist.

Within moments of his movement, Elizabeth startled awake. She shook her head and sat more upright. "I was dreaming," she said, smiling to herself. "We were in the Netherfield library, together upon the settee in front of the fire." She looked at Darcy, who was entranced by her sleepy countenance.

"Are you always this pretty when you awaken?"

"Good gracious, no, sir! I should warn you, I look a fright in the morning."

Darcy chuckled. "Madam, I do not believe you. I expect you judge yourself too harshly."

"That is exactly the proper response for a new husband. I am proud of you!" She laughed at him.

Darcy leaned his face down, kissing her smiling lips, and followed his inclination to pull her into his lap.

"Are you happy, Fitzwilliam?" she asked shyly.

"Indeed, Elizabeth." He squeezed her a little. "I am happy. I plan to hold you all the way to Coventry."

"Even when we stop to change the horses?"

"We have a picnic hamper from Netherfield under the other seat. I was advised it would be prudent as we would have little appetite at the breakfast, although I observed we both ate more than Bingley and Jane."

Elizabeth blushed to think Jane and Bingley would be having a normal wedding night at Netherfield in a few hours. Her eyes searched Darcy's countenance. He seemed mirthful. She asked, "You have not changed your mind?"

"About what, my love?"

"Tonight. Our wedding night…" Her blushes continued, and she looked away. "I am sure that is why Jane was nervous."

Darcy smiled mischievously. "Has napping with me so filled you with desire that you would rather we not wait to be at home?"

"Mr Darcy…" She turned, shaking her head at him. "I am well aware of the liberties you attempted whilst I slept. But as we are married, it was not really a liberty, I suppose. It is you, I fear, who may not be able to wait."

"I will have you know that I, like you, was asleep when my hand moved."

She nodded exaggeratedly with an arch look. "Oh, I am *sure* it was all most innocently done. The chill when you moved your hand away awakened me."

"I can easily warm you again…" Darcy looked hopeful and started to move his hands to her bosom.

Elizabeth squirmed and giggled, sliding herself off his lap, back onto the padded bench seat, blocking his hands with the shawl. "Now you have made me giggle, and I do pride myself on not giggling like other girls. Unforgivable, sir!"

"If you would not resist me, you would not giggle. But if I may say, Elizabeth, you have a pleasing giggle. It does not alter my opinion of you."

"My concern is my opinion of *myself*, sir. I am quite certain I have *your* good opinion," she teased.

He laughed. "You are very sure of yourself, Mrs Darcy."

"That is because I *am* Mrs Darcy. Mrs Darcy must be sure of herself on every occasion." She looked at him, and he was smiling at her. *He is so handsome when he smiles.* She turned her face up and closed her eyes.

"You look as if you are sure I would like to kiss you, Mrs Darcy."

"What I would like you to know is that *I* would like to be kissed, sir."

"Ah, I see. That makes me even happier. But you now have leave to kiss me; you needn't wait for me to read your thoughts." Darcy kissed Elizabeth gently, teasing her lips with his tongue.

They rode for another hour, kissing and laughing, before the coach slowed to a stop in a little village. "Never have I enjoyed such a pleasant carriage ride, Mrs Darcy," her husband murmured in her ear as he handed her down, and Elizabeth was lead to a presentable little inn to stretch her legs and refresh her person whilst the horses were changed. Once the coach was on the road again, they ate from the picnic hamper. Elizabeth was surprised to find she was ravenous once presented with food. Darcy sat opposite her as they ate, but as soon as the hamper was stowed away, sat next to her again.

"Did you bring a book to read?" he asked.

"You know how I love to read, and I feel the flaw in my constitution very keenly that I am not able to read much in a moving carriage. I can look at a map or pictures, but to read to pass the time, I become quite ill. It is vexing, but it cannot be helped."

"This is not so very great a flaw, dearest. I shall happily converse with you instead."

Just after they left the village, the clouds made good their threat of rain, but this did not last long and proved the air was warmer as they travelled north, away from the clear, freezing weather in Hertfordshire. The area had not had a recent rain, so the road was not much muddied by the current shower.

They talked of matters great and small: their discussion of the situation in France lead Darcy to reveal something of Colonel Fitzwilliam's history, which in turn lead to a discussion of Georgiana's childhood. Darcy mentioned some details about his parents, which steered the talk to Pemberley, and Elizabeth asked Darcy many questions about the history of the house.

As Darcy expected, Elizabeth had a reasonable grasp of foreign affairs —they interested her—and her questions about his family showed a perceptive awareness of him, which he found pleasing, for it gives any man in love pleasure to know his beloved has been observant of his person and character. She asked him about the grand tour he had taken at the end of his days at Cambridge—where he had gone, what he had seen—although Darcy suspected there was some unspoken, underlying question, which she seemed occasionally poised to ask.

In truth, Elizabeth overheard a conversation between Bingley and Darcy as she passed outside the Pemberley billiard room the day before Jane arrived. She had dirtied her hands in the conservatory and sought a washroom. She was returning to Georgiana when she heard the male voices. What she heard caused her to pause outside the doors, which she knew was very wrong, but acknowledging her inappropriate curiosity about a private conversation did not stop her from listening.

Bingley was concerned that his tour of Europe, just three years prior, had not yielded the sort of lessons for a gentleman's intimate conduct, as he put it, as Darcy's had. Bingley worried he would not strike the proper tone once alone with Jane; he wished to be confident. When Bingley asked Darcy to recommend a brothel in London where he might gain some knowledge quickly, Elizabeth was appalled. Darcy suggested a book instead, saying, "I know of nowhere in London to send you. When I came back from the Continent, there was an establishment recommended to me, but you know my nature, Bingley. I had a horror of meeting men of my acquaintance there. I have no current knowledge."

"Are you saying the gossip in the society pages has been entirely fabricated? That you have no particular penchant for blonde-haired, blue-eyed actresses?"

"Indeed, I am. I do not care for the temperament of actresses. If I marry properly to a lady with a nature capable of feeling passionate affection, I shall never have want of a mistress."

Elizabeth blushed furiously, willing her feet to withdraw, but her ears told her feet to stay exactly where they were.

"Darcy!" Bingley sounded scandalized. "You have changed what you require in a wife from when last we spoke of it at Netherfield?"

"I did not understand myself then as well as I do now. I have learnt lessons of which I was sorely in need. I have come to believe a felicitous marriage and a socially advantageous marriage may likely be mutually exclusive."

"Because you have fallen in love with the daughter of a mere country squire, as have I, but now *you* must reconcile your ideals to what your heart desires. My inclinations suffer no such qualms." Bingley said this as a statement of fact.

"My hope, Bingley, is that a lady who has despised me with such justified determination may come to love me with the same degree of vehemence."

"You know my opinion on that subject, Darcy. You will need to declare yourself before I am proved right. She cannot run at you, you know."

"At this point, Bingley, I would not think any less of her if she did, and in point of fact, I would be greatly relieved."

Elizabeth was, at last, embarrassed enough to successfully tiptoe away. That Darcy had not acknowledged the red chrysanthemum confused her.

Now, she was sitting in his embrace in his carriage, as Mrs Darcy. "Fitzwilliam, at the inn...tonight, will you have your own room? Since we plan to um...not, er..."

"Consummate our vows until tomorrow night?" He finished her sentence for her. "I do not plan to awaken upon my first morning as a married man in an empty bed, if that is what you are asking. We have taken two rooms but we shall use one as a dressing room and sleep in the other, whichever has the bigger bed. In most inns, the beds are too short. It is my design to sleep in rather more clothes than I am used to"—Elizabeth felt the colour rise in her face at this—"and I hope your nightgown is modest. We shall get you tucked into bed properly, and I shall sleep next to you, but only between the counterpane and bedclothes, so I may hold you, but with many layers of cloth between us."

Still blushing, she turned to look up into his face. "My impression is you have given this evening a great deal of thought."

"Not nearly so much thought as for tomorrow night, darling Elizabeth, I assure you."

Remembering the overheard conversation and the look of desire she often saw in his eyes, she murmured, "I can well believe it," without realizing she had spoken aloud.

It was indeed long after dark and another change of horses before they reached Coventry. Elizabeth and Darcy each travelled with one small case and no personal servants. Elizabeth's clothing had all been sent on to Pemberley except for an exceptionally modest Welsh flannel nightgown and a warm travelling ensemble of fine claret-coloured wool for the next day. Darcy ordered a simple dinner be readied immediately and served in a small sitting room across the hall from their rooms. They both exhibited a hearty appetite. A fire was lit in the room in which they chose to sleep, and Darcy ordered a bottle of the inn's best wine, hoping it would help them both be easier with each other.

A maid arrived at their door at nine o'clock to assist Elizabeth in her preparations. Darcy had, he thought, quite generously offered to undress his new wife, a suggestion that brought forth more of the giggles Elizabeth so loathed. They jovially gave up the idea as a bad bet.

Elizabeth emerged from the smaller bedchamber in a nightgown that was indeed completely without allure. The heavy pink flannel had long sleeves tied at the wrists and buttoned from the unstructured waist to the high band collar at the base of her neck, with many tiny shell buttons securing the placket. The bodice, from shoulder to waistline, was detailed with pin tucks so close together that the decoration formed a breastplate of flannel armour, and the fabric fell in vertical folds to the tips of Elizabeth's slippers. The pout of her unsupported bosom could barely be detected. Elizabeth had not removed her silk wedding chemise, which had been the garment closest to her skin all day.

246

Darcy heard the door creak open and stood as Elizabeth entered. She stopped when he turned to her, and his eyes unabashedly searched from head to toe for any sign of her form being further revealed. He had hoped at least he might lose himself in her long dark hair, but it was woven in a heavy braid curving on one shoulder and down over her arm to nearly her elbow. "You are very modestly dressed, Mrs Darcy. I suppose I should appreciate that tonight you do not wish to excite me."

"Indeed, Mr Darcy, this nightgown was selected to have just that effect, once we decided to wait to be at home." Her smile widened. "I think you will be entertained to know this gown was a special wedding gift from Mrs Collins." She raised her eyebrows at Darcy. Elizabeth watched with delight as he, at first, tried not to chuckle but finally guffawed with a deep natural laugh she had not heard before. He sounded unrestrained, relaxed and thoroughly amused.

When he regained his composure enough to speak—they had both laughed quite boisterously—he took her hand and turned to settle them on the settee in front of the fire. He handed her a glass of wine. "I recall a conversation we had about how fortunate Mr Collins was in his choice of wife. Do you remember it?"

"I do. We were in the parsonage at Hunsford." She did not mention the conversation had been most awkward and disjointed.

"You said Mrs Collins had an excellent understanding but you had a devilish look in your eye as you said it."

"Did I?"

"You did, and I longed to ask more, but to do so would have been unseemly. Does this style of nightgown coincide with your opinion of the Collinses' marriage?"

"Am I to understand that Fitzwilliam Darcy, of all people, wishes to lure me into gossiping about another married couple?" She gave him a rather saucy sidelong glance.

"Yes, about *that* particular couple, I am all curiosity. How does such a thoughtful woman bear such a pompous nincompoop? Is this the sort of nightwear that drives him wild with desire?"

Elizabeth grinned and tried to suppress—not for the first time—the vision of her cousin wild with desire. After a deep breath, she said, "Charlotte has contrived to only have marital relations once a week—on Saturday night. The rest of the week, she has him gardening vigorously or walking to and from Rosings to the point of near exhaustion. And she is not to be disturbed when in her sitting room. I think she has managed her husband very well."

"'Managed her husband!'" Darcy repeated her words. "Is that what wives do? *Manage* their husbands? Is that what you intend to do with me, Mrs Darcy? Manage me?"

Elizabeth leaned forward and looked over her shoulder at her husband, her eyes bright with merriment. "You are tall and well-made; Mr Collins is short and squat. You are handsome; he is ill-favoured. You are well-educated and clever; his education was limited, and he is foolish. You have cared to improve your flaws; he admits to none, yet they are legion. There is simply no comparing you. I foresee no need of management such as Charlotte must employ. She must curb his ardour to maintain her sanity. I think I will want to encourage yours to serve my nature."

"By this, do you mean I will not be consigned to exercising my rights as your husband merely once a week?" Darcy's eyes darkened, and he gazed intently at her.

Elizabeth looked down with a maidenly blush and did not answer.

"Elizabeth?" He sensed she was suddenly contrite.

"I…I spoke words just now I thought you would want to hear, but you must know, I have not the knowledge or experience to speak so. I do not know what it means to encourage your ardour…what such encouragement entails. I do not know. I wish it were not so." Her insides were all aflutter.

Darcy leaned forward to her. "You wish what, exactly, were not so?"

She compressed her lips. "Let me just say, Fitzwilliam…let it be known to you that the things in the world I fear most are the things of which I know too little. Maidens enter the married state with far too little information."

Darcy's look was serious. "You fear me?"

She took in a deep breath then looked into his eyes. "I fear appearing stupid, silly, artless. I fear embarrassing myself. I fear disappointing the man I love and wish most in the world to please."

"Dearest Elizabeth…" She preferred to tease him rather than speak of loving him, thus whenever she *did* speak of her affection, Darcy felt over-whelmed with tenderness. He kissed her forehead and gathered her into his arms. He held her quietly for a moment before responding, "I cannot comprehend how you could possibly disappoint me."

She seemed to relax into him, but he sensed a tension remaining that, until they were alone in their chambers in Pemberley, would be present within her. Then he would be able to show her, so she would believe it, how groundless were all her fears.

"I slept but little last night," Elizabeth finally said. "Perhaps it would be best for me to try to sleep since we are to make an early start. Finish your wine, sir." She motioned for him to stay seated; he disregarded her.

"I slept very ill last night, myself. I kept dreaming that various inanities were making me late to our wedding. It was a poor night."

They were now standing, and Elizabeth smiled gently into his eyes. "We *are* a pair, are we not?"

"We are." Darcy swept her into his arms and carried her to the bed. He had already turned down the bedclothes and laid her upon the clean sheeting. She kicked off the little slippers she wore before burrowing her feet into the blankets. He covered her to her chest, and she raised her arms to lay them atop the counterpane. "Will you be cold?" Darcy asked.

"Not if I am holding you," she said, smiling.

"I must go prepare myself. It shan't take but a few moments." Darcy disappeared into the second room. When he reappeared, his coat and cravat were gone. He wore only a fine lawn shirt, and instead of trousers, a pair of soft knee breeches with no stockings or shoes.

Elizabeth gazed at his bare neck as he approached. He was carrying a blanket from the bed in the second chamber. Darcy pulled back the counterpane and climbed under it, half-sitting to spread the blanket over himself. He lay back and turned to Elizabeth, who rolled on her side to face him.

"Will you be warm enough?" she asked.

"If I am not, there are more bedclothes to bring from the other room. And, as I said, I am wearing more clothes than usual...for me, at night." He was trying to prepare her for the next night, and the nights to follow, when he intended to sleep naked beside her.

Elizabeth impulsively touched his neck with her fingertips. It was warm and slightly rough with a shadow of unshaven beard. She placed her whole palm on his throat. "You know what a curious creature you have married, sir..."

"Yes..." Her little, soft hand upon his neck thrilled him.

She snuggled towards him and placed several reverential kisses upon his throat before cuddling against him. "There," she said. "Now I know what that feels like, I can sleep peacefully."

Darcy chuckled. "But you see, Elizabeth, now *I* cannot." He turned her face to his with a hand under her chin, noticing she had undone the top half dozen buttons of her nightgown. He claimed her mouth, kissing her deeply, and as he felt her tongue responding to his explorations, he ran the back of his hand down her throat, until the closed buttons stopped his progress at the middle of her chest.

He released her mouth and whispered, "You are lucky, madam. I am not yet dexterous with tiny buttons."

Her eyes darkened with a desire fighting through her drowsiness. "Or perhaps unlucky..." She initiated a new kiss. When she released him, she whispered, "Tell me about tomorrow night. How shall it be different from this?"

Darcy met her eyes sheepishly. "I must warn you, I am becoming aroused."

Elizabeth was not precisely sure what this meant, but did not care to admit it. "You needn't," she replied.

"Turn with your back against my chest. If I cannot see your eyes, I may be able to say somewhat of tomorrow night."

She rolled away from him, looking toward the fire. He drew one arm under her neck and partially under her pillow, and with the other, covered her left arm and rested his hand upon the bed in front of her, but not touching.

"This is very pleasant. Very pleasant, indeed," she murmured.

Darcy smiled. "So...when you come to me tomorrow night..."

"I will come to you?"

"Or when we meet in our bedchamber, I would like your hair to be unbound. And I would like your nightdress to be a good deal less confining."

"This nightgown is quite ample, sir. You needn't fear I am confined in any way." She chuckled.

Darcy was comforted to feel her laughing in his arms. "Less modest, madam, I meant less modest."

"I know."

Darcy moved her braid and played at biting her neck. "Vexing woman," he growled. "And I would request that you not wear the little cross from your father."

"I have already removed it."

"You have?" Darcy moved his hand from her braid to the throat of her nightgown, and felt gingerly around just inside the open placket at her collarbone. "So you have..." He encountered the chemise. "You are wearing yet another layer of armour?"

"At the risk of tempting you, I must confess I often become too warm in the night, and assume all this flannel will increase that tendency. I may need to shed a layer and this chemise is not too immodest."

Darcy drew in a hissing breath, fighting the urge to shed her layers with all due haste. "Elizabeth, you had better hope such an action in the middle of the night does not awaken me. You may find yourself taken at an inn after all." He murmured into her ear then proceeded to kiss her earlobe, the skin in front of it, and strained against her to reach a kiss onto her cheek, which felt fiery to the touch of his lips.

"Is my wife blushing?"

"No." She giggled.

"Yes, you are."

"Yes, I am."

"Blushing and giggling in my arms in bed; you are pleasing me, Elizabeth."

"I am shocked at this proclivity to giggling: three times in one day. You ought not encourage it, Fitzwilliam. I must give myself a stern talking-to."

"Might I be making you unsettled?" he asked, before nibbling on her ear, drawing her earlobe into his mouth, and thinking about other parts of her person he hoped to draw into his mouth.

"You? Making me unsettled? You must know I would never admit to such drivel, even if it were true." She laughed.

Darcy chuckled in her ear. His hand went to her waist and he pulled her against him more forcibly. "Suit yourself. I am not inclined to argue the point." He was glad the layers of bedclothes kept her from any awareness of the potency of his desire. He longed to rub himself against the soft skin of her derrière, and the more he thought it, the more he feared he would act upon his cravings.

"Will you tell me more? You would have my hair loose and wearing a more revealing nightgown. I have already proved compliant with regard to my little cross. Anything else?"

Darcy could barely breathe. "That will have to do for now."

"Oh."

It took several minutes to quell his desires, and when he returned attention to Elizabeth, he found she had fallen asleep. He nuzzled his face into her hair and joined her in slumber.

About an hour later, Elizabeth awoke. As she feared, she was now much too warm. Darcy was draped partly over her, his rhythmical breathing indicating he was fast asleep. She reached to the neck of the nightgown, which she was rapidly coming to regard with a hearty dislike, and released a few more buttons. With careful slowness, she rolled slightly away from him onto her back, and inched away from the mass of bedclothes separating them; the blankets had absorbed and held the warmth. Darcy stirred but did not awaken. His leg lay over the tops of her thighs and his warmth was felt directly by that part of her where she knew he had an interest. *This is not unpleasant, but these must be sensations I ought not to have. Is this what he means by becoming aroused?* His elbow was behind her neck but her head was supported by the down pillows and she saw no need to move his arm. His other arm was on her waist and she felt no harm would come of it either. She opened the neck of the nightgown to expose more of her skin to the cool air. *This should be safe enough.* As sleep again overtook her, the focus of her mind on the parts of her person under his leg impelled her to dream.

Elizabeth awoke upon a strange bed in a very dark room. The last embers of a fire produced the only light except for the frantic sputtering of a waning candle. She was naked under heavy bedclothes, and her husband, Fitzwilliam Darcy, was asleep, mainly on top of her and between her legs. She was too warm, but it was the bedclothes covering their bodies that constituted the annoyance to her comfort. She welcomed Darcy's weight, and felt an odd, aching heat build in the hidden place between her thighs. She moved her hips, spreading her legs further and bending one knee. Darcy was not naked; she could feel his shirt in wrinkles against her skin. Her arms were not encumbered and she slid the blankets down his back. His cheek was upon her shoulder, but as she rolled her hips—the sensations between her legs seemed to necessitate this—his hand opened flat upon her chest. It did not touch her bosom but his arm settled between her breasts, and he whispered, "I love you, my dearest Elizabeth."

Elizabeth felt full of the tender emotion his words of affection always inspired, but there was something more, rising from her soul, a sense of wanting, even needing, to give herself to him. She placed her hand over his upon her chest. "My handsome Mr Darcy, I love you."

She drifted into a deeper, dreamless sleep.

Darcy awoke with cold feet. He became aware of his hand upon her warm chest, and when she placed her hand upon his, he heard her murmur "Mr Darcy" in her sleep. Under his leg, her hips seemed to be rocking. He was enraptured. *She is dreaming...of me! Maybe of us, together.* Darcy felt a sudden potent development between his legs. The delicate hand lying upon his clenched and Elizabeth sighed. The little hand then flung over her head onto her pillows. *Is she giving herself to me in her sleep?* Darcy watched as her movements stilled.

He longed to explore her bosom—all of her, in truth—and he knew he must move his hand; temptation was too strong even with a substantial layer of pink flannel covering most of her person. That she had moved so invitingly in her sleep was a revelation to him. He lifted his hand away. Elizabeth stirred and turned with a little moan onto her side, her back to him. He carefully pulled his arm from under her neck and lifted his leg off her. *I shall build up the fire, fetch a blanket for my feet—and will my urges under better control.*

Elizabeth awoke again, a crackling fire providing the focus for her eyes. Darcy was sleeping on his side behind her, and the only part of him touching her was a comforting hand upon her waist. *Fitzwilliam must have built up the fire again. He may be cold, but I am roasting. There is nothing for it but to remove this ludicrous nightgown.* She eased out of bed. The floor was chilly, but she decided against her slippers, fearing their little heels would announce her movements. She walked behind the settee, untying the ribbons at her wrists as she went.

Darcy awakened as Elizabeth pulled herself from under his hand. He watched her walk away from the bed, wondering if she would disappear into the second bedchamber. She stopped behind the settee, and he could see she was untying the long sleeves. *Is she removing her nightgown?* His heart started to beat so loudly he feared she would hear it.

Elizabeth stood with her hands in front of her, unbuttoning the remaining little buttons down the placket. She flapped the loosened fabric to fan herself before pulling her arms from the sleeves and letting Charlotte's gift drop unceremoniously to the floor. She stepped from the puddle of flannel, catching it upon one foot and giving it a kick, which sent it aloft ten feet across the room. "Asinine, damned thing," she muttered.

Darcy had to turn his face into the pillows to keep from laughing out loud. *She is her father's daughter.* He was afraid she might turn and see him shaking with mirth.

Elizabeth looked down at her more exposed bosom. The chemise was of a finer quality than she usually wore next to her skin; it was made of the same fabric as the under-layers of her wedding gown and it clung to her curves. It had wide shoulder straps and one drawstring cinched the neckline, while another pulled the garment close under her breasts. The hem fluttered around the middle of her calves, revealing slender ankles.

Darcy peeked from the pillows in time to see Elizabeth, now slightly facing him, untie the neckline ribbon and retie it more snugly. She thought this would pull the neckline higher, which was true, but it also drew the fabric more closely around her breasts, lifting them a little outwards. *Oh dear. That was not entirely helpful,* she fretted to herself. She felt more exposed than she was.

Her husband detected yet another erection building. *How can I be expected to resist her? Look at those little ankles, her perfect bosom. And I know she was dreaming of me.* Darcy groaned and rolled away.

She looked at him. *It is a shame he must be cold tonight, our first night together.* She turned and tiptoed into the second room, closed its door and made use of the receptacles there. Afterwards, she refreshed herself with lavender water. When she stepped back into their bedchamber, she studied him as he lay facing the wall. His shoulders were appealingly broad and his legs long and lean. His feet had tossed off the blanket he brought in to cover them.

Darcy was wide-awake. He felt her wrapping the fallen blanket around his feet. He could not discern what she did next, but it felt as if she were smoothing the bedclothes on her side of the mattress. *What is she about?* He felt her lift the blanket and counterpane covering him, and crawl in. He could feel her bosom pressed against his back. She snaked one arm under his neck to pull into closer contact with him; her other arm wormed its way under his, and her hands opened on his shirt. Her right hand reached inside, touching the skin of his chest. The air was filled with the scent of lavender. He savoured a moment in her arms before warning her.

"You are treading a dangerous path, Elizabeth." He reached into his shirt and withdrew her hand, holding it in his, raising her palm to his lips.

"I do not believe myself in danger, Fitzwilliam. You are an honourable man. But you are too cold to sleep well, and I am too warm. If lying in my arms is disturbing you, I can recommend, by way of substitute, a certain flannel nightgown that will keep you very warm indeed, I promise you."

Darcy closed his eyes, smiling. "You are an obliging wife."

"Or," Elizabeth continued, "*you* should sleep under the bedclothes, and I should remain as I am now."

Darcy sighed. "How I long for my own bed, with you in it." He released her hand, reached behind him, and felt the length of her thigh from hip to knee under a layer of smooth silk. His virile member was urgently alert. *Do I ask too much of myself to wait? How I long to make her truly mine and have done with it.*

Her hand returned to the opening of his shirt. She kissed the nape of his neck. "If you do not wish to wait, Fitzwilliam, I will not fault you."

"I may be an honourable man, but I begin to question whether I have married an honourable woman. You would be willing?" He held his breath.

"Indeed, sir, I hope you will always find your wife willing." She leaned her cheek against him.

"That is not quite the answer I was hoping for. Fitzwilliam Darcy wishes to know if Elizabeth Bennet is willing to give herself to him, to become his wife in every way. Do you want me?" His voice was a tense whisper.

Elizabeth became alert and pulled her head away. *How can he ask? Why does he ask? Why does he not simply take me if he is so filled with desire?* "Fitzwilliam, I love you, but I fear I do not quite understand myself well enough to know whether I want you. I must learn what that means."

Darcy considered this. As delicious as she felt as she lay against his back, Elizabeth was still an innocent. If he was stirring feelings within her, she could not yet give them words, nor did she have knowledge enough to understand her body. *Stick to your plan, Darcy, marshal your self-control, and wait for Pemberley. It is in every way preferable.* "I think there are very few hours of sleep left to us, and tomorrow we will be in the carriage all day. As much as I long for you, Elizabeth, I want to be at Pemberley, where we have shared so much already, when we take this final step to bind ourselves together."

Elizabeth was relieved. "It *is* where I realized you were the *only* man I could ever be prevailed on to marry." Darcy started to chuckle, and again pulled her hand from his shirt and held it. She asked, "Now are you more comfortable? Can you sleep?"

Darcy closed his eyes, willing his manhood to quiet itself. "Yes, I am a little drowsy." He was conscious of telling her what she wanted to hear, but not the truth. It calmed him that she was soon asleep.

Elizabeth slept soundly for several uninterrupted hours but every move she made awakened Darcy from fitful catnaps. When she rolled onto her back, he raised himself up on his elbow to gaze at her as she slept. One arm was tossed over her head in a rather child-like pose, but her bosom, held somewhat in place by the tightened chemise, created a round and rosy exhibit of her womanly attributes. He felt himself under some enchantment, and gave in to the urge to stroke her there, above the neckline. His arm grew tired of supporting him and he nestled his cheek upon her breast, the steady beating of her heart soon bringing him an hour's sleep.

ELIZABETH STIRRED BUT DID NOT awaken. Her arm was around him, her hand on his shoulder. Darcy was wide-awake and quite certain he was too wakeful to sleep again—and he had another erection. *Damn it, man*, he chastised himself. *You have all the patience of a whistling teakettle.* Once he determined Elizabeth was still asleep, he turned and kissed the flesh where his cheek had rested. It was warm and slightly moist from the perspiration of skin on skin. *She does indeed sleep hot. Irresistibly hot.* He kissed her bosom again, this time tasting her a little with his tongue. *Stop, Darcy.* He leaned to her and rubbed his manhood, still bound in his breeches, against her hip. *God, man, you must stop.* Finally, with a low groan, Darcy rolled out of her loose embrace. He lay back upon the pillows with a great sigh. *I shall make up the fire, light a candle and read for a time.* He sat up and looked back at his sleeping bride. Elizabeth's face was angelic, the curls around her forehead slightly damp and the hand he abandoned settled in a graceful arc over her bosom, her fingers where his cheek had reposed for an hour. Watching the rise and fall of her chest claimed his attention, but the logs on the fire shifted, the flames grew lower and the room darkened.

After lighting a candle, Darcy crept into the second bedchamber and brought his pocket watch into the candlelight. Four o'clock. *The footman will awaken us at five. It is no use trying to sleep.*

Darcy read. Time passed, and he decided to dress. He was buttoning his frock coat when a strange, strangled whimpering sound could be heard coming from where Elizabeth lay dreaming.

She awakened in a dark cold room, with no Darcy in the bed. Wearing only a chemise, Elizabeth wandered the halls of Pemberley, worried where he had gone. Like a disquieted ghost, she called him, panic rising with each corridor crossed and stairway ascended. She arrived at the portrait gallery gasping, and felt a moan forming in her chest that she could not still. There, at the end of the grand hall, captured in cold moonlight, Darcy embraced a woman, locked in a mutually devouring kiss. As if she was the woman in his arms, Elizabeth could feel the intensity of his embrace and ferocity of his kiss, and experienced the sensations of returning his desire. Yet she was staring, not participating; she was not that woman. It was her worst fear: he had taken a mistress. Elizabeth screamed in anguish but could not force the sound from her throat. She backed away, desperate to shriek, yet barely able to breathe.

Darcy rushed into the bedchamber. Elizabeth was sitting up in the bed, wild-eyed, still in the power of the dream. She was making sounds of stifled horror. "Elizabeth!" he called to her as he approached.

She rose to her knees and, hearing her name, fully awoke. Seeing him, she wailed, "Fitzwilliam! Fitzwilliam, where were you?"

"Elizabeth, darling!" He embraced her, burying his face in her neck. "You had a bad dream. There is nothing to fear." He pulled back and beheld her eyes, still full of panic.

She struck him, hard, on the upper arm with a closed fist. "Where were you?" she demanded. Darcy watched as tears formed at the corners of her eyes. "If you make me cry on the first morning of our married life, Fitzwilliam Darcy, I shall never forgive you." She blinked rapidly, but a few tears escaped and ran down either side of her nose. "Damn you," she murmured, and collapsed onto her haunches, her head hanging in defeat.

Darcy sat next to her as she sank. "Elizabeth?"

"Where *were* you?" The tears were flowing freely, but she did not sob.

He stared at her. His throat tightened, and he could make no response.

"What could possibly have compelled you to leave our bed on our first morning together? Why would you?" Her liquid eyes searched his face. She was exquisite in her dishevelment: one strap of her chemise had slipped down her shoulder, leaving a breast nearly revealed. Her braid was frazzled; her cheeks were moist from tears and glowing with heat. "Did you not say you wished to awaken in my arms?"

It was as if she had kicked him in the chest. A wave of guilt consumed him. "And so I did…an hour ago," he confessed. "You were so beautiful as you slept; I stared at you for some time. I read for a while then decided it might speed our departure if I dressed before you. It did not occur to me that *you* might wish to awaken with me in *your* arms. I am a selfish creature." Then he whispered, "Elizabeth. Forgive me. I…I can offer no excuse. I have so much to learn."

What a horrible start to the day, she fretted silently. *And now I am causing a scene he is not likely to forget. I must be calm. I must look a great mess.* Elizabeth smiled crookedly at him. "Indeed you do. Let me warn you, sir, tomorrow morning when I awaken, you must still be in my bed. I absolutely insist."

There was a tapping at the door. "Damn," muttered Darcy as he strode to it. "Yes there! We are awake," he announced to the closed door.

A man's muffled voice replied, "Where will you and Mrs Darcy take your breakfast, sir?"

"In the sitting room across the hall. We shall be ready in half an hour." His voice was curt.

"Very good, Mr Darcy, sir."

Darcy turned to see Elizabeth had risen to her knees again and pulled the corner of the counterpane to cover herself lest the servant enter, but not in a particularly efficient or thorough manner. Her wild loveliness drew him back to her side. He pulled the counterpane from her hands, tossing it aside, and embraced her ardently, kissing her in the way he had been kissing the unknown woman in the dream.

At first, Elizabeth was too perturbed to respond, and then, against her conscious wishes, her body melted against him, one hand buried itself in his curls, the other pressed against his back. His tongue ravaged her and she moaned her approbation, hungry for more, when he moved to withdraw from her. "Yes, like that," she murmured, then held his head between both of her hands and kissed him in return, feverishly. *That is how he was kissing her. How I long for him always to kiss me as if he cannot resist.*

When she released his head, he smiled with wonder. "Do you have the least notion of how beautiful you are? If it were not for our breakfast being imminent, I would have all of you, immediately, Pemberley or not." His voice was low and tense.

"I look a fright, just as I warned you."

"No, madam, you most certainly do not. You look wild and tempting, and it is my lot to tame you." His hand touched her naked shoulder, his fingers grazing her warmth lightly; he raised the strap of her chemise, touching all the skin of her upper arm and shoulder as he did so, and feeling the pleasing weight of her breast as the strap lifted it. *If I cup her breast in my hand, would she stop me? Would I stop myself?*

Her eyes were soft and kind. She knew she had tried him. "Thank you, Fitzwilliam." She blushed and looked down. "I must dress. We have not much time."

He held out his hand, taking hers and assisting her to stand. "May I attend you? Lace up your corset? Brush your hair?"

"Fitzwilliam…I have chosen an ensemble for the day that allows me to see to myself. I will not be long." She stopped and looked back at him before disappearing to dress. "I am sorry for being so addled when I awoke. I would not have you think yourself burdened with a fretful wife."

"You were quite justified. It was my own fault. I will not make that mistake again. Is it true that had I stayed in bed holding you, you would have awakened in a happier dream?"

"I am sure of it." She smiled enigmatically and was gone.

And I would have made you my wife utterly…

Sweet Marjorum
"Blushes"

Chapter 16

Coventry to Pemberley

Darcy and Elizabeth boarded their carriage and were away before the pale sun was clear of the horizon. Although Darcy seemed lively and attentive enough at breakfast, he quickly became drowsy once the horses settled into a regular gait when the bustle of Coventry receded.

"I am sorry, Elizabeth, to be such poor company as we travel. I slept very ill last night."

She looked out the window. "Oh. I am very sorry to hear it. This morning is not going at all well."

Darcy reached for her chin and gently turned her face back to his. "I have so looked forward to sleeping with you, but I am not yet used to sleeping with anyone. You were delightfully cosy and generate an appealing warmth when you sleep."

Her cheeks coloured, and although, for a moment, she thought of resisting her impulse to smile, she could not. "That was a very pretty speech, Fitzwilliam. It will certainly take some time, but I believe you may not be such a tedious husband as others have predicted."

His eyes sparkled at her. "You might practice acting the martyr, Elizabeth, or my reputation as a disagreeable man will be in ruins. It would be a great disappointment to your father to have me revealed as an amiable fellow who dotes upon his favourite daughter."

260

Darcy leaned his head against Elizabeth's shoulder; it grew heavy. He awoke as Elizabeth slid to her left to give him more room on the seat.

"Hmm?" He sat upright again.

"If you weren't such a great tall fellow, Fitzwilliam, we could devise a way to stretch you out for a proper nap. What can we contrive for your comfort?"

"I am sure I would doze nicely with my head in your lap."

Elizabeth studied his countenance and was not surprised to find some mischief there. "Yes, I am sure you think you would, but we would have to fold you in half. Oh, let's try this…" She leaned forward and pulled out the picnic hamper, now loaded with provender from the inn at Coventry, and put one of the unused lap robes upon it, which she left folded in several thick layers. She slid it into the empty space between the two seats, in front of Darcy. Then she pulled another lap robe from the wicker bin under the seat beneath her. "If you will put your head in my lap and sleep on your side, you can stretch your legs to the opposite seat with your knees supported on the hamper. That might be comfortable for a time…"

His sleepy eyes smiled at her. "Clever girl," he said, assuming the prone position she suggested. He laid his head upon her thigh, on top of the lap robe she spread over herself when their day's journey commenced.

"Shall I pull the window shades?" she asked.

"No, I am sure I shall sleep perfectly well, and you would like to watch our progress, I expect."

Elizabeth fussed at covering him with the blanket she had just retrieved. "Delightful…" Darcy said. He smiled and closed his eyes.

Elizabeth looked down at his face with fondness. The odd ache that centred in her bosom when Darcy seemed at his most vulnerable returned. After making sure it was warm, she laid her hand upon his cheek, and before she knew what she was about, she began softly singing a lullaby. When the song ended, she whispered, "I love you."

Darcy remained quietly awake through her serenade, his throat tightening when she whispered to him after she finished. *Never did I imagine anything as wonderful as this,* he thought. He took her soft hand into his and settled their joined hands under his chin. The soothing smell of lavender seemed to rise from her. He was soon asleep.

Elizabeth leaned into the corner of the carriage where she had wedged herself to give Darcy more room. They rolled through forests of trees now bared of their autumn colour, occasionally passing harvested fields. The sky was a dull grey, though it did not rain. She was pleased when Darcy slept through the first change of horses and put a finger to her lips for quiet when the footman looked in when they did not emerge. He saw the master's head on the new Mrs Darcy's lap and nodded with a fleeting smile.

As the journey resumed, she mulled over the morning's dream, still confounded by its implications. There was a vague sense of holding back when she was in Darcy's arms, until his masterful kiss caused her to feel quite pleasantly overpowered. That night there would be no reluctance, no reason to wait. Elizabeth did not completely understand what caused her disquiet and the utter panic in her dream, but she knew it was past time to give herself to him in such a way that he would never desire another woman. Too tired to follow any proper logic, at last she slept.

Darcy was enjoying his dream.

He was standing at the end of the pianoforte in the Pemberley music saloon, wearing evening dress. Elizabeth was singing and playing for him, wearing a gown that reminded him very much of one she had worn at Netherfield. The last of their holiday guests departed that morning. Georgiana left the day before for London to partake of music lessons with a master harpist visiting from Vienna. Darcy and Elizabeth were alone as they had not been since the first three weeks of their marriage.

The aria Elizabeth was performing was from a tragic opera, and her countenance matched the sadness of the words she was singing. She rearranged the music into simple chords to enhance the melody, and her mellow mezzo-soprano voice was well suited to the emotions. Darcy watched, spellbound. He hoped there would be many evenings like this —just the two of them, dressed beautifully for each other, Elizabeth playing, singing, and displaying her tempting attributes.

On impulse, Darcy moved to sit by Elizabeth's side on the floor and leaned his head upon her leg. The vibrato of her voice reverberated through her. Darcy believed he could hear her even better with one ear pressed against her thigh. Her right hand dropped to his head, her fingers playing idly through his hair as her left hand softly continued the bass chords of the song.

The smell of lavender rising from her thighs and between her legs was intoxicating. After two months of marriage, the scent had an aphrodisiac effect, and Darcy reached under her gown to caress his wife's leg. Her stockings were held by satin garters not far above her knees and he stroked the luscious bare skin above the tie.

Without looking at her face, Darcy could surmise the effect of his actions upon Elizabeth. He knew she was fighting a smile, which changed the timbre of her voice. He smiled and closed his eyes, inhaling. So many pleasing options presented themselves: to venture his hand higher to tease her most private place, to turn her piano chair towards him and lift her skirts completely that he might explore her with his mouth, or to rise up on his knees and disarrange the low neckline of her gown, suckling her to begin their love-making. But the idea that pleased him most was that they were at home, alone, and he could take her hand and lead her to their bedchamber, to do all the things the scent of lavender bid him do.

WHEN ELIZABETH AWOKE, DARCY WAS still sleeping. It was colder and she hugged the cashmere shawl about her shoulders. Her hand was still under Darcy's chin but his hand was no longer holding it. He rubbed his cheek against her thigh, settling the back of his head against her belly. She suddenly felt an alarming movement upon her leg. His hand had burrowed under the lap robe, and trespassing her pelisse, gown and petticoat, lay upon the bare skin of her thigh just above her stocking. She looked carefully at his face as he shifted his shoulders in sleep. *Is he truly asleep, or is he playing?* Her heart started to race. This was too much—his hand upon her clothed breast the day before and his cheek resting upon her chest in the night were nothing to this—and there was no possible method to extricate his hand. Even when he returned to wakefulness, there would be embarrassment. She sat in complete stillness, for how many miles she knew not. The nearness of his motionless warm hand to her secret place became the locus of her consciousness. When the carriage jostled, the hand slid to her stockinged knee and she breathed a sigh of some relief. Rocking in another direction stirred Darcy enough to replace the hand in its previous location but not enough to waken him.

The carriage slowed through a small village and the ride became more jarring. Still very much asleep, Darcy slipped his hand higher still to settle under his cheek, which rested over the many layers of fabric. The rocking of their conveyance grew more pronounced.

Elizabeth watched as his eyes slowly opened, unfocused at first. He started to smile, inhaled deeply from the layers of cloth separating his cheek from his hand. Finally, awareness intruded and his eyes flew open in abject mortification. "Good god!" he cried. He pulled his hand from under her skirts, rising to a half-sitting position and looked at it as if it were a foreign object. Darcy was glad the lap robe covering him from his waist to the top of his boots kept his arousal well hidden. He met her surprised gaze with a countenance illustrative of profound shock.

Elizabeth suddenly felt herself very much her father's daughter—she was highly diverted by Darcy's display of discomfort, and as his expressions of apology poured forth, she started to chuckle.

"Elizabeth!" Darcy huffed, "Why are you laughing? You should be furious with me."

"I was indeed alarmed when I awoke and found you were making free with my legs, sir, but it was clear you were sound asleep. I hope your dream was a pleasant one, at least." Her eyes were lively.

The dream recalled itself forcibly in full detail, and Elizabeth watched as he blushed from cravat to hairline. Her laughter grew nervous. "Oh, my, Mr Darcy! I hope you were not dreaming of tonight." She wanted to sound light of heart and careless but was not at all sure she succeeded.

He shook his head. "Worse, I am afraid. I dreamt of an evening, months from now."

She continued to smile, although she could not yet imagine with any veracity what filled his dreams—marital relations, obviously—but of the particulars she was ignorant. Was there an all-encompassing kiss as she had dreamt? The place where his hand rested upon her skin now felt cold, and she was chagrined at the fleeting wish that it was still there. She became bemused and quiet. If she could not understand her own body, how could she ever aspire to understand or inspire his?

Darcy sat upright and stretched his legs as best he could as Elizabeth watched. The lower corner of her lip was caught by her upper teeth—the pondering aspect she assumed when perplexed—and Darcy noted an unusual look in her eyes. He did not understand that she was trying not to laugh at her own folly, but she did finally chuckle. Without pausing to consider, he pulled her into an ardent embrace and kissed her with rather more recklessness than finesse.

Her response was instant and passionate. He was warm and his mouth demanding; he moaned a little as he plundered her willing lips. Her arms clasped his neck, and her hands ran through his hair.

She tried to recover some of her composure when he at last released her. "What was *that* for?" she whispered, and her eyes issued a challenge. She wanted him to kiss her again, just like that, as soon as possible. *How can I be so confused?*

"I found your laugh impertinent, Mrs Darcy, and I moved to silence you. However, since you give the appearance of enjoying your punishment, I will have to find a different way to censure you."

Her lips were lovely, full and bruised by his vehemence. She leaned towards him playfully. "Indeed so, sir, for if *that* is your idea of punishment, you shall make of me an excessively impertinent and even, may I say, insolent wife."

He growled, "Come here, insolent wife." He captured her shoulders to kiss her again when the carriage jounced and she landed on top of him as he was thrown back into the corner.

The lap robes tumbled away and Elizabeth found herself lying upon Darcy, his hands still holding her shoulders. They both laughed at the abrupt change in their posture until she became aware of a hard ridge against her hip. *Oh! That is his...he is...* Her eyes flared open in surprise. She pulled away and looked down at his lap involuntarily.

Darcy's eyes followed hers. When Elizabeth recoiled to her previous position at the opposite corner of the seat, Darcy, attempting to appear calm, lifted the corner of a fallen blanket to cover the obvious erection stretching his trousers. He ran a frustrated hand through his hair.

After a deep breath, he said calmly, "I will not apologize for responding ardently to my own wife, Elizabeth. I am done apologizing for desiring you."

Her eyes widened. She instinctively reached a hand to his knee. "Oh, no, Fitzwilliam, no. No. Do not think I meant any rebuke. It is myself I chastise. I want you to desire me, believe me, I do. I am too ignorant of these things. I am aware of what is to happen between us tonight, at least the theory of it…but I am mortified to reveal such ignorance…for that is what it is."

"It is innocence, Elizabeth. That is all. I never think you ignorant." He put his hand over hers on his knee.

Her eyes were pleading. "You are too kind, Fitzwilliam. But look at the imbalance between us. Until last night, I had never seen an adult gentleman's bare feet or lower legs. I had not seen your neck without the hindrance of your blasted cravat and those high collars." Darcy smiled at this. "I still have not seen your arms. Yet think of what you can say of me. You have seen my arms, my neck, my feet, my hair braided, and what with the current evening fashions, and this morning's aberration in my normally even temper, why, you have seen me nearly naked from the waist upwards!"

Darcy was chuckling. Shaking his head ruefully, he pulled her close and said, "Not nearly naked enough to suit me, Elizabeth."

"Fitzwilliam…" Her exasperated sigh only amused him further.

"I so rarely get the advantage of you, Elizabeth. You really must allow me to enjoy it while it lasts. After tonight, you will know only too well your power over me and how to wield it."

She cocked her head at him. "Will I?"

"Yes, I thoroughly believe you will. That is the irresistible danger of loving an intelligent woman."

Elizabeth's mouth opened to ask a question, her eyes full of disbelieving wonder. She closed her mouth, her upper teeth tucking up the corner of her lower lip. *Whatever can he possibly mean?*

The rumble of the carriage changed tone as the wheels rolled onto the cobbled streets of Derby. "I must have had a long sleep. We are coming into Derby already. We will be stopping at an inn the family owns and change horses to make the best possible time. Perhaps we will arrive before dark."

"*You* own an inn?"

"Yes, and since yesterday morning at ten o'clock, so do *you*, Mrs Darcy. We employ a fine family to manage it. They are former house servants from Pemberley. My father wanted a comfortable and trustworthy place for our guests and ourselves to stay when weather or time kept us from getting to Pemberley, so when he bought the Black Kite Inn, James and Sophie offered to manage it, to be nearer their grown children. The scheme works well for all concerned. On occasions such as this, we keep a spare team of carriage horses here. I can tell by the time we're making, that this team must be spent."

Elizabeth straightened and shook off her nerves. To own an inn in a convenient town, to keep several spare teams of horses lying about—all this would take getting used to. "Are you not hungry, sir? We have not touched the hamper."

"Other than to sleep upon it," Darcy said. "Let us stretch our legs and refresh ourselves. We can eat immediately once we're on our way."

When they stood together at the entrance to the inn, Elizabeth was introduced to the innkeepers. She cast a brief glance at the front of Darcy's trousers. The effect of whatever she had done to provoke him before was subsided. *It seems at times his...ardency...can be controlled, and sometimes it is beyond him. What a remarkable thing.*

The innkeepers presented Mr and Mrs Darcy with ornate white ribbon rosettes with bountiful steamers to affix to the four corners of the carriage, announcing to those along the route that the bride had arrived in the county. Darcy smiled at them. "Thank you, James, and all your family, but must we? You know I had hoped to avoid this."

"Aye, sir, but 'tis the tradition, and everyone betwixt here an' Pemberley knows yer comin' home today with the new missus. Let folks pay their respects an' best wishes, Mr Darcy. You do not want to bring bad luck upon yerself."

Darcy looked to Elizabeth, who raised her eyebrows. "It seems there is nothing for it, sir, but to follow tradition. I see no harm in it."

Darcy sighed and indicated with a defeated wave of his arm that the footmen should assist James and Sophie in decorating the coach.

The innkeepers asked to introduce the new Mrs Darcy to the important members of their staff before Darcy and Elizabeth were left alone in a sitting room with a cheerful fire. They each had a glass of hard cider. "From Pemberley apples," Darcy boasted.

When they returned to the carriage, Elizabeth felt a numbness at her cheeks. "That was strong cider, sir," she said.

"Think of it as an aperitif. You won't feel it so much if you eat enough."

They settled down to a meal of cheese and crusty bread with potted pheasant and some fruit. Darcy pulled more cider and two heavy cups from the bottom of the hamper. "This will be Coventry cider, I cannot vouch for it. Shall we try it?"

Her cheeks were still flushed and she touched them with light taps of her fingers. "For my part, I will forego it. My cheeks are still numb. I cannot feel them."

"Are they?" Darcy leant over and kissed her cheek. It was warm. "*I* can feel your cheek perfectly well."

The cider coursing through her removed a layer of inhibition. "I am your wife. You should feel whatever part of me you wish... I must confess that my leg felt a little sad and cold earlier when you moved your hand away." She paused, trying to cast out her trepidation. "Oh, Fitzwilliam...have we waited too long?"

Darcy looked at her with concern. "Elizabeth? Is something wrong?"

She pushed the hamper away. "How far is Bakewell?"

He continued to regard her with confused curiosity. "Twenty miles, or about two hours, but we have fresh horses and good road, so our pace is brisk. Where do your thoughts tend?"

"You have not asked about my terrible dream, which seems to show a lapse in your usual curiosity, sir."

"It was not my wish to bring such alarm back to your mind."

"I see. If you will not ask, I will tell you. I was running through Pemberley in the cold, looking everywhere for you, and I found you in the portrait gallery, in the arms of another woman. You were kissing her in a way you have never kissed me. The utter abandon of it...I cannot explain. It was as if I could feel you kissing me, but you were kissing her. There was a sense of having lost you, because I had not given you enough."

A phrase Darcy had heard once at his club was brought to mind: "sexual frustration." A husband of a very fine lady spoke the words, saying when he was away with his family, his mistress complained of this. The senselessness of the man turned Darcy's blood cold, and he no longer approved the fellow's company. But in addition to feeling the effects of the Pemberley hard cider, was his bride, the lively Elizabeth Bennet, feeling the strain of having waited? Was too much now riding upon the coming evening? Did she think his expectations might not be fulfilled? He looked very particularly into her eyes: so wide and earnest they were.

He placed his hands gently on either side of her face. "I do not doubt you." She closed her eyes, and her lips parted as his mouth claimed hers. His tongue filled her mouth, and she welcomed it. His hand slipped to the back of her head, the other slowly travelled down her neck, and he did not avoid a long descent over her bosom, revelling in the firmness of her clothed breast.

His hand lingered only a moment, but Elizabeth moaned into his mouth, pulling away long enough to murmur, "Yes. Want *me*."

Darcy's hand came to rest on her hip and he pulled her body to his. "Do not doubt *me*," he growled. "Never doubt me." He kissed her repeatedly, whispering her name.

Finally, he pulled away just far enough to see her eyes. The hand upon her hip began insistently to raise the skirt of her gown. This time, however, they were both awake. If she became embarrassed, he meant to know it, but he did not mean to stop. His hand reached the top of her stocking. "Raise your leg," he murmured. She did so as his fingers circled her leg, first one way, then the other, gently exploring the soft skin of her thigh just above her garter.

His hand was only inches above her knee, but Darcy could see the nervous anticipation in Elizabeth's eyes lest he dare venture higher. Instead of enticing her deepest places with his fingers, he chose to do so with words. Making sure her eyes were locked to his, he explained what would happen to her, saying, "Tonight, my love, when you are naked in my arms, I will ask you to wrap this lovely leg around me, and I will explore every part of you with my fingers. When you have opened yourself to me, I will fill you up, and we will be one, you and I."

At first her expression was unreadable, as if she could not believe he would speak so explicitly, but then he saw a subtle change. She was pleased, and he could see her desire. Her cheeks coloured. He moved his hand higher, to her bare thigh. "Will that convince you I desire no woman but you?"

He did not wait for an answer. She opened her mouth to respond but was silenced as the back of his hand brushed against the hair between her legs, the merest touch. Her eyes widened as he smiled seductively then removed his hand and smoothed her skirts into propriety.

He raised his hand to his nose and inhaled briefly, still forcing her eyes to meet his. "Lavender," he whispered. "You intoxicate me, dearest Elizabeth. How delightful to know *all* of you smells this way."

He saw the shock in her eyes, but it did not concern him. He waited.

"Perhaps you are not as much a gentleman as I thought, Mr Darcy," she finally said. There was the barest glimmer of mischief in her eyes.

"That gives you leave to be less than perfectly ladylike, Mrs Darcy."

She smiled. "I am glad to hear it, sir." She leaned forward and kissed him passionately. Her mouth plundered his and her arms moved around his neck, pressing her upper body against his so he could feel her heat through their clothes.

Darcy closed his eyes, envisioning many future carriage rides when he would take her at his whim, fondling her thighs, disordering the necklines of her gowns, urging her to express her pleasure. *Soon, Darcy. She will make you as happy as a man can be.* "Elizabeth Bennet…" *will make you an admirable wife.* He did not realize he said her former name aloud when she released his mouth.

"I love you, and I ought to tell you oftener," Elizabeth said. She smiled at him, stroking his cheek.

"Surely you do not expect me to argue with *that*, or offer any discouragement." He turned and kissed the palm of her hand gently then moved to hold her palm to his mouth, wetting it in his ardour. He made them both breathless. "If I kiss your bare shoulder tonight with such abandon as this, or the back of your neck…if I kiss you here," he touched her breastbone just above her bosom, "will you still love me?" His low voice lured her to share in his desires.

Again her eyes met his, and he continued, "My theory of ensuring marital felicity is to behave in a frightfully ungentlemanlike manner when we are alone. I may shock you, and I hope to please you, but I promise, you will never doubt I desire you." He deftly opened the frogs holding her pelisse across her bosom, and was saddened to see the gown she wore underneath did not allow access to her skin. Still, just the action of his opening her coat thrilled her, and he could see her heart pounding through the fine woollen cloth. "Never doubt your power to fascinate me." He cupped one breast in his hand. Her eyes widened. "Last night, I let you sleep. Tonight, I will not be so kind. When I am awake, I will be touching you." He leaned so his lips were at her ear. "Kissing you, tasting you, coaxing your body to welcome me, until I exhaust us both. And then, if you wish, you may explore me."

She was speechless.

"What do you say, Elizabeth Bennet? I know we are husband and wife, but that was a mere formality, a necessity to get what I want."

"What do you want?"

"I have made you the mistress of Pemberley because there was no other honourable way to have you become *my* mistress. Will you allow me to have you for my mistress, even though you are my wife? Will you allow me the liberties most men do not ask of their wives?" The motion of his hand became more demanding as he continued fondling her.

"It was me!" His question was the catalyst of her epiphany. As if she was again dreaming, the woman in Darcy's arms turned to face her. It was her own ravenous reflection: hair about to fall, lips bruised, eyes smouldering, looking upon her panicked self as a silly little fool.

"It has always been you…" He began kissing below her ear.

"In my dream, the woman you were kissing was me."

"You make my point." He kissed her without restraint.

DARCY AND ELIZABETH TRAVELLED FOR miles in a passionate embrace. Had he chosen to take complete possession of her, she would have mindlessly complied. When their lips were not locked upon each other, his deep unrelenting voice, in carefully chosen words, explained his intentions for their first night as husband and wife. Elizabeth was quite thoroughly seduced and Darcy suspected as much.

After pausing for breath, they stole a glance out the carriage window. Little cottages were passed with more frequency. "We are entering Bakewell," said Darcy. "I suppose I should move my seat, since I am known here."

Elizabeth smiled, besotted. It was an expression Darcy longed to see on her face almost from their first meeting. He said, "I needn't," just as she said, "You needn't." He returned her look of fond tenderness.

Darcy did shift position to sit snugly next to her, rather than be seen nearly trying to mount her, or so he feared it would look should they be glimpsed. He slouched comfortably, his arm around her shoulders, his legs stretched to the opposite seat.

On the empty gentlemen's side sat his tall beaver hat and her wine-dark bonnet, side-by-side, appearing quite companionable. The vignette made him smile.

"What makes you grin so?" Elizabeth asked, looking up at him.

"See my hat and your bonnet? Do they not look well together? Do you remember the morning I visited you at Lambton to ask your help with Bingley? I sat my hat next to your bonnet upon the table there. The intimacy of it thrilled me, for I never thought this day would arrive."

"Are you as sentimental as that? I am surprised, but it is a most becoming revelation. I give you leave to remember any such charming details of our past acquaintance as give you pleasure."

The carriage slowed as they passed through Bakewell. Two or three merchants stood at their doors and waved. Elizabeth and Darcy returned the gesture. "A tailor I have employed and the bookshop," Darcy explained.

The coachman called down, "Pardon, Mr Darcy, sir, but will we be wanting the Lambton road, or Kympton, sir?"

"Kympton, Mr Bains." Darcy called up to him.

"And then the shortcut, sir?"

"Yes, Bains, from here take every shortcut you know. Slow down in Kympton only to keep from running anyone over."

The coachman smiled to himself, and the footman sitting next to him on the box chuckled.

"The front outriders will make for Pemberley now," Darcy explained. "Mrs Reynolds will muster the troops, and you shall be grandly welcomed by every chambermaid, stable boy and under gardener. Then we will have dinner. The mistress's room has been refreshed with new draperies, rugs and bedclothes; there is also a new mattress. I hope you will make whatever adjustments you wish. I tried to account for your tastes rather than mine, but my assumptions may have been wrong, and I have not been here to attend to the work."

"Will I have time to change clothes and bathe? I have a lovely new gown to wear for our first dinner at home."

He looked down at her meaningfully. "Save it for tomorrow night. I would not take so much of our time tonight, when it might be employed differently." His voice dropped to the low insistent tone he used earlier.

Although his meaning was clear enough, she felt a wave of nerves beset her. She thought it best to leave her remarks at a nonchalant, "Oh, yes, of course."

"Mrs Reynolds has selected a maid for you, but she fully expects you to make your own choice when you are ready to do so. We shall have our baths after dinner." *And it may be the last time you bathe alone for quite some time, Elizabeth Bennet.* He did not tell her he indulged himself with a new, very large, bathtub.

The carriage rolled through Kympton without stopping, although there were so many townsfolk along the street that Elizabeth could not catch anything like a detailed glimpse of the church. Once through the village, they picked up speed, which pleased Darcy.

THE SKY WAS DARKENING WHEN they pulled to the front entrance of Pemberley. As the carriage slowed, Elizabeth moved to take up her bonnet, but Darcy stilled her hand. "Leave it. You look lovely."

"Nonsense, I'm sure I look a mess. My hair must be untidy."

"I have not removed a single hairpin. It took every ounce of restraint." He smiled into her eyes.

"That would explain everything *else* you did." She was mischievous, and Darcy was glad of it.

He smoothed the curls off her forehead and into their usual position as the frame of her face. "You have never looked more beautiful. You will charm them all, and of course, several are not strangers to you. Let us enter our home hatless, and cast off a little of propriety now we are here."

Darcy moved to the carriage door, and a footman from the house opened it for him. With his feet on the ground, he turned and handed Elizabeth down then stepped away and held out his arm, presenting her.

"Ladies and gentlemen of Pemberley, let me present your new mistress, Mrs Elizabeth Darcy."

His new wife blushed prettily, he thought, and smiled at their staff. Mrs Reynolds came forward to greet her with a handshake, saying, "Welcome back to Pemberley, Mrs Darcy," but Elizabeth would have none of it, and hugged the housekeeper briefly.

"Thank you, Mrs Reynolds, for everything."

Mrs Reynolds, her cheeks infused with pink, turned and introduced Elizabeth's new maid, Anna. Then Mr Grayson introduced Darcy's valet and moved with Elizabeth down the row of footmen. Elizabeth looked further on and found the scullery maid, Sarah R. who helped her the day she made her furtive visit to the stillroom, which ingratiated the new mistress with the lesser servants. Darcy hung back, speaking in a conspiratorial manner to Mrs Reynolds.

The head gardener came forward and introduced the under gardeners who maintained the house gardens. Next came the stable master, and the stable hands were introduced. At last, Elizabeth was allowed to approach the house, and Darcy caught her up. The personal servants bustled around, taking her pelisse, gloves and reticule, and Darcy's greatcoat and gloves. A footman entered with their hats, which Darcy took, to his valet's surprise, and set them side-by-side under a large arrangement of autumn seedpods and foliage on the oak entry table.

"Leave them, Garrick, will you? To humour me…" Darcy whispered to his valet. Elizabeth heard and was quietly charmed.

As he took her arm to lead her up the stairs to a sitting room, she whispered, "You are quite a pleasanter person when we are at home. I may never allow you to leave."

Darcy looked down at her merry eyes. "I could say the same of you."

They entered a small sitting room Elizabeth had seen when Georgiana was showing her the house during her visit in July. Doors were opened into another room beyond, which was bright with candlelight. It was a tiny —by Pemberley standards—private dining room. Elizabeth peeked in and saw servants laying out dinner on the sideboard. The little table was round and would seat no more than six but was set for two, sitting rather close together. She smiled and turned to Darcy, who was standing near a table in the sitting room fitted with a selection of beverages.

"Would you share a toast with me, Elizabeth?" he asked. "What would suit you?"

"Some wine will suffice, sir, but not a full glass. Remember the cider."

"I consider the effect of the cider not so very detrimental if it allowed you to let down your guard a little." He handed her a half glass of wine and poured himself a short portion of brandy. He stood and turned to her, raising his glass. "To us: Elizabeth and Fitzwilliam Darcy."

Their glasses touched and they drank. Darcy stepped closer and lowered his face to hers, kissing her briefly, but not so briefly that they noticed a footman enter the sitting room entrance from the dining parlour. He cleared his throat, and they jumped apart, looking like naughty children.

"Ahem…sir, madam. Mr and Mrs Darcy, your dinner is ready. We shall not disturb you again unless you ring for us."

"Thank you, Williams." Darcy smiled.

"We shall not see any more of the household staff tonight except my man and your maid. They are aware, as is Mrs Reynolds, that tonight is our *true* wedding night." He watched her face carefully.

"Oh…" Elizabeth looked fleetingly alarmed. *Why does anyone have to know?* She then took a deep breath and lifted her chin.

Darcy knew this turn of her countenance well, and it comforted him to see it, needing no words to confirm she was marshalling her confidence. He held his arm for Elizabeth, but as the servant had withdrawn, she clasped his hand, entwining their fingers, and they proceeded hand-in-hand to dinner.

Honeysuckle
"Generous & devoted affection"

Chapter 17

Mr and Mrs Darcy at Last

D arcy stood barefoot in a robe, partly hidden by the open door joining the master and mistress's bedchambers, watching Elizabeth. He told her, when they had given up trying to do justice to a dinner they were too unsettled to eat, he would join her in her bedroom in an hour. He bathed quickly and assumed his post amongst the shadows to watch for her. He enjoyed observing when she thought herself alone since the previous April at Rosings Park, when she wandered the paths of his aunt's estate. He had watched her from his balcony when she set out for a walk during her brief stay at Pemberley. Now they were home—and she mistress of the estate —and he looked forward to seeing her become as accustomed as he to the beloved pathways, woods and rocky peaks.

When Elizabeth hurriedly entered the bedroom, it was clear she thought she had taken too long in her preparations. His heart raced, and he had to still his breathing to remain undetected. She was breath-taking with her dark glossy hair cascading around her shoulders and down her back, catching glints of auburn from the firelight. She wore only a nightgown of the thinnest creamy satin with sheer loose sleeves fluttering to her elbows, although she carried a dressing gown. Darcy thought the fabric of her nightgown exceptionally fine. The garment was a shift with no collar and a placket open to her waist, held together by three slender ties, which did not bring the two sides wholly together. The gleaming material hugged her bosom and hips with the hem just covering her ankles. Darcy was a visual man, well able to imagine what he was not shown, and the nightgown thrilled him by implying much but revealing little. He would have to untie the front and reach in to cradle her breasts in his palms. His hands itched. *I hope her bosom is sensitive for her sake, as I intend to pay it a good deal of attention.*

When she turned away, he saw that the back of the gown conformed to her trim waist, and just below her backside, an ample fabric insert created a fishtail skimming the floor as she walked. It clung and draped over her pear-shaped derrière. *Soon*, he promised himself, *I will be caressing that beautiful backside to my heart's content. What a charming nightgown. I cannot wait to remove it.* He felt himself growing more aroused. *At last, at long last, I do not have to hold myself back...*

Elizabeth put on the dressing gown, a fluffy garment, and presented herself in front of the only mirror in the room on a shelf over a tiled dry sink, which showed her reflection from the shoulders up. The dressing gown had layers of ruffles over the shoulders and at the wrists with gauzy lace long sleeves; it was a sickly shade of pale green. Darcy silently deemed it hideous. She frowned and disappeared into the dressing room again.

This will not do, she thought. *My mother never could select clothes for me. This looks like something* she *would wear.* Once in the dressing room, she regarded herself in the full-length mirror and laughed aloud at what she saw. Darcy heard her and smiled, surmising what she was about. Deciding to forego the time it would take to find another dressing gown, she shrugged off the offensive robe with a sigh of bother, preferring to face her bridegroom in the nightgown alone. She looked at herself again without the dressing gown and blushed at her immodesty, but she was pleased. *After a night of me buried in heavy flannel, he must find this an improvement.*

Elizabeth re-entered the bedroom, looking around a little cautiously, and began to tour the room, which was lit only by the fire. Darcy watched her wander, smelling the last of the autumn flowers in a vase on a table, which included red chrysanthemums, and saw her smiling at the bowl of lavender potpourri as she sifted the flower buds through her fingers. There was another low bowl filled with silvery foliage, a card in Darcy's hand inserted into it. 'Southernwood' it read. Next to this, lay an herbal like Georgiana's. Elizabeth smiled, looked up the reference and murmured aloud, "Jest. Bantering.

Maiden's ruin, taken to enhance virility." She chortled, "Oh my!"

Darcy smiled and was tempted to step into the firelight, but he waited.

Elizabeth looked at the painting of Pemberley woods over the mantle. She approached a window and drew back the curtain, noticing a drizzle had started and the sky was dark. It seemed indecent and dissolute indeed to be preparing for bed at what seemed only dinnertime. Darcy planned to enter the room when she climbed into bed, but now it appeared she was taking a minute survey of the room and everything in it, perhaps to calm herself.

Elizabeth opened a little wooden box on the mantle to find matches and began lighting the candles scattered about the room. Darcy could not see her when she approached the head of the bed, but the room grew brighter, and he knew she lit the candles on the night table. There was a little table with candles next to the door hiding him, but she did not approach it. She walked back to the middle of the room, swishing the tail of her nightgown. She half-turned to him and her eyes looked into his directly through the shadows, full of mirth.

"Will you spy on me all night, or do you plan to join me?"

Darcy chuckled and stepped into the room. "When did you see me?"

She smiled fully. "When I first entered. Your bare feet are very white, sir, like beacons in the dark." She laughed at him. "The bath water was slow to arrive. I thought I had taken more time than I ought…" Her voice trailed away as she remembered to be uneasy. Whatever advantage she felt she had gained by calling him out of hiding seemed lost in the light of the candles. *He is impossibly handsome… How could a husband of mine be so handsome? I want to throw myself upon him, but what would he think?* She looked down, feeling her face colour, then could not help admiring him and met his intense gaze.

"Lizzy," he whispered, calling her so intimately for the first time. "*My* Lizzy."

She looked quizzically up into his face and then smiled. *Now I am 'Lizzy' to him.* "That is the name I use when I talk to myself, you know." It was the most intimate disclosure of her thoughts she had ever made to him.

"Is it?" He understood.

"I am pleased to hear you speak it. Another threshold has been crossed."

"Lizzy, then, when we are alone." He nodded at her.

Time seemed to stop. They were five feet apart, both rooted where they stood. He was wearing only a robe and, from what she could see, seemed to be naked under it. There was a suspicious bump below the tie that held the robe together. *Oh! There it is… What should I do? Where should I look?*

"What is it you wish to ask? You have questions on your mind; I can see you do in your lovely eyes. Now we are married and alone in our bedchamber, you may ask me anything you like. Here you are *my* mistress, not just the mistress of Pemberley. Say anything. Say everything." He smiled encouragement.

Elizabeth looked away from him with an impatient toss of her head. "I do not know where to begin!" She felt at a distinct disadvantage and woefully ill informed. "I do not know the words to use to frame the questions…"

Darcy took a step closer, longing to begin exploring her. He spoke in a low voice, "Perhaps I should start. What have you been told?"

She took a deep breath and looked up at him. There were tears of frustration forming in her eyes. "I do not like what I have been told; it does not seem right. After last night, it certainly does not make any sense. I am confused and impatient with myself for being so silly."

Darcy quite understood the tears poised on her eyelashes were formed from vexation rather than fear. Perhaps he could work her annoyance at her ignorance to his advantage; perhaps he could make her laugh again. *If she is most relaxed when she is laughing at me, so be it.* He stepped closer and held out a hand, which she took after staring at it a moment as if it were the head of a venomous lizard. He drew her forward until her breasts were just an inch from his chest. Her nipples had become obvious points under the gossamer satin.

One corner of his mouth tipped up as he asked, "Have you been told just to lie there and submit to whatever I may choose to do to you?"

She smiled ruefully. "Yes, exactly. But that is not what you indicated would be expected. And you do not seem to be that sort of man."

"What sort of man would that be, Lizzy?" He put his hands on her waist. She felt fit and strong and did not shy away from being held so intimately.

"The sort of man who would be content with that sort of wife."

"And what sort of wife would *that* be?" He rested his forehead on hers.

"A timid wife." She looked down, feeling bashful.

"I do not imagine I have saddled myself with a timid wife. If I have, if I am mistaken in you, then I am bundling you back to Longbourn before we are alone one minute more, for I will make a very grave error indeed if I consummate a marriage to a timid wife." He tried without much success to sound grave. "You are not one, are you?" His question was accusing, but he was smiling.

"Indeed, I hope not. I do not intend to be timid, but I do not know what is allowed." She looked imploringly into his eyes.

How adorable, he thought. "You made a declaration of sorts by dispensing with the ghastly dressing gown, so we know your instincts are sound. Perhaps, when in doubt of acting upon your inclinations, you might ask yourself what a timid wife would do and behave contrariwise."

This finally produced a chuckle from his bride. *He is teasing me!* They looked fondly into each other's eyes, and Darcy decided it was now safe to kiss her. He raised her soft chin with a finger and kissed her very thoroughly. He felt her hands grasp his sleeves, and her mouth responded to his with every bit of the enthusiasm she had shown in the carriage. He drove his hands into her hair, as he had been longing to do since seeing her arrive dishevelled at Netherfield so many months before. The memory of her tumbling hair, high colour and defiant spirits never left him, and he knew he had been a simpleton to think it ever would. He kissed her earlobes, whispering, "Have I told you I have always admired your lovely hair?" Then he kissed her cheeks and closed eyes, and turning her head gently with her hair, kissed her mouth again. Finally, he pulled away. She was glowing a little, her breathing quick and shallow.

"Here's my suggestion. I shall show you what I expect of you and what I desire, and then you can decide for yourself what sort of man I am."

Elizabeth was breathless. His kisses caused an unfolding feeling within her. She nodded up at him, too awed by her body's response to speak. There was a heat and moisture between her legs that confounded her, and from her breasts, she discerned the most fervent desire for his touch as if his hands would relieve their strange ache.

"But you must promise me this, Lizzy, that as I touch you, you must let me know if I do something you like particularly, and conversely, you must speak immediately if you find yourself alarmed. I would not have you afraid of me. Will you tell me? Both the good and the bad?"

His eyes were intense. She saw he was serious and found her voice. "Yes, sir." Darcy started to protest, and she corrected herself. "Yes, Fitzwilliam, I will tell you what pleases me. But what of you?"

"Me?"

"I am your wife. I am here only for your pleasure, or so I have been instructed." She seemed uncharacteristically solemn.

Darcy looked into her eyes and laughed gently. "Who on earth told you such nonsense? I assure you, if I can give you pleasure, it will go a long way to ensuring my own. If I can persuade the famously difficult-to-impress Miss Elizabeth Bennet, when she is in this room as my wife, to give herself over to physical sensation and become the wanton Lizzy of my dreams, I shall count myself as having married very well indeed." One hand untangled from her hair and slid slowly to the small of her back.

Her eyes widened and her mouth formed an "oh," which Darcy kissed. Moving away from her mouth, he began kissing down her neck slowly, tasting her at each point with the tip of his tongue between his warm lips. He pulled her body more firmly against his.

"You are warm," she murmured. Her arms found their way under his and wrapped around him.

"Is that good?" He continued his kisses until his lips reached the fabric at her shoulder.

"Yes. Everything so far is very good."

"I am relieved to hear it." He smiled against her skin.

She felt Darcy's hands caressing her backside through the nightgown, and he moaned in approbation. With agonizing slowness, his hands travelled up her back and down the front of her shoulders, reaching the first tie of her nightgown. He untied it and folded the limp fabric away from her collarbone.

Elizabeth inhaled and raised her chin in a little show of bravery. He was watching her eyes for any sign of misapprehension, and he was charmed to see, instead, the typical summoning of her courage.

"You intend to undress me?"

"I do indeed, madam, whenever I get the chance, but you must own you are not much dressed at present." His hands settled lower, at the next tie at the top of her cleavage. "If you did not wish me to see you, you should not have lit every candle in the room. You should rather have jumped under the counterpane and hidden yourself. That is what a timid wife would have done."

She smiled a little and looked up from under her lashes. "I wanted you to see me in this nightgown. I thought it would please you."

"Indeed, it does." He slowly pulled the second bow apart.

"But what if I do not look so well without it?"

"That, Elizabeth, is a question not worth answering." Darcy was enraptured. With his face buried in her hair, he untied the final bow, just below her breasts. He reached for her sleeves, and pulled the silk down to her elbows, then stretched his hands so his thumbs brushed her still-covered nipples. She gasped.

"Bad?" He pulled away enough to see her face. *Have I gone too fast?*

Elizabeth looked down at his hands poised over her breasts and drew in a deep breath. "No," she murmured. "Not bad." *It is as if his fingers burn me, yet I want…I want to feel his hands on my skin. Surely, a timid wife would not feel so… Oh, I am lost.* She slid the fabric down further out of his hands, revealing her bosom to him, and pulled her arms from the gown, which settled to hang about her hips. She looked up see his reaction.

His eyes were alight in admiration of her naked breasts. Her nipples were rosy brown, a natural colour he had never seen before. *I should have guessed as much; a country maiden of no experience would not colour herself. Thank goodness I will not have to endure the taste of rouge.* He unconsciously licked his lips.

Elizabeth nearly swooned at the notion of his mouth upon her…*there, where his eyes are looking.* She took his hands in hers and placed one on each breast. "Better."

"Better?" He began stroking and cupping them, pleased with her daring.

"Better than being stared at…" she muttered. "Oh, my… Oh, Fitzwilliam." His hands inspired feelings more intense than anything she had ever experienced or expected.

"You should know, Lizzy, looking at you is very…stimulating. You are exquisite." Darcy was watching what his hands were doing, his erection growing adamant.

She closed her eyes. Never had she felt such rushes of sensation. The more he touched her, the more she craved he would continue. Her chest warmed, and she placed her hands over his, urging him to caress her with more vigour. He began rolling her nipples between his fingers. "*That* is exquisite," she murmured.

"I must compliment you. You are not timid in the least," he whispered into her ear. His warm breath on her bare neck released a frisson of pleasure; he felt it move through her.

"So you will keep me, Mr Darcy?"

"Thus far I am most pleased, but we shall see…" His dimples deepened when he saw the smoke of desire enter her eyes.

He kissed her deeply as she reached up to place her hands upon his neck. When their lips parted, she whispered, "May I touch you?"

"Of course. Please indulge any passing curiosity that occurs to you. I am yours to do with as you wish, just as you are mine."

Darcy became dizzy when she pulled the shawl collar of his robe apart, and moved his hands off her breasts, pressing her body to his chest and resting her cheek upon him. He could feel her panting breath in his chest hair. Her hands travelled inside his robe, along his muscled ribs, and stroked his back.

Darcy bent one knee, pushing apart the overlap of his robe, and slowly rubbed his bare thigh between her legs. She moaned, pushing her secret place against him. He felt her knees buckle, and his hands went to her waist, holding her upright. "Fitzwilliam!" she cried softly. She looked at him wordlessly, her mouth open to voice a question that would not come.

"Lizzy?"

Her eyes closed. Darcy began pulling up the skirt of her nightgown with one hand while the other returned to her breasts.

"Fitzwilliam! I want..." she cried. She writhed against him. She could not feel enough, nor separate the sensations from her breasts and the heated place between her legs. Her torso ached.

"Tell me what you want, dearest Lizzy." Darcy's voice held a note of insinuation as if he knew exactly what she wanted.

"I only know I want..."

Darcy's hand reached her derrière and stroked her, fearing he would spend himself, for her skin was softer than the silk of her gown. She was every bit as he had dreamt: lush, firm, and warm. As he bathed before joining her, he had gratified himself as he heard some men did before meeting their lovers in order to prolong lovemaking, but now he felt sure the exercise had done him no good. He drew in a deep breath and tried to restore his control even as he searched for new sensations for Elizabeth. She pulled her hips back from his thigh, as if to meet the hand behind her. When he slipped two fingers into the place she had pressed to his leg, massaging the little ridge of moist tender flesh where her desire was centred, the shock of the touch drew from Elizabeth the response he promised himself she should feel before he took any pleasure for himself.

Elizabeth's head lolled back, her hands clasping the collar of his robe, and the rest of her rocked with a shudder of met desires. "Fitzwilliam, Fitzwilliam..." she murmured his name repeatedly, but he did not think she knew what she said. Darcy gazed at her adoringly. Her chest and breasts were an enchanting rosy pink.

Elizabeth lifted her head, and started to rouse from the wave of pleasure that had engulfed her and now ebbed away. She opened her eyes and met his loving smile. "Was that supposed to happen?" Her face was suffused with wonder.

Darcy did not answer her directly. "I have never in my life seen anything so beautiful as my dearest Elizabeth discovering passion. My darling, darling Lizzy!" He embraced her as tightly as he could.

"So that is a yes? You meant for that to happen?"

Darcy laughed, still holding her as if she might evaporate, his cheek against the top of her head. "I was not sure it would happen; I only hoped it would."

They stood in each other's arms quietly for a few moments. "So, as I understand it, what I just felt, a timid wife would not feel?"

"No, a timid wife would not allow herself such an indulgence, and the sort of man she would marry would not care whether she felt such sensations or not."

"Poor, timid wife…" Elizabeth smiled and looked up at Darcy. He had a look of relief on his face that surprised her. "Were you worried?"

He shook his head a little. "In truth, I am still worried. There are many ways I can give you this pleasure, now I know you will allow it of yourself, but I fear when we completely join together, it may give you pain, at least the first time, and I do, with all my heart, want you to welcome me when we are alone together. You know I have been with courtesans, Lizzy, and have some experience."

She blushed. "I know it for a certainty now. It is common, I understand, for men to learn of such things before marriage."

Darcy nodded. "But this is *your* first time, and I have not been…a maiden's…a lady's deflowerer before."

Elizabeth laughed nervously. "Deflowerer? Is that a word?"

Darcy cleared his throat. "My hope is that, if I can seduce you into a moment of extreme sensation and time my actions accordingly, you would feel passion and not pain when…well."

"Wait. Let me hear you rightly. Through your manipulations of my person, you may bring about these extreme sensations within me whenever you like? Now you have done it once, you may do it again? And there are different ways to arouse these feelings in me?"

Darcy looked into her eyes, which were alive with flickering candlelight. "Yes, as many times as you and I may manage, whenever we are alone."

Her countenance became almost feral. "Oh, it is *I* who has married well,

Mr Darcy, and it has nothing whatsoever to do with estates or gowns or pin money. Let us get to the bed! I almost fainted the first time."

Darcy was laughing as she pulled him by the sleeve, clutching her nightgown around her waist with the other hand. He sat and pulled her between his legs, turning her back to him. His hands loosened the nightgown over her hips and sent it slithering to the floor. Presented with her naked derriere, he informed her she was just as exquisite from the back view as the front, excepting he could not see her eyes, and began kissing the small of her back. Slowly he turned her until he was kissing her navel. The scent rising from between her legs was exhilarating: lavender and something womanly. He sat upright and looked up into Elizabeth's face. She had the entranced countenance he had seen when he fondled her breasts.

Her nipples were just above his mouth. He pulled her closer and kissed the undersides of her breasts; again, her breath grew shallow.

"Oh, oh. Fitzwilliam," she murmured urgently.

"Lizzy?"

"Please?"

He smiled. "Please? What desire has made you so polite?"

She turned slightly and pressed a nipple into his mouth. "Ah!" she cried rather more loudly than Darcy expected. He suckled noisily and felt his manly organ emerge from his robe. Her hands tousled his hair, pressing his face into her bosom.

"Oh! Oh, I love you!" she cried. She had no other words to express her joy. He changed breasts and drew the second nipple into his mouth. "I love you! Fitzwilliam…"

He could not resist teasing her and pulled away, delighted that her eyes were full of astonishment. "Good?" he asked.

"One is hesitant…" she paused, gasping, "to bestow too much praise upon so excessively proud a man…but 'good' is a mean and paltry little word for you, Fitzwilliam Darcy."

He started to laugh, but Elizabeth, overcome with the sight of his mouth at her breast, bumped her left nipple into his mouth and begged again, "Please?"

As he licked and tugged at her, he untied his robe. Holding Elizabeth to his face with one arm around her waist, he approached the cleft between her legs with his other hand. She was moist, and as he rubbed the centre of her sensations, she collapsed against him, crying his name loud enough, he was sure, to alarm the servants. Her cries enflamed him. He slowly moved his hand until he could tentatively extend a finger inside her, and although he could sense where her maidenhead was, it was not so tight that he felt his finger would harm her. He felt a release of moisture upon his hand as he pushed with one finger. She inhaled sharply, but did not exhale. Her hand released his hair and followed his arm to its end, where his finger was within her, and her hand pressed him deeper. She exhaled with a great sigh and he felt her tremble. Her hips rolled against him and away. He longed to laugh with delight, but her other hand kept his head pressed firmly to her breast.

When the movements of her hips gained urgency, he turned his head and whispered, "Crawl into my lap, Lizzy, astride me."

He removed his hand from her, but tried to keep his mouth upon her breasts. Guiding and supporting her, Darcy helped her knees come to rest on either side of his thighs. Her hands grasped his shoulders and pushed his robe down his arms. Shaking off the sleeves, he held her lower back with one hand, and with the other, he rubbed the tip of his member against the seat of her desire. He took a nipple into his mouth and applied himself with renewed attention. When he sensed she was nearly delirious, he began to enter her.

Darcy had to force himself to stop from thrusting brutally, but it took every fibre of his concentration. That Elizabeth was in the midst of a moment of bliss was obvious, and he did not want it to end in distress. He pushed a little further and felt her entire body grow rigid.

Elizabeth thought she would swoon as the swirling awareness of intimate contact increased. She felt the action of his hand between her legs was highly improper…a gentleman ought not touch a lady so, but they were far beyond such considerations, and he did, after all, warn her in the carriage. She did not know what part of him was arousing such stimulation now that she had scrambled astride his lap, but suddenly, as he started to enter her, she realized the moment had come, that they were consummating their union. It stung, and she did not wish to transmit her pain to him but it was too late. She felt her body stiffen and the passion that filled her with frenzy was quite suddenly gone.

Darcy stopped. "Oh, Lizzy…Elizabeth. It cannot be helped. Shall I withdraw?" Only his swollen manhood suffered no misgivings.

Her decision was the work of an instant. Darcy was perfectly still, and although it continued to sting, Elizabeth willed herself to push down upon his upright member, forcing him deeper within her. She slowly exhaled against the pain, and found doing so beneficial, like breathing against the cramps she occasionally endured during her monthly courses.

Darcy was astonished at her fortitude. She was distractingly tight, and he longed to give himself free rein but continued to remain stoic as she pressed herself onto him.

Elizabeth's forehead had dropped against his shoulder, but now she looked at him, her deliciously bruised lips forming a line of temper. Her eyes were intense as they met his. "My virginity will be offered to you only once, sir, I think one of us should enjoy the taking of it. Or are you going to just sit there?" A tense smile started to play upon her lips.

His hand slid down to the depression at the top of her derriere as he began thrusting slowly and gently, watching her. Elizabeth closed her eyes, determined to hide any evidence of pain he might see there. She leaned to his face, kissing his firm cheek and then found his mouth. She kissed him to offer encouragement; she kissed him to distract herself.

Once Elizabeth was kissing him, Darcy could not hold his animal desires at bay. His tongue explored her lips as he repeatedly drove himself further inside and gave himself over to wonder and eagerness. *This woman was Elizabeth Bennet—now and forevermore, she shall be mine, Elizabeth Darcy.* "Elizabeth Darcy," he repeated aloud between their kisses.

Despite relieving his urges during his bath, he knew taking Elizabeth would not last as long as he hoped—although, undoubtedly, the sooner it was over for her, the better. He ceased to care, and finally thrust with abandon, allowing himself to enjoy her thrilling tightness. She spread her thighs and he had the odd feeling of falling into her, even though he was pushing upward.

Elizabeth, too, was experiencing odd sensations, and she wondered vaguely whether this was akin to riding astride a runaway horse. She was breathless. The pain was easing, and she could feel, from the ardency of Darcy's kisses that he was giving himself over to pleasure. It seemed the discomfort she felt was lessened if he were more deeply within her, and she squirmed as best she could to open herself further. In a moment, she knew she had done the correct thing. Darcy ended the kiss and began softly calling her, both as Elizabeth and Lizzy, in a most insistent manner in her ear, reverential yet lost to reason.

Quite suddenly, his hands were on her waist, and he pressed her down forcefully as he pushed inside. He growled, "Elizabeth, my god!", and she could feel his warm seed filling her, then spilling from her as his thrusts continued. She knew he had taken the gratification he needed, and they were now completely husband and wife.

Darcy's pinnacle ended with one last sharp thrust, and Elizabeth felt it as an awakening, as if his potency unlocked a deeper core of desire lying secretly within her, waiting to be found. The spilling of his seed soothed the stinging of her stretched flesh, and she began stirring herself upon him.

As his wits returned, he realized his member had not slackened—*maybe it was a good idea to sate myself before*—and his wife seemed to be finding new satisfaction in it. Her panting breaths returned. Given what pleased her before, he knew to suckle her closest breast, tugging at her as he continued rocking her with his hips. Her back arched, her hands buried in his hair, and his lips teased her.

"Fitzwilliam, yes! Oh yes! Please, please…" She became incoherent. With one final flex of her thighs, she impaled herself as completely as possible, shuddered, and rolled her hips against him, slowing until she was still.

Darcy was grinning, although she was entirely unaware of it. Elizabeth's head was on his shoulder, looking away into space, and she was smiling. Her arms were around his back, embracing him tenderly. She did not notice or respond as his spent member slipped out of her. Darcy realized the evidence of their consummation was now besmirching his lap and the inside of his robe upon which he was still sitting.

"Lizzy?" he whispered, stroking her hair.

"Hmm?"

"Are you well? You are not too much hurt?"

She lifted her head and met his gaze. Darcy was relieved by what he saw. Her expression was eloquent of affection and praise.

"No, Fitzwilliam, I do not think I am much hurt. You were very kind."

"And you were very generous. Would you ever be willing to do this again? It was not so terribly bad?"

"Dearest…it was *not* so terribly bad. After you, uh, had your way…as they say, I was greatly soothed, and so…"

"Yes, you then had your way with *me*." He chuckled.

Her hands found their way into his hair, and she studied his face. "Fitzwilliam Darcy, have I ever told you that you are the handsomest man I have ever seen who was not a statue?"

"No, you have not. As it happens, up until this minute, you are the only woman of my acquaintance who has not praised my looks. But now that you are my wife, I would like you to consider it your duty to tell me so at least once a day."

Her eyes met his, imploring in an exaggerated way and teasing him. "You mean you *will* keep me, Mr Darcy? It is a decided thing?"

His countenance was full of love and admiration, as she had not seen before, even as they met at the altar of Longbourn church. "Yes, Elizabeth Darcy, it is indeed a decided thing."

Her smile broadened. "Well then, if we have moments together like this once a day, I will not forget my duty. It will be my pleasure to tell you how very handsome you are."

"But what if we have moments like this *more* than once a day? Will you tell me I am handsome more than once a day?"

"Is such a thing possible?"

Darcy shifted his weight under her, pressing his renewed ardent member against her leg. He was pleased with this evidence of his prowess. Never had he been able to restore an erection so quickly. He knew it was due to the years he had waited for a wife, Elizabeth's tempting body, and the rapture of being intimate with the woman he loved. "Whilst I am a young man, a young man violently in love with his new wife and physically able to do so, I believe we may enjoy many opportunities for you to tell me how handsome I am every day. Will you lay with me, Lizzy?"

"Whenever it pleases you, dearest, handsomest Fitzwilliam."

DARCY AWOKE IN THE MIDDLE of the night to find Elizabeth's back tucked against his chest, exactly as they had fallen asleep after lovemaking. He suddenly wished to be in his own bedchamber with her. He slid from the bed, noticing in the sputtering candlelight that there was some slight evidence of blood where they had joined the second time. It was not as dramatic as on his robe, which he carried into his bedchamber. A fire had been laid, and after stirring it to blazing, he stood before it with the robe loosely folded. He, in good conscience, could not bear the thought of its being laundered and worn again, which would somehow demean the deeper connection now binding them. *Do I put this away and cherish it always as the token of this night, stains and all? Or should I burn it to keep the memory between Elizabeth and myself?* Being a fastidious man at heart, Darcy placed the robe on the fire, watching it for a moment before turning to his bed. *The servants will see all the evidence they need from her bed.* He folded down the counterpane and blankets and returned to the other room for Elizabeth.

She stirred as he gathered her into his arms. "I am carrying you to my bed or, more properly, our other bed. You do not mind?" he whispered.

"Mmm, lovely." She tucked her cheek against his shoulder without opening her eyes. "Nightgown?"

"No, I think not. After last night, I am quite done awakening with you in a nightgown."

She sighed contentedly as he carried her. "Most improper."

"Yes. I hope you will not be shocked by how improper I prove to be when we are alone." He smiled.

He laid her onto his bed and stepped back a moment to admire a vision he had seen before only in dreams. She stretched and opened her eyes. For the first time, she took in the full view of Darcy's naked body in a state of nearly complete arousal. She grew more alert and smiled with a dubious raised eyebrow. "It would appear, sir, that you are wishing me to say you are handsome again. When you said 'many opportunities,' I thought you might be exaggerating to impress me favourably with your ardency in case I had any doubt of it." Her voice seemed disapproving.

Darcy stepped to the bed, leaned upon it with one knee, and did not resist the urge to stroke her thighs, just below the triangle of dark hair that hid so many delights. "Lizzy...darling..." He found himself preparing to beg, or even grovel. He could only think of being accepted by her again. He met her eyes, which revealed she had been teasing. They smiled at each other for a moment.

She reached a hand to him and pulled his hand to cup her breast. "If you will kiss me, *here,*" she said, "I will not be inclined to object to anything else you might wish to do, I assure you. Your person is far too handsome for me to refuse or even resist."

Darcy complied, and so, quite willingly, did Elizabeth.

ELIZABETH OPENED HER EYES IN the darkness. The fire had consumed itself, but she was still too warm. She was on her side in Darcy's arms, his sleepy breath at the back of her neck. Slowly and carefully, she slipped out of the bed and crept to her dressing room. After using the water closet and freshening her nether regions with a cloth moistened in lavender water, she found herself not much harmed by the night's events.

The last time Darcy had stirred from sleep, he had appealed to her for another consummation. He was apologetic but unrelenting, and he guided himself inside her before she had time to express her willingness. His progress was slower, his embrace gentle, and he was most attentive to her comfort. When he had finished, he whispered she should not expect such frequent performances in the future. "I imagine this is all because I have waited so long for you…to have a willing wife," he whispered. "Thank you, Lizzy."

She went to peek out the window. The weather was still, and she could see the barest glow of a red sunrise. *Red sky at morning, sailors take warning.' Perhaps I shall just sail back to bed.* She picked her nightgown up off the floor as she passed through the mistress's bedroom, surprised at the ease with which she was adjusting to wandering naked in the dark. She laid the garment upon the long bench at the foot of the master's bed.

Elizabeth crept back amongst the bedclothes and lay on her back, higher on the voluminous pillows. She pulled the blankets over from Darcy to cover herself to her chest, but he stirred in his sleep. He cuddled next to her, depositing his head on her shoulder and chest, and covered her private parts—*they are no longer so very private. I can no longer think of that place as mine; he has taken such possession of it*—with the masculine thigh of a bent leg. The bedclothes uncovered her bosom as he moved, and she did not pull at them again.

The sky lightened. Elizabeth realized his first view upon waking would be her breasts, and that would not be a bad thing. She did not wish to dwell overmuch upon those feelings Darcy awoke from between her legs during their conjugal relations, which seemed beyond understanding, but as she lay there, she did wonder at the overpowering yearning stirred in her bosom when he looked at her, touched her or, marvel of marvels, pulled a nipple into his mouth. Her own desires started there, and as his warm breath now washed rhythmically over her bare skin, she found herself hoping he would rouse.

THE FIRST LIGHT OF MORNING entered the room though a tiny gap in the dark curtains, illuminating Darcy's face and Elizabeth's bosom. His breathing grew sonorous just before he awakened.

Darcy inhaled lavender, which made him smile. He sensed the soft cosy body under him; his head was nestled upon his Lizzy. One arm was under the pillows, the other crossed her waist, and his thigh covered that place where his pleasure was now centred. He could feel her cheek leaning against his head. He was undeniably erect. He opened his eyes and could see only her exposed bosom, milky pink with large relaxed nipples in the day's first sun.

"Lizzy?" he whispered as his hand stroked her breast. Her nipples immediately responded by forming hard points. He was amazed.

"Fitzwilliam." Elizabeth kissed his forehead. "You are *finally* awake," she said, accusingly. "I thought you were going to sleep all day."

Elizabeth turned more towards him. She wiggled down the bed to claim his mouth and curled her leg around his waist. He placed his member at her entrance and met her eyes. Elizabeth nodded with a smile; she was ready to welcome him, though he had done nothing to stimulate her. *What an astonishing creature I have married*, he marvelled. *She awakens as aroused as I do.*

As he entered her, he felt her frisson of pleasure. She looked up at him, not yet delirious enough to prevent speech.

"I awoke thinking how remarkably handsome you are, and how very much I wanted to tell you so."

"Good morning, then, Mrs Darcy!" Darcy chuckled as he grasped her hips in his hands, pushing further into her as he rolled, holding her in place, onto his back.

Elizabeth found herself on top of him, with his potency driving further within her than it had yet been. The summits of ecstasy she reached were far more profound than she had experienced in the night.

As Darcy feasted his eyes upon her, her eyes closed and her mouth opened with cries of passion. His several exertions of the night before were allowing him to last longer. He found a new source of pride in how often he could bring his willing, nay, demanding wife of just two days to further heights of bliss. At last, as she bent over him, murmuring rather incoherently of her love for what he was doing to her, he pulled her shoulders down and captured a lovely nipple in his mouth. He allowed his eyes to close, and amidst her gasps, remembered all of the past when he despaired of ever kissing her, let alone sharing a moment such as this. Even now, he wondered, *does she love me, or is she merely overcome with pleasurable sensation?*

Elizabeth straightened and opened her eyes, gazing at him. His expression was one of desire and a strange anguish. She willed him to look at her.

Darcy opened his eyes. Her beautiful face filled his vision. He could sense by her movements she was again near another pinnacle, but she held his gaze and started to smile with such love that he could not help but return her emotion in full measure. It was the first time he felt that, though she was transported by desire, she was aware of him, she was truly with him, she loved him deeply, and she had given herself to this profound moment without reserve just as thoroughly as had he. With a shudder and stronger thrusts, his seed released within her. He cried, "Elizabeth!" and found himself laughing for joy when he realized she was crying, "Fitzwilliam, Fitzwilliam…" with him as she crested a summit of desire.

They grew quiet together. Darcy drew the counterpane over Elizabeth's back and she snuggled down, still astride him. "I have not told you," she began, "but the night of the Meryton assembly, as Jane and I readied ourselves, we spoke of our futures, of marriage. I told her I would only marry for the deepest love. Of course, I had no real notion what those words meant. I merely liked the sound of saying it. But it must have been a charm, Fitzwilliam. I invoked some sort of spell and did not know it."

"You must have been ready to be loved, and I was the first man to lay eyes upon you and recognize it, although it was unconsciously done. But I knew soon enough, irrational though I was to fight it."

"Perhaps that is why I could not trust you. You were trying to fool yourself. When you said I was not handsome enough to tempt you, I had the singular impression you were expressing an opinion that was not your own." She lifted her head and laughed at him.

Darcy laughed with her.

Artemisia
"Jest & banter"

Chapter 18

Seven Months Later

It was mid-June, just at sunrise. Darcy awoke in an empty bed for the first time since his wedding. He heard the sound of water—a bath being filled—coming from Elizabeth's dressing room. His bleary eyes opened and traversed their bedchamber. No Elizabeth.

This was the room they both preferred as it had the biggest bed in the entire house. The former mistress's bedroom had been converted to Elizabeth's dressing room; her former dressing room beyond it was now a pretty sitting room, hung about with botanical drawings and a framed vignette of dried flowers and leaves, Darcy's nosegay to her from the previous July. The rooms were refitted while the Darcys were in London for six weeks of the Season, as much to-doing in the *ton* as Darcy could tolerate. There was a small pianoforte in the new sitting room for Elizabeth to play for Darcy alone. The servants laughed to themselves when the mistress never played more than one song through. The master always interrupted a second.

Darcy listened, and he was alerted to what sounded like Elizabeth attempting to stifle sobs. *What is this? She has not cried since we married.* He flung back the bedclothes and noticed the evidence of blood where she slept. Her courses had come, but this was nothing to Darcy. *She is regular in her habits.* To him, it meant she was healthy.

Picking up his robe, he stole to the nearly closed door. He paused to rap on it. There was a need for politeness in the air. It swung open at his touch and revealed Elizabeth in her bath with one arm on the rolled edge. Her other hand covered her mouth. Her eyes were closed but tears escaped. Darcy saw there was no maid and tossed aside the robe he had held to cover his tumescent attributes.

"Lizzy?"

She rolled away from his gaze and cried harder.

"Lizzy!" He knelt at her side. "What disturbs you so, my love?"

Elizabeth drew herself into a ball. He touched her shoulder tenderly. "Lizzy, darling, why do you bathe so early? Why alone? This is not like you."

She choked. "I, I...I am so sorry." She spoke in huffed gasps without turning to him. "Oh, Fitzwilliam..."

He shook his head, thoroughly perplexed, but she did not see his face. "Lizzy?"

She drew in a deep breath. "I am not..." She sobbed again before finishing, "I am not with child." Her tears redoubled.

"I saw you are not from our bedclothes." He turned her by her shoulders to face him. "What of it?"

"It is time I should be. I am afraid..." She could not speak her thought aloud. *I am afraid you will put me aside if I am barren.*

"Afraid? Of what? We have only been wed just beyond six months."

"Seven cycles of the moon." She would not meet his eyes. "In Jane's letter yesterday... She is three months along and ready to tell everyone her interesting news." Elizabeth was taking deep breaths as she tried to calm herself. She did not mention Lydia Wickham had delivered to her scoundrel of a husband a fair son now over a month old. And some two weeks older than Lydia's son were the twins, William Lambton and Elizabeth, born to Aunt and Uncle Gardiner.

Darcy smiled knowingly. "Is there some sisterly competition of which you have not made me aware?"

"We were married on the same day," Elizabeth bleated.

"Of that I *am* aware," Darcy chuckled. "But if you recall, she and Bingley had a one day start with certain matters."

Elizabeth attempted a withering glare, which only provoked further chuckles. "You laugh, but what will you think of me if I am...if I cannot..." Her voice grew fragile. "I was told that no small part of what attracted you was my appearance of health."

"Indeed, madam, you have not been ill a day since our wedding. I do not feel myself misled."

"You know that is not what I meant."

He knelt behind her and massaged her tight shoulders. "Lizzy, it does not signify. I will always love you. Please do not alarm yourself unnecessarily." After a few moments, when she seemed to relax, he asked, "May I join you?" Her tub was smaller than his, but he had squeezed into it before.

She sighed, still disheartened. "You better not. There is blood here."

"We have bloodied my sword before. Why are you timorous now?"

He moved to face her and saw her forming a response. "Today, or in a day or two, I shall have a letter from Mama. She started two months ago, hectoring me. She knows my time. She keeps a calendar. She *will* ask. She says I am lucky there is no entail, and any child will do, but I must get to it or you will put me aside, or take a mistress." Her expression was woeful.

"Oh, hang your mother." Darcy leaned forward and kissed her forehead. "My dearest, *you* are my mistress. You allow me anything. Your generosity and playfulness astonish me still. You have done so since our first night."

Elizabeth considered this. She looked down, embarrassed. She slid to her neck under the water to shield her bosom from his covetous gaze before saying, "I own I astonish myself, sir. You have made me accustomed to sensations most unseemly." She knew from their brief season in town that their marital relations were unusually varied. She allowed him much more freedom with her person than was normal. Most women were not led to the joy Darcy insisted she experience. She listened to the other wives but stopped speaking of her own marriage when she saw how they looked at Darcy after she once made the effort to be explicit.

Darcy's dimples deepened. "You think us indecent?"

"I think we must be. Jane and Bingley do not behave so."

Darcy's eyes twinkled. Clearly, he had different information than did she. "Or perhaps someone is not saying. These things are best left between a man and woman alone."

"Oh! I would not have you think I asked for any particular information of Jane. I speak only of what I infer."

"I know, Lizzy. Do not fret." He moved to capture her gaze. "Indeed, this may all be my fault."

"How so?" She looked dubious.

"The morning after we arrived home, after our wedding night, when we awoke together and were so happy, I said a little prayer that you would not become with child too soon. It was selfish I know, but I wanted to continue having my way with you at my will before we stop for your confinement and the altering of our habits becomes necessary with children in the house."

Elizabeth let out an exasperated breath. "You might have told me."

Darcy laughed. "You already thought me ungentlemanly for the way I touched you."

"Yes, but did that stop you? And now you are *much* worse." At last she smiled.

"So are you. You do things to me, Lizzy, for which I would have had to pay a great deal in the finest brothels of Vienna eight years ago. And I have never imposed upon you; you just seem to know what I want."

A flush of pink spread over her face and down onto her chest. "What a thing to say to Mrs Darcy," Elizabeth scolded but looked pleased.

Darcy was delighted he could still make his wife blush. "If you will not let me bathe with you, then come out of there." He pulled her to standing and dried her with the ready towelling. Looking at his wife's freshly bathed and rosy body, Darcy smiled seductively. "This month, let me answer your mother. I shall send her news she never would dare repeat. You told me what the old hens of Meryton said of me—what they told you to expect." Darcy unpinned her hair. "Were they so very wrong?"

She looked into his smiling eyes. "What they failed to take into account is *my* nature. Are we *both* incorrigible?" She entered his embrace.

"Lizzy," Darcy sighed, running his hands through her hair. "I would have your mother find us so."

As Elizabeth predicted, a letter from her mother arrived with the evening post. Darcy purloined it, and he would not reveal its contents to its intended recipient. It was full of praise for Jane and worried criticism of Mrs Elizabeth Darcy.

MRS BENNET WAS SURPRISED TO receive a letter from Pemberley in handwriting other than Elizabeth's. She was mortified by its content, which was terse and explicit.

20 June, 1813

Dear Mrs Bennet,

This letter is the humble request of your son-in-law that you immediately desist writing to my wife regarding the getting of children. These letters discompose her. They set you at odds with the wishes of her husband that she learn the arts of Europe's finest courtesans, from my instruction, for my pleasure and, I hope, hers, before we consume our time with child rearing. Your daughter has proved to be everything her husband wishes, both wildly adventuresome and charmingly acquiescent. She denies me nothing and is a quick study. Elizabeth has not disappointed me in any particular, and I would not have you influencing her otherwise.

Elizabeth finds your letters on any other topics to be highly diverting; this is the only amendment I would make to your correspondence with her.

Respectfully,
F. Darcy

An immediate case of the fidgets beset Mrs Bennet. She paced her rooms, flapping the letter, and sighing loudly. She rang for tea and sent it away. There was no one with whom she could disclose this disturbing and repugnant missive. It was too improper for Mr Bennet to know his darling was being trained as Mr Darcy's fancy woman. Mrs Phillips or Lady Lucas would trumpet the news far and wide. Lydia was lately delivered of her first child, and she loathed hearing about the Darcys and their wealth. Lydia wanted nothing more than to think Darcy dreary and Elizabeth unhappy. Mrs Gardiner already thought Mrs Bennet foolish enough for taking so decided an interest in the procreative accomplishments of her daughters, and could be counted upon to side with Darcy.

After changing her clothes three times, Mrs Bennet called for her carriage and directed the driver to Netherfield. She could rely upon Jane to be suitably shocked, and Mrs Bennet longed to share her disapproval. Perhaps Jane would hear her with the proper attitude of righteous indignation.

When Mrs Bennet sallied into Netherfield unannounced, the servants were sent into turmoil. No, Mr and Mrs Bingley were not from home, but no one would say precisely where they were. It was noon, and Mrs Bennet knew the couple had formed the habit of taking some light refreshment at midday.

298

Without hesitation, Mrs Bennet flung open the small dining parlour doors. Jane was alone but appeared extremely disturbed as her mother entered the room. Jane's chair was at an odd angle to the table and she seemed to be rearranging her skirts.

"Mama!" Jane's cheeks were heated and florid but Mrs Bennet did not notice.

"Jane! I have received such a letter from Mr Darcy as will shock you to your tender heart. Indeed, I do not know if I ought to tell you in your delicate condition."

"Mama, calm yourself. If you will go to the drawing room, I shall join you in a moment."

Mrs Bennet ignored her and pulled out a chair to sit. "You will not believe it, Jane. I am myself so upset I can scarce speak of it." Yet she gave every appearance of settling in to do so at great length.

"Mama, please. If you will just…"

"It seems he is training Lizzy to be a columbine. No, that isn't the word… concubine? Courtesan? That's it! It is just as I feared. He does not care for children. He only married her for"—Mrs Bennet lowered her voice but whispered as if on stage—"*fornication.*"

There was a loud bump that sounded like a head hitting the underside of a dining table. It was followed by Charles Bingley muttering, "Ouch! Damn it!" and a peal of nervous laughter. Jane sat for a moment in stunned silence; then the present situation began to be comical. Forever more, betwixt just themselves, she and Charles would refer to Lizzy as "the columbine." Jane was trying so intently not to laugh that her eyes watered from the strain.

Mrs Bennet grew quiet. She stepped back from the table, drew up the tablecloth and looked underneath. She was met with the fair prospect of her son-in-law's bare buttocks, his trousers bunched around his knees. She stood bolt upright, all colour drained from her face. Her eyes narrowed and her lips pursed.

"Jane! For heaven's sake, it is the middle of the day, and you are with child," Mrs Bennet hissed.

No further words were exchanged as Mrs Bennet flounced from the room with all possible haste. Within fifteen minutes, she was at Longbourn, and she took to her bed for two days.

IN LATE SEPTEMBER, MRS BENNET received another letter from Darcy, short and to the point as ever.

Dear Mother-in-Law,

We thought you would be relieved to know that, after enjoying conjugal relations rather constantly throughout July and August, my dearest Elizabeth has missed her monthly bleeding for two months running. Her bosom is becoming so voluptuous that I have decided, rather than viewing the getting of children with misapprehension, I will now endeavour to keep her increasing as often as God wills it—and Elizabeth allows it —for the foreseeable future.

Nature has taken its course, Madam, as I always knew it would.

Yours respectfully,
F. Darcy

In spite of its good news, this letter was met by its recipient with the same disapprobation as the previous one.

Columbine
"Folly"

Epilogue

Elizabeth and Fitzwilliam Darcy raised six children. Their eldest was a boy, Charles Richard Darcy, followed in quick succession by three girls, Jane, Georgiana and Madeleine. As soon as Charles Darcy learned the meaning of the term 'harpy,' his three sisters became "The Harpies," much to the amusement of their parents.

It began with Jane's birth, for she had the temerity to be born on her brother's second birthday. He was taken to see his baby sister and, with shrill alarm, uttered the word, "No!" for the first time, being a jolly and good-natured baby until that moment.

All his sisters richly deserved their appellation. They seemed born into a conspiracy, visiting upon their brother every manner of indignity and mortification that was within their considerable means to produce or procure. They were intelligent lively girls, all three very much their mother's daughters.

There was a period of several years before the last two Darcy children were brought forth, Thomas Bennet Darcy and Edward Gardiner Darcy, born only a year apart. The Harpies doted on them to the point that Elizabeth and Darcy despaired of the baby boys ever learning to walk. Their sisters carried them around like rag dolls.

When Charles Darcy reached marriageable age, the Harpies went from one extreme to the other. They appointed themselves his staunchest defenders from grasping females and their greedy mamas. It was a source of wonder to their elder brother that, for eight years, from his eighteenth to twenty-sixth birthdays, his three sisters knew the full history and every particular of all young ladies introduced to him no matter where he went.

301

They rendered an instant opinion bolstered by facts. How they contrived it, he never learnt. The Harpies scolded their mother if she suggested a young lady for her son whom they deemed wanting. When Charles did marry, just before his twenty-seventh birthday, it was with the unanimous consent of the Harpies. He would not have proposed without it. The approval of his parents was *pro forma* by comparison.

Thomas Bennet outlived his wife by eight years, sparing her the indignity of seeing Longbourn pass into the hands of William and Charlotte Collins and their one son. Mr Bennet visited the Darcys as often as he felt like it, whether they were in London or at Pemberley, and took great delight in watching the Harpies harass poor young Charlie. He was known to aid and abet them—his pack of Lizzies.

Fitzwilliam and Elizabeth Darcy were married for nearly fifty years. Although they squabbled and teased each other throughout their marriage, no one ever heard them truly quarrel. It was not until both Darcy and Elizabeth passed away that their children and grandchildren, nieces and nephews and Gardiner cousins, realized the Darcys had enjoyed the happiest of marriages. It was an elderly Charles Bingley who explained to them at his final Christmas that Elizabeth and Darcy plagued themselves with many vexations and absurdities during their courtship, thus relieving married life of most of its usual trials.

Open Rose
"I still love you"

Georgiana Darcy married into another Derbyshire estate, becoming Georgiana LeFroy. She married for love into a family of quality. She was not as suited to childbearing as she was to music and was survived by only one child, a tall, fair-haired son. It was she who secretly placed bouquets of red chrysanthemums upon the graves of her brother, and then his wife, in the churchyard of St. Swithin's in Lambton—during the season when those flowers were in bloom—and open roses in the spring until the year of her death.

Red Chrysanthemum
"I love"

CPSIA information can be obtained at www.ICGtesting.com
Printed in the USA
BVOW05s1136100316

439670BV00002B/104/P